Moonlight in Odessa

Janet Skeslien Charles

B L O O M S B U R Y

LONDON · BERLIN · NEW YORK · SYDNEY

First published in Great Britain 2010

This paperback published 2010

Bloomsbury Publishing, London, Berlin and New York

36 Soho Square, London W1D 3QY

A CIP catalogue record for this book is available from the British Library

ISBN 978 1 4088 0287 8
10 9 8 7 6 5 4 3 2 1

Typeset by Hewer Text UK Ltd, Edinburgh
Printed by Clays Ltd, St Ives plc

www.bloomsbury.com/janetskesliencharles

For my sister, Kathy Skeslien

'Language ... remains a highly ambiguous transaction, a quicksand, a trampoline, a frozen pool which might give way under you ... at any time.'

Harold Pinter

Part I

Mail-order marriage is not a new phenomenon – it is an inseparable part of North American history and the settlement of the United States.

– from a 1999 report to Congress on International Matchmaking Organizations

Chapter 1

M R. HARMON HAD BEEN driving me mad for six months, three weeks, and two days. From Monday to Friday, nine to five. He actually timed me when I fetched our morning coffee. Best time: fifty-six seconds. It had just been made. Worst time: seven minutes forty-eight seconds. I had to prepare the coffee myself, though he insisted that I'd wasted time flirting with a security guard. Perhaps, but I was also watching the coffee perk. I always had to keep one eye on my work, the other on Mr. Harmon. If he wasn't sneaking up on me, he was listening in on my phone conversations. If he wasn't looking over my shoulder (and down my blouse), he was at his desk plotting to get his hands on me. But so far, I'd been faster.

These irritations were nothing compared to his latest machination. A month ago, he'd finally agreed to have the Internet installed on my computer. Actually, he'd been prodded by the head office in Haifa. I was dying to have it (even though I didn't know what *it* was exactly), but Mr. Harmon always found a way to stop the connection. Today, I let myself feel a glimmer of hope. Perhaps I would finally be connected to the world. The third computer technician I'd hired walked in wearing Ukrainian cool circa 1996 – carefully ironed jeans that came up past his navel and a brown leather jacket – and introduced himself with the easy smile of a man who still lived with his mother. He sat a little too close while explaining how to dial and connect; I inched my chair away, knowing it would upset Mr. Harmon. I saw flashes of his dark blazer as he paced his office, glaring out at us.

'Daria, get in heeeeere!' he bellowed.

The technician's brows rose, I rolled my eyes and excused myself.

'That man is flirting with you,' Mr. Harmon said.

True. But in Odessa, everyone jokes and flirts. It's our way. Even if I'd been a pensioner with bulging eyes and thinning hair the technician would have winked and repeated the same jokes. *Four fonts walk into a bar. The barman says, 'Get outta here! We don't serve your type.'* Or, as he patted the computer monitor on the head like a wayward child, *Be careful with this thing. Computers let you make more mistakes faster than any invention in history, with the possible exceptions of Kalashnikovs and vodka.*

'He's just doing his job.' I pointed to the man as he redialed the access number for the tenth time. Everything takes time in Ukraine. And money. If Mr. Harmon didn't dismiss this one, we would be among the first offices with Internet in all of Odessa.

'I don't like him,' Mr. Harmon said.

'You don't have to. In twenty minutes, he'll be finished and we'll never see the man again.'

'Fire him. And don't pay him! He hasn't done his job.'

'Please don't make me fire another one,' I whispered.

'Don't argue, Daria.'

Red-faced, I returned to my desk and said in Russian, 'I'm sorry. You have to go.'

The technician looked upset. 'The old boy is jealous, eh?'

I nodded. It was hard to be dependent on the fickle desires of Westerners. They had the power, we had the desperation.

'It took me over an hour to get here,' he said. 'You know how it is. I need this job. My mother … her medication –'

'I know. I'm sorry.'

'What are you whispering about out there?' Mr. Harmon yelled. 'Speak English!'

I grabbed some money from my purse and tried to pay him. He refused the bills and invited me out for a drink, his Odessan bravado restored. We are so good at faking it. Feeling Mr. Harmon's intent stare between my shoulder blades, I shook my head. 'Go. Before he calls security.'

This was not the first time that Mr. Harmon had dismissed a man for speaking to me. I'd tried to find a female technician, but there simply weren't any. I tried to find a homely old man, but in Odessa, only young people know anything about computers. Whenever I hired a new one, Mr. Harmon paced around my desk, sniffing and growling like a bulldog at the handsome, yet interchangeable men, making sure that they weren't coveting me, his bone.

The only man he couldn't object to was Vladimir Stanislavski who was so daunting that Mr. Harmon didn't dare say a word. After all, he knew that the last person who'd been rude to the gangster had been evacuated to an emergency room in Vienna.

I sighed. Would I *ever* have Internet?

None of the other prospective employers I'd met with had come close to matching the salary that Mr. Harmon's firm, an Israeli shipping company, offered: three hundred dollars a month when the average was only thirty dollars.

During the job interview for this position, I'd actually thought that Mr. Harmon was handsome. Different. Better. Threads of silver at his temples made him seem scholarly. He wore a well-cut suit. He was shorter than me, but then most people are. He had a mustache and was rather robust, yet when his face broke into a grin, he looked so happy that he scarcely seemed older than me, though as a director, I knew he must have been nearly forty. Mr. Harmon was certainly more interesting than Ukrainian bosses. He'd traveled. He spoke English and Hebrew. His fingers were long and elegant, his teeth perfect. He smelled fresh and clean like a meadow. And – most importantly – he was foreign.

While he spoke about the job, I discreetly caressed the soft leather of the boardroom chair and marveled at everything about the room – the satiny paint, the bright lights, the sleek cordless phone. It felt as if we had left the dismal, dark former Soviet Union and arrived on Wall Street. Mr. Harmon stared at me and seemed to savor every word that came out of my mouth. He even invited me to have lunch right there in the boardroom. A middle-aged woman scurried in and laid out a fine repast on a white linen tablecloth. I'd never had cheese from France before. The Brie melted in my mouth. And the wine! After we finished the first bottle, I picked it up and placed it on the floor, since an empty bottle on the table is bad luck. When he opened the second I noticed it had a real cork, not just a plastic stopper like our wine. The food was all so good, but the best was the hummus. It tasted like sunshine – golden, warm, and light. I closed my eyes and felt it slide down my throat.

'It's the olive oil,' he said, watching me. 'You don't have that in Odessa, I imagine. We bring all this food on our ships. If you worked here, you could eat like this every day.'

To stop myself from smiling, I rubbed my fingers on my chin as if I were carefully considering whether I wanted the position. If Boba, my grandmother, had been there, she would have grabbed my hands and put them in my lap.

'We have branches all over the world,' he continued. 'Germany. America. There's no reason a smart girl like you has to stay in the same office all her life …'

America! I couldn't believe it. I smiled, and quickly put my hand to my mouth. 'To speak English all day … It would be my dream.'

'Your English is impeccable,' he said. 'Did you study in England?'

I shook my head. No one in this country went anywhere. Didn't he know that? Everything we needed to know was learned here. He could not imagine the pains we had endured in Maria Pavlovna's class. She was a difficult mistress. Her thin gray hair pulled back into a tight bun only made her bug eyes and thin lips more prominent. She was the only Odessan I ever knew who didn't smile or joke. But we did learn with her. She scared even the biggest, baddest boys into studying. We had to memorize texts and recite them in front of the classroom. When we made a mistake, Maria Pavlovna banged her meter stick on the desk. If we slipped up again, we feared she would strike the back of our thighs. She played records on pronunciation over and over. Though. Thought. Bough. Bought. Once, when I hadn't pronounced the 'ou' sound correctly, she grabbed my jaw and pulled my lips until the sound she wanted came out.

She kept a metronome on her desk, and we recited the irregular verbs to a tick-tock that sounded faster and faster each day. Tick-tock, tick-tock. Ticktocktick. Tockticktock. Arise-arose-arisen, begin-began-begun, break-broke-broken, burst-burst-burst and cut-cut-cut (our favorites because they stayed the same), eat-ate-eaten, fight-fought-fought, get-got-got, etc., etc., etc. Years later, the ticking of a clock still made me unbearably nervous, and when I was nervous, I couldn't stop myself from reciting her list of one hundred irregular verbs randomly in my head.

Drink-drank-drunk. My thoughts started to spin, and I put my wine glass down.

'There were no trips abroad,' I explained. 'But we had rigorous teachers.'

He frowned, which made me think perhaps he, too, knew something of discipline at school.

'The other candidates I interviewed could barely say "hello." '

I'd seen the girl he'd 'interviewed' before me. Where had he found her? The casino?

The woman returned with espresso. I inhaled the steam that billowed from the white porcelain cup. It smelled so good, so rich and dreamy, that even though I was full, my mouth began to water. Mr. Harmon handed me a square of dark chocolate. I accepted it gingerly. Of course we had such luxuries in Odessa, Mr. Harmon was wrong to say we didn't. It was just that people like me – 98 percent of the population – could not afford them. Hoping he wouldn't notice, I slipped the chocolate into my purse so that I could share it with Boba.

'Have you ever had champagne, my dear?'

I shook my head. When he ordered the woman back into the room with two snaps of his fingers and asked her to bring a bottle, I couldn't believe my luck. Wait until I told Olga and Boba that I'd had champagne, real champagne! From France! In my family, we only drank *champagnskoye* once a year, to celebrate the New Year. 'A drop of sweet *champagnskoye* makes life sweet.' That's what we say in Odessa. Everyone knows that if you don't drink *champagnskoye* on December 31, the New Year will be a disaster. Ask Boba if you don't believe me. The one time we didn't meet the New Year with *champagnskoye* was the year my mother died.

He poured the champagne. The bubbles glistened like tiny *brillianti*. Diamonds.

We clinked glasses and he proposed a toast, 'To a significant ... partnership.'

Did that mean I got the job?

He watched as I took my first sip. It was bitter. I wanted to cough, but held it in. He extended his hand and I placed mine in his, feeling that our meeting was destiny. Feeling that after so much struggle and loss, something good would finally happen. Then he winked and said, 'Of course, sleeping with me is the best part of the job.'

I snatched my hand away. He'd made it sound like a joke, but he was serious. Suddenly, he resembled a walrus in a puce jacket that he'd been quick to point out was Versace. The silver threads at his temples became dull smears of gray. He was just like other men, only with shinier teeth and fancy cologne. We stared at each other. The only sound in the office was the ticking of a clock. *Weep-wept-wept. Win-won-won. Withdraw-withdrew-withdrawn. Stop it!* I shook my head. *Think!* In addition to fetching his coffee and translating his documents, was I capable of sleeping with him? Could I do *that* for a job? The thought of his meaty hands touching me made my skin crawl – I'm a vegetarian. Behind his tinted glasses, he observed me with hot black eyes, waiting for me to decide.

He'd come from Israel and quickly got used to being treated like a VIP. Many Western men came to the former Soviet Union because of the clout they had here. At home, they were invisible and barely eked out a living. Here, they were considered rich and had large apartments, cooks, cleaning ladies, and plenty of other 'ladies.' (For Odessans, everywhere from Tel Aviv to Tokyo is considered Western; geography is not dictated by the compass but rather by abundance.)

I thought of my friends. Of Olga, who had three children but no husband, no job, and no money. Of Valeria, a teacher who went to work every day but didn't get paid, like most government employees. Of Maria, a conservatory graduate who'd recently become a waitress and had to wear a skimpy skirt as part of the job. I thought of ten, twenty others. I didn't want to end up like my girlfriends, with no choices and no money. Maria, with her beautiful voice, was mistreated by her boss and the bar patrons. If I took this job, at least I would be harassed by only one man.

I'd graduated from the university six months earlier and still hadn't found a full-time position. I needed to support myself and my Boba, who'd taken care of me since I was ten. Our situation was dire – Boba's pension was only twenty dollars a month. (Ukraine had declared its independence in 1991; five years later our currency was still unstable, so we used dollars.) I shouldn't have been surprised by his proposition – it hadn't been the first. I just hadn't expected it of a Westerner. Maybe Boba was right. Maybe we were cursed. I looked at Mr. Harmon again.

Chess. There's a reason the former Soviet Union has more world champion players than any other country. Chess is strategy, persistence, cunning, and the ability to look farther into the future than an opponent. The bloodlust of killing off others, one at a time. Chess is every man for himself. Building traps and avoiding them. It is mental toughness. And sacrifice. In Odessa, life is chess. Moves. Countermoves. Feigns. Knowing your adversary and staying one step ahead of him.

I took the job.

An hour after the interview, I found myself wandering around the city center on trembly legs. What had I done? If only I could afford to sit at a café and have a tea, just the time to collect my thoughts. Home seemed so far away. I found myself walking towards the sea, towards Jane. She was so positive, so encouraging – like no one else I knew. Odessans are fatalists and pessimists. Whenever I spoke of travel, my friends would say, 'Wake up! There's a reason they call it the American dream.' My Boba's friends shook their heads at me and said, 'Horses dream of sugar,' the Odessan way of saying that good things are for other people. With Jane, I could talk about my hopes and dreams and she made me believe that they would come true. Her flat in the city center, only three blocks from the sea, was a haven, a heaven. High ceilings, parquet floor, a balcony with grape vines. She had her own kitchen, her own space. No one else our age lived independently. Maybe it was easier to be an optimist when you had so much.

An *Americanka* who'd come to perform what she called 'community service,' Jane had tried to teach Odessan pupils about democracy. She lived like she'd never learned the meaning of the word 'no.' She wore trousers to school. It was as if she didn't know that it was against the rules for females – even the teachers – to wear them. I'd seen her win a shouting match with a bureaucrat *and* punch a corrupt cop! I kept a notebook of words and phrases she taught me. Awesome. Cool. Fuck. Whatever. It's easier to ask forgiveness than it is to ask permission. Go for it. Just do it. Her vocabulary was as colorful as her red hair. And the stories she told. I loved hearing about America. Even her impressions of Odessa were interesting to me. In this shady city famous for its shades of gray, Jane saw only black and white. She made life seem so … uncomplicated.

I slipped into the courtyard and tiptoed into her building, but the babushka on the first floor heard me anyway and opened her door a crack.

In Odessa, there is always someone watching.

'Going to see Janna?' she asked.

'*Da*,' I replied, though it was none of her business.

'Well, don't stay too long. She needs her rest. The poor thing's been packing all day.'

I didn't need a reminder that my dear friend was going home. I walked up to the third floor. Jane opened the door before I could knock.

'How did the interview go?' she asked and pulled me inside.

'I got the job.'

'Awesome!' she said and hugged me tight. She put on the tea kettle and we sat at her table. The pure joy on her face, the way she said, 'I've been so worried about you and I was leaving and felt like I was totally abandoning you. But now I know you'll be okay.'

'I'll miss you,' I said, looking into the living room at the piles of clothes and books – her two years in Odessa reduced to two suitcases. 'You're so different from my other friends.'

'Friends,' she snorted. 'I know they mean well, but don't listen to them, especially not to that Olga. Don't listen to anybody.'

'You're right …'

' "Nothing I do matters. Nothing ventured, nothing lost," ' she mimicked the fatalist Odessan refrains. 'No. Don't let the bastards get you down. You need to believe in yourself. Not your Odessan superstitions, not your Boba's curses, not fate. Yourself. You're stronger than you think you are.'

'I'm not so sure ...'

'Believe it. I would have died without you. I was so lonely and scared when I got here, but you called every evening, you helped me learn Russian, you taught me all I needed to know about Odessan men ...'

We laughed.

She stroked my cheek. 'God, what would I have done without you? I'll miss you. But now I know you'll be fine. You've got a good job. No, a great job. You'll be speaking English all day, your dream.'

'Do you think my English is good enough?'

'Hell, yes. You speak better than most native speakers. Your vocabulary is better than mine. You've mastered the language. You even know differences in British and American English. I'm telling you, you know more than I do. Remember how disappointed my colleagues were when they learned I was "only an American" as they put it? When they were disappointed because I didn't speak "real English," who helped me learn the vocabulary?'

I basked in the glow of her praise. And decided to quiz her. 'What's a "flat"?'

'An apartment,' she shot back.

'Queue!'

'A line. Or to wait in line.' She squeezed my hand. 'What would I have done without you?'

We sat in silence and doubt crept back.

'But what about my accent?'

'How many times do I have to tell you? Everyone has an accent. I have an accent – you can tell right away I'm American. British people have accents. Canadians have accents. Yours is almost imperceptible – that's not something New Yorkers can say!'

I laughed. She knew how to put a person at ease.

'My God! Think about it. You'll be earning a huge salary. You'll probably be running the place within a year. I'm so proud of you.'

So how could I tell her the truth? That nothing in Odessa is entirely good. That this contract had a cost. For excellent-paying jobs, candidates paid a bribe, which Odessans called 'an investment.' And with this position, my investment would be more personal and painful than most.

Chapter 2

On that first day, I went to work filled with great trepidation. When? And how? At the office? Or some hotel? Right away or after lunch? How do these things happen? How could I put him off? It's that time of the month. That time of the year. I don't feel so good. Let's get to know one another. It could take years …

I sat at my desk, tense, ears pricked, waiting for Mr. Harmon to pounce, ready to fight him off with words or fists. But he didn't even want to sleep with me. He said he didn't like my teeth. (I'd been careful not to smile during the interview. Napoleon's wife Josephine also had bad teeth. But aside from being married to a murderous dictator, Josephine was lucky. She was born in an age when fans were a popular accessory. She held one in front of her mouth when she smiled. When Mr. Harmon summoned me to his office, I imagined holding his electric fan in front of my face and I started to giggle.)

Like many Odessans during Soviet times, my grandmother had had to choose between luxuries like buying food and going to the dentist. (Philosophically, health care in the former Soviet Union was free. In practice, however, things were slightly different. You had to take a gift to the doctor. No gift, no treatment. No present, no future.) My teeth weren't perfect, but at least I'd never gone hungry. I was surprised when Mr. Harmon said he would pay to have my smile fixed. I declined, he insisted. I declined, he insisted. I declined, he insisted. Thus, I knew he meant it and I made an appointment. For the first time in my life I went to the dentist, who sat me down in the gray leather chair and pulled a light over my face. To evade the glare, I turned my head and saw a menacing arsenal of picks, hooks, and pliers on the table next to him. I looked away and saw that in the sink, there was dried blood and spit. (In Odessa, the city 'conserved' water by turning it off during the day.)

I clenched my teeth.

'Open up,' he said.

I couldn't. I didn't want him to see my blackened teeth.

'It's not that I don't appreciate a tight-lipped woman,' he joked, 'but I have a job to do.'

I smiled. He frowned and said, 'It's worse than I thought.'

'Can I come back tomorrow?' I asked, barely opening my mouth.

'What difference will a day make?'

I returned the next afternoon and sat down in the chair. The dentist shone the light in my eyes. I stood – I knew what he would do. I didn't know if I could go through with it.

'Today's not the day?' he asked, hiding his annoyance fairly well.

It took one more appointment before I felt comfortable on that chair with the light blaring in my face, highlighting my foremost imperfection. I'd spent my life hiding my teeth, never smiling without my hand in front of my lips. It was hard for me to open up.

'There, there,' he crooned, 'that's not so bad. So your teeth are crooked and black. Soon, you'll have white, straight ones.'

He promised the process would take less than a month. But the sooner I had beautiful teeth, the sooner Mr. Harmon would be interested, so I told the dentist to take his time. This tactic alone bought me four months. I was happy to have a nice smile. Though I was sad when the dentist yanked all my teeth out.

I loved those first days, working in English, the international language, communicating with our branches all over the world. Growing up, I'd learned English sayings and songs and sonnets, but never thought that one day I would *need* English, that this knowledge would be useful: we Odessans lived on the Black Sea but we'd been landlocked by the Soviet Union. English had been my pastime, my passion, my solace. I loved everything about the language. I read the English dictionary the way nuns read psalms. I craved new words the way Russian leaders crave power. I loved

13

the alchemy of English, how a 't' and an 'h' come together to form a completely different sound. Thistle. Thunder. I loved how speaking English made me feel. Smart. Sophisticated. Foreign. Better.

I loved answering the phone in English. I loved running my hand along my computer monitor. Everything in the office was of the best quality. Quality that I, and most Odessans, had never seen before – even our light bulbs gave off a dingy, sad light. I felt proud to be a part of a company that imported space heaters, washing machines, and videocassette players from the West. I enjoyed speaking with the ship's captain in English as the sailors unloaded the large metal containers filled with our yearnings. Mr. Harmon took a photo of me at the helm, then the captain snapped one of us together. I didn't even mind that Mr. Harmon snaked his hand around my waist. In Ukraine, having our picture taken was very special. Most people didn't own cameras. We didn't even have color film until the eighties.

It was a challenge to get our products through customs, but I soon learned to deal with the agents – who could blame them for wanting to taste the food or watch the films or wear the clothes our company brought to Odessa? I found that when I offered samples, our goods cleared customs quickly. This exchange seemed perfectly reasonable. After all, at the post office you pay more for first-class postage.

I admit to being seduced by the high-quality pens, sleek black cordless phone, and pristine company stationery, so unlike our rough, gray paper. The whiteboard and markers in the boardroom and the colorful packs of Post-its seemed remarkable to me. The first month, I put neon pink ones on documents to remind Mr. Harmon where he had to sign and when shipments were coming in. These tokens made me realize how much better and brighter things were in the West, and I yearned to discover that world. I hoped my new job was a step in the right direction.

Our offices weren't on the Black Sea. Mr. Kessler, the company director in Haifa, called the rent at the port 'extortion' and instead leased a nondescript building in the city center on bustling Soviet Army Street, where cars and faded red trams fought for space, where gypsies begged in front of the blue Orthodox church with golden domes, where young women selling bouquets called out to passers-by. The plain exterior of our office belied the posh interior, though the presence of a hairy security guard hinted at our prosperity. Near the entryway, there was a state-of-the-art kitchen for coffee breaks. The refrigerator was filled with Finnish vodka, German chocolate, and French cheese. Down the long corridor with shiny white walls was my work station. Mr. Harmon's spacious office, with his large black desk covered with expensive gadgets, was through the door on my right; the boardroom, with the long, sleek table and leather chairs, on the left.

I bought a palm tree and placed it beside the window. Sometimes I daydreamed about California. Sandy beaches; warm, salty water rolling over my body; the sun soft on my skin. There'd be no thoughts of money, of letches, of whether I was Ukrainian or Jewish. I would be just me, alone – anonymous on a beach. I looked towards the palmetto and sighed. The metal bars ruined the effect. Because it was an Israeli office, the panes were covered with steel shafts and security guards stood at attention twenty-four hours a day. Despite the protection money we paid the Stanislavskis.

I have always been a good worker. I never missed a day, even when I had gaping holes in my mouth. I just kept my head down as though the documents on my desk were fascinating. My hair curled around my face to hide my lips curled around my gums searching for the missing teeth. I went into the office early and wouldn't leave until the last person had gone for the evening. During these weeks, Mr. Harmon fetched our coffee – I refused to venture into the kitchen.

I was not entirely suited to the position of secretary, since my degree was in mechanical engineering. Still, I learned to make excellent coffee and type. I improved my English and studied Hebrew. Mr. Harmon asked me to teach him Russian, but after three lessons, I realized that some old dogs can only bark or whine.

After my dentures were in, Mr. Harmon started to pursue me. He'd already worked out that propositions were not the way to win this young lady's body, so he tried another approach: subtlety. In the afternoon, when the city cut the power, he and I sat in the darkened boardroom, he at the head of the table, I at his right side. We sipped cold coffee and waited for the computers and fax machine to switch back on.

'Can't we bribe someone?' he asked.

I nodded approvingly. He was finally thinking like an Odessan. 'We'd have to pay at least three people at the electric company, which would cost roughly four hundred dollars per month.'

'Extortion!'

'The price of doing business in Odessa,' I corrected.

'Same thing,' he muttered. 'Maybe I could bring in a generator.'

He drank the last of his coffee and we sat in companionable silence for a moment.

'I never go out in the evening,' he said.

'Not even to the opera or *philharmonia*?'

'No.'

I couldn't believe it. Most people come to Odessa for the entertainment – the ballet, the beaches, the concerts, the cafés, the casinos, the discos … 'Don't you have a good *compania*?'

'What?'

'This is how we say a "circle of friends" in Russian. Many Odessans would love to be friends with you. The girls in the office have certainly been … friendly.' Odessans don't always speak directly. We have a certain code. Distracted means crazy. Direct means abrasive. Friendly means slutty.

'True,' he said. 'But when they crowd around me, I know what they're after.' He rubbed his fingers together to indicate money.

I shrugged, the Odessan way of saying nothing and everything. I hoped I looked sympathetic, but inside I wondered why he didn't take one up on their very obvious offer.

Unable to trust anyone, he said, he sat alone in his flat, a foreigner far from friends and family. When he invited me to the ballet, of course I went. I felt sorry for him. And I loved going to our opera house, the third most beautiful in the world after Rome and Prague's. We sat in a private box. He inched his gilded chair closer to mine, telling me he couldn't see. I moved closer and closer to the edge of the box. *Leave-left-left*. His forehead shone with perspiration. He stared at me, not the stage. I knew what he was thinking and I knew what he wanted, but I sat, ankles crossed, knees firmly together; spine straight, exactly two inches from the red velvet backrest; chin slightly lifted, lips fixed in a slight smile; eyes never leaving the stage. Teeth grinding, heart pounding, stomach heaving, brain berating, 'Fool! Never let your guard down! Everything in Odessa has a price.' After the performance, people around us talked and laughed, but we were silent. In a hoarse voice, Mr. Harmon said, 'Come home with me.' I pretended not to hear. I thanked him and said goodbye, then slipped through the crowd in front of the opera house, down the 192 granite steps of the Potemkin Staircase to the bus stop at the port.

I couldn't afford to be indignant. I couldn't afford to offend him. I couldn't afford to lose my job. I remembered those six months of searching – two interviews a day and lines like, 'Maybe I'm old-fashioned, but in these hard times, when conditions are so tough, I need to give the job to a man with a family, to a breadwinner.' Boba's pension barely covered her heart medicine let alone our food and bills. We couldn't afford candles, so when they cut the electricity in the early evening, we sat in the dark in the kitchen because it was a little warmer than the rest of the flat. At bedtime, we felt our way to the bathroom to wash our faces, then back to the living room/bedroom to change into our pajamas and convert the sofa to our bed.

I had to do everything in my power to keep my job and that meant keeping Mr. Harmon content. I found a young professor with big hair and bigger breasts to try to teach him something of our language. When he showed no interest in her, I took it upon myself to hire a curvaceous charwoman, telling her to linger in his office and that if she played her cards right, she'd have a flush bank account. But Mr. Harmon had no interest in poker. To keep him at bay, I used a careful mixture of geography, denial, and guilt. I always made sure that there was something between us. When he started coming too close and had that look in his eye, I got up and walked to the opposite side of the boardroom. We circled the table slowly, both of us pretending this was perfectly normal, as many as five times before he gave up. Seeing that he would never win a race of endurance, Mr. Harmon changed his tactic and wooed me with hummus and baba ganoush as well as a battery-operated flashlight/radio for the nightly blackouts. He asked me to call him David, but I avoided doing so. When he stood too close to me, I

17

looked at him with wide eyes and said, 'You're like a father to me.' His hands tightened into fists, and he stalked back into his office. I exhaled and hoped I could last another month.

In time, he put up photos of us together. On one of our ships. In front of the opera house with clients. His arms slithered around my shoulder, his hand poised near my breast. Everyone in the office looked at the pictures and assumed I was his mistress. He was pleased – the men respected him more and me less, the women were either jealous or admired my good sense. For a time, he seemed satisfied and stopped pursuing me, as if the rumor of our involvement were good enough. I resented the fact that colleagues thought of me as his private reserve or that I was hired, not to translate the most important, strictly confidential papers, but to sleep with the boss, yet I appreciated this period of détente. We no longer circled each other warily, trying to gain the advantage. A holding pattern emerged; when we sat in the darkened boardroom waiting for the electricity to switch back on, we really talked.

'It's my daughter's birthday next week.'

I looked at him in surprise. 'You have a daughter?'

'A daughter. And ex-wife. An ex-house. An ex-dog.'

'How old is she?'

'Eighteen. I don't know what to get her.' He sighed. 'She hates me.'

I smiled. 'Is there anyone harsher or more intimidating than an angry eighteen-year-old girl?'

'You went through that phase?'

'Didn't we all? What's she like? What does she like?'

He looked at me, and his hands fluttered helplessly, as if what he was trying to convey was too much for him. Finally, he settled on, 'She's nothing like you.'

'Could you be more precise?'

'Well, you're so together, and she … she's not. She struggles at school, struggles with her weight. She dyes her hair black and listens to punk bands that make me suicidal.'

'My Boba would say that music is a cry for help. Write, even if she doesn't write back. Phone, even if she doesn't say much. Let her know that you love her. Call her best friend. She'll know exactly what your daughter would want for her birthday.'

'You're right,' he said.

'Those words sound so good coming from you.'

He laughed.

I looked at my watch. Time will show, my Boba always said. Time will show.

'I never wanted this,' he said, pointing to the black boardroom table, to the white board.

Board, bored.

'I know, I know. You hate Odessa.'

'No, I don't, and that's not what I meant. I wanted to be a writer, to study poetry. I didn't care about business.'

Know, no.

'Then why are you here?'

Here, hear.

'Family.'

That one word said so much.

'I wanted to study English, too. But Boba said, "Who'll pay you to stand on the street corner and recite Shakespeare? No one, that's who. English isn't a career, it's a hobby. You'll study engineering or accounting – something with a future." '

'Did that make you angry?' he asked.

'Why would it?' I shrugged. 'She had my best interests at heart.'

'You're a much bigger person than I am. After years of therapy I'm still not where you are. I hated that my father tried to control me. Made me get a business degree. Made me ...'

'Made you what?'

'It doesn't matter.'

Bite-bit-bitten. The strange edge of anger in his voice made me nervous and my fingers flew to my mouth out of habit.

'You don't have to do that anymore,' he said, still sounding annoyed.

I put my hand on my lap. He didn't say anything more. I wanted to fill this strange silence, to banish his sudden anger, so I spoke of Odessa. 'If you love poetry, you should read Anna Akhmatova. She was born in Odessa, you know. Or Babel. Also a native Odessan. Who did you study?'

He told me he majored in business and literature. He didn't know how lucky he was. In Ukraine, you study one thing. Classes

19

are laid out for you and there is no choice about it. He told me about his favorite authors: Hemingway, Steinbeck, McCullers. I was relieved by this talk of writers, this common ground we had found. He could have been more aggressive. He could have fired me for not complying with the criteria he'd laid out at the job interview. The devil knows other men in his position would have. Instead, he waited and would not stray, even though I constantly put voluptuous pawns in his path.

Vita and Vera, two trouble-making secretaries who seemed to know everything, said Mr. Harmon had been sent to Odessa as a punishment for screwing up so many shipping orders in Haifa. When colleagues repeated this rumor and asked if he was as inept as he looked, I sharply reminded them that what Vita and Vera did not know, they simply made up. As long as he didn't force me, I remained loyal to him. But inside, I acknowledged that Mr. Harmon still couldn't do much without my help. He didn't even know to make three copies of the books – an accurate copy for the accountants, as well as fake sets for the Stanislavskis (showing 50 percent of our profits) and the government (showing only 25 percent). What had they taught him at that business school?

As always, before Mr. Harmon arrived, I made coffee, getting in and out of the kitchen before Vita and Vera turned up. But today, just as the coffee started percolating, I heard them cackling down the hall. So far, they'd caused three girls to quit – or get fired – because of their cruel gossip, and I didn't want to be another of their victims. *Run-ran-run.* When they entered the kitchen, they looked at me like I was a stain on the wall. As usual, both were wearing too much make-up and not enough clothing. Boba would never let me leave the flat wearing a skirt so tight it looked like sausage casing over lumpy bits of meat. These girls had spent more time applying their make-up than applying themselves in school. They barely spoke English and had no computer skills. One didn't need to think too hard about why they'd been hired – the same reason I had.

Vera asked me, 'What do you do?'

'I beg your pardon?'

'What do you do in bed?' Vera asked. 'We want to know.'

'I sleep.' I gulped down the last of my coffee and tried to leave, but they blocked the door.

'How did you get so much money?' Vita pressed. 'Why do you get so many presents?'

'I'm sure I don't know.' Perhaps it was rude to think of these girls as prostitutes, but it was naïve *not* to think of them in that way. I didn't feel guilty about my uncharitable thoughts, since they considered me a whore, too. A superior one at that.

'You look like a frigid bitch, but you must be doing something right.' Vera stared at me, as though she could somehow decipher my tricks. 'Do you lick it? Do you like it?' she continued, trying to embarrass me. And succeeding, though I would never show them. I took a deep breath and willed myself not to turn borscht red.

'What do the two of you talk about?' Vita asked.

'Does he dress you up? Tie you down? Does he buy you lingerie just so he can rip it off your tight, little body?' Vera asked, running her fingers across my chest. I hit her hand away.

As I walked down the hall, I heard Vita ask softly, 'Does Mr. Harmon love you?'

Her question stopped me. Love? He spoiled me with trinkets and treated me like a precious object when he wasn't jealously guarding me from the eyes of any male in our office. He pursued me until he grew dizzy, like a dog chasing its own tail. That wasn't my idea of love. Was it his?

I longed for love. For passion. For ecstasy. I knew what the words meant, but not how they *felt*. Love. Was it dancing in the moonlight to music only two people hear? Was it washing socks and peeling potatoes? Was it sex? Was it tender? What were the exact ingredients? How do you make it grow? How do you kill it? How long do you have to suffer when it dies? I'd read Russian novels full of beauty and anguish. I'd discovered American romances with their happy endings. But nothing in my life was like that. Love. Boba said love was blind, deaf, and dumb – mostly dumb. She also said that the minute a woman fell in love was the minute trouble began. And that the women in our family were cursed. But that didn't stop me from longing. I wanted a husband. I wanted to hold an infant to my breast. I wanted a real family – the kind I'd never had. The kind with a mother *and* a father.

Vita's question softened me. Of course, I wanted friends at the office. Of course, I hated that they were jealous. I returned to the kitchen threshold and admitted, 'I haven't slept with Mr. Harmon,' then added, 'My grandmother says that sex gets you dinner and an evening at the opera, but saying no to sex gets you respect, or at worst, a wedding ring.'

Vera laughed bitterly; Vita still didn't understand, the poor dear. Some women never get it. Of course, they repeated what I'd said. Fifty-one minutes later, when Mr. Harmon realized that he'd gone from the office stud to the office joke, he was angry. Very angry.

Late every evening, after her three children fell asleep, my neighbor Olga, an artist, came down for a quick bite – she couldn't stay long, as she didn't dare leave her babies alone. Olga and I had been in the same grade in junior high, I'd been the head of the class, she the tail. We'd stuck together through thin and thinner. Both our fathers deserted us. We were put in the worst section because neither of us could afford to bribe the teachers. We both wanted to practice ballet, so we pooled our money together to buy one pair of satin slippers. Later, the dance instructor said my body was made for playing ping-pong, not dancing. My feet kept growing; Olga kept the slippers.

In high school, Olga was so popular she didn't have time to study. I wrote her essays and let her copy my math problems with pleasure. In exchange, she told me all about her dates, including her rendezvous with the geometry teacher. (That term, she didn't need to copy my math homework.) Olga, petite and pretty, sat on the boys' laps, giggling and cooing as they stroked her curvaceous bottom. I was the tallest person in school and so skinny the boys called me 'frizzy-haired matchstick.' Olga fell in love as often as it rained. I hadn't fallen in love yet – not even once.

Five years later, she was the only classmate who had any time for me. Though Odessa is a fairly level city, a great divide exists: marriage. Boys are spoiled by their mothers and expect to be pampered by their wives. As a teen visiting my friends this is what I saw: Men go to work, then return home and read the newspaper with their feet up. Women go to work then return home and work some more. Marriage is all-consuming.

And now my former schoolmates spent their evenings and weekends looking after their husbands: cooking daily feasts from scratch; canning the vegetables and fruit of their labor; washing clothes and linens by hand, then ironing all items – even towels and underwear – as a proper wife should. In Odessa, girls' night out doesn't exist for married women.

Olga, despite her three little ones, was like me – never married. Of course, she said she was divorced so that people wouldn't think there was something wrong with her.

As usual, Olga wore her sheer cotton robe and our tattered ballet slippers. There was blue paint on her cheek and some in her yellow hair. She carried little Ivan, who was bundled up like a Siberian Eskimo.

'Olga, come in. For God's sake, eat something.'

We entered the kitchen, my grandmother's domain. The orange linoleum on the walls and floor was of poor quality, but immaculate. Boba had scrubbed the surfaces with her special lemon-bleach concoction so many times that they were tangerine-colored. I pulled a stool out from under the table and sat Olga down, then fixed her a plate of hummus, red peppers stuffed with feta, and *lavash* bread.

I took Ivan in my arms. 'He feels hot,' I said and gently pulled off the sweater and cap Boba had knit him so I could touch his soft skin.

'I swear, you're in love with that boy,' Olga said.

She seemed to force herself to eat slowly, so that I wouldn't know – or wouldn't mention – that this was the first meal she'd had all day. 'I get so involved in my work and forget about the time,' she said.

For my birthday, Olga always gave me a small abstract painting. She was talented, it's just most people were struggling to survive and couldn't afford art anymore. Principles were also very expensive. As she finished eating, I poured the water from the purifier into the electric kettle (both presents from Mr. Harmon). The electric kettle was easier to use than the gas stove, and the filtered water tasted much better, though we still had to boil it to kill the bacteria. Olga asked about my day, so I told her about Mr. Harmon, Vita, and Vera.

'Wake up!' Olga yelled. 'Every bite you take is thanks to Mr. Harmon. Everything you have – down to your fancy toilet paper – comes from him. You know what he wants, just pay up! You're being rude. He's made more effort to seduce you than all my lovers combined!'

It must be said that all of Odessa knows how easy Olga is.

'What's the big deal?' she continued. 'If I had a rich foreign man who wooed me, I'd be thrilled.' Olga slammed her plate in the sink, then turned and said, 'You just don't know how lucky you are.'

I did know. Boba taught me to look for moments – or seconds – of grace. She often reminded me that we were lucky to live in a one-room flat, when many people lived in *kommunalkas*, communal apartments. She said we were lucky to have enough to eat and instructed me to give coins to pensioners begging in the streets and to feed Olga, who could barely nourish her three children. (Unlike most women, Olga was too tenderhearted to abort. I'd never met any other Russian or Ukrainian woman with three children.)

Olga opened the front door and yanked Ivan from my arms. 'You owe it to Mr. Harmon to sleep with him. After all, you took the job knowing the requirements. Pay up.'

The door slammed in my face.

Perhaps she was right. After all, I had accepted the job and the conditions.

I thought about what Olga said and decided to ask Jane. After Mr. Harmon left for the day, I called her in America and explained that a 'friend' was having trouble with her boss. Although she sometimes surprised me with her uncanny analyses, Jane was sometimes so obtuse she couldn't see through plastic wrap (another gift from Mr. Harmon). This was one of those times. Jane said, 'That's harassment! It's against the law for her boss to demand sexual favors,' as though the laws of the civilized world counted here.

I laughed at that phrase, sexual favors. A favor is an act of kindness or help. It wasn't a favor, it was an economic form of dominance that many Western men applied in Odessa. But

Americans are not precise in their language. Jane could meet someone and five minutes later call him a friend. For me, this same person would remain an acquaintance for a very long time.

'Don't let her be taken advantage of! In the States, laws protect women and children against predators.'

I liked it when she spoke of her country. It sounded like a lovely place full of laws and security for everyone. Even trees and flowers are protected in America.

Mr. Harmon was no fool. He didn't speak much Russian, but he understood that everyone was laughing at him, and he was furious with me. I'd managed to hold him off for six months, yet I could feel my days were numbered. He noticed Vita and Vera giggling when he entered the kitchen. It occurred to me that they exhibited this behavior to get back at me or get rid of me. They were jealous that I had a higher salary and unlike them, I hadn't slept with my boss as a contract clincher.

For days, he glared and barked at me, more than usual. 'Quit typing so loud, dammit! I have a headache!' 'What are you smiling for? And who do you think paid for that smile?'

My hand flew to my mouth.

After lunch I sat at my desk, typing as quietly as possible. He slipped behind me. I kept typing. 'Ship arrived a day late, on the 25th.' He didn't say anything, he just stood there. I didn't know what to do. I was afraid to speak. Afraid to move. *Freeze-froze-frozen.* Somehow, this quiet assault was more terrifying than his blundering and blustering. 'Customs cleared on the 29th.' I felt unsettled, as if he had tied a ribbon around my neck and pulled it tighter and tighter until I could no longer breathe. Still I typed. 'Two hundred empty containers loaded on to ship.' Only when Yuri the security guard lumbered down the hall on his rounds did Mr. Harmon retreat. I continued to type. 'Await next delivery on the 2nd.' Quietly.

The next morning, I stalled. I stood in the bathroom and gripped the cracked sink and looked in the mirror. How much longer could I take it? What would it take to make him stop? I was afraid. And weary of constantly watching my step. But I needed this job. Boba and I were finally living like normal people.

In Odessa, there's a saying: Moscow is known for its winter days and frosty females, Odessa for her summer nights and hot women. The plain truth is that Odessans are drop dead out of this world gorgeous. Maybe it's the sea air, maybe the sunshine. We have silky hair, flawless skin, and cheekbones with sharper edges than our tongues. How could I make myself less attractive? I pulled my dark hair into an austere bun at the base of my neck and washed off the mascara that highlighted my green eyes. Pairing a white blouse with a loose black blazer and long skirt, I looked like an anemic nun.

When Mr. Harmon stood in front of my desk to tell me the day's schedule, he snapped. 'You owe me!'

Sick of feeling as though I were walking barefoot on broken glass, I, too, snapped. I stood, so that I towered over him. 'Do you want me to show you what I owe you?'

'Yessss.' The word came out of his mouth like an enraptured sigh, as if he really expected me to lift up my blouse and bare my breasts.

'This is what I owe you.' I pulled out my dentures. 'Take them.'

I forced myself to smile, revealing my bald, ugly gums. Deflated in every sense, Mr. Harmon retreated to his office. My hands shook so hard that it was difficult to put my teeth back in. The constant pressure was starting to get to me. I knew that I had to leave this office – and eventually Odessa – if I wanted to build a normal life for myself. Although at twenty-three I was rather old, I still wanted a family. If I had a little girl, I'd name her Nadezhda – Hope – after my mother. Of course, to have a child, you need a man. I was so busy with work, I had no time to date. And anyway, Boba said Odessan men weren't worth a kopeck. Jane had praised American men because they built a foundation of friendship before 'taking it to the next step.' I loved my native city, but how I longed to escape, to go to America – a land full of eligible men, a land free of harassment at work.

I thought of how I'd repelled Mr. Harmon, embarrassed that I had been lowered to such a vulgar display. Until now, I'd thought of him as a nuisance, but after his outburst and strange behavior the day before, I had to reconsider this stance. He was a danger. It would not be possible to out-maneuver him forever. I just didn't realize that his retribution would come so quickly.

That afternoon, I was standing at my desk revising the quarterly report when he strode up behind me and spun me around.

'Hey,' I yelled and shoved him.

He shoved me back and I fell back on to the desk. My breath left my lungs and wouldn't come back. I gasped for air. I tried to move my leg to kick him in the groin. Impossible. I tried to formulate a complete thought. Impossible. I tried to find the words to dissuade him as I had so many times before, but when I opened my mouth, only a sad whimper emerged. I stared up at him like a butterfly full of ether, waiting for him to stick his pin in and finish me off.

But Mr. Harmon looked at me with wide eyes; he was just as scared as I.

For once, being Jewish in Ukraine paid off. The thump of my body hitting the metal desk must have reverberated throughout the building because someone came to see about the noise. As an Israeli office, we received phone threats all the time. Despite our security guards, bombs had been placed in our offices. Any strange squeak or thump raised the hairs on the back of people's necks.

'I'm sorry,' he whispered hoarsely. 'I never meant ...'

He tried to help me sit up, but when he moved to touch me, I flinched.

I turned my head to see who'd come to investigate the noise. Thank God it wasn't Vita and Vera. It was only Mr. Kessler, the director from Haifa who'd come to inspect our offices. He looked at me flat on my back, at my boss standing inert between my legs. He shouted something at Harmon in rapid-fire Hebrew. My breath came back with a vengeance, and I started coughing. Harmon stepped back; I rose and righted my skirt, then ran.

Cold and strangely restless, I stood at the kitchen sink, trembling. This was the first time that my voice – and indeed, my mind – had ever failed me. I felt like crying, but knew any display of weakness would be used against me in the court of Vita and Vera. In Odessa, what others thought was more important than the truth; you learned to think fast and never show your feelings. People had heard the commotion and were milling around the halls; they would learn of the incident and my response would be talked about. I pretended my eyelids were hummingbird wings that flicked away my tears. I wanted to flee, to get another job, even another life. *And how soon is the sentence to be carried out? Why does nothing work out for us?*

I didn't know what to do with myself, so I took a white filter, filled it, and watched the coffee drip into the carafe. I concentrated on the rich smell, this small taste of daily luxury, so that I wouldn't embarrass myself. Before working here, I'd never tasted real coffee. Boba and I only had lumpy Soviet instant. When I'd told that to Mr. Harmon, he gave Boba and me an espresso machine and a three-month supply of coffee.

I filled my small cup, which I had to hold with both hands. Suddenly, everyone wanted coffee, and they came into the kitchen. Vita and Vera smirked; their bosses, slightly younger versions of Mr. Harmon, leered. My legs couldn't hold me any longer and I sagged on to a stool at the table.

Minutes later, the presence of Mr. Kessler dispersed the crowd, and he apologized on Mr. Harmon's behalf. I covered my face and berated myself for the moment of honesty in which I'd told those tarts that I hadn't slept with Mr. Harmon. I'd just been so sick of people looking at me like a slut. I should have remembered that telling the truth just gets you into trouble.

Mr. Kessler mistook my reaction for shame and patted my shoulder awkwardly. He offered me a small raise and said he hoped I wouldn't be litigious. Apparently, he didn't realize there was no law and order in Ukraine. I wouldn't be the one to tell him.

'It won't happen again,' Mr. Kessler promised.

He would be gone in a week. Then what?

I stood and smoothed down the long wool skirt that Boba had sewn for me, then walked down the empty hall, back to my chair, back to my life.

You needn't pity me.

Chapter 3

I congratulated myself for looking as though nothing had happened. Dry eyes, faint smile. Vita and Vera would have nothing to report. Though I'd stopped trembling, I felt as if I would throw up or pass out. I looked at the numbers on the quarterly report but didn't see them. It took all my concentration to remain calm. This was difficult. As the minutes passed, I became aware of my tenuous position, and it terrified me.

I wasn't scared of Harmon. Not in the physical sense, anyway. He hadn't meant to hurt me. Rather, he'd come to his senses or lost his nerve before he could do his worst. But his intentions weren't what mattered. What mattered was what Mr. Kessler saw. Harmon was now in trouble with the hierarchy, and in a true trickle-down system, that meant I was in trouble with him. If he fired me, I would lose the salary and the security I'd gained. If I wasn't careful, I could end up a waitress like my friend Maria, or worse. Without this job, Boba and I would go back to the way things were before, when we could only dream of oranges and espresso, when Boba had taken in laundry and we'd spent evenings and weekends washing, wringing, and ironing Party people's garments for a pittance.

I was keenly aware of Harmon and his rituals. As usual, he uttered the number of days he had been here: 183; and how many left to go: 547. As usual, he counted out fifteen one-hundred-dollar bills and muttered that it was worth living in a 'third-world country' since he didn't have to declare his earnings to mother Israel. I heard him stuff the bills back in his wallet and snap it shut. He refilled his stapler and lined it up with his Waterman

29

pens. He cleared his throat and blew his nose. He sighed. If he was counting the days, I was counting the minutes, looking at the digital alarm clock that he'd given me. (Twenty-three minutes to go.) It gave the day, the date, and the temperature inside as well as on the street. It said that the office was 70 degrees, but it felt well below zero. I picked the dead strands off the palm tree and organized my desk drawer. At 5 p.m., I picked up my purse and said, 'I'm going.'

'Go.'

I was not able to decipher his tone.

The security guards smirked at me as I walked out of the building. Vera and Vita had been efficient. Why had I said anything to them? *Never trust anyone. Never say anything. The walls have ears, the birch trees have eyes.* How many times had my grandmother warned me? Why hadn't I listened? I feared that the moment Mr. Kessler went back to Haifa, Harmon would fire me. One thing was clear: I needed to look for another job, though none would pay as well. I thought about earning only thirty dollars a month and felt sick. How would we manage? Only a month ago, the world had felt so full of promise. I had a good job and felt reasonably secure. Now I was back to where I had been just months before: no money, no security, no future.

Unless.

Unless I found Harmon a mistress … But who? He'd rebuffed every woman in the office. Perhaps now guilt and shame and Mr. Kessler would make him reconsider, I thought as I stood at the bus stop. Who? Olga? She needed money; he needed sex. He would appreciate her flashy hair, petite body, and lively spirit, though I worried that she wasn't educated enough. She only spoke Russian and didn't know how to hold a fork. No. I could never ask her. What if she was offended and said no? What if she said yes?

As always, the bus was twenty minutes late. As always, passengers were packed like Black Sea sardines into the seats and aisles. We couldn't open the windows: they'd been nailed shut as a safety precaution. The glass was already fogged up, and we hadn't even left yet. I took off my blazer. Perspiration ran down my face; my arm stuck to the girl's beside me. I hated beginning and ending my day with this forty-five minute bus ride to and from the sleeping district. (Jane called it the suburbs of the suburbs.) Once, I invited an American missionary to my flat. When she stepped off the bus, she looked around and said, 'It's like a cemetery. Look at all the gray tombstones sticking out of the ground.'

I'm sure she didn't mean to hurt my feelings.

Before, I hadn't thought about it. Home was just home. But afterward, I couldn't help but see my neighborhood through her eyes. Ugly. Gray. Dead. At my stop, I got off and wound my way through the rusty kiosks and crude cement high-rises that hurt my soul to look at.

As always, the lift was broken. I trudged up ten flights of stairs to the one-room flat Boba had received for thirty years of faithful service at the rope factory. Of course, now that the Soviet system was abolished, no one gave anyone anything anymore. I unlocked the first three locks and Boba opened the final two. I'd never unlocked all five. It was like a game. I tried to be quick, but she was always there for me, waiting. I took off my pumps and wiggled my toes. (The city was so sooty that when Odessans got home the first thing we did was take off our dust-covered shoes.) Boba had already laid out my blue slippers, which she'd knitted for me; I handed her my blazer, purse, and briefcase.

'Look at you in just a blouse! You must be freezing! No wonder you're practically catching a cold! Put on your sweater and I'll feed you.'

It was no use telling her I'd just taken off my blazer and that I wasn't cold and was perfectly healthy. She always makes a fuss.

To my mind, Boba looked like the great French singer Edith Piaf, whose nickname was 'the little sparrow.' Boba dyed her cropped hair as black as Stalin's soul. Her skin was dark and leathery from a lifetime of Sunday afternoons at the beach. She was sixty-three but had more energy than a teenager. She wore a housecoat and had a dish towel slung across her shoulder, always prepared to clean up one of my messes. Her one extravagance was a silver necklace with a medallion of a sad-looking saint.

'Oh, Boba, I had such a hard day,' I told her, trying to hold back the tears. I wanted to tell her what had happened, but didn't want to worry her. She carried enough burdens. Not only had Boba

31

brought me up, she'd raised her daughter alone and taken care of her as she died.

'There, there,' she said and stroked my hair. 'I'll get your sweater. Everything will be fine. I made you a chocolate cake.'

I washed my hands at the kitchen sink. I wore the sweater though I was hot. She beamed at me – Ukrainians liked to see people bundled up. She handed me the dishtowel that rested on her shoulder.

'Tell me everything, Dasha.' Boba called me by my diminutive. In Odessa, we have the inside world and the outside world, the informal and the formal mode of address. Like shutters on a window, the formal is a form of defense. Diminutives are for friends and family, a sign of affection. I was so glad to be home with Boba after such a difficult day. If only she could keep the outside world at bay, like she did when I was a child.

We sat together at the small Formica table. She put her hand over mine; I looked into her concerned eyes and told her that the work load given to me was stressful. She patted my hand and began, 'I remember my boss Anatoly Pavlovich at the rope factory. He was so grouchy and hard to please …' I listened to her voice, so soothing, but not the words.

Late that evening, when Olga came with little Ivan, we sat in the kitchen. I pulled a tablet of German chocolate out of my purse, she handed me Ivan. I cradled him in my arms, whispering the same words Boba used to say to me. He opened his eyes, then his lids fluttered shut again. He nestled closer and as the heat of his little body seeped into mine, I felt the events of the day recede. My heart stopped twitching and started to beat steadily again. My breathing calmed. Such is the magic of children.

Olga slowly opened the beautiful gold foil and put a square in her mouth and sighed. 'I haven't had chocolate in ages.'

I felt guilty for not giving her more of these little pleasures. Olga radiated a sensual bliss, her eyes closed, her neck arched. She chewed slowly to make it last. Watching her savor my offering, I realized how much had changed for Boba and me. I wondered how to broach the subject of Harmon.

'You're awfully quiet,' she said.

I didn't know what to say. I turned the question over in my mind ten times in thirty seconds. *My virtue or my friend? Maybe she needs the help. Maybe you're a terrible person. Maybe you should let her decide what she wants. Maybe you should find someone else.*

'What already?' she asked.

'Olga, was what you said true?' I blurted out. 'You know, about being thrilled to have a foreign man woo you and spoil you? Even if he was a bit older?'

She snorted. 'As long as he puts food on the table, I'll gladly welcome him in my bed. I've had it with Odessan men! Do the math – three kids, three dead-beat dads, and zero help. I'm not smart like you – I'll never make a living sitting on my ass all day. I'm willing to make it on my back – God knows it's faster.'

'You're a talented artist,' I protested.

'That no one needs.' This was a common refrain after perestroika. Singers, artists, and scientists had talent and training but no jobs. And they weren't the only ones. Odessa was full of the Red Army's cast-offs, big men who'd been so important now felt useless. Many committed suicide – some with a gun, others slowly drowning in vodka. Factories closed, leaving men and women – thousands of whom had worked thirty years at the same machine – broke and bewildered. There was no safety net, or safety, for any of us.

I patted her shoulder, wishing that things were different.

She shook off my hand. 'Leave me be.'

Poor Olga. It was so hard for her, for everyone, right now.

'Are you ever going to start dating?' she asked. 'When are you going to do something with your life?'

I shrugged.

'I mean, what do you have to show?' She looked pointedly at my non-existent chest and flat belly. 'You know, a woman who doesn't have children might as well be a man.'

Tears pricked my eyes as if she had slapped my face.

Worthless. She didn't say it, but that's what she meant. Who but your best friend will tell you the truth?

I stroked Ivan's cheek. Just looking at him made me feel better.

'Keep going the way you are and no one will ever want you.' She took another square of chocolate. 'I just hope your uterus doesn't start to shrivel up. That's what happened to my friend Inna. She's practically thirty. You know her, she lives on Kirova Street.'

Don't listen to that Olga. You're stronger than you think you are.

'What about your boss?' she continued. 'He must be loaded. If I worked there ...'

People often said I didn't see things the way others did. Perhaps it was thanks to Boba, who encouraged me in my studies and shielded me from much of the ugliness of Soviet life. She had made me feel secure, despite the blackouts and shortages, and she constantly reminded me how lucky we were. Perhaps it had to do with Jane, an alien from another world (America!) who showed me that it was all right to be different. But maybe I wasn't so different after all. Here I was asking if my friend wanted to be my boss's mistress. I took a deep breath and asked, 'Do you want to meet Mr. Harmon for lunch tomorrow?'

There. I'd said it. Now it was up to her.

When her expression stilled, it was clear she knew what I was really asking.

'If he wanted you, he'll never want me! I'm not smart and I'm no beauty like you. With your tiny waist and big green eyes, it's no wonder you got the job!' She sighed. 'Who would want me, a single mother with a flabby gut? No one, that's who.'

'No, Olga, no! The boys at school always preferred you.'

She smiled at the memory. 'You were just a skinny splinter with your nose in a book. Look at you now. Shiny dark hair, brows like an archangel's wings. A mouth made for kissing, even if you only use it for arguing. If only you'd shut it, they'd be lining up to date you. Look at your skin with no stretch marks! How can I compete? As far as romance goes, I'm on death row.'

Yet another thing we had in common.

'Olga, you're talented and pretty. Men always like curves.'

'They go for your bony ass, too.'

We laughed together.

'All I want is a sliver of security,' she said. 'Is that too much to ask?'

I shook my head. We sat in silence.

Boba came into the kitchen and brewed us a pot of chamomile tea. Olga looked at the cup as if she had never seen one before.

When she had drunk her tea and made up her mind, she simply asked, aware of my grandmother, 'What would I wear?'

'I might have something,' I said to acknowledge her response.

She ransacked my armoire with glee. 'You have better things than the bazaar! Such quality!' She tore out dresses then ran to the mirror and held them in front of her. Finally, we found a skirt she could hem. Olga looked longingly at my sandals, but I wore a size ten, she a six. Olga could never fill my shoes.

Perusing the Western perfumes that clients had given me as thank you gifts, she grabbed a bottle of Dior off the shelf and said, 'I'll take it for luck.'

For the first time ever, Harmon was already in his office when I arrived. He'd left a ten-page logistics report on my desk with a note to translate it into Russian. I started immediately, hating the strange tension, but relieved that I didn't have to deal with him. At 10.30, I heard him get up for his morning coffee, then plunk back down in his black ergonomic chair. Perhaps he was as embarrassed as I was – he didn't even come out to look over my shoulder like he usually did.

When Olga walked though the door at noon, her squeaky voice cut through the tension. 'Such a beautiful office. Superior light fixtures, satiny paint. Look at these bare walls! You need some artwork. *Ooh tee!* What a fancy desk!' She caressed my cordless phone and the snowy white paper, surely thinking of her rotary phone with the beat-up cord and the rough, gray Soviet paper she used as her canvases. I could almost see Harmon's nose twitch at *my* perfume – it smelled like she'd used the whole bottle. I went to the door of his office, but did not cross the threshold. 'Olga and I would like you to join us for lunch.'

Would Olga change her mind? What would she think of him? When he came out of his office, she greeted him effusively with a kiss on his cheek. 'Daria has told me so much about you – such a *kind* and *generous* gentleman.'

When I translated Olga's words, Harmon looked at my face sharply, expecting to find irony. He found none – I had told no one about the incident.

'How many times have I told Daria she's lucky to work for such a boss?' I translated the words, but this time Harmon's eyes remained fixed on Olga's face, feasting on her plump raspberry lips. She took off her rain coat to reveal velvety thighs in *my* blue skirt and a silver lamé halter that barely contained her breasts. Harmon ushered her into the boardroom and seated her on his right side, where I usually sat. When I returned from the kitchen with the hummus, pitas, crab, and avocados, Harmon was leaning over Olga, practically sitting in her lap. He'd taken off his glasses and I could see that his eyes sparkled with interest.

'You nice,' she said, trailing her finger along his cheek. 'I like. You need girlfriend?'

Harmon looked at me as I finished setting the table; I scowled.

When he saw me frowning, he smiled and looked back at Olga, 'I need girlfriend.'

She cooed.

I crossed my arms and bit my lip. This wasn't at all how I'd imagined it.

That evening, as usual, I waited for Olga. I expected her between nine and ten after her children fell asleep. But she didn't come. At half past ten, I put together a plate of food and took it up to her flat. No one answered, though I heard faint voices. I left the food in front of her door. I waited every evening for two weeks, but she never came. Not even to give back our plate.

Before returning to Haifa, Mr. Kessler asked me to give him and his three Israeli colleagues a tour of Odessa. He surely asked out of pity. Harmon was happy with Olga, if his baby talk and her giggles were anything to go by. Still the office atmosphere was tense. Harmon was terse, I nervous. Vita and Vera hovered in the hall, waiting for the next installment.

Feeling like a prisoner unexpectedly released on parole, I stood on hustling bustling Soviet Army Street and raised my face to the sun. I closed my eyes and listened to the voice of the city: babushkas perched on overturned pails coaxing passers-by to buy sachets of sunflower seeds, 'Come, come, a taste of sunshine!'; the gypsies begging in front of the sky blue Orthodox church; the whispers in the park across the street where people watched the old-timers stare at their queens and make their moves.

'I didn't realize chess was a spectator sport,' Mr. Kessler said.

His comment returned me from my reverie. Under a canopy of majestic acacias, I guided the men past the dark brick *philharmonia* (formerly the stock exchange – ours was founded in October of 1796, earlier than New York's), past the apartment of the white witch who could cure any complaint (from a cold to a curse). Sharing my love of Odessa – the most beautiful, cosmopolitan city in the world – with foreign colleagues was the best part of my job. 'Odessa is the humor capital of the former Soviet Union! It's no coincidence that Odessa Day is on April the first. Odessans love wordplay and jokes. For example: In Russian, what is the plural of "man?" '

The men looked at me expectantly.

'Queue!'

They laughed and continued to look at me with warm interest as I guided them down the boulevard of pastel neoclassical architecture.

I continued: 'Odessa was founded by Ekaterina the Great in 1794. Legend has it that she gave an order to name the city for Odysseus, the hero of the Greek epic. They even say that there was once an ancient Greek colony here. Visitors are surprised to learn that we Odessans speak our own blend of Russian, mixing in Yiddish phrases, a bit of Ukrainian, as well as a little German and French. Odessa was a part of a region called 'Little Russia.' But Odessa is not Russia! Russia is cold and hard – a nation of czars, madmen, and tyrants. Odessa is a warm, welcoming harbor that thrives thanks to the Black Sea – and the black market.' Thinking of another black aspect of our history, I added, 'Odessa is beyond the Pale.'

'What does that mean?' the youngest asked.

'Didn't you read any history books?' Mr. Kessler responded. 'Because of the Pale of Settlement, Jews weren't allowed to settle in Moscow, St. Petersburg, or Kiev, so they came to Odessa.'

The men looked at me with pity in their eyes. I straightened my spine and met their gaze. I didn't want anyone feeling sorry for me.

Four emaciated soldiers – they were no more than nineteen years old – wearing gray uniforms three sizes too large, approached us on the street. 'Please, just a slice of bread,' one said.

I emptied my pockets of candy and apples, which I carried because in Odessa it was important to have something to smooth over bureaucratic difficulties. I called this goodwill; Jane called it bribes. She learned quickly that a box of chocolates could open doors more quickly than arguing.

'Thank you, miss!'

The Israelis were shocked. I explained that all young men, except those who paid large sums to be 'medically unfit,' were drafted. Unfortunately, the military couldn't afford to feed its conscripts. It was true we had problems with poverty. But what city doesn't struggle to feed its poor?

'When I look at the detailed ironwork on the balconies, I think of New Orleans,' Mr. Kessler said.

The others agreed, and I felt proud that they compared Odessa to an American city. Afterward, I took my parole board to a seaside café. As his colleagues chatted up the waitress in their basic Russian, Mr. Kessler handed me an envelope and said, 'Thank you for such an interesting tour.'

Of course, he was really saying that he was sorry about the incident.

Two months later, the office atmosphere still hadn't improved. Vera and Vita kept stirring up rumors that I'd spurned Harmon because he was impotent. He fought back by inviting Olga to the office and by snapping relentlessly to show our colleagues that he was the boss of me. ('You're five minutes late!' 'Daria, get me a coffee!' 'Dammit, it's not hot enough! Make me another!') If the gossip didn't die a natural death soon, he'd fire me to regain face. With Mr. Kessler in faraway Haifa, there was no one to stop him. I was careful not to raise my voice, talk back, or even smile. Sometimes, I even held my breath.

And Olga. Olga never came back to visit Boba and me, though I did see her in the office. As always, she arrived in a burst of designer perfume.

I smiled and stood. 'Hello, Olga,' I said tentatively. 'You look lovely today.'

And she did. Quality make-up. Sparkly dress. White go-go

boots. Shiny platinum bob styled at a fancy salon. No blue paint in her hair.

She breezed by me into Harmon's office, never looking me in the eye or saying more than hello. I didn't want to press, to make her feel uncomfortable, but I didn't want to lose her, either. It made me sad. I didn't know what to do. How did she feel? Was she embarrassed? It was true that everyone from the security guards to the junior executives knew about her. Did she hate me for using her as a shield to protect myself?

During this tense period, something wonderful happened. Harmon became slightly less jealous of the computer technicians, and after several trying weeks, I finally got the Internet! You can hear about something, then be disappointed, but the Internet was much better than I'd imagined! The technician showed me how to fly from page to page and to navigate the sites. I could see why it started with a capital letter, like a country or a city. It was a whole new galaxy, like the Milky Way. I could read the BBC news, see the latest fashions from Paris, and read Edgar Allan Poe's poetry. I could search for a new job on Western employment sites. I could plan my escape.

What Jane said about America flowed through my mind like fluffy white clouds. *Wide open spaces. Courtesy. Kindness. Everyone had a car. Marriages were partnerships. People were treated the same. Laws and the police protected people, all people.* I wanted this for myself. Jane had seen my world. Now I wanted to see hers.

I wrote dozens of letters and résumés with Harmon breathing down my neck. 'Why are you typing so much? I didn't give you any typing to do.'

I felt as if I'd joined the ranks of our great writers. Penning cover letters was as challenging as writing a novel. But Tolstoy could go on for pages, while I had only four paragraphs. Of course, I was no Pushkin, but Harmon acted like a czar, threatening, snapping and spying on me.

After weeks of no response, I asked Jane what I was doing wrong. She e-mailed me a revised résumé that made it sound like I'd been elected president of Ukraine while eradicating world poverty with my bare hands. The minute Harmon left the office I phoned her. 'Such bragging. It makes me uncomfortable.'

'People who have no scruples about showing how great they are are the ones who get hired.'

'That's depressing,' I said.

'That's life.'

Maybe that was life in the rest of the world. But everything was the opposite here. When I wrote to Jane, I put her name, street address, then the city on the envelope. When Jane wrote me, she put the city, then the address, then my name. When Americans ask questions, they are phrased in the positive: Do you know? Will you help me? In Russian, they are negative: Don't you know? Won't you help me? If I gave a Russian employer the résumé Jane wrote – even if it were the truth – he'd think I was uncultured, the worst insult, the worst offense, in the entire former Soviet Union (that's almost nine million square miles). In Odessa, no one passed around résumés. When he hired me, Harmon had no information about my academic background. He probably told people he was looking for a pretty secretary. His neighbor, a friend of Boba's, told him I was a smart girl who could keep her mouth shut and help him navigate the black sea of corruption in Odessa.

I spent another month researching positions and writing letters. It was worth it – in the West, I could earn in a month what I earned in a year in Odessa. Though new banks were popping up every week, Boba and I didn't believe in them – we kept our money in the icebox. I tried to imagine the size of the freezer we'd need to hold the salary of my new job in America. It would surely take up our whole kitchen. I laughed.

'You crazy girl!' Harmon yelled from his office. 'What are you cackling about?'

Sigh.

Finally, I got a response. Apparently, I was a strong candidate, but they weren't able to hire me because I didn't have working papers. They wished me much success. Another, then another wrote the same. Perhaps my friend Florina was right about emigrating to Germany. She said it was easy for Jews to get citizenship.

While searching for engineering positions, I'd seen many advertisements for Internet dating services. The photos of smiling, happy couples made me envious. And curious. I'd spent some time in the Odessa dating pool, which was slimy and black. Perhaps I'd have better luck dating someone abroad – I certainly hadn't had any luck dating Ukrainian men. In the last year, I'd had only first dates – an alcoholic, a mama's boy, and a snout (Russian slang for 'pig' – one pink body part represents the whole). Of course, I'd spent time with Vladimir Stanislavski, but he could hardly be considered a date. Not a respectable one, anyway. In designer sunglasses and black cashmere coat – the typical mob uniform – he sailed past our security guards each week to collect the protection money. As always when he saw me, he took off his sunglasses. I looked at his dark eyes and sensual mouth. As always, he asked me out. As always, I rolled my eyes and pretended to be annoyed. Who could take him seriously? Odessan men flirt with anyone in a skirt. As always, he smiled, a sexy, confident smile. It was the best part of my week.

Just then, as I handed Vlad the envelope, I heard giggling behind Harmon's door.

'What's that horrible sound?' Vlad frowned.

That horrible sound was my friend simpering for my boss. What had I done? She'd gone from a sensitive artist and friend to a stranger. The door opened and Harmon and Olga came out. She wrapped herself around Harmon. His eyes widened when he saw Vlad. Olga continued to stroke Harmon's lapel but eyed Vlad with interest; he dismissed her. I supposed that was one point in Vladimir Stanislavski's favor.

Once, Jane teased me for having a crush on her boyfriend, Cole, a Peace Corps volunteer stationed in Khmelnitsky. Of course I didn't. That would have been rude. He was just so courteous and handsome, hardworking and sincere, smart and funny. I wanted to find someone just like him. Maybe it would be possible on the Internet.

Since Harmon spent much of his day shut away in his office with Olga, I had time to look at matchmaking sites. Dates.com offered a free membership, so I filled in the questionnaire, then looked to see what the men wrote. Some profiles were incomprehensible, like TurboGuy who wrote,

'I love NASCAR.' When asked the question, 'What are you most grateful for?' Pirate37 replied 'presents.' I smiled at that. One offered no photos of himself, but did post three of his red truck. When asked about his job, another wrote, 'I drive a school bus because I love to hug little kiddies.' I started corresponding with seven. (Odd numbers are lucky.) Jeff, a construction worker in Bend, Oregon, loved Jesus and wanted to know if I was saved; Al in Albany wrote in abbreviations, 'HOPE 2 C U CUZ I M LONELY'; Davis, a Tolstoy fan, seemed more preoccupied by war than by peace; Shakir wrote, 'I want to come to your cuntry.' As diverse as they were, all had one thing in common: they wanted to see 'a pic.'

How could I feed my photo to the computer? I saw an ad for an evening computer class and signed up. I was tired of being dependent upon computer technicians. Harmon agreed to buy a scanner for our office, and I hooked it up. He complimented me on my new skills as he went out the door to meet Olga. Perhaps things were looking up.

I sent the photos. Upon receiving them, all seven proposed. Boba was right. Men are so superficial.

I still tried to talk to Olga when she came to the office. After three long months, she finally started to acknowledge me – and my belongings. All the tokens that Harmon used to shower on me, from the videocassettes and clothes that came on our ships, to the perfume and trinkets that clients gave me as a thank you, now went to Olga. Her appearance had improved; she looked well rested. Unfortunately, her style had not – she was wearing a gold lamé top and no bra. And she watched me suspiciously, as though I hadn't spent months avoiding Harmon, as though she expected me to steal him back. Of course, I tried to remain on pleasant terms with my boss. Did she really expect me to stop talking to him entirely?

Now all she talked about was money – the first word she'd learned from the English tutor Harmon had engaged for her. '*Ooh, tee!* How much this cost?' she asked with her eye on my phone. Harmon had hired a nanny so that she could paint, but instead, she shopped. She showed me her new purse and matching gloves.

I admired them. As always, I asked after her little ones. 'How is little Sveta doing in school?'

'Fine, fine,' she replied, perusing my desk.

'Has Ivan stopped teething?'

'I think so.'

Her eyes darted from object to object. If she could have fit my computer into her new Escada clutch, she probably would have taken it.

'He's surely waiting for you in his office,' I hinted. She certainly had him in her clutches, I thought sourly.

'Ah! Just what I need,' she said, and grabbed my stapler and stuck it in her purse.

'That's *mine*. Give that back!' I whispered furiously in Russian. 'What do you need a stapler for anyway?'

'*Jadna!*' she said, the word for cheap or stingy, then grabbed my tape. 'What do you care? You can always get more.'

'So can you. He's your sugar daddy.' I regretted the words as soon as they left my mouth.

'Uptight bitch. You're just jealous.'

She eyed my digital clock, so I put it on my lap.

Olga drove me crazy, always ignoring me in the office, always taking my things. The worst was that I hadn't a leg to stand on – I'd chosen her. I realized that I should be patient with her, that this new life of hers was easier in some ways but more difficult in others. But my resolve snapped when Harmon came out of his office. Before he could greet her, I complained in English, 'She stole my stapler *and* my tape. Yesterday, she took the bouquet and box of figs that Playtech sent me. The day before that, my favorite CD.'

Harmon used to take me seriously, but now he just smiled.

Olga's brow wrinkled when she didn't understand, which he seemed to think was adorable. She'd been trying to learn English so that they could communicate. But so far her vocabulary was limited. When I'd asked him about it, Harmon said he didn't mind, sighing, 'It's like she graduated summa cum laude in massage.'

'Please tell her to return my belongings,' I said stiffly. 'Don't you think you should send her home so that we can go over the logistics report? The deadline is tomorrow. I need you ... your help.'

Olga shot me a dirty look and moved to Harmon. 'Hhhhello.' Like a cat in heat, she rubbed her body against his. 'Daria, be a dear and make us a coffee,' Olga said condescendingly in Russian. 'And go get me a pack of cigarettes.' She reached into Harmon's pocket and stroked his thigh before pulling out a money clip and throwing three one-dollar bills in my direction. I let them fall to the floor at my feet. I looked to Harmon, but he didn't say anything. Perhaps he wasn't used to women fighting over him. Not that we were fighting over him, exactly.

He was the most security she'd ever had.

He was the most security I'd ever had.

Neither of us would give it up without a fight.

'What about the report?' I asked. 'We need to do it together.'

He looked at the stack of invoices on my desk. 'You're right. It has to go out tonight.'

Good. He'd sided with me. He turned to tell her, 'I work. Bye, bye,' but just as he opened his mouth, she kissed him and plastered herself to his body.

If English was my weapon, sex was hers. He went cross-eyed with lust and she pulled him into his office. Olga gave me a pointed look and laughed. Clearly, she'd won that battle. She continued to cackle and I left, taking my clock with me. Thankfully, the kitchen was empty and I could sit and let my temper cool. If only I could understand *what* exactly I was angry about. Was it just the office supplies? Or the loss of control? I watched the minutes pass. When I returned to my desk, I could still hear Olga, even though the door was closed. She was saying in her pathetic English, 'She no work. Daria lazy. She go. I work.'

What was Olga up to? Could she be attempting a takeover?

I looked past my palm tree, past the bars on the windows and waited for five o'clock. I had to face the truth: I'd lost my friend, I'd wasted months applying for jobs I'd never get, I'd never find love in Odessa or anywhere else, and I'd probably lost the most security Boba and I had ever had.

Chapter 4

Moonlight. I love this word. So romantic. There is a hint of secrecy, of deeds done at night when no one can see. I love its transformation from noun to verb. To moonlight: to work a second job on the sly.

When I told Boba I needed a second job, she said, 'But I barely see you now. You don't eat enough – look at you! Skin and bones and not much else. And you certainly don't get enough rest!' But Harmon was a man and if history had taught us anything, it's that you can't depend on a man. I needed to feel secure. At the shipping company, the waters were choppy and a storm could come in at any time.

I also like the phrase 'to put out feelers.' I imagined that Boba and I were caterpillars, putting out our feelers to find me another job. Our neighbor's cousin needed a waitress. One of Boba's former colleagues told us that his son-in-law in faraway Kiev was looking for an engineer. My friend Florina's aunt was looking for someone to translate letters from American men to our women at her matchmaking agency. This job would be an opportunity for me to practice my English and maybe even meet someone. The office was located on a quiet street five blocks from the shipping company. Three times I passed the ground-floor flat with lace curtains made of thread as fine as any spider's before I realized that the agency was located in someone's home. I glanced at the scrap of paper with the address written on it. This was the place. I rang the bell. My friend's aunt answered the door and introduced herself with a hearty Western handshake.

Valentina Borisovna was of indeterminate age, had large pink glasses that slipped down her nose, calculating blue eyes that could sum up any situation, a blond bouffant shellacked into place, and a bullet-proof brassiere that made her ample breasts seem like pointy weapons aimed at the person in front of her. In a previous life – that is to say, before perestroika – she'd been an influential Party member. However, connections hadn't protected Valentina Borisovna from poverty – her bank account had been emptied like everyone else's. So this once ardent communist became an entrepreneur and named her agency Soviet Unions. It was like she hadn't wanted the Party to end, so she'd created her own.

'I need full-time help to sort things out. Some of my girls are nuclear physicists, but some of them! Look at what they write!'

She handed me a questionnaire filled out in pink ink. I read, 'Name: Yulia Shtunder; Age: 19; Sex: Yes!! All the time!!'

I couldn't help it, I laughed. She did, too. 'If I showed the men looking for a bride that questionnaire, they'd be lined up at her door, but marriage wouldn't be on their minds,' Valentina Borisovna said. 'So you see, I need help with some of these girls. I want them to be as classy as the women in Moscow. You could teach them manners and basic English, couldn't you?' She looked approvingly at my chignon, lightly made-up face, and black business suit.

I nodded. Let the haggling begin.

'Is this your first job out of college, dear?'

Code: I won't have to pay you a decent salary since you need the experience.

'No,' I sat up a little straighter and preened. 'I work at ARGONAUT.'

Code: I'm smart enough to land a job with a foreign firm.

'The shipping company?'

That had her attention. Ha!

'The Western shipping company?'

And her respect.

'Well, if you have a job, you certainly don't need this one ...'

Code: You won't be my twenty-four-hour-a-day slave.

Clearly, I was dealing with an expert negotiator.

'I have plenty of time to translate letters at work. We could train the girls in the evenings and on weekends – after all, most of them have jobs, too.'

Valentina Borisovna couldn't know that I spoke English better than most people in Odessa, that I was determined to make a life for myself and Boba. All she knew was that her niece trusted me. Of course, she'd just seen that I could fend for myself.

'You're hired,' she said.

As we say in Odessa, it's not what you know, it's who you know and how much money you have.

Valentina Borisovna and I continued to wrangle, this time over salary. When the deal was concluded, she gave me a packet of letters to translate. I almost regretted not being able to work in her office. She had orchids and ferns in front of the large windows. On the shelf behind her mahogany desk stood a stout silver samovar surrounded by a tea service. The cups were so fine I could almost see through them.

After the interview, I walked toward the bus stop, hugging the packet of letters to my chest. This second job made me feel lighter, more in control. Even if I lost my job at the shipping company, I wasn't totally lost. It didn't matter that I had to work in the evening and on weekends. The money would help us buy a flat in the city center. I was sick of the long commute home.

I felt a shadow pass over me. A Mercedes slowed on the cobblestone and sidled up to me. The blacked-out back window descended.

'Care for a ride?' Vladimir Stanislavski called out. *Ride-rode-ridden. Forbid-forbade-forbidden.* His golden eyes shone from the dark interior. His smile was sinful and he was as seductive as he was arrogant.

'Still sitting in the back?' I asked. 'When are you going to learn to drive?'

'Oh, I can drive,' he assured me.

'Backseat driver,' I mused, careful to look straight ahead so he wouldn't think I was interested.

'Are you getting in or not?'

'Not.'

The car sped off.

Standing in the jam-packed aisle of the bus, overwhelmed by the smell of sweat and diesel, I admitted the ride home would have been faster and more comfortable in Vlad's car. But mobsters were just plain trouble. Plus, a neighbor would surely see me get out of the Mercedes and then everyone on the bloc, including my Boba, would find out. Gossip was a four-course meal to neighbors on a feeding frenzy. You couldn't cough without them telling everyone you had pneumonia.

As the bus bumped along, I wondered about the letters. What did strangers looking for love say to one another? I wanted to take a peek and wished the bus wasn't so crowded. Had the men enclosed photos with their letters? Were they handsome? Perhaps, just perhaps, I would find an American man of my own. The pensioner next to me started coughing and didn't even cover his mouth. I tried to inch away from him but there was no room. I sighed. I longed to see Jane's world of sparkling streets and cars for everyone.

Jane. My Jane.

Came, saw, went.

Going, going, gone.

Friends and neighbors emigrated to Israel and Germany.

The American missionaries I befriended stayed for a year, then moved on to the next sad spot in the world.

Eventually, everyone left.

Even Jane.

I remembered the day I accompanied her to the airport. She nearly vibrated with giddiness, so happy was she to leave. But in the shadow of my long face, she was sensitive enough to hide her joy. She was going home to a real family. I'd met her parents and sister when they'd come to visit. Jane was so lucky. And when I was with her, I felt lucky.

She hugged me tightly one last time – her fingers spread, aligned on my ribs – before dumping her huge black purse onto the conveyor belt of the X-ray machine.

She stepped through the metal-detecting arch.

'I'll write!'

She'll forget me.

'I'll call!'

They always do.

'I'll be back!'

Nu, da. Yeah, right.

She passed through the door that led to the West. I remained. Bereft. Standing in the gloomy Soviet airport, staring at that door. People went in and never came out. One more person gone from my life. My feet were so heavy I couldn't move them. My soul hurt. It felt brittle and black and sad, like a burnt blini – no, a charred blini that was at least a hundred years old. People jostled me and I knew I should leave. I just wanted to stay in the same building as her a little longer. Just five more minutes.

What would I do without Jane? How was it that a farmer's daughter from the other side of the planet understood me better than the girls I grew up with? I remembered all the times we sat in Boba's kitchen and talked. When I'd told her about my father abandoning us, she clasped my hands in hers and said, 'I'm so sorry. It must be very difficult for you.' This sympathy is like dew on the soul: it refreshes and cleanses. If I'd told Olga, she would have replied, 'So what? You think you're the only one with problems? Let me tell you ...' And she would have listed every disappointing man she'd met or seen on television since she was ten. ('Can you believe Pugachova's husband? A cheater, I'm sure of it!') Of course I didn't mind listening, but it was a relief to be with Jane, to talk and be listened to.

I barely registered the shouting behind the door. In Odessa, there is always some commotion or another. Then I heard Jane's voice. She flew back out the door, broke the grasp the security guard had on her upper arm, and hugged me again. 'Dasha,' she whispered fiercely into my ear. 'I know you think that once people leave they never come back. I will. I promise.'

'You'll miss your plane,' I chided as she caressed the tears on my cheek.

'Always so proud,' she chided right back, touching her cool forehead to mine. 'I'll miss *you*.'

At my stop, I got off the bus and wound my way past the crude concrete high-rises, past the rusty kiosks, past Harmon's beat-up BMW. How long would he visit Olga here, so far out of the city? Was it just sex? Or more? Did her little ones call him Papa? Neighbors grumbled because of all the *remont*, remodeling, going on in her flat. They were fed up and jealous of the incessant hammering.

He had never come all the way out here to see me.

After dinner, Boba and I sat on our worn blue sofa. 'Where is Olga? I haven't seen her for weeks. You must miss little Ivan.'

'She's probably busy painting,' I replied, hoping I sounded nonchalant, hoping she wouldn't dig further. 'Do you want to see the letters? Maybe there are photos.'

Distracted, Boba chose a 'valentine' and opened the envelope gingerly. We were surprised to see the letter was typed. A pity. So much is revealed through handwriting. Boba looked at the photo while I translated the letter aloud to her. 'Hello. My name is Brad. I have a ranch in Texas. I'm looking for someone dependable and sincere, and pretty ...'

'Look at him.' Boba held up a photo. 'He's not too bad. He has kind eyes.'

'Just what any girl wants,' I chided gently, 'someone who's not too bad. Listen to this. "Hello, my name is Matthew. I'm a dentist and live in Colorado where I enjoy skiing and rafting. I have four Great Danes ..." '

'He sounded good until he mentioned the dogs. Think of the fur you'd have to sweep up.'

That was my Boba, ever practical. What would I do without her?

I knew exactly what Olga would have said about Brad. 'Look at him! He could crack a concrete wall with that forehead!' She would have held the photo of Matthew next to her face, batted her eyelashes flirtatiously, and said, 'What do you think? A good match?' I smiled as I thought of her mischievously putting Brad's photo in with Matthew's letter and vice versa. I sighed. What had I done?

'How interesting that they want our women,' Boba said, looking at the letters and photos spread across the coffee table. 'Why can't they find wives in America?'

I didn't know. After translating six letters, I took a break, stretching my neck and shoulders. Anywhere I looked in the room, stern icons stared back. I was careful not to say anything about religion. Boba had suffered as a Jew in the Soviet Union

– it had been noted on identification papers that we were not Ukrainian, but Jewish. We were not just of another religion, we were of another race. An inferior race.

Boba said that Mama hadn't been allowed to study at the university because she was Jewish, that there had been a quota on how many Jews were allowed a college education. I don't know how she did it, but Boba went from the Jewish nationality to Ukrainian on her documents (bribes?) and to the Russian Orthodox religion in her heart (denial?). As with everything, she did it for me, so that I would have the right last name and the opportunity to pursue a higher education. So I didn't dare say anything about the nine icons watching me.

Reading words of hopeful men and wishful women was more interesting than writing business reports for Harmon. I didn't mind spending my evenings with these letters, translating the men's thoughts and yearnings. Boba and I sat on the sofa, she looking wistfully at the photos while I wrote. I became quite good at reading between the lines – or so I thought.

On Saturdays, when I met with clients at the Soviet Unions office (Valentina Borisovna's living room) to teach them English and translate their letters, I told them about my online dating experience and urged caution. But they were convinced that American men were richer, kinder, and in every way superior. Granted, in comparison to our men – macho lechers, alcoholics, layabouts all – it wasn't much of a contest.

It was hard not to get involved. I sat across from Yelena, a thirty-year-old blonde with a worry line that divided her forehead in two, and translated her letters: *Dear Yelena, I am a Mormon living in Wilbur, Washington. My wife is dead and my three children need a mother.* Clearly, he wanted a nanny and a cook, but I couldn't convince Yelena. She dictated her response: *Dear Randy, I, too, am widowed* ('Strictly not true,' she confided, 'I was never married.') *and worry about my son. I long to have a strong man to take care of me and my boy.*

A few more letters and off she went to Wilbur on a 'fiancé visa,' a three-month permit that the American government grants to foreign women so they can live with their future spouse on consignment. A trial period. She was brave to go to a country when she didn't speak the language or know anything about the man she was to marry.

When we received a wedding invitation from Yelena, we were thrilled for her. And even jealous. She explained that two weeks had been enough for her to decide she wanted to stay in America for good. In her next letter, she wrote that since her husband didn't drink he took the *champagnskoye* she'd brought to celebrate their nuptials and poured it down the drain. He also 'didn't hold with' tea or coffee since it was caffeinated. Poor Yelena wrote that she couldn't live without her morning tea. A month later, she announced that she was saving money to come home – Randy didn't respect her and neither did his children. Then we received a card telling us that she was pregnant. Then came the letter explaining that she didn't miss caffeine and actually felt healthier following Randy's 'guidelines.' Then she wrote no more. To be honest, Valentina Borisovna and I didn't miss her letters. It made us sad to realize that she'd not only learned to live within her new husband's rigid rules, she'd embraced them.

Harmon spent more and more time with Olga, less and less time at the office. I'd finished my tasks and his for the day and decided to look at the Internet, but it was difficult to concentrate. Swiveling nervously in my chair, I wondered where he was. When was he coming back? What if he gave my job to her? He wouldn't do that to me, would he? The longer he stayed away, the more nervous I became. Curious, I dialed his home number.

No answer.

Where was he?

I swiveled back to my computer. The free membership had expired, but I continued to write half-heartedly to the men who'd given me their personal e-mail addresses. Unfortunately, the one who said he loved Jesus seemed to love 'porn' even more. The capital letter man started asking, 'DO YOU LIKE TO CUM?' I wrote, 'I prefer to go,' and blocked his address. Some wanted to visit me in Odessa, Texas, though I'd stated several times I lived in Ukraine.

The women at Soviet Unions who received letters on paper seemed to have better results than I. Their men wrote sentences containing real sentiment. But none of the correspondence touched my heart as much as the letters from Will in Albuquerque to Milla in Donetsk. When I read his words aloud, I heard poetry. His photo reminded me of Jane's American boyfriend Cole – a dark-haired, gap-toothed gentleman.

Every other week, Milla took a ten-hour bus ride to Odessa. She plowed into our office with a bottle of home-made vodka which she tipped into Valentina Borisovna's tea cups before plopping down in the chair across from me. 'Well, girl? Do I have any more suckers?' A forty-year-old chain-smoking former prostitute, Milla talked like a miner and her teeth were as yellow as her sallow skin. She had nine men sending her letters, money, and gifts. (When they asked for a photo, she sent them one of her daughter, last year's Miss Donetsk.) When I told her I liked Will, she replied, 'Take him! Hell, girl, he's cheap. I couldn't get anything out of him. I'll probably go with Monty from Palm Springs or Joe in L.A. Where the fuck is Albuquerque anyway?'

To be sure she wasn't offended that I took one of her men, I gave her a bouquet of yellow roses and slipped her ten dollars. I didn't like to owe anyone. Will stopped writing Dear Milla and started writing Dearest Daria. It was easier to correspond by e-mail, so I wrote my letters at work. When Harmon came into the office at eleven, he patted me on the shoulder and complimented me on my diligence. Pleased by his thoughtfulness, I smiled.

'You have beautiful teeth,' he said. 'You should smile more often, so I get my money's worth.'

I expected to see an ugly expression on his face, like he'd worn so often in the days after the incident, but he looked at me in an avuncular way. This pleased me. I didn't want to be his enemy. He'd given me a job. Thanks to him, I could correspond with Will and Jane and save to buy a flat in the city center. Though there were still tense moments, our wary circling had become an awkward dance as we worked together to run the office. He saw himself as a kindly boss, who complimented my work and let me go home early on Fridays. He hadn't spent a year pursuing me. He'd never been jealous of men who looked at me or – worse – talked to me. He'd never attacked me. He didn't care that I was a procuress of flesh. He was not the first man to rewrite history. I liked this version much better and decided to believe it.

The chess game seemed to be over. A stalemate.

A relief is what it was.

He spent the morning taking down the photos of him and me at the bazaar, in front of the opera house, at the port. He whisked the pictures out of the frames and slid in prints of him with Olga. The poses remained the same, only his paws roamed her body instead of mine. He stood in front of my desk, staring at the photos of us in his hand, unsure what to do with them. Perhaps he considered tossing them into the bin. Suddenly, he extended the handful of memories and asked, 'Do you want them?'

Had he finally forgiven me for turning him into the office joke, something that wasn't my fault? It was unlucky to throw photos away, so I accepted them. When he left for lunch, I glanced at the photos and wanted to make a gesture towards peace. 'Wait!' I called after him. He turned around. 'Wait.' I wasn't sure what to say. I stood. 'Um, would you like to have coffee?'

He glanced at his watch. 'Olga's waiting. Later?'

'Later,' I echoed.

He left, and I felt that we could go on, not as friends, but as colleagues with peace between us. I was relieved that five months after the incident, the awkward moments were slowly disappearing. If only I could say the same about my relationship with Olga. Was she still angry with me? Did she really want my job?

I opened my briefcase and pulled out a salad that Boba had made for me, packed in a Tupperware container from Harmon. As I ate, alone at my desk as usual, I checked my inbox and found a letter from Will: 'My darling girl, leaves swirl, trees dance, love's delight, a moonlit night. When I think of you, I think of Pushkin and poetry. I think of *War and Peace* – only with a happy ending. I am so lonely lonely lonely but when I think of you, I am healed.'

Will was alone and lonely. I, too, felt lonely. Jane was in America, Olga was no longer speaking to me, and Florina had emigrated to Germany. My other friends were married and lived in another world as well. Of course, I had my Boba, but there are some feelings a girl can't share with her grandmother. Sometimes I really missed having a mother.

I wondered what Mama would say about my Internet beau. Or any of the other boys I'd dated. I was not completely without experience. I'd had two boyfriends – both handsome snouts who felt that since they bought me dinner and took me to the opera I owed them sex. I dated them because everyone expects you to have a boyfriend and to marry by the time you're twenty, twenty-two at the latest. A woman's shelf life is extremely short in Ukraine. How many times had I been told that a ripe fruit like me is only hours away from rotting? If you don't have a *cavalier* people think there is something wrong with you. Only my Boba told me that I shouldn't marry the first man I slept with, that sex wasn't love. But she also said that we didn't need a man. She said looking for love was like looking for wind in a field. She never talked about her own husband. I didn't even know if he deserted us or if he was dead. She never had kind words for my father, who'd disappeared long ago. Once, I heard her tell a friend that all my papa knew how to do was get women pregnant and lose money gambling. I didn't even know what he looked like. Sometimes, I wished that I had a photo of him.

Although he wasn't in the picture, I bore his first name and would for life. In Russian, adults use patronymics, a name derived from the father's. Women add the suffix –ovna to their father's name. Valentina's father's name was Boris, this was why we called her Valentina Borisovna. It was a relief to work in an office where we used only first and last names – I'm Daria or Miss Kirilenko – like they do in the West. Another reason I was grateful to Mr. Harmon: unknowingly, he saved me from this daily reminder of my father's perfidy.

What would Jane think about Will? About meeting a man on the Internet? When I met her, she was twenty-three and had no interest in getting married. I was fascinated by this *Americanka* who was nearly a spinster and didn't even care. When I asked her about it, she laughed and said no one in America gets married before they're thirty. Boba was right – life was different elsewhere. And I wanted to go elsewhere, just to see. While with Jane, I'd stopped worrying about getting married, or not getting married, even though all my girlfriends were tying the knot. Of course, it was hard to not worry about them, when Boba told me that they had tied nothing but a hangman's noose.

In the meantime, Soviet Unions earned less and less. We checked the mailbox several times a day, waiting, hoping for correspondence that didn't come. No men, no money. If the situation didn't change soon, I would be let go.

'Those damned Americans changed the law,' Valentina Borisovna lamented. 'Now men must actually meet their brides before importing them. No more deliveries. They have to come here to pick up the merchandise, or at least to order it.' In a flash of self-pity, she looked up at the ceiling, her bosoms heaving in her dove-gray knock-off jacket, and cried, 'Why? Why are they doing this to me?' as if the Americans had enacted new regulations to slow her profits.

To take her mind off this cruel blow from the American government, she took the train to Moscow to visit one of her former sisters-in-law for a week. She came back full of good food, good vodka, and with a good scheme. When she walked through the office door, the first words out of her mouth were English. 'Soooo shall. Soooo shall. Soooo shall,' she said.

'So what shall we do?' I replied in kind, surprised she was speaking English.

'Darling!' she said, back in Russian. 'The future is in Moscow. But we can have it here, too. Soooo shall. I haven't the slightest idea what it means. But it's our salvation.'

She poured us both a *kognac* and described what she had seen, speaking so quickly the words bounced off my forehead. Men. Lots. Foreign. Rich. Women. Ours. Sexy. Young. Find mates. Expensive for men. Free for women. Music. Money. Alcohol. Sooo shall.

It all became clear. Never one to let the law get in her way, Valentina Borisovna had quickly found a new, more lucrative kind of traffic. We began organizing 'socials' which were advertised as a way for American men to meet one thousand beautiful Odessans in just five days. I looked up the word in my pocket dictionary and found, 'having to do with the activities of society, specifically the more exclusive or fashionable of these.' When I told Jane about my new job, she explained a social is what people used to call dances in the 1950s, when people used to dance with a partner and good grooming habits were in style. And there was nothing exclusive about them. She then muttered that socials were 'the ultimate meat market.' (Perhaps she meant 'meet market.') Her definition only made me more curious. Two days later, I received a dictionary that she sent by Federal Express and learned that a social was just a party with a pretty name.

Late Saturday afternoon, I helped Valentina Borisovna coordinate our very first social in the ballroom of the Literary Museum, home to Pushkin and Gogol and Tolstoy. The Grande Dame had bribed the curator to close the entire mansion to the public. She somehow procured frilly American wedding decorations for the pristine white walls topped by scalloped molding. She brought in a well-stocked metal bar and a CD player. After we covered the scarred tables with white tablecloths, we hung the disco ball from the crystal chandelier.

'Daria,' she said in her haughty voice, 'make sure that we have enough punch. Spike it with a fair amount of vodka. We don't want any awkward moments. Turn off most of the lights – we don't want the girls to see how old some of the men are! You'll have to check the bathrooms from time to time to make sure there's no hanky panky going on. I want these girls to behave themselves!' She pushed her pink spectacles back onto the bridge of her nose. 'I just hope the Stanislavskis don't learn about my socials. I can't afford to pay protection money yet.'

Chapter 5

A darkened room in a former palace. A music box set to play. A strobe light sends flickers across the parquet. The Literary Museum was about to become the setting for a garish high-school prom for thirty- to sixty-five-year-old men. On the website, the Grande Dame had advertised these socials as five evenings, one thousand women. Of course, she didn't mention that it was the same two hundred women five times. I wondered if the men would notice. Valentina Borisovna was wearing her very best – a pink, simulated Chanel suit garnished with a pink pearl necklace and pink pumps. Even I'd dressed up in a black cocktail dress.

When the girls arrived, I felt as if we were backstage at a Miss Universe pageant. Tummies tucked in. Bosoms thrust out. Hips swaying so hard, I was reminded of the back fin of a fish swishing by. There was more make-up on these faces than in an entire cosmetics factory. The smell of two hundred competing perfumes was overwhelming, so I opened a few windows. The women practiced pouts and sultry looks. Sitting around the tables, they joked and laughed, sized each other up and tore one another down.

'Masha, you'll get someone right away.'

'With that hair and those turkey drumsticks for legs, Louisa will never find anyone, poor dear.' Cackle, cackle.

'Do you think American men are as well hung as ours?' one asked.

'I for one will find out tonight – a walrus dick or a tiny radish!' another responded before taking a drag on her cigarette.

'No smoking, girls! No smoking!' Valentina Borisovna shouted. 'Americans don't smoke and they certainly don't want smelly dates!'

Immediately, the girls threw down their cigarettes and ground them underneath their stiletto heels, except for one, who exclaimed, 'Ahhh, Americans! They don't know how to live!'

The Grande Dame glared; the girl put out her cigarette. The floor looked like an ashtray. Valentina Borisovna swung open the doors and fifty Americans entered. The room went silent. I peered at the men in the semi-darkness. Some looked confident. And rightly so. They were a rare commodity here. We looked at them and saw three-course meal tickets with cell phones and credit cards. A direct flight to the American Dream: money, beautiful homes, stability.

The men stood in huddles near the door, the women sat at the tables. Nervous anticipation surrounded us. We all want love. The men had flown thousands of miles for it. The Odessans had come to the table to place their bets on an American, ready to gamble everything for a better life elsewhere.

The women broke the silence. 'They look as nervous as I feel,' one whispered.

'Who helped them dress?' another asked, looking at the numerous flannel shirts and faded jeans.

'Why whisper?' a third asked. 'They don't speak Russian.'

We women laughed to cover up our nervousness.

'They're older than I thought.'

'Girls, I'm here to tell you that older lovers are better – they last longer and think each time is the last, so they're just thrilled and grateful!'

More laughter.

One of the youngest, in a miniskirt that barely covered her bottom, said to her friend, who wore a top that barely concealed her breasts, 'I'll need a few drinks before I find these guys attractive.'

They fled to the bar. Larissa, a stout, older woman, said, 'Let them wait a year or two and see what life with an Odessan man is like!'

Her words underlined the women's reason for being here. Galya, a nineteen-year-old with wide eyes and a nervous expression, asked, 'Does that mean romance doesn't exist?'

'Of course it does, sunshine. In lovey-dovey American novels,' Larissa replied.

Galya looked to me. 'Have you never trembled under a man's touch?'

'Yes, the dentist's.'

The women laughed at the old joke. I remembered how my teeth were ripped out by pliers, and my hand moved to my mouth. *You don't have to do that anymore.* I put my hand on my lap.

Most men were still standing near the entryway. I gave them credit for this. It is proper to be reserved. They stared at the women, some of whom preened, some of whom struck a pose of nonchalance, some of whom danced with each other. The Grande Dame wanted me to create a website as well as a catalog, featuring a profile for each girl with a photo and her vital information – horoscope, height, weight, likes and dislikes (not unlike *Playboy*) – but I hadn't yet entered all of the information into the computer. She would charge men $100 for the program, which they could buy before the evening of the social to narrow their list of 200 candidates to ten contenders to cross-examine.

Some men looked intimidated when they heard the women laughing. And rightly so. They were in a foreign city, outnumbered in a room of women, some of whom were sociopaths who felt no remorse about using their bodies and faces to ensnare. Men who should have known better, and who were smart in so many other ways, became victims.

Take my former classmate Alexandra. She wore a tight, low-cut turquoise top to match her eyes. Every time she leaned over – and she leaned over a lot – her breasts reached out to mesmerize the eyes. She rubbed herself, seemingly unconsciously, and the men followed her fingers as they crossed her neck, shoulders, her hips, her hand as effective as a hypnotist's medallion. She'd learned enough English to ask the right questions. Where do you live? (Initials need only apply – N.Y. or L.A.) What do you do? (Only three possible occupations: dentist, lawyer, and/or oil.) She could ask other questions using her elementary English, but didn't care about the answers. She smiled attentively and rubbed her hand up and down his arm, her eyes never leaving his. Sirens, these women.

I watched her go in for the kill. Bells should have gone off in that man's head, but Alexandra had already dismantled his alarm system. Jane and her American friends had called these women 'Robo-babes' and said that you could shoot them or set them on fire, but they'd repair themselves instantly and keep moving towards their target. Why am I talking about these women? They are common: girls who think their looks will carry them through life as easily as foam floats down a gentle river. Surely they are everywhere.

I played romantic Western music, from 'The Sea of Love' to Stevie Wonder's 'Isn't She Lovely?', but the dance floor was nearly empty. A barmaid in a short black skirt and a white see-through blouse ran to the Grande Dame. 'Valentina Borisovna,' she said in a panic, 'some men ordered rosé, but we only have red and white wine. What should I do?'

'Fool! Don't you know that red and white make pink? Just mix a little together. No one will know – just be discreet. Why isn't anyone dancing?' She put on a techno CD and cranked up the volume. The men moved towards the women, choosing partners using the only index available to them – looks.

I'd been assigned to five women, the first of whom was Maria, a woman twice divorced who took care of her elderly parents while raising her young daughter. They all lived in a two-room apartment. Maria made forty dollars a month as a waitress, though her degree was in physical education. English and math teachers made extra money by giving private lessons. Unfortunately for Maria, there was no call for tutors in dodge-ball. I looked at Maria; her eyes told me that she needed to make a match. Tonight.

An old man, his every facial capillary broken, approached and asked my name. I made it clear that I was not the one available by instantly introducing him to Maria. He took in her brown eyes and tight figure and barked, 'How old?'

Shocking. Not even a hello. No Odessan would ever be so rude. I could not bring myself to show how uncultured this man was and translated, 'He says, "Delighted to meet you. You look like a teenager. Just how old are you anyway?" '

'He said all that?' she yelled over the techno music.

'Remember the English you learned in school. Americans use contractions,' I replied.

She nodded knowingly and said, 'Twenty-six,' lopping nine years off her age as efficiently as my grandmother trimmed ears off potatoes.

I split the difference and said, 'She's thirty.'

'How much money does he have in the bank?' she asked.

Odessans did ask blunt questions. Perhaps it was best not to generalize.

'Maria says she welcomes you to Odessa. She wonders what you do for a living.'

'Engineer,' he replied. 'Does she have kids?'

I nodded. He walked away.

'I don't need a millionaire,' she said, looking relieved. 'Just a nice man who is closer to my age. One who will respect me. And be a good father.'

I squeezed her hand. 'Don't worry, Maria. We'll find you that man.'

Over the next hour, we talked to James, Pat, Michael, Kevin, and George. Too old, too immature, too vague, too intense, too much talk about sex. Maria was hopeful, since I didn't exactly translate word for word. I started to despair.

I surveyed the room and saw a shy, gentle-looking man. I looked into his eyes and could see his yearning. I grabbed Maria's hand and pulled her towards her destiny. But before we reached him, a Siren appeared. It would have been easy to get rid of her with a whisper, 'There's a dentist with a Porsche on the other side of the room.' But a scene was definitely the best way to proceed – Odessans love drama. Our opera house is the third-most beautiful in the world after Venice and Bratislava's and we have dozens of theaters. I yanked Maria in front of me so she was standing at the side of the Siren and declared, 'She is the one for you,' gesturing to Maria. 'She is the kindest woman in the room and will make you an excellent life partner. I sense that friendship and love will grow between you.'

The man looked at both women. His gaze fixed on Maria. 'That's what I want.'

The Siren stalked off. Maria was buoyed because in her eyes the man had been gallant and chosen her over a younger, more beautiful woman. We spoke. Or rather, they spoke and I interpreted – this time no need for lies.

The Grande Dame witnessed the scene I'd orchestrated, and later that night she gave me a small raise, sighing, 'If only everyone were as dedicated to the cause of true love.' We stood in silence for a moment, watching the scene unfold. She gestured to the men, who were slowly approaching the women. 'Look at them! My vodka punch has finally taken effect! Can you help Anya?'

I interpreted for Anya, Masha, Vera, and Nadia. The Americans seemed pleasant enough, a little rough around the edges, but nice. Of course many needed guidance on clothing, haircuts, and flattering spectacle frames, but what man doesn't need a woman's touch? It was strange that their relationship depended on my English. I advised the girls to start studying. By the time we locked up the ballroom, my ears were buzzing with the questions that had been repeated over and over.

'Does she like candle-lit dinners?'

'Find out if he likes kids. (I've got two, but don't tell him just yet.)'

'Does she like going to plays?'

'Does he earn a good pay?'

'Tell her I think she's beautiful.'

'Find out if he lives independently from his parents.'

'Does she like going to the gym?'

'How old is he?'

'Does she like to travel?' (Raucous laughter followed this question; most women hadn't left the city in years.)

'Ask him in a nice way if he drinks, I don't want a drinker.'

All fifty men came away with dates, even that rude old man, but over one hundred women went home empty-handed. As usual, the odds weren't good for our women.

Meanwhile, at the shipping office, work relations were complicated. Olga circled like a shark on steroids, making sure I didn't talk to Harmon, making sure he didn't look at me. She eyed everything on my desk while ignoring me. Olga swiped the digital clock – the only one I owned that didn't tick, that didn't make me nervous. I stood and tried to grab it, but she held it behind her back and hissed, 'You owe me. If *I* weren't doing the job *you* were hired for, *you*'d be known as the office slut instead of *me*.' I let her keep the clock. And sat down, stunned. Why had I cared so much about the trinkets she'd taken? Didn't she deserve them?

I watched Harmon and Olga with a mixture of curiosity and animosity. How could I help but watch and wonder especially when they were back and forth and in and out of my work space? How much was passion? How much irration? How much was commerce? How much carnal? How much convenience? After all, he'd spurned half of Odessa while he pursued me. How is it with her? I wondered. Easier, without a doubt. She didn't speak English, so they couldn't argue. They couldn't even talk. She tried, and the result was, 'David, I like. David, you so good, so nice.' 'No,' he replied, 'you so nice.' Her English wasn't improving, his was disintegrating. In the evening when they left the office, they didn't even notice me sitting there. Didn't even say goodbye. He forgot me so quickly. It's embarrassing how quickly.

I translated Harmon's documents by day, and two evenings a week, I interpreted the longings of desperate women and lonely men at socials. I corresponded with Will from Albuquerque and, in my more foolish moments, hoped that this friendship would lead somewhere – maybe even to the altar. Not because he was The One, but because most of my former classmates were married, and I felt left out. I craved the love they described. I was ready to start my own family. *Dearest Daria, During my break at work, I wrote another poem in your honor. 'Purple twilight, fast asleep, dusk's promise on the steppes of the Ukraine. I will come my darling one to save you from the Hun.' Your new job certainly sounds interesting. Hope you aren't working your loverly self too hard. Maybe I could visit this summer so we could get to know one another. No pressure, I would stay in your guest room. Where there's a Will, there's a way ...* What guest room? We didn't even have a bedroom. Boba and I made the couch into a bed each night. Will and I really did come from different worlds. His was not quite tangible, his letters not quite gibberish, but they were enough to keep a deep-seated loneliness at bay. When men asked me out I could honestly say I had a boyfriend, even if we'd never met.

The socials were so popular that the Grande Dame begged me to interpret more and more. 'I need you,' she cajoled, and

I fell for it. So I agreed to work three more nights a week. Faces, professions, and questions blurred. I was so tired. Work all day, work all evening, the grocery shopping on Saturday. Between the pickpockets, gypsies, and vendors who cheated clients to see if they were paying attention, the bazaar was an arduous outing. Regardless of my schedule, Boba and I always took breakfast together. Over tea, she scolded me gently about working too much and eating too little. I knew that this chastisement was her declaration of love – the more one is scolded the more deeply one is loved.

One evening, Valentina Borisovna pointed to a well-dressed man with gray hair, gray eyes, and gray skin and said, 'Help him.'

I offered the client a glass of *champagnskoye* to put him at ease and asked what he was looking for. 'I want a beautiful woman with a small jaw.'

'Pardon?'

'Like you, you have a small jaw.'

When he looked at me with eyes as cold as Siberia, I felt something very disturbing, something very wrong. Most men who came to Soviet Unions were a little awkward, but seemed genuinely kind. This man was different.

'I have a boyfriend,' I said, grateful to have Will as a screen.

Valentina Borisovna hovered, discreetly hissing, 'Help him.'

'Can you be more specific?' I asked, swallowing my misgivings. 'I know a lot of the girls here. The more you tell me about what you desire in a spouse, the closer I can come to finding her.'

He surveyed the ballroom and said, 'It's like a sea of breasts, thighs, and hair. And I'm the captain.'

What a snout. He must have paid a lot because the Grande Dame was still circling. I gave her a pleading look and she responded by tightening her lips and narrowing her blue eyes.

'I like blondes,' he said after a moment.

I rolled my eyes. Any woman could be a blonde.

'What do you like to do on the weekend?' I asked. 'Read? Go sailing? The opera?'

'I'm a lawyer. I don't have hobbies. Time is money.'

I nodded. 'Katya,' I called out and spoke quickly in Russian. 'Here's the kind of guy you were looking for – a rich attorney who's never home.'

She looked him up and down. 'Perfect,' she said in Russian to me, though he looked old enough to be her father. 'Hhhello,' she said to him. She wore a brittle smile and her eyes were as hard as Soviet concrete.

I couldn't do this work anymore. Suddenly it all seemed wrong. And I was exhausted and missed my Boba. How long had it been since I'd been to the sea? Since I had time to think about something other than work? Since I had read a book? I marched up to the Grande Dame and said, 'I resign.'

'You can't quit; I need you. So you're a bit disabused and cynical. That's life, my sweet little fish.' She swept her hand out, gesturing at the people in the room. 'This isn't love. It's commerce, for the most part. But remember dear Maria? You did right by her. She's wildly happy in America.'

True. Once a week, we received a thank you from her. Valentina Borisovna decided to create a testimonial page for our website. I was glad for Maria. She gave us all hope. Yes. Perhaps it could work out for me as well. 'My Russian beauty, I hope to meet you soon,' Will had written. Would he really come all the way to Odessa? I rubbed my eyes. The days seemed longer and longer. *Lonely night stood around me. I wanted friends. I wanted myself.*

'Darling, you look tired,' the Grande Dame said. 'Help one more, and you can go home. Have I been working you too hard?'

I shook my head.

'The computer technician created a program to match up our women with Westerners. Why don't you give it a chance?'

'I already tried computer dating. It didn't work. Besides, I'm still corresponding with one of Milla from Donetsk's men.'

'If you refer to him as Milla's man, he must not have a place in your heart. I'm sure this time will be different – the technician promised a simple questionnaire with fool-proof results. I need you to do it. For me. For research purposes. I'll give you a bonus,' she smiled winningly. I could see why she'd been an effective Party leader. And why I was here five nights a week.

'Fine. For you. I'll try it,' I said as one of the clients joined us.

'Hello, I'm Robert,' he said nervously and held out his right hand. I shook it. He was what Jane would call a geek – a sweet, intelligent guy. He was tall and thin, and boyishly handsome, though he needed a haircut and more flattering clothes. Why do men wear XXL shirts and scuffed shoes?

'You seem a bit young,' I commented.

'People always say that. I'm actually thirty. Ready to settle down and start my life. I have a good job and a nice house. I want to share that with someone.'

I nodded. 'Anyone in particular?'

'I'm not like most guys here. I can't just pick a girl out of a hat. Or out of a room. I was hoping you could ... help. I want someone who is smart, kind, and not too pretty.'

'Not too beautiful?' I asked. This was certainly a first.

'Looks aren't everything,' he said.

'When you work in this atmosphere you certainly forget that is true. Mostly, the prettiest girls find mates first.' For the first time, I actually enjoyed conversing, even commiserating, with a client.

He nodded. 'Ideally, she'd already speak English.'

'What do you like to do in your free time?' I asked.

'I like to read, cook, and garden.'

I looked at Robert speculatively, and wondered if he could be the man for me. Then I remembered Will from Albuquerque and felt disloyal. The Grande Dame put the cherry on the cake when she chose that exact moment to say, 'Daria, you're my best interpreter – the only one who wouldn't dream of keeping a client for herself. Thank you for your trustworthiness. You're a good girl.'

Guilt and shame – two strong motivators.

I helped Robert find a shy, sweet English-speaking girl and left them to it. Valentina Borisovna reminded me to hurry so that I wouldn't miss the last bus to my district. I needn't have rushed. As always, it was late. When the woman standing beside me saw the bus arrive, she groaned. Nearly midnight, and it was packed. We made eye contact and shrugged, as if to say, what else? I'd ridden this bus for years and had never had a seat. I almost wished Vladimir Stanislavski would drive by and offer me a ride. He often did in the evening, but I always said no. I stared straight ahead so he wouldn't know that I knew he followed me to the bus stop, then trailed the bus to make sure I got home safely. Once, when I'd wanted to sit on the seashore and watch the waves, I accepted his invitation. We drove to a deserted beach and sat on the sand, looking out at the horizon. He held my hand. I told no one.

I sighed. At my stop, I stood and looked at the tall buildings in the moonlight. If Will came, this is what he would see – tombstones sticking out of the earth. I didn't want that. It occurred to me that between my jobs and the thank yous for helping get shipments through customs, I'd amassed nearly enough to buy a flat in the center. The thought excited me. I had come to hate our building. There were even moments I'd come to hate my life, though I suppressed these feelings deep, deep inside of me.

The parking lot was full. Harmon's car was parked on the sidewalk right in front of the door. He'd mentioned that having Olga live with him would be convenient. There were even bets going on which day she would move in. Vita and Vera had picked next Friday. I'd picked two months hence. I looked up at her flat. The lights were still on. I sighed. And went into the gray tomb. And trudged up the stairs.

As always, Boba opened the last of the locks. She took my purse and slid my blazer off my shoulders. Jane told me that in America, there were many 'latchkey kids' who came home to an empty house. I felt sorry for these children, who did not know how it felt to be met by a loving grandmother.

'Such a hardworking girl,' she said with a smile. 'I made you a special dish for dinner.'

'You always spoil me, Boba. Thank you,' I said and kissed her cheek.

'It's been ages since we've seen Olga.'

I bent down to pull off my heels. 'She's busy.'

'Probably found another pigeon to pluck,' Boba muttered.

So she'd heard the rumors about Harmon.

She escorted me to the kitchen and turned on the water so I could wash before dinner. She pulled the dishcloth from her shoulder and I dried my hands. As I ate oven-roasted red peppers and kasha, Boba peppered me with questions. She was fascinated by the socials – we certainly didn't have anything like them before perestroika. If someone had told me that in the future men would be able to choose a bride from a catalog, I would have told him to quit drinking so much home-made vodka.

Boba didn't have any respect for Odessan guys, but in the evening while waiting for me to come home, watching American movies with their beautiful homes and happily-ever-afters, she got the impression that their men were hardworking and serious. She hoped a rich, cultured foreigner would fall in love with me and take me back to his American mansion by the sea.

'*Nu?*' she asked. 'Did you meet anyone good?'

'Boba, how many times have I told you that I am there to help other girls find husbands, not to find one for myself?'

'It doesn't hurt to look,' she said.

I hugged her and said, 'You know I have a boyfriend. We correspond by computer.'

'Comb-poo-tair,' she scoffed. 'How could that possibly work?'

It could work quite well. Will in Albuquerque wrote that he couldn't come after all and asked if I wanted to visit him. *Yes! Yes! Yes!* I wrote. *It's my dream to go to America! I would love to meet you!*

I buzzed around the office until Harmon tried to swat me like a fly.

Now that he no longer hounded me, I found myself missing our talks in the boardroom when the lights were out. No one had ever exasperated me as much as Harmon, but no one but Boba had ever trusted me as he did – I was the only person in Odessa who had the keys to our offices and to his flat. He'd given me both sets the first month. Even Olga didn't have them. Though I hadn't respected the initial agreement, he still had food from our ships delivered to my flat. Boba had never eaten so well in her entire life – even though we had a little money now, she refused to spend it on luxuries such as strawberries out of season. I was relieved that he was with Olga. That he left me alone. Yet I felt sad. Surely it was because I had lost Olga's friendship.

'Fuck! Fuck! Fuck!'

I heard something smash against the wall in Harmon's office, then drop to the floor.

'Why have a state-of-the-art phone if the telephone lines are shit? I can't believe this place. I'm supposed to have a conference call and I can't hear a goddamn thing!'

I tiptoed in to see the damage. The phone was in pieces on the parquet. Harmon sat at his desk, his shoulders slumped, his face buried in his hands. It scared me to see him like this. I backed out.

On a normal day, he seemed invincible. Maybe because his barrel chest made him appear commanding and strong. Maybe because his appearance – suits expensive, hands soft, thick hair perfectly coiffed – indicated that he was not one of us. Because unlike Odessans, who watched the bazaar prices climb and their salaries freeze, he didn't have to worry whether he got paid on the thirtieth of this month or of the next, whether there was a sugar shortage, whether he could pay for medicine. Anything he wanted came on our ships. And like them, he could set sail.

What did he know about hardship?

'Coffee?' I yelled from my desk, then reentered and swept up the batteries and pieces of plastic.

He looked at me. His tie was crooked, his breathing ragged. The expression on his face. He looked like he wanted to yell. Or kill someone. Or bawl.

'Better make it a double,' he finally said. The words came out hoarsely, like a sigh.

I knew what that meant and poured a splash of cognac into both cups.

We sat in the boardroom like we used to. He took a sip and said, 'The only good thing about living in Odessa is that you can drink at work and it's totally understandable. In fact, it would be surprising if you *didn't* drink.'

I laughed. 'Surely it's not the only thing.'

He looked at me. 'No.'

His gaze was hot like it used to be. He closed his eyes and shook his head as if he were reminding himself of something. 'That writer you recommended. Babel.'

'What did you think?' I asked, grateful to be back on safer ground.

'Ferocious. My God. "Just forget for a minute that you have spectacles on your nose and autumn in your heart. Stop being tough at your desk and stuttering when you're out in the world. Imagine for one second that you raise hell in public places and stammer on paper … If rings had been fastened to the earth and sky, you'd have seized those rings and pulled the sky down to earth. And your papa ... What's a papa like him think about? He thinks about gulping down a glass of vodka, slugging someone in their ugly mug, and his horses – nothing else. You want to live, but he makes you die twenty times a day. What would you do?" '

I just looked at him. This is how we Odessans entertain ourselves – a clever joke, a snippet of poetry, a passage of prose. It's easy and natural for us. Reciting texts in front of an impatient class is a learning technique. I still remember poems I memorized when I was eight. But I never expected my boss to quote Babel.

' "You want to live, but he makes you die twenty times a day." That's Dad.' Harmon sounded bitter. And looked disheartened. Like a real Odessan.

After a year of working for Harmon and saving nearly every kopeck, I finally earned enough to buy a flat in the center for Boba and me, after selling ours in the sleeping district. It wasn't difficult to find one with so many Jews emigrating to Germany and Israel. Most were happy to leave their lives and their homes in Odessa behind. Our new flat had a bedroom, parquet flooring, high ceilings, and large windows. A person feels better when she lives amidst beauty.

I loved being closer to Park Shevchenko and the sea, and it was liberating to be able to walk to work rather than taking public transport. Some of our buses came from the West, where they'd been retired because of gas leaks and mechanical problems. Often passengers vomited or passed out because fumes seeped inside. Asphyxiated by the misery. The decrepit buses lumbered down streets that hadn't been maintained. Travel time was long. But the commute wasn't the only reason I was glad to leave our building. I was glad because I would no longer hope Olga would visit. Here I knew she wasn't coming.

Boba and I had packed my mother's fashion magazines, thin towels, a brush with her hair nestled in the bristles. Basically, everything Mama had ever touched. We had so few photos of her. I put them in my purse so that they wouldn't be lost. I pulled the small canvases Olga had given me from the wall and wrapped them in bed sheets. I followed the course of her development – from drawings in high school to neo-classic surrealism to gothic kitsch. I found a book I'd given her five years ago. As usual, we had exchanged presents a day before New Year's Eve. She gave me a two-inch by two-inch painting. I gave her a book filled with photos of Albania. She took one look at it and threw it at my head. I ducked. It ricocheted off the chair and onto the floor.

'Quit giving me fucking books!'

Who could blame her? Growing up in the Soviet Union, every New Year's, every birthday, every International Women's Day, I gave and received books. If you had no money and lived in a country where the shop shelves were empty, what else could you buy? Books were cheap and plentiful.

If you couldn't leave your country, no matter how you longed to escape, what could you do? How could you travel? Through books. This is why Odessans start nearly every sentence with, 'I read that' or 'Apparently …' We couldn't go anywhere, but we could read. *I read that the Bible is a translation of a translation of a translation, so no one can be sure that the stories are accurate. Apparently, Sofia will soon be the new Paris. According to one poll, Edgar Allan Poe is the most famous dead poet of all time.* Yet our shelves were filled with novels we didn't have time to read set in countries we would never see. The only state we could travel to was the state of irony. To remove ourselves from the office of wanderlust and longing, we made jokes. We made Odessa the humor capital of the former Soviet Union.

I packed the book on Albania. And so many other things I should have left behind.

In our new neighborhood the buildings were only five stories high. Ours was painted Tuscan yellow. This warm color, in addition to the wisteria vines and small wishing well, made the courtyard feel inviting. The new flat was closer to everything – my job, the main bazaar, the polyclinic, the beach, Boba's friends. Perhaps I was unconsciously planning my departure by making things easier for my grandmother to get along without me. I wondered how things would work out with Will. We had a bedroom for him if he changed his mind about coming to Odessa. I didn't tell Boba that he wanted me to visit. I didn't tell anyone. How I missed Olga. I wanted to tell her all about Will, that I was going to America. To ask her advice about redecorating our new flat. To share my happiness with a friend. I'd been so wrong to introduce her to Harmon. Without Olga, there was no one to tell.

I knew that Boba would be happy for me when Will sent the ticket. She said I should go abroad and encouraged me to find a man at the socials. She wanted me to get married and have kids, and she knew that in Odessa, I was unmarriable – what man would want a woman who works more and earns more than he does? Maybe a Western man wouldn't mind, but an Odessan man would.

Olga hadn't been to the office in three days. Vita and Vera said her kids had the chicken pox. I worried about her little ones, but was glad that she couldn't come in. Harmon and I worked side by side, getting more done in a week than we had in a month. It felt good.

After work, I walked to Soviet Unions. In front of the office, a wiry man in black leaned against a Mercedes. I hoped that the car was the Grande Dame's, but feared that the Stanislavskis had finally heard about her matchmaking operation and wanted their unfair share. Something told me that even if she could afford a new car, she wouldn't have a driver/bodyguard with a Kalashnikov.

When I walked in, I saw three dark-haired brothers in designer sunglasses and identical long cashmere coats. Vlad was the tallest and the best-looking. The middle brother was passable, and the youngest was ugly and, as my Boba would say, far from being the sharpest knife in the drawer. The Grande Dame stood behind her desk, wringing her hands.

I tried to move towards her, but Vlad was in the way. 'You're like a scarecrow in a field of melons,' I hissed.

He smiled. I frowned, which made him grin. He really was incorrigible.

'Do you want to go for a walk on the beach?' he whispered.

'We already did.' I was with Will now. Will who'd invited me to America.

'That was months ago,' he protested.

That day had been divine. But then any walk on the Black Sea is superb. The gentle lapping of the water, children building sand castles, babushkas selling *boobliki*, the ships in the distance. Life.

My heels had sunk into the sand, so we had to walk slowly. Of course at the sea you breathe more deeply. You relax, you let your guard down. When your sleeve brushes his, it sends a jolt up your arm straight to your heart. You let it happen again and again, wondering does he feel it, too? I tried to ignore him but it was hard. Something in me responded to him. Lethal charm, lethal looks, lethal to my heart. I couldn't help the way I felt, the way he made me feel, but I could hide my feelings so that no one – especially him – knew that they existed.

'Good afternoon, gentlemen,' I said as I moved around Vlad to Valentina Borisovna's side. 'Looking for wives? We've got a fine selection.'

I looked at Valentina Borisovna, but I could feel his eyes on me.

'Daria, you know these men?' she asked, clearly surprised.

'They visit the shipping firm for "rent," too,' I whispered.

'Does Mr. Harmon know you work here?' The youngest asked.

I could just see the little snout trying to hold it over my head.

'Of course,' I lied. Tomorrow, Harmon would have to be told before he found out from someone else. I cringed when I thought of his reaction. The yelling and foul language. The accusations of divided loyalty. I hoped he wouldn't fire me.

'Sorry, gentlemen,' poor Valentina Borisovna tittered, 'but I just can't let you introduce ... ladies of the night into my socials. I have a sterling reputation abroad and don't want to sully it.'

The men hadn't moved or changed expression, but the room was charged with menace. Business owners who balked before the Stanislavskis had turned up dead. One of Harmon's colleagues – a foreigner who did not know our ways – had told them to 'sod off' when they'd first come to our office. The next day, Harmon had found him alive, but unrecognizable. A helicopter came and took him to Vienna for treatment. Harmon had never described what they'd done to the man, but our cleaning lady said it took days to remove the blood from his office, which became a large, mostly empty storage room. I didn't want to imagine what they would do if she refused them.

'Valentina Borisovna, it's a capital idea and will certainly liven up the dull evenings,' I said.

She looked at me as though I'd grown a red, bulbous nose like Yeltsin's.

'Listen to Daria, Valentina Borisovna,' Vlad said. 'She understands business. She's a very intelligent young woman. You're lucky to have her.'

His words warmed me.

Resigned, she handed over the money with a schedule of the next three socials.

After they left, the Grande Dame sat down in her chair and started to cry. 'There, there,' I said, standing behind her and patting her shoulder. I chanted the Ukrainian mantra, 'Everything will be fine. We'll think of something.'

'But what? Things were going so well,' she sniffled into her limp hanky. 'I don't want our girls mixing with call girls! Some of the men who went to the Moscow and St. Petersburg socials said that I had the highest quality, prettiest girls. Better than Moscow! Do you realize? Now all is lost!'

'Everything will be fine,' I repeated, whether I believed it or not.

'Daria, it wouldn't surprise me if you found a way out of this disaster. You're so smart, I bet you never had to bribe your university professors to get your degree.'

'High praise, indeed!' I said, and we both laughed. Of course, she was wrong. Professors refused to correct exams if students didn't slip a twenty-dollar bill between the first and second pages. Everyone had to pay 'reading fees,' though the dumb and lazy had to throw in a bit more. I didn't go for my master's in engineering – I could have afforded the tuition, but not the 'fees.'

'Didn't you want to show me something?' I asked.

'The technician finally finished it,' she said.

She turned on the computer and pulled up the Soviet Unions website. Its homepage featured close-ups of demure young women – a blonde with cheekbones that could cut glass, a brunette with sparkling hazel eyes – as well as a few full-body shots taken at socials. The women looked like models, tall, lithe, sexy. On closer inspection, I saw that one was me. 'Valentina Borisovna! How could you? You know I have a boyfriend.' *And he's invited me to go to America,* I thought to myself. I couldn't stop smiling and had to wrap my arms around my body to contain my excitement. I loved these moments when I was happy, even giddy, and could imagine leaving all my troubles behind.

'Back to earth, darling! There's more.' She gave my shoulder a little shake. 'Where do you go when you're gone?'

I shrugged and reluctantly pulled myself out of the clouds. We continued to look at the website together. It was impressive. In addition to the girls, there were links to the prestigious Krasnaya and Londonskaya hotels, a list of restaurants, and photos of the beach, opera house, craft fair, and philharmonic. Because some of the women who applied for a fiancé visa had been denied, the Grande Dame asked me to research the process. She sold an information packet on getting a 'girlfriend visa' with everything from the forms (both the G-325A and the I-129F, not to be confused with the I-129, no F) and fees (currently ninety-five dollars). The packet also listed the requirements, including color photos of both petitioners, ways to establish proof that the couple has met, and a sample statement written by the U.S. petitioner. *I met Julia through Soviet Unions, a serious matchmaking organization based in Odessa. Julia and I corresponded for three months before I traveled to meet her. She is planning to visit me in the States and hopefully, we will be married there. In my file, please find photos of me and Julia at the beach, at her home with her parents, and at a Soviet Unions social. Etc. etc. etc.*

Everything on the site was written in English. It looked so professional. In the 'About us' section, there was a large photo of Valentina Borisovna that was more repainted than touched up. I scrolled down to her bio, which was a paragraph on her desire for everyone to find true love and to make matches between lonely souls. Directly underneath were my photo and the title 'vice-president.' My eyes watered.

'Brava, brava,' I said.

She hugged me.

Still, I couldn't help worrying about our next social. What would happen? Mobsters only brought trouble. That night, I fell asleep thinking of Will in America and how exciting it would be to go there, but I dreamed about Vladimir Stanislavski.

Chapter 6

I made coffee, turned on my computer, and read through the faxes
that had arrived – all the time wondering how to tell Harmon
about working at Soviet Unions. How angry would he be? As
usual, he was late. I stewed in the juice of my guilty conscious.
Guilty conscience. I tidied my desk and the boardroom. I even
arranged the papers on his desk. Where was he? It seemed that
every time I wanted a moment of privacy, he was there, looking
over my shoulder. Then when I really needed him, he was AWOL.
(I love this expression.)

I checked my e-mail; there was a message from Will.

'Dear Daria, This is the hardest e-mail I have ever had to write.
The truth is, I have found your American equivalent and decided
to marry her. I know you'll be happy for us. We both wish you the
best. Sincerely, Will.'

My mouth slightly open, I stared at the words until the
screensaver transformed them into a school of cartoon fish
swimming around a fake sea. America, I whispered. Would I ever
get there? My throat constricted and tears welled. I swallowed.
And swallowed again. I tilted my head up and looked at the ceiling
so that the tears wouldn't fall. *Please don't let anyone see me upset.*
Breathe. Just breathe. I tried to inhale deeply, but the air came and
went in jagged little rifts.

I hadn't loved Will, though I liked him. It had been gratifying
to think that an articulate, non-alcoholic man was interested
in me. More than that, he was the thin membrane between me
and solitude. I told myself that we'd never met, that he was just
a figment of my computer. But this truth didn't take away my

feelings of hurt and disappointment. I was surprised at the ache in my chest. I heard Boba's voice telling me to look for something to be grateful for. It took time, but I found it. I hadn't told anyone that I was going to America. How mortifying it would have been to tell people the trip was off.

I erased every e-mail Will had ever sent. There. It was like he didn't exist. I looked at the inbox, still full of messages from Jane and my ARGONAUT colleagues. Some revenge. Eradicating him from my inbox didn't make me feel better. I still felt sad and rejected and a million miles away from America. I hadn't even realized how much I was counting on Will, on the trip to America, until it was taken away from me. I had been faithful, barely looking at the men at the socials, thinking of him. Apparently he hadn't been as loyal. Men disappear. How many times had Boba told me that? Why did I think an American man would be different?

Suddenly telling Harmon I was working a second job didn't seem like such a big deal. The day couldn't get any worse. I didn't know what to do with myself and made my way to the kitchen and prepared a chamomile tea. Unfortunately and as usual, the kitchen wasn't empty.

'Herbal tea?' Vita said. 'Stomach problems?'

'In the family way?' Vera asked. 'No, wait. That's not possible, you don't even have a boyfriend.'

Strike-struck-struck.

'Shut up, you syphilitic piece of road kill,' I said to Vera and stalked off.

'What's wrong with her?' I heard Vita ask.

Back in my work space, I watered my palm for the third time in a week. I looked out the window, hoping to see Harmon. He would probably just disappear, too. Nothing was keeping him in Odessa. I sat back down and pulled out a sheet of paper. *Dear Jane*, I began. And didn't stop until I'd covered both sides with my maudlin thoughts and ridiculous feelings.

When Harmon sauntered in, he took one look at me and asked, 'What's wrong?'

'I have something to tell you,' I said, looking up at him. 'To supplement my income, I've been working at Soviet Unions.'

I held my breath and waited for his reaction. I even cringed, thinking of how he could yell.

Instead, he smirked.

'The matchmaker?'

I nodded, still waiting for the worst.

He burst out laughing. Laughing!

'What's so funny?' I demanded.

'The irony.' He gasped for breath. 'Here you work in imports. Over there you deal in exports.'

I felt at once offended and relieved. He slapped his thigh and repeated, 'Imports, exports.'

He continued to laugh – a hearty sincere laugh, which made me chuckle, too. He really was starting to think like an Odessan. I looked at him, at his jolly eyes, his lips curved in a smile, his tender throat framed by his snowy white shirt. And just like that, he became handsome to me again.

'What you do on your own time is fine with me.'

I'd forgotten that we were now living in a revised history where I could do as I pleased.

'Just promise me you won't get mixed up with those losers,' he said. 'There must be something wrong with them if they can't find dates at home.'

'No danger there,' I said, thinking of Will.

My tone of voice must have given something away, because he patted me on the back awkwardly and said, 'You're an amazing young woman. Someday you'll find a man worthy of you,' before settling into his office.

I devoted the rest of the morning to forgetting Will and finding a solution to the Stanislavski puzzle. Or tried to. Strange noises came out of Harmon's office. 'Bah! Bah!'

'What?' I asked, peeking in.

'This thing,' he said in a disgusted tone of voice, gesturing to his computer. 'It's just like you! It has a mind of its own.'

I was actually glad that Harmon was having technical difficulties. It was humorous and frankly, it felt good to be needed. I walked around his desk to look at the screen. I clicked on the mouse a few times. 'When it freezes up like this, you just turn it off and on again.'

Ten minutes later, he called me into his office again. He couldn't open Word. I put one hand on his shoulder, the other on his mouse, and re-explained the concept of double clicking. He smiled up at me. I smiled back.

And this was exactly how Olga found us.

Harmon and I said hello, he in English, I in Russian, but she didn't answer.

I tried again. 'It's good to see you, Olga. Did you go to the Vigée-LeBrun exhibition?'

Nothing.

'All her portraits from the Imperial collection of the Hermitage are at the museum ...'

Still nothing.

I straightened and returned to my desk. She slammed the door behind me. Which, of course, did nothing to muffle the screaming. 'I no like. She bad, Daria bad. She go. I stay. She go.'

I heard Harmon's deep voice soothe her. When she giggled, it was like a high-pitched jackhammer on my skull. I crept out of the office and made my way to Soviet Unions. Over lunch, I told Valentina about Will's defection. She cracked the safe and pulled out a bottle of *kognac*. 'To God with him,' she said. 'You can do better. Now will you give my matchmaking program a try?'

I scoffed; she laughed.

When I returned to the shipping company, Olga had gone, but Harmon was hovering near my desk. He cleared his throat and looked at the floor. 'I, uh, have something to tell you.'

I swallowed hard. Was the axe about to drop?

'I'd like you to start dressing more conservatively. You know, turtlenecks, baggy trousers.'

Relief was quickly followed by anger. I crossed my arms and raised my voice. 'My clothes are neither tight nor revealing. They are entirely appropriate in the business world.'

'I know, I know. You always look fabulous. I mean appropriate. But you know how other women are. They get jealous.'

I felt my mouth tighten and barely got the words out. 'Other women or the other woman?'

Silence.

I had my answer. 'That witch,' I muttered in Russian.

'What did you say?'

'You're no fool. Use your imagination. And since when is she the boss of you? Or of me?'

'She's jealous. She sits at home all day, imagining things.'

'Whose fault is that? She could get a job, or she could fire the nanny and actually take care of the three children she brought into this world.' With each word, my voice got sharper. I couldn't help it. I worked *hard* to keep this job. I'd done everything – submitted to Harmon's flirtations, dealt with damning office gossip, handled a physical attack, and found the old dog a new bone. And now his mistress wanted to dictate to me? We'd just see about that. I decided to allow myself to brood for the rest of the day. I looked at my palm tree, but my eyes focused on the bars that covered the windows. There has to be a way out of this prison, I thought to myself.

After bringing me a tray with cookies and coffee exactly the way I liked it – two spoonfuls of sugar and a splash of hot milk – he asked about Boba. This was usually more than enough to coax me out of a snit. When he saw I was still angry, he magnanimously told me he would write the weekly logistics report himself (something he was supposed to do that I always ended up doing). I just stared at him standing in front of my desk, shifting his weight from one foot to the other, running his fingers over the top of his hand, trying to figure out what else he could say. Looking at my furrowed brow and jutting jaw, he realized that he would get nowhere and wisely left for the day. Good riddance. 'The mare's work is easier when the farmer gets off the cart,' I yelled to no one in particular.

I took a sip of café au lait, allowing myself this pleasure. He made the best coffee.

At five o'clock, I left the office. Vera ran after me and said, 'You lose!'

'What?' I asked.

'The office bet! Olga moving in with Mr. Harmon. I won! I had the fifteenth!'

'How do you know? He didn't say anything to me.'

She smirked. 'You think he tells his secretary everything? I heard him talking to my boss. You were way off.'

'Congratulations,' I said bitterly and handed over the money.

After work, I went to work. Valentina Borisovna had a liter of vodka on her desk and an ice pack on her head. She moaned and downed a shot. I was worried that she'd switched to the hard stuff. 'The Stanislavskis dropped by,' she said.

'I know you're scared, but anyone could walk through these doors,' I reminded her gently.

Immediately, she snapped to and the Grande Dame persona was back. In Odessa, illusion is everything. She whipped her fake Chanel compact out of her fake Louis Vuitton purse, tidied up her make-up, then put the vodka back in the safe. She only had thirty dollars in cash and photos of her grandchildren in there. Anything of value, she tucked in her bullet-proof bra. She put her pink glasses back on and looked up her nose at me.

'What can we do?' She covered her face with her plump, manicured hands.

'I have an idea.'

She looked up at me. Her blue eyes narrowed.

Just then, two girls in fluffy angora sweaters walked in and asked how much our services cost. The Grande Dame pasted a smile on her face and gave them her spiel. 'We make the men pay! Give it a try! What have you got to lose? Americans are richer and more stable than any man you'll find in Odessa.'

On cue, I handed them forms. Name, rank, marital status. Likes, dislikes. Age, profession, etc.

'What if I'm married?' one asked.

'Write divorced,' the Grande Dame advised.

While they filled in the forms, I whispered the plan in Valentina Borisovna's ear. She looked up at me in disbelief.

'It will work, you'll see,' I said.

'I hope you're right.'

When the women handed me their forms, I typed their profiles for the program. 'Vika, 25, originally from Odessa, enjoys playing tennis and taking long romantic walks. She seeks an athletic man who wants to have a family.'

The Grande Dame snapped their photos. (If a girl was plump, she took a headshot. If she was svelte like Vika, the photo revealed the girl's body.) We thanked them for choosing Soviet Unions and handed them the list of upcoming events.

After they left, I continued the conversation as if we hadn't been interrupted. 'I've dealt with the mafia for over a year at the shipping agency. You can't go through them, only around them. Trust me.' Still, I was nervous and hoped that if Vlad figured out our ploy, he would only be annoyed, not angry.

She nodded. 'In the meantime, Daria, our girls must look pristine next to the prostitutes. We'll have to call them and explain.' Of course, when Valentina said 'we,' she meant me.

'Explain what?' I asked.

'That we have a planeload of rich, *conservative* men arriving.'

I phoned the first number on our list. 'Irina? It's Daria. Listen, this weekend we have a group of rather wealthy traditional gents, I thought I should warn you ... Yes, yes, Irina. You're absolutely right, conservative clothes, natural make-up. Smart girl. See you Friday?'

'Only 199 to go,' Valentina Borisovna said.

I groaned and slipped out of my heels. I supposed that soon Harmon would want me to start wearing orthopedic shoes. And why not curlers in my hair? I sniffed. That man. And Vladimir Stanislavski was no better.

Seeing my day had gone just as well as hers, Valentina Borisovna dialed the safe combination and brought the bottle back out. 'To unexpected occurrences and mitigating disasters.'

'To mitigating occurrences and unexpected disasters,' I seconded, and we downed the shot.

I called the second number. 'Allo, Sveta? Daria. You should know that we have a large number of Mormons attending the next social ... you might consider wearing less make-up and more clothing, that's all ... No, no I'm not telling you what to do. You're an adult. It's just ... we don't want anyone mistaking you for a hooker.'

Valentina Borisovna chortled at that, but number two was not amused. 'Fuck off,' she said and slammed down the receiver.

'You call number three,' I said.

'Vera? Verochka, listen ...'

We were so worried about the women that I'd forgotten we had to say something to the Americans. Most had arrived a few days early and if they explored the city at all, they'd seen prostitutes in front of the hotels and the *vauxhall* – the train station. What to say?

I poured two more shots. Vladimir Stanislavski could drive any woman to drink.

I was relieved we had to spend the whole evening on the phone so Valentina Borisovna couldn't show me her new matchmaking computer program. I needed a break from men.

The evening of the next social, I gathered all forty-seven Americans in the ballroom. I checked the microphone and cleared my throat. 'Gentlemen, welcome to sunny Odessa. You have spent a day or two in our fair city and have seen that we have a minor problem with ... ladies of the night.'

They nodded.

'Unfortunately, the police send provocatively dressed agents to our socials to try to trap foreigners. Please do not fall into this ambush. If you are propositioned by an 'undercover agent,' simply walk away. Trust me, you wouldn't like Ukrainian prisons.'

They chuckled nervously. I hoped my warning would work.

When our girls entered, for the most part, they looked as wholesome as country maidens, which only made the prostitutes stand out in their worn thigh-high boots, cheap lingerie, and excessive make-up. Each was branded with hard eyes and a mouth set in bitterness. Like a Mercedes or Rolex, they were owned by the mafia but not treated half as well. I didn't blame these young women, I pitied them. For they were not like the floozies in the shipping office who slept with their bosses and tried to make trouble for the rest of us. They were fighting for their lives. I imagined that they'd sold off their valuables first – a mink hat, a silver serving spoon – displaying them on a small towel on the ground at the bazaar. Then went possessions of little value: books, Soviet knick-knacks, a grubby childhood toy. With nothing left, they sold the one possession that remained: their bodies.

At first, the prostitutes lolled against the wall, certain that the customers would come to them. They seemed surprised that for over an hour, the men stuck to the marmish misses. Girls like Sveta, who had not heeded our advice and wore a leather mini-skirt and high, high heels, were having serious difficulties.

Usually, with her teased-up platinum hair and glossy lips, Sveta was chatted up straight away. But tonight when she approached a man, he walked away. Eight times, I watched her advance and the men retreat.

She came to me and said, 'Daria, for what it's worth, I'm sorry. I never thought that … well, I should have listened to you. You were only trying to help.' She looked at the professionals leaning against the walls, then at her own clothing. Unfortunately, she'd chosen the same footwear as one of the working girls – shiny silver sandals with tinsel hanging off the four-inch heels.

'It's not too late,' I told her. 'Wash your face in the bathroom and take off those shoes.'

She did as I bid her and had more success. One man referred to her as 'my barefoot princess.' Valentina Borisovna nodded in satisfaction as she looked at our demure girls, 'Ah, the chaste are chased.'

After an hour, the intruders slinked over to proposition the men, who repeated the one Russian word, besides 'vodka,' that they knew, 'Nyet, nyet, nyet.'

Both our girls and the prostitutes were impressed by the men's disinterest when solicited, and we made many matches that evening. It is a sad commentary on society when a man becomes a hero simply for saying no to a prostitute. A few of the prostitutes asked to become clients. Valentina Borisovna gave them forms to fill out on the spot. Trust her to find a way to turn adversity to advantage.

Harmon and I knew each other by heart. When he hummed he was in an excellent mood, when he sighed he needed a square of dark chocolate to bolster his courage. I knew he hated scenes, cheap coffee, and bureaucracy. He knew that I had my moods, and when my brows came together like angry thunderclouds, it was better to let me be. He knew that the best time to convince me to do a task was after a meal, when I was sated.

Monday, he set lunch on the boardroom table: olives, hummus, rice pilaf, garlic dip, dolmas. *What did he want?* He watched me soak the *lavash* bread in the creamy dip that he'd topped with the most decadent olive oil. He watched me gingerly take a plump black olive. I closed my eyes and gnawed at the flesh. And sighed. And forgot that he was after something. He poured us each another glass of Bordeaux. He knew everything I could not resist.

That afternoon I was heedless, my belly full of bliss. Harmon used this to advantage, asking: 'Where should one go in Odessa to buy a ring?'

I told him the names of a pawnshop and three jewelers known for their high-quality gold without realizing there was only one reason he would need a ring. Harmon – this job – was the one rock of financial security I had. I should have protected this interest in the same way the Soviet government protected Lenin's carcass.

Unwise.

I had been unwise.

When I arrived at the Soviet Unions office, the Stanislavskis were already there. *Win-won-won.* The Grande Dame was in Party con mode, her blond bouffant shellacked up even higher than usual. On the long ledges of the windows, her ferns and orchids were dewy. She sprayed and watered them when she was nervous. I was afraid we'd have plenty of plant cadavers on our hands if the Stanislavskis started visiting regularly. The younger two looked at her gravely, like she was talking about a cure for cancer or their take of our profits. Vlad was flipping through one of our new programs, scanning the faces and statistics of our girls.

'What can I tell you?' Valentina Borisovna looked up at them with a poorly hidden smirk. 'We have virtuous men who are interested in ladies, not tramps.'

'Virtuous men don't exist,' Oleg, the youngest, said.

'Surely you gentlemen realize that our clients come to find a wife,' I seconded. 'If they wanted a prostitute, they'd go on a sex tour in Asia. They chose a matrimony expedition for a reason. Picking up a prostitute in front of two hundred potential spouses is not a good tactic.'

They nodded and were silent for a moment.

'We could send the whores to the hotels,' Oleg suggested. 'They can find out what rooms the Americans are in and knock. That's what hookers in Moscow do. Russian room service!'

The Grande Dame sputtered, and I gave her a look to quell her objections. If they talked about their strategy, we could combat it.

Seeing I hadn't flinched at their lewd idea, Vlad put down the program, took off his sunglasses, and put his face one inch from mine. We were nearly the same height. His black hair was slicked back with too much Western product, but he was handsome for all that. 'The scythe meets the stone,' he said, meaning *You've met your match.*

I refused to blink or to look away. It seemed to me that the air between us sizzled like piroshki in Boba's frying pan. I could avoid him, tell myself a hundred times that he was only interested in the chase, but I couldn't stop myself from thinking about him. I could only hope he wasn't aware of my feelings.

'I'm thirty, maybe it's time for me to settle down,' he said. 'Find a woman. I want *you* to find me a suitable wife.'

His brothers snickered.

'The fee will come out of the money we give you,' I replied.

'Fair enough.'

'Our bro's going to be wearing epaulettes – Daria's,' Oleg said.

I gasped and stepped away from Vlad. This despicable phrase refers to the sexual position in which a woman's ankles rest on the man's shoulders.

'Now just a minute!' Valentina Borisovna yelled. In her outrage, she didn't care that she was dealing with killers. 'Daria is a well-bred, cultured girl, and I insist she be treated with respect. Apologize at once, you jackal!'

She moved to my side.

'Apologize!' The middle brother seconded as he glared at his brother.

'I ain't gonna apologize to the heifer or the train-station whore,' Oleg said.

'Oh!' Valentina Borisovna clamped her arm protectively around my shoulder and shoved my face into her bosoms, trying to shield me from the ugliness. No man had ever spoken to us in such a manner. The Grande Dame and I were used to chivalrous words from men, but gangsters respected no one.

'What the hell is wrong with you?' the middle brother asked.

Vlad turned to Oleg and hit him in the face with such ferocity that I could have sworn that his nose was not just gushing with blood, not just broken, but actually concave.

'To hell with you!' Oleg screamed as his hand moved to his face. Blood spurted onto the Persian rug. I clutched Valentina's arm, never expecting to witness such violence. She squeaked out the incantation, 'Everything will be fine, everything will be fine.'

'I apologize on behalf of my brother,' Vlad said.

'It's nothing,' Valentina blathered. 'The blood matches the rug. No one will notice.' She rubbed it into the rug with her pink pump. 'See? No harm done.'

Vlad grabbed Oleg by the scruff of the neck and shoved him out the door.

I took a step forward, wanting to thank him for defending me, but didn't know what to say. Instead I thrust out my chin, put my hands on my hips, and demanded, 'Will you kindly send someone to clean up the mess?' to their retreating backs.

Vlad looked back at me with a wolfish grin.

After they drove off, Valentina Borisovna cracked the safe. We both sat down. 'Vlad was right to discipline his brother for insulting you. He seems quite taken with you. Is it possible you were ... flirting with him?' She said this non-committally, but her eyes fixed on me like a bazaar vendor's on a gypsy girl.

I fought the urge to smile. I didn't know why, but I liked giving Vlad a hard time. He seemed to like it, too. Valentina Borisovna dug around in her purse and handed me a book that looked like it had been read about a hundred times. 'Promise me you'll read this. It got me through three ugly divorces.'

I looked at the tome. It was called *Smart Women Foolish Choices* by Dr. Connell Cowan.

A half an hour later, a middle-aged woman dressed in a housecoat and slippers got out of Vlad's car. When she walked into the office, she looked at the bursts of blood on the side of the desk and exclaimed, 'What happened here?'

'Vlad punched Oleg,' Valentina Borisovna replied.

'He's never done that before,' she commented, pulling a rag and square of lye out of her pail.

Valentina Borisovna explained that Oleg had been *nogli*, a Russian word that combines rude and obnoxious.

'I didn't think anything could come between those brothers.'

'And nothing will,' Valentina Borisovna said. 'Boys will be boys, that's all.'

But she eyed me speculatively. I said I had a headache and went home.

Italy is well known for its mafia, but most people don't realize that our mob is much worse – and much wealthier. In Italy, there is a hierarchy, a tradition, and family counts. In Ukraine and Russia, where money and opportunities are new, there is no hierarchy, there are no traditions, and family doesn't count for much. Our mobsters have mansions all over the world, collect things like Fabergé eggs and B-52s, and are strangely proud of how quickly they can throw away money. From reading the news on the Internet, I had the impression that in other countries, the mafia controlled prostitution, underground gambling, and the drug trade. However, in Odessa, it controlled all commerce, not just illegal trade. Maybe living conditions were fine in Kiev, where all the politicians and foreign journalists worked, but outside the capital, if you wanted heat, electricity, or a telephone, you went to the mafia. If a doctor needed supplies, he went to the mafia. In a sense, Odessans needed the mob, who rebuilt the infrastructure of the city – granted, at a high price – more than they needed the government, a group of self-inflated old communists who filled their pockets as fast as they could, and unlike the mafia, gave nothing in return.

Which is not to say that the mafia didn't have a negative side. After perestroika, there was a period in which drive-by shootings were common. All *businessmeni* needed bodyguards. It had been a free-for-all as the mobsters fought for the top spot. Things were calmer now, since many of the contenders had been shot, fled the country with their illegal gains, overdosed, or become politicians. Vlad had crowned himself the king of the Odessa hill. And it seemed we'd be seeing more of him.

I was never so happy to find Boba standing in the doorway of our flat. She must have heard me trudging up the stairs. 'Oh,

Boba!' I hugged her – she smelled of freshly made sugar cookies. 'So glad to be home.' I took off my shoes and kicked them under the hall table and handed her my jacket and briefcase. The things I normally would have told Olga, I told Boba without thinking; the events of the week burst from my mouth. 'I got dumped by my Internet boyfriend. Olga is trying to depose me, and Harmon is so whipped he may well go along with it. A fight broke out in the Soviet Unions office. And to top it all off, that gangster Vladimir Stanislavski wants us to set him up. How would he know how to treat a lady? I bet he only frequents tarts!'

Boba took my hand in hers. 'First things first, Dasha. Have you had dinner?'

I'd been too upset to eat. Boba led me to the kitchen, sat me down at the table, and gave me a loaf of black bread to slice. She lit two burners to heat the pot of borsht and the pan of aubergine caviar, then sat down. 'Now tell me everything.'

When I explained about Will from the Internet, Boba reacted just like I thought she would, she blamed The Curse.

'That other woman stole him! Why can we never be happy? It's the curse, the curse, I tell you.'

'More likely he got more affection from a real woman than from his computer,' I sighed.

Anytime anything went wrong, Boba started in about being cursed. The Curse caused milk that seemed perfectly fine at the bazaar to sour once the pail crossed our threshold. The Curse was responsible for babies crying, clocks stopping, and men leaving. The Curse had ruled my life. When I got dumped, the flu, or a bad mark, clearly it was The Curse.

Neither Boba nor Mama ever said why we were cursed. Was our family cursed more than any other? In our neighborhood no one had had much food or money. 'Have we done a terrible deed?' I asked Boba years ago. Everyone knows if you're cursed, it's because you brought it on yourself. She averted her eyes. 'Well?' I insisted. 'What did we do?' She admitted to nothing, saying only, 'We were born here. That's curse enough.'

I thought of Will, about how I'd almost gone to America. How the mirage had been real for me. Tears welled in my eyes. Boba looked at me quizzically and said, 'I'm sorry you feel sad, my little rabbit paw, but I don't understand how you can be upset at losing something you've never seen or touched.'

I could only smile at her confusion. She'd never seen a computer, so she didn't know how e-mail worked. She didn't know that I went to work in hopes of having a message from Will. She didn't know how happy his letters made me. It felt real to me.

'Eat, child, eat. You'll feel better.'

She served two steaming bowls, each with a dollop of fresh sour cream and a handful of parsley, which she grew on the windowsill. It smelled delicious – like springtime at our neighbor's dacha. We ate in silence. It's true that her borscht is a form of solace.

When Boba asked about Olga, I admitted that I'd set her up with Mr. Harmon, who'd in turn set her up in his flat. 'She's changed, Boba. It's my fault, but she's changed. She's become so jealous that Mr. Harmon asked me to wear baggy trousers and turtlenecks instead of my usual clothes. She's ignored me for months.'

'Can't you reason with her?'

'I've tried. But the only thing that counts for her now is money.'

'Try to talk to Olga again,' she advised. 'Maybe she'll come around.'

I nodded. As I finished Boba tipped the bowl so that I could scoop up the last spoonful. 'What were you saying about the Stanislavskis?' she asked.

'The youngest … was rude to me. And Vlad hit him in my defense.'

'You're on a first-name basis with Vladimir Stanislavski?!'

She sounded alarmed, so I said, 'Hardly. I mean, I don't call him anything.'

She served the aubergine caviar. Boba was an amazing cook, but I'd never learned how. Her friends thought it odd, but Boba told them all, in a snippy tone of voice, that I'd been much too busy with my studies. To be honest, I'd never even boiled spaghetti or made an omelet. What would I do without my Boba?

That evening in my bedroom, I made a list of things to do.

1) Find Vlad a girlfriend.
2) Warn American men not to open the door when the prostitutes come knocking.
3) Confront Olga.

Confront Olga and tell her what? I'd tried to get her to talk to me when she came into the office, though not lately, since I'd been distracted by my work at Soviet Unions. Maybe I let myself be sidetracked because I didn't want to think about how much it hurt to lose a friend. I just had to try one last time. Maybe when she saw how much I missed her, she would relent. Perhaps she was embarrassed by the compromise she had made. God knows I felt guilty for having compromised her. We had both struggled, yet I hoped there was a way we could go on as friends. For the first time, I prayed. *Please God, don't let me lose Olga, too.*

At work the following day, I warned Mr. Harmon, 'I'm going to pay a visit to Olga directly after work. If you don't want to walk in on a scene, you'd better work late.'

I translated documents, sent faxes to the main office in Haifa, took notes in a meeting, tried to train Vita and Vera to use Excel, and ran to the port to walk our shipments through customs, all the while thinking of what I would say to Olga. *Think-thought-thought. Tread-trod-trodden.* It was only when I finished work for the day that I realized I'd spent more time thinking about Olga than Will, and I understood the pain – so sharp and sudden – I'd felt yesterday was actually hurt pride.

From the port, I zigzagged down my favorite streets, walking past flower sellers cajoling, 'Miss, miss, buy my flowers!', past babushkas selling hot, honey-glazed buns, past artists on the pedestrian street selling portraits of our opera house, the Black Sea, and naked women in odd poses. I walked through the dusty courtyard of Harmon's newly renovated building, where his flat was on the top floor. I took the stairs, as someone had peed in the lift. Olga opened the door, expecting Mr. Harmon, not me. She was dressed in a red negligee trimmed in white marabou. She was still the pretty, petite girl I knew, but her eyes seemed different somehow.

Harder. Colder. Distant.

'I'll just go get my robe,' Olga said and stalked off. She didn't invite me in, so I stood in the foyer. If Olga still considered me her friend, she would have invited me into the kitchen for a tea. No woman in Odessa leaves someone waiting in the corridor.

Everyone has an extra pair of *tapochki*, slippers, for their guest to wear, so that they feel at home, like a member of the family.

I peeked into the living room, which had been completely redone since I'd last been here. Harmon had favored dark walls and black leather furniture, while Olga preferred pink wallpaper and red loveseats. *Bend-bent-bent. Bind-bound-bound. Break-broke-broken.*

'We have to talk,' I said loudly. My voice echoed in the large rooms of the flat.

'I don't have anything to say to you,' Olga said when she returned in a tattered cotton robe she must have saved from her former life.

'Olga, Olga, we used to be such good friends,' I said in my kindest, softest tone of voice. 'Boba and I babysat your little ones. You came for tea all the time. Boba was just saying how much she misses seeing you.'

I saw a shadow of a smile cross her face, but the clouded expression quickly returned.

'Are you mad at me then?' I asked, looking down at my pumps. If she was unhappy, it was my fault. I'd thought with her money problems, Harmon would be a solution – granted, one I'd wanted no part of.

'I just get so jealous.'

'But Olga, why? You *know* I ran from him for a year.'

'Oh, you think you're too good for him?'

'No, Olga, no.' Clearly, this was not an argument I would win, so I focused on his selling points. 'Mr. Harmon clearly cares about you. Look at all he's done for you: hired a nanny so that you can paint, let you redecorate his bachelor pad to your liking, paid for a whole new wardrobe. Since you've come into his life, he's had no other woman. Trust me, I would know. I take care of the books.'

She sighed. 'He's always saying how smart and funny you are.' The way she crossed her arms reminded me of a five-year-old left out of play time at the children's garden.

So this was all Mr. Harmon's fault. 'He doesn't mean any harm,' I said. 'He thinks that you're interested because we used to be – because we're friends.'

'I'm sick of competing with you,' she said, her voice hardening. 'I know how clever you are.' It sounded like a compliment, but wasn't. In Russian, clever was often used in conjunction with another word: Jew. In this context, clever didn't mean smart, it meant sneaky.

Competing with me? Clever? I wasn't sure what to do or say. Olga solved my problem. She reached behind me, opened the door, and shoved me out onto the landing. Eyes that had once sparkled with humor and friendship now burned with anger. Her robe fell open to show her tacky negligee and heaving chest. She sneered at me as I stood agape, my fingers clutching at each other as if they needed to touch something solid, since my friendship with Olga seemed to disintegrate before my eyes. 'I don't need you any more. I'll get rid of you if it's the last thing I do, you damn Jew,' she hissed and slammed the door in my face.

Chapter 7

That night, I didn't sleep. I just tossed and turned my relationship with Olga over and over in my mind. How could I have been so blind? I'd loved her and thought that she cared about me. We'd shared so much. The same ballet shoes, the same classes, the same hopes for love. How often had I helped her with her homework? How many hours had I spent with her children? How many slippers had Boba knit for them? I thought that she was my friend. But then as I looked carefully, I saw that when we were schoolgirls, she barely spoke to me in class. She only spent time with me after school in our apartment, where no one could see, while she copied my homework. Later, in the evenings, she didn't come for conversation. She came for food. When I told her my problems, she was never supportive. Her advice was more harmful than helpful. When I told her about Harmon chasing me, her response was, 'Pay up.' Who would advise a real friend in such a way? Why hadn't I realized this earlier? I hated myself for being so blind. There were many interpretations of her words and actions, but I'd always given her the benefit of the doubt. I'd always had faith in her.

I finally understood why Boba had denied her faith – because she was tired of losing. Losing not because of something she did or said, but because of something she was. How could I tell Boba that we'd lost again?

At breakfast together the next morning, I wondered what to do. Boba sat in her pale blue robe; I was dressed in my gray business suit with a turtleneck underneath, as per Harmon's request. Harmon. He should know the truth about Olga. Yes. That would settle the score. She'd be sorry when he kicked her out on her plump ass. I pictured her without a kopeck in the street and felt better. Until I saw her three children sitting on the curb with her.

'You look tired, my little rabbit paw.'

I tried to smile. Should I tell Boba? I had to tell someone. As I drank the last of my coffee, I described the confrontation. Boba just shook her head. 'This is why you have to leave Odessa,' she said sadly. 'You mocked me when I suggested you find an American, but now you see why I want you to find a man who can take you away from this world of hardship and hatred. I lived my whole life among two-faced people like Olga, never knowing who I could trust. I don't want you to live like that. I've shielded you from so much, but I can't protect you from everything. And everyone. And I won't always be here ...'

'Oh, Boba ...' I embraced her, folding my body around hers. I didn't want to think about life without her.

For the first time in a long time, Harmon and I took our morning coffee break together. We sat in the boardroom, and he asked how 'the talk' went. I was prepared to tell him the truth, even relishing it, until I looked at his face – his warm eyes, his tentative smile – and realized that he was just as hopeful as I had been that the situation could be smoothed over. I remembered all the gifts he gave me and how he put up with my moods. I couldn't tell him. 'She wasn't home. I'll try another time.'

'Good girl,' he said, patting my hand awkwardly.

I went to the bathroom so I could cry in peace.

Once again I gathered the Americans into the ballroom. This time, I told them not to open their hotel doors to any beautiful women who came knocking, citing the undercover agent pretext again. I then added a dose of oozing venereal disease for good measure.

The upside of the confrontation with Olga was that it had kept me from thinking about Vlad coming to the socials. I didn't see how we would find him a wife. I doubted that he even wanted one. Despite not wanting to think about him, I *felt* the moment he entered the room. I looked up and his eyes met mine. Of course, he was dapper and young, he spoke Russian, and had a Rolex and a Mercedes, so the Sirens made a bee-line to him. Unfortunately, he came straight to me. I was interpreting for Alina, a sweet young divorcee, and Jim, a physicist from Nevada. Vlad stood beside me quietly and watched.

'You're so sexy when you speak English,' Vlad told me when Alina and Jim moved to the dance floor. 'Of course, you're sexy when you speak Russian, too.' When he said this, his lips curved into a gentle smile.

I ignored his compliments as best I could and asked, 'Do you want me to introduce you to some of the girls? What kind of wife are you looking for?'

'I want her to be smart, tall, able to speak English and Hebrew, hard-working, and sexy as hell,' he told me.

'Are you going to be serious?' I asked.

'Oh, I'm serious,' he replied, taking my hand.

I shivered and didn't know if it was because I was excited or scared.

Or brain dead. Didn't chickens twitch and shake after their heads were severed?

'I'm working,' I hissed, and pulled my hand out of his warm grasp. 'You're like my shadow! I can't get rid of you.' I called to one of the Sirens waiting in the wings, 'Tatiana, do you know Vlad?'

She knew he was rich and smiled at him ingratiatingly. I could see that it grated on his nerves. To be honest, I was surprised that he was annoyed. I assumed he'd welcome the attention.

Tatiana had already been to fifteen socials and still hadn't found a mate. 'We usually have a good turnover of our stock,' said Valentina Borisovna, clearly puzzled. Tatiana was beautiful with her thick shoulder-length chestnut hair, slim nose, and full lips. One couldn't help but notice her firm breasts, the erect brown nipples jutting out through her sheer white blouse. Unfortunately, she wore an overpowering perfume, probably from a bottle that someone had used, then refilled with mosquito repellent. (This kind of swindle happens frequently at our bazaar. Just because the box says 'Chanel' doesn't mean it is.)

'Vlad was just telling me he loves to dance,' I lied.

She grabbed his hand and pulled him towards the dance floor. He glowered at me and I smiled brightly back at him. She pressed her body to his, but his eyes remained cool and fixed on me.

The Grande Dame noticed the by-play and said, 'You've got to be careful, Daria.'

'How am I supposed to get rid of him?' I asked.

She smiled. 'Are you sure you want to?'

She knew me so well. Vlad and I stared at each other as he danced with Tatiana.

In the moments I forgot everything I knew about him, I was drawn to Vlad. He came to the shipping office, without his brothers, just to say hi. When I pretended to be annoyed and asked what he was doing there, he joked, 'Daria, I'm your roof,' which means mob protection, but also shelter or respite. 'More likely your roof's blown off,' I responded, the Odessan way to say you've gone crazy, like the American phrase, 'The lights are on, but no one's home.'

Odessan banter. Harmless, yet anything but simple. You see, if English is straightforward, then Russian is twisted. In English, there is one form of address: you. In Russian, in every interaction, there is a choice to be made: *vui* or *tui*, formal or informal, foe or friend, work or pleasure, indifference or interest, gatekeeper or girl his age. No or yes. The formal establishes distance and keeps a man away; using the informal is like opening the door a crack. I always used the formal with Vlad, at least at first. But he joked and smiled until I slipped up and said *tui*. The expression of pleasure – the intimate twist of his lips, the softening of his gaze – was enough to jolt me back into the formal, back into the role of gatekeeper. I crossed my arms and said, 'Mr. Harmon isn't here, I'll tell him you stopped by.' Formal. Austere. I kept pushing him away, he kept coming back. He'd give up and leave soon enough.

Vlad returned when the song ended. 'Happy?' he asked, a look of irritation on his face.

'I'm just doing my job.'

'Will you dance?' he asked. This is one word in Russian. *Tantsouyesh?*

'*Tantsouyou,*' I replied.

He put his palm on the curve of my lower back and led me to the dance floor. It was the first time I danced at a social. 'When a Man Loves a Woman' by Percy Sledge came on. After I'd played it for Jane at my old flat, she explained it was the number one song played in

American supermarkets because it lulled women into buying more. I confess, as I wrapped my arms around Vlad's shoulders, I would buy whatever he was selling. He held my hips between his hands and I allowed myself to melt, just the time of a song. He looked into my eyes and I saw a shadow of a smile cross his lips.

When the music ended, I looked for a way to ruin the moment. 'How's your brother?'

'Fine ... I assume.' He kept his hands on my hips.

Intrigued, I asked, 'What do you mean?'

'I sent him to Irkutsk.'

'What? You sent your brother to Siberia?' I screeched.

'Hey!' he protested. 'Irkutsk is the Paris of Siberia.'

'I hope you didn't send him there because of me.'

'I didn't like the way he spoke to you.'

'You sent your brother six time zones away because you didn't like the way he spoke to me? Are you nuts?'

'I didn't like the way he spoke to you,' he said, trailing his finger along my cheek.

I just stared at him with my mouth slightly open.

'He can look after our family interests there,' he said, then kissed me, a soft tantalizing caress.

'You're crazy. You could have any woman here,' I gestured to all the beautiful girls. 'You only have to choose one.'

'I already have,' he replied.

I stalked off, but didn't get far. Valentina Borisovna gestured for me to go to her.

'So you see, Valentina Borisovna,' Katya, one of our sweetest girls, said, 'Mick was my date and that slut Yelena stole him.'

'They should be pissed upon from a great height! No loyalty there! You're better off without him!' she exclaimed as she put her arm around Katya. 'Surely you realize there are more bulls in the pasture! Go out and find a few. Daria will be happy to help.'

I scanned the room, but Vlad had left. Good. I could do my job in peace. I interpreted for Katya, Tanya, Irina, Masha, and Natasha, then walked home. Boba greeted me at the door and asked how my evening went. I didn't tell her about my dance with Vlad. She would only worry.

* * *

The next morning, Boba remarked that I was rather pensive and I tried to smile. '*Vsyo budyet khorosho*,' she said. Everything will be fine.

I walked to work, avoiding the cracks and potholes in the dusty sidewalks. On the corner before our office, I saw a pensioner wearing a bright scarf with a bandage on her earlobe. She sat on an overturned pail, selling sunflower seeds wrapped in squares of newspaper for a few kopecks more than the going rate at the bazaar. When I gave her a dollar instead of a few coins for a packet, she was thrilled. Our poor, poor pensioners. I was too young to understand life before perestroika because Boba had protected me from the worst of it – the lines for food, people being taken away, the constant police state. She made it seem like a game. When I asked questions, she said, 'Sshhh. Even the birches have eyes. Let's count them.' We touched the alabaster skin and counted the ebony eyes that looked out in every direction. Still, I felt that post-perestroika life was not an improvement for old people in our country. Their monthly pension barely got them through a week.

Crime was rife, and defenseless pensioners were the first to suffer. I saw more and more old ladies with bandages on their lobes. Hooligans ripped the gold earrings – heirlooms that had been passed from mother to daughter – right out of the earlobes of babushkas as they walked down the street. In broad daylight. How could young men be so wicked?

I walked past the security guard, down the hall to my desk, sat down, and started to read the faxes sent from Haifa. Harmon and Olga arrived at ten. He came in later and later. She stayed longer and longer. I was getting tired of covering for him.

'Daria, quit being so lazy and go make us a coffee,' Olga said in a condescending voice as she stole a box of tacks from my desk. It was the first time I had seen her since she had thrown me out of the flat, and it was like I was seeing her for the first time – as a stranger. A heartless stranger. She wasn't my friend. She'd never been my friend. I had tried to make peace and had accepted her treatment of me because I felt guilty about introducing her to Harmon. But no more. I hadn't forced her. She'd made her own decision. Pay up? You pay up!

'You know, he's Jewish, too,' I said.

'Listen, little hole, in the dark, men're all the same – weak fucks who think twitching their asses makes them great lovers.'

I just looked at her, dumbstruck. How could I have counted her as a friend?

'Go get me my coffee!'

I lowered my head and replied in Russian, 'Yes, your majesty.'

'She rude. Daria rude,' Olga said in baby babble that Harmon seemed to love.

I went to the kitchen and found that someone had already made coffee. The pot was nearly full, but lukewarm. A devious angel whispered in my ear, and I couldn't resist. War. If that's what she wanted that's what she would get. I wouldn't just give up. I unbuckled my sandal, grabbed the pot, and marched back to the boardroom where Olga and Harmon were sitting. Just as I reached them, I tripped and poured the coffee all over her lap. She yowled, expecting the coffee to burn her.

'Oh, Olga,' I said in English for Harmon's benefit, 'did I burn you? I'm so clumsy! The strap on my sandal came loose. Forgive me!'

'Feces-soiled cunt,' she said in Russian, in a sing-songy voice, equally aware of him. She used the handkerchief he proffered to wipe the coffee off her legs and white leather miniskirt. When he was sure that she hadn't been burned, Harmon left to find the cleaning lady.

'The next time you order me to serve you, the coffee will be burning hot,' I told her, really getting in her face, lowering myself to her level. 'Don't look at me, don't talk to me. Don't take anything off my desk, not even a tissue, and quit stealing my presents from clients. If you don't leave me alone, I'll tell him how you really feel.'

'Bitch! You wouldn't dare. I'll get David to fire you!'

'I'd like to see you try. Your precious David can't sent a fax without my help,' I said, then gulped. Because of the brouhaha, I hadn't noticed the fat diamond on her finger.

After five, I went to work at Soviet Unions. The people passing by looked at me as though I was a little off and kept their distance. I admit, I was muttering to myself, asking questions that had bothered me all afternoon. What kind of idiot marries his mistress? Why didn't I see it coming? What was I going to do? Would Harmon really fire me? Should I tell him the truth? Would he hate me?

Valentina Borisovna was waiting for me at her desk. Her black suit hid a multitude of sins. Her signature pink pearls around her neck did nothing to detract from her cleavage.

'Ahh, Daria. With the Stanislavski business, I nearly forgot all about my new matchmaking program. The technician and I put your profile in the computer and it gave these responses,' she pointed to the screen. I sat down and looked at the words without really seeing them.

'Which one looks good?' Valentina Borisovna asked as she called up photo after photo. 'Steve from Cincinnati? Billy from Austin? Peyton from New Hampshire? Nate from Minnesota? James from Seattle? Tristan from San Francisco?'

'I don't care, Valentina Borisovna. Just choose one,' I said, watching the parade of photos. 'Wait! Did you say San Francisco?' Jane had told me that her boyfriend lived there.

'Yes, San Francisco, California. I like the sound of that. You're a real Odessan. You need the sea. That's why it never would have worked with that Will. Where did he live? Nowhere, that's where.'

'It doesn't matter who I write to. It won't change anything.'

'Dasha, dear, you're meant for bigger and better things. You're intelligent, hardworking, and cultured. You will find love. You will find a husband and start a family. You just need to read this.' She handed me a book called *The Seven Secrets to Attracting Bliss*. The author was a 'psychologist-like guru' from Chicago, according to the back cover. 'Americans do give the best advice.'

Her words barely registered. I was tired, sad, lost. Harmon would hire Olga and fire me as easily as he'd sacked the computer technicians. Boba and I would be destitute again and it would be my fault for giving away the one piece of security we'd had. I bit my lip so that I wouldn't cry. San Francisco indeed. Nothing I did mattered.

Valentina Borisovna looked at me and must not have liked what she saw, because she pulled the bottle of emergency *kognac* out of the safe and poured two glasses.

'Za nas,' we said and clinked glasses. To us.

'Tell Auntie Valya all,' she urged. This phrase let me know that it was all right to use the informal with her, that I no longer had to use her patronymic. I felt closer to her, as though she had taken down a barrier between us, as though we were friends.

I swallowed the *kognac*, reveling in the sensation of it burning my throat. I told her everything. Everything. Harmon's first stipulation. My teeth. His advances. The incident. How I found him a mistress. How Olga turned from a sweet-natured Russian spaniel into a real bitch. How she stole things, how I tried to talk to her, how she ordered me around, how I'd responded. How Harmon gave her a diamond ring. Then I told her about the drop of water that made the vase overflow: she'd called me a damned Jew.

Valentina's shrewd eyes took in my facial expression. She listened for what I didn't say as well as what I said. She was silent for a moment, then rendered her verdict. 'You did exactly what I would have done, what any smart woman would have done. Right or wrong, who knows? You have nothing to reproach yourself for, my dear. Nothing at all.' Then she laughed and added, 'The trick with the coffee was inspired! I may have to use that warning myself. How I would have loved to see the look on Olga's face when her expression turned from fear of being burned to anger at being tricked!'

I felt relief that she understood, but then I looked at the cut-throat survivor who lauded my line of defense and attack. She was a snake who shed her skin when needed – she'd been a communist when it had been necessary to survive, and now she espoused democracy because it allowed her to make loads of money. She was conniving, always looking out for herself. I liked her, but did not want to be like her. Not at all.

I didn't dare ask what she would do next. Luckily, she volunteered her tactic. 'I assume Harmon has adult children. Dasha, you must call them and congratulate them on their new stepmother. They'll be so pleased.'

That evening, Valentina called and told me that I'd forgotten to take Tristan's e-mail address. I wrote it down with no intention of contacting him.

'Promise me you'll do it,' Valentina insisted. I wondered if she felt guilty about my indentured servitude and was trying to set me up. 'For research purposes.'

'Fine,' I sighed.

At work, I had plenty of time to write to Tristan, since Harmon was over an hour late coming in. Again. I walked into his office, which was larger than mine. His desk was larger than mine. His chair was more comfortable than mine. I turned on his computer. It felt right to sit at his desk. *Dear Tristan, Thank you for your interest in Soviet Unions. We are happy that you have chosen us, Ukraine's premier matchmaking organization.* I reread the lines and shook my head. I'd been spending too much time on Valentina's PR. I erased the letters and started over. *Dear Tristan, Why can't you get a girl at home?* Perhaps the direct approach wasn't the best. I hit backspace. *My name is Daria. I work as a secretary* – Secretary? Translator, computer technician, accountant, and juggler would be more accurate. *and enjoy going to the beach in my spare time.* What spare time? I tried to think of something else to write. *Write-wrote-written.* My life seemed ridiculously small.

I love the sea ...

The ringing phone cut through my thoughts. I answered Harmon's direct line without thinking. It was Mr. Kessler calling from Haifa. When I told him that Harmon was in a meeting, he sounded skeptical. He'd heard that excuse from me too many times. I also used 'He's at the port' and 'He's at the doctor's office.' I was not creative when it came to new and plausible reasons why my boss was absent. I admired Mr. Kessler and hated lying to him.

'Daria, you would tell me if I need to replace David, wouldn't you?'

I didn't say anything. In Odessa, we don't like change. Something about the devil you know being better than a new boss.

'Daria? Is there something you want to tell me?'

I didn't say anything.

'That's all I need to know,' he said and hung up the phone.

Thirty minutes later, Harmon walked in, whistling and in a good mood. I glowered at him, so he'd know that I was angry.

'What's your problem?' he asked. 'And why are you at my desk?'

'I'm doing your job – might as well have your office. I can't keep doing this. Mr. Kessler keeps calling and you're never here. He's suspicious. When I lie and say you're in a meeting, you can bet that he calls Pavel and Yuri. When they're in their offices, he knows I lied! I can't keep covering for you.'

'Well, if that's your foul attitude, maybe you shouldn't work here anymore.'

I called his bluff. 'Maybe I shouldn't.'

'Anyway,' he said, 'I've been meaning to talk to you. Kessler said that the monthly reports have been late. What do you have to say about that?'

So this was how it would end. He would blame me for things that were beyond my control. He would fire me and hire her. I strode up to him, until our faces were two inches apart. I drove my finger into his chest to drive home my words. 'Let. One. Thing. Be. Clear. My job is to scream cockle-doodle-doo. Don't blame me if the sun doesn't rise.'

'What the hell does that mean?' he yelled back.

'It means it's not my fault that the electricity goes out most afternoons and that the post is slow. I've done my job and yours. I can't help it if documents don't get to Haifa on time.'

Harmon didn't know what to say to that and went into the boardroom. I checked my e-mail and saw that I already had a response from Tristan. *Dear Daria, I was so happy to get your e-mail. I saw your photo on the website. You're beautiful. And intelligent! I can't believe you speak three languages. You should work at the UN!* At least someone appreciated me, I thought, glaring in Harmon's direction. *I love the ocean, too. I live near San Francisco and camp at the beach as often as possible. Of course, I also love to hike in Yosemite. Its the most beautiful place on earth, so quiet and peaceful. You would really like it. I would love to show you.*

Maybe I should tell you a little about myself. I'm a schoolteacher. I teach science to 11–14 year olds. I'm also a scout leader and spend time teaching boys how to do everything from pitching a tent to helping them with their hunter safety classes. As you can see, I enjoy teaching and I like kids.

Well, that was a huge point in his favor.

I have never done anything like this before …

Harmon stalked into his office to grab a stack of files. 'You really are the most infuriating woman I have ever met.'

'You can't break a wall with your forehead,' I muttered to myself. And to him. In other words, don't deal with stubborn people. And don't be stubborn yourself.

I needed to get out of this office, out of Odessa. And San Francisco suddenly sounded appealing. I wrote back immediately.

An hour later, Harmon came out of the boardroom as though we hadn't fought and said, 'You know, I was thinking this place needs a little something. I never thought this branch would last more than a month, so I didn't bother decorating. But we've been here for well over a year now. What do you think about getting some paintings?'

'Fine,' I said. Another chore on my list. 'I'll take care of it.'

'No, no, you're so busy. I can do it.'

I should have known that Harmon had something up his Gucci sleeve. He never volunteered to do any extra work. He never volunteered to do any work, period. The following day, when I walked down the hall towards my desk, there were paintings on nearly every inch of the wall. Splatters of yellow over blots of black entitled *Bruise*. A canvas painted monotone blue called *Sky*. I didn't need to see the signature to know that they were Olga's post-modern spree. The prices were marked on cards tucked between the canvas and the frame: $100, $75, $150. Exorbitant in a country where an average monthly wage is thirty dollars.

We don't say 'That's the last straw' in Russian. Who has a camel? We say 'the last drop.' As in the drop of water that makes the vase overflow. Everyone has a vase. The last drop came when I looked up from my desk and saw the three by three foot painting of a large red stiletto with someone crushed underneath it. I looked closer. It was me beneath the heel, extinguished like a cigarette. *Sudden Death* for only twenty dollars. That bitch. And Harmon. How could he let her get away with this? I went to the kitchen to escape the art gone bad. The paintings there were equally ugly, but at least I wasn't being snuffed out in them. I waited for Harmon. This vase had overflowed.

When he came in at ten, he was grinning. 'Well, what do you think? Don't all these paintings liven up the place?'

'Did you see my portrait?' I grabbed his tie, pulled him down the hall to my office space and pointed to the offending shoe.

He squinted. 'That's not you.'

'The hell it isn't,' I said, using a phrase I'd learned from the captain of one of our ships. 'Take it down.'

'Olga thought you'd like this painting best and insisted we hang it in front of your desk.'

'One needn't think too hard why.'

'It's not a big deal,' he said.

'Easy for you to say, you're not the one being squished under her shoe. Of course, if she painted your portrait, you'd be under her thumb.'

'Enough!' he roared. 'The painting stays.' He strode into the boardroom and slammed the door. Looking around, I realized that I was surrounded by photos of the Barbie and the Bulldog and tacky paintings. I moaned. Why couldn't I have just one ordinary, boring day?

When Harmon's daughter Melinda phoned a few minutes later, I looked at the discount *Sudden Death* canvas and felt no compunction about saying, 'Ah, yes, your father is in. Let me be the first to congratulate you ...' I was so mad that I didn't think about the ramifications. I just wanted to hurt him.

'Congratulate me on what?' she asked.

'Oh, dear,' I said, 'didn't your father tell you he's engaged?'

When she started to scream, I bellowed, 'Harmon, it's for you.' Although in my mind I'd referred to him as simply Harmon since the incident, this was the first time I dared to address him without the respectful title of 'mister.' It was the first time I walked out of the office before the end of the day. It was also the first time I put my fist through a work of art.

I wasn't worried about going to work the next day. I knew that Harmon wouldn't mention his daughter or the painting – he hated confrontation more than my Boba hated dust. But I also knew that my days were numbered and that I had probably started the countdown myself with that stupid stunt.

For the first time since the day after the incident, he arrived before me. He'd even made coffee. I appreciated this gesture, especially since I knew that of the two, I was the one who should have made the peace offering. He put the carafe on the tray along with cups, spoons, Scottish shortbread, and the bowl of sugar and carried it to the boardroom. He sat at the head of the table, I on his right side.

I poured the coffee and waited for him to speak. 'I don't blame you for telling Melinda that Olga and I are engaged. I'm sorry for not telling you. Maybe you knew before I did myself.'

'I saw the ring.'

This is what I'd wanted all along: Harmon attached to some other woman. Then why was I miserable? Because of what Olga had said? Because she'd never been my friend? Because I was jealous? Jealous that she was getting married and I wasn't?

'Thank you for introducing me to Olga. I care for her and her three children.' He looked into his white porcelain cup, imported all the way from France. 'I haven't always made things easy for you. Especially at first. I'm sorry. For everything.'

I didn't know what to say. I never expected an apology from him. Never expected him to have real feelings for Olga.

He continued, 'I want you to know, about what I said ...' *Sleeping with me is the best part of the job.* The words hung in the air. 'That's not me. I've never said anything like that before ... It's just my first night in Odessa, I met this guy Skelton and he said ...'

I groaned. Not Skelton. Anyone but him.

It all became clear. Odessa is like a village. Everyone knows everyone. And every village has an idiot. Ours is Skelton, a loud redhead, red-faced lout, the owner of a Tex-Mex restaurant. Anyone with a little money went there – missionaries, mafia, sailors, teenage children of New Russians. I swear he opened the restaurant just so he could hit on the waitresses and female customers. Friday was Miss Tex-Mex night. He actually held a pageant – contestants were whoever happened to be eating there. Skelton was a Texan with a skewed vision of the former Soviet Union. True, women slept with him because they hoped he would marry them. But that happens everywhere.

'How could you have listened to Skelton?' I yelled.

'I know. I don't know. I met him my first night at the casino. He seemed nice. Like he knew what was going on.'

Casino! That was just an Odessan euphemism for whorehouse.

I could just imagine the scene. The two men, drunk, watching strippers gyrate to throbbing Russian rock. Harmon, the fragile newcomer, stunned by the foreignness of Odessa, unable to read the street signs, speak the language, decipher a menu, order a drink. Charismatic Skelton, the old pro, only too happy to relay his vast experience, to give warped advice, to order Harmon plenty to drink, to give him the wrong impression about Odessa and her people. I could just see him telling Harmon that all the women were easy, that they *wanted* to mix business and pleasure. That this was a place you could get exactly what you wanted without even trying.

'Anyway, he told me –'

'I can't believe you listened to Skelton,' I said. 'He's an idiot. *You're* an idiot!'

'I know that.'

'Being under the influence of Skelton isn't an excuse. A man in your position . . . what you did . . .' No one can understand what it feels like, what it does to you when you're scared to go to work when you're scared to quit. Why try to explain? I shook my head.

'I realize that. I'm not trying to make excuses. I'm trying to say that I was wrong. Period. After what happened, when I hurt you, I thought the best way to prove I was sorry was to back off entirely. That's why I stayed out of the office or came in with your friend Olga. To show you were safe. So that you would feel comfortable at work.'

'You mean you started dating Olga for me?'

'Well, yeah.' He stared out the window, as if the answers were out there on dusty Soviet Union Street. 'I thought it was what you wanted, since you brought her here. But now ...'

I didn't want to hear how much he loved her. 'Congratulations. My best wishes to you both,' I said. The words scorched my mouth. He looked up from his coffee. I continued, 'I'm sorry, too. For my behavior towards your daughter.'

'I'll have to go to Haifa to sort things out,' he acknowledged.

'I already booked the ticket.'

'I can always count on you.' When he gently grasped my hand, it felt as though someone squeezed my heart.

Chapter 8

It was a day of unexpected arrivals. Bright and early, Harmon's daughter walked through the door and stood directly in front of my desk. To my mind, she looked like a pudgy punk, all glower and sneer in black baggy clothes with green hair that stood on end. I didn't appreciate the fact that she referred to Odessa as the 'slum' where her father worked. Odessa is one of the most beautiful cities in the world. Everyone knows that. She came to visit her father for a week every few months and was nasty to everyone in her path.

'Aren't you surprised to see me?' she asked.

'Not particularly.' I went back to my logistics report.

'Go get me an espresso,' she said.

Another one who wanted me to get her coffee.

'The kitchen's down the hall,' I said. 'Help yourself.'

'I said, go get me an espresso.'

The director stood in the doorway and watched Melinda. After the strange phone conversation in which he had asked about Harmon, I shouldn't have been surprised to see him. Still, I was. In Hebrew, which sounds guttural and rough during a scolding, Mr. Kessler said, 'I don't like how you're speaking to Daria. If you say one more word, I'll have security remove you.'

She opened her mouth, then closed it again, looking like a fat Black Sea carp.

'Wait for your father in his office,' he dismissed her.

'Thank you,' I said. 'Coffee?' God knows I needed one.

He nodded.

110

When I returned with the tray, he was looking at the canvases in the boardroom. 'This is truly the ugliest excuse for art I've ever seen. Whose idea was it to put up all this crap?'

Crap. The perfect word. I nodded, happy that we were in perfect agreement.

'Mr. Harmon is just doing his part to support local artists,' I murmured.

He sat down and I pulled our paperwork out of the cabinet.

'The downside of having three sets of books in different languages is that it's time-consuming; the upside is that your common thug or government employee can't read Hebrew,' I told him with a smile.

'People have told me the mafia is worse here than in New York. You haven't had any problems?'

Personally or professionally? Here or at Soviet Unions?

'No. The payments aren't so high and their protection keeps the skinheads away. Since they made it known that we're under their roof, the office hasn't received as many threats and we haven't found any more bombs on the premises. I hate to say it, but it's money well spent.'

He glanced at his watch and cleared his throat. 'I know this is a delicate subject, but we need to talk about David.'

I hoped that he would arrive; already he was an hour late. And again I had to cover for him. I started to grind my dentures, which only served to remind me how much I owed him. And I didn't like to owe anyone. Thus, I chose my words carefully. 'It's true ... that ... he's been somewhat ... distracted. But as a newly engaged man, can we blame him?'

I could see the informal announcement, and my defense of Harmon, surprised the director. Perhaps the nuptial news worked in Harmon's favor. Who doesn't want to believe in happy-ever-after? Perhaps the director remembered me in an altogether different position concerning Harmon, and thought that if I, of all people, stood up for him, then he was defensible.

Harmon and Olga came in together as usual. When she saw that I wasn't at my desk, she said, 'Daria bad worker. I good worker. She bad. She go, I stay.'

111

I rolled my eyes. Despite daily English lessons, Olga's language skills remained as crude as Soviet architecture. But as long as she had a limited vocabulary, she couldn't come straight out and ask for my job.

Completely oblivious to Mr. Kessler and me, the happy couple went into Harmon's office, where Melinda was cooling her cloven hooves.

'Papa, how could you marry this whore?'

I was glad that Olga couldn't understand what was being said about her. Harmon's daughter had called me a whore plenty of times and it was never a pleasure. She must have thrown herself at him because there was a dull thump and a gasp from Harmon. I couldn't blame Melinda for wanting her father all to herself.

'I suppose it's too late to escape,' the director noted wryly and closed the door of the boardroom, which did almost nothing to muffle the scene.

'I told you over the phone, honey, I care about Olga,' Harmon said.

'How could you give this cow a bigger engagement ring than Mummy's? You're just a dirty old man,' Melinda sobbed.

'Olga makes me happy. Don't you want me to be happy?'

'Noooooo,' she wailed.

What surprised me most during this altercation was that Olga remained silent. I expected her to start wailing as well. Instead, she said, 'I go now. You talk.'

Her grace only reminded me that my role in this little play was contemptible.

'How long do you think we'll be trapped in here?' Mr. Kessler asked.

I shrugged. He could leave whenever he wanted, I was the one stuck here. My skin so hot, my longing so fierce, my days so long. *I hunched by the window, my forehead melting the glass.* I was weary. Weary of poverty. Weary of intrigue. Weary of manipulation. Weary of working two jobs and never seeing Boba. Weary of constantly having to remind myself that I was one of the lucky people, with a nice flat and a good paying job. Because lately I didn't feel lucky. Not at all. *Gray raindrops on the windowpane.*

I wanted someone to lean on, someone strong to shelter me. I wanted to live in a place where the laws were not made by the mafia, where policemen, schoolteachers, and doctors were not corrupt, where people treated each other with dignity and respect. Could a place like that exist?

According to Tristan in California, it did. His letters convinced me that his world was a kinder, gentler one. 'On my way to work this morning, I got a flat tire. The first car that drove by stopped to help. Its things like this that make me happy to live where I live. But I bet folks are nice where you live, too. People are people, right?

'This weekend I went to Yosemite National Park. Have I told you about it? It holds the largest living things – Sequoia trees. There so wide that long ago a man cut a large hole at the base so that cars could drive thru it. There so tall that they surely must touch the heavens.' I loved this image of a tree so tall that its branches tickle God's feet. But I didn't believe that a car could drive through a tree though – that's just silly.

At first, what he wrote was lighthearted and even superficial. But as time went on, the tone changed, 'It was a awesome day in Yosemite. The fresh smell of leaves, the light filtering thru the trees, but all I could think of was you. You mean so much to me.

'Im forty. My friends have all hooked up. They have families and kids to go home to. Like them, I want someone to share my life with ...'

Tristan was becoming dear to me. I wrote that I looked forward to reading his letters, that they made going to the office bearable and that it seemed like we wanted the same things: love, companionship, a family. I asked if he wanted children. After I hit the send button, I berated myself and tried to get the letter back. But it was gone. He probably thought I was too forward. I'd probably never hear from him again. Still, I checked my e-mail account every ninety seconds, hoping. I realized only an obsessional fiend would do this, yet I couldn't stop myself. And I couldn't concentrate on anything else. When his response came, relief washed through me.

Dear Daria,

   I would love to have a family, to have children, especially a little girl who looks like you.

   All my love,
   Tristan

For the first time, I printed his letter. And caressed the words.

Meanwhile, Vlad became more and more persistent. He had flowers delivered to the office. Harmon said they gave him hay fever, so I offered them to Vita and Vera. He sent chocolates. I slipped them to a pensioner begging in the street. Then jewelry. But as I looked in the mirror with the five-carat emerald around my neck, I reminded myself that mobsters proffered jewels the way normal people handed out breath mints. I gave the ruby bracelet to Valentina, the emerald to Boba.

He tucked scraps of paper under my keyboard and in between file folders. I found them at unexpected moments during the day. Quotes from Pushkin.

   I remember the sea before a storm:
   How I envied the waves,
   Running in turbulent succession
   With love to lie at her feet!
   How I wished then with the waves
   To touch those dear feet with my lips.

I kept his notes under my pillow.

Tristan wrote, 'The most important thing to me is having a wife and children. More then anything, I want a family. I don't need tons a money or a fancy car. My dream is simple – I want to love and be loved by my wife and children. Is it too early to talk like this? Should I of waited?' I wrote that I shared his dream. I wanted a home of my own and children – what woman doesn't? I hesitated to hit the send button, thinking of Vlad. Although I'd never admit it aloud, I liked him. I really liked him. He was smart and sexy and I felt so … alive in his presence. 'Twitterpated,'

Jane would say. But Vlad disappeared for long periods at a time, and his money was as dirty as the streets of Odessa. He certainly wasn't father material. And if I wanted a life that didn't include bodyguards and body bags, Tristan, my Californian teacher, was the more intelligent choice.

I hit send.

Not that body bags didn't have their appeal, I thought as I sat at my desk and prepared our quarterly report, half-listening to Harmon corner colleagues in the corridor to coerce them into buying Olga's delusions of art. Sometimes, it was so tempting to tell Vlad everything and let him deal with it. I imagined Olga's blue-tinted skin, eyes wide open, faint bruises around her throat where she'd been strangled, a bloody dent in Harmon's head where he'd been hit with a shovel. Who could say that these images didn't appeal? But I never said anything about work to Vlad, even if some days I was sorely tempted. And never more than today.

When Harmon walked back into the office after dealing with Melinda, Olga, and Mr. Kessler, he said, 'We need to talk.'

Are there any four words that strike more fear into the heart?

I folded my hands and waited.

'Daria, there's no easy way to say this. Olga wants your job.'

He closed his eyes, perhaps waiting for my wrath to rain down upon his wavy brown hair.

'I'm willing to negotiate,' I said and moved into the boardroom. I'd known this day would come and had prepared for it. Harmon followed me and sat in his black leather chair at the head of the table. I sat at the opposite end.

'When I told Kessler that you were interested in getting your master's, he authorized me to give you six months' pay as a bonus.'

I smiled sweetly. Of course, he'd made it sound like leaving was my idea. If Harmon quoted six months, Mr. Kessler had undoubtedly said nine. I'd find out.

'Six weeks,' I replied. 'I give you six weeks with that woman in the office. If you survive, and are actually happy with her work, I'll give you my "bonus." Call it a wedding present from your matchmaker.'

'Fine!' he said gleefully, mentally putting the money in his wallet.

'If after those six weeks you find that you can't do without me, I'll return. You'll double my salary. And ban her from the office.'

'Double or nothing? I can live with that,' he said and stuck out his hand.

I held his hand in mine and asked, 'So quickly? You can barely open your e-mail account without me. Who will deal with the Stanislavskis? Who will wipe the pornography sites off your computer history before the executives from Haifa inspect our office?'

'That was you?' he asked, sounding impressed for once.

'What did you think happened when you couldn't find your "Busty Gals" link? Of course it was me. What if she sees Vlad Stanislavski and decides to trade you in for a younger model?'

'She'd never do that,' he sputtered. 'She's with me.'

I'd raised just enough doubt. 'You don't know her like I do,' I said bitterly.

He looked at me, still holding my hand in his. Did he want to say more? We stood like that, for what seemed like minutes. I looked into his eyes, felt his hand warm mine, and I wanted to say something. I wanted to tell him the truth about her. It felt like it could be the right moment. But I was afraid that he wouldn't believe me. Or that he'd be angry. So I just said, 'I'll take a six-week leave of absence and then we'll see.'

'You're pretty damn sure of yourself,' he grumbled, releasing my hand.

'You need me.' I would never admit that perhaps, just perhaps, I needed him, too.

'Not anymore, I have Olga.'

Was it just wishful thinking, or did his voice warble at this last sentence?

'Do you want me to train her?'

'No, she said you've helped her enough.'

I looked at Harmon for a long moment. 'Goodbye, then.'

I had no personal belongings at the shipping office. I looked under my keyboard and went through the papers sitting on my desk to be sure I hadn't missed a message from Vlad. Harmon said goodbye. I glared and strode out of the office to Soviet Unions. When Valentina heard that I was all hers, she crowed gleefully, 'That fool's loss is my gain! At least for the next six weeks! Look how wan you are! You work too hard.'

Perhaps she was right. I would have more time with Boba. I thought of Olga, Vita, and Vera. It would do me a world of good to be out of the viper's nest. While I looked over bills from the caterer and the liquor suppliers, Valentina made up a 'to do' list for me. 'Since you're here full-time, I've decided to add a Wednesday afternoon tea and a Thursday tour. You'll be in charge of both. I want you to create new sections on our website called "Frequently Asked Questions" and "Tips for Finding the Love of Your Life." You can take pictures of the happy couples for the success stories page –'

The ringing phone interrupted her list. 'Allo,' she answered and handed the phone to me.

'Daria. You have to help me. My computer froze up and I don't know what to do.'

'Turn it off and turn it back on again.'

'Oh, right. Right. Should have thought of that myself. How are things going?'

'You mean since I saw you last, an hour ago?' I asked, looking at the mother of pearl watch he'd given me to celebrate our first six months together. 'Fine.'

He cleared his throat. 'Well, then. Goodbye.'

I put the receiver back in its cradle.

'So he misses you already?'

'Computer problems.'

'As I was saying, you could interview couples.'

The phone rang again. 'Vladimir Stanislavski is here, and he's upset that you're not. He wants to know why you've gone. How do you say "She's not fired" in Russian?'

'You did fire me.'

'It's a trial period!'

'You can't call here every ten minutes. It isn't professional. Have Olga talk to him. How did you get this number?' There were no white or yellow pages in Ukraine. He was resourceful when he wanted to be.

I hung up the phone and apologized to Valentina.

Ten minutes later, a sleek sedan parked in front of the window. 'And here I thought having you full-time would be an advantage,' Valentina joked. At least, I hoped she was joking.

Vlad stormed into the office and asked, 'What happened? I couldn't get any information from Harmon. That idiot can't put two words together.'

Of course, Harmon was usually quite smooth, he was just a bit intimidated by Vlad. I gestured for him to sit down and gave him the abridged version.

'Do you want me to get your job back for you?' he asked.

'Absolutely not. I don't need anyone to fight my battles for me.'

'You know, it's okay to lean on someone. I have broad shoulders.'

I bit my lip. I'd noticed his shoulders when we'd danced together.

'Come for a walk with me after work,' he cajoled.

Valentina watched speculatively, so I agreed just to get him out of the office.

'She said yes!' Vlad winked at Valentina on his way out the door. His eyes narrowed the slightest amount. He must have noticed that she was wearing the ruby bracelet he'd given me. It went so well with her black angora sweater.

'So, for the website, a section on frequently asked questions, tips, and success stories,' I said, hoping Valentina wouldn't ask about Vlad.

'Plus a description of the Wednesday afternoon tea and Thursday tour of Odessa. You'll have to interview for two more interpreters – they keep running off and getting married. Can you believe I pay these women to interpret, then they find a guy they like and sabotage his relationship with the girl they're *supposed* to be helping? It's like I'm paying them to apply for a green card. Unbelievable!'

She fumed about an ungrateful generation of youth, and I sank into my chair, relieved that she wasn't going to bring him up. Then she smirked and said, 'I had no idea that having you full-time would bring such excitement. A date with Vladimir Stanislavski?'

'It's not a date. It's a walk. He's invited me to restaurants and to the opera, but I refused.'

'You love the opera. What's wrong with dating a young, handsome man?'

'Who's an extortion king, mafia don, and possibly a killer?'

'No one's perfect,' she said. 'At least he doesn't smoke.'

*　　*　　*

118

At five o'clock, Vlad returned for our walk. He extended his arm, and I laced mine through his. It would have been churlish not to. We walked down Pushkinskaya Street then turned on Malaya Arnutskaya towards Park Shevchenko, an immense, neglected oasis with tall trees and long grass. Even in the summer, its paths were dark – perfect for clandestine meetings.

'What were you ... before?' I asked as we walked along the leafy boulevard.

'A marine biologist,' he replied. 'I studied dolphins in the Crimea. We even had a program for children of Chernobyl who came in the summer and swam with them. Those kids were great, so strong and optimistic despite cancer and the other illnesses they faced. When you looked at them, serious eyes stared back. They were already old souls. The treatments and doctors' visits had sucked the youth right out of them. But they loved the sea and watching them play with the dolphins at our center was like watching them become children again, even if it was only for an hour.'

What was he doing to me? I could feel my body swell with empathy and even love ... for those children. I felt my mouth soften and form an O. I turned my head so that if there was any tenderness radiating from my eyes, Vlad would not see it.

'If it was so great, why did you stop?' I asked sharply.

'I loved it, but my salary was barely twenty dollars a month, if I got paid. Hell, we could barely afford to feed the dolphins. It wasn't a life. So I came back to Odessa.'

His quiet answer only intensified my desire for him. I resented this surge of emotion and tried to expunge my feelings. First, I thought of Tristan, but his crinkly, blue eyes and soft smile paled when compared to Vlad. I repeated phrases I'd read about California: bordering the Pacific; possessing a beautiful climate and immense resources; San Francisco has a magnificent harbor; Los Angeles, the largest city, is the center of the moving picture business; nickname: the Golden State. I remembered that in America Jane earned in a week what I earned in a month. I repeated the litany of charges I'd filed against Vlad: an extortion king, mafia don, and possibly a killer. A powerful, rich man who would never be content with just one woman. Again, I tried to turn my thoughts to Tristan, my gentle schoolteacher. Tristan, modest, simple Tristan, the opposite of Vlad – he wanted a quiet family life in beautiful California. No bodyguards required.

'How can you live like this, being watched all the time?' I asked, gesturing to the man trailing us. Vlad tensed. And stopped walking.

'You get used to it,' he shrugged. We continued toward the sea. After a moment, he said, 'When you weren't at the shipping office today, it was a blow. I realized how much I looked forward to seeing you.'

At the beach, he turned to me and ran his hand through my hair, then caressed my face and neck with the back of his hand. And I craved his touch. I closed my eyes and let the tips of his fingers trace my cheeks, eyelids, and lips. I listened to the waves approach and retreat. I inhaled the salty air.

'Why did you give the bracelet to Valentina Borisovna?' he asked.

'Are you angry?' I asked, my eyes still closed. His fingers traced my neck and jaw line.

'Surprised. You're the only girl I know who isn't crazy about jewelry.'

My eyes snapped open. 'So you give jewelry to lots of girls?'

'Not anymore. I have a past. You do, too. I can't do anything about the past, but I can work on the future. With you.'

Chapter 9

Monday

He is forty-six. She is twenty-four. His hair is salt, hers pepper. He only speaks English – fast and with a heavy nasal accent. She only speaks Russian. Near the opera house (the third most beautiful in the world), at the Bondarenko restaurant (the best in all of Odessa) they sit next to each other. I sit across from her. She fiddles with her fork. He looks at the ceiling and clears his throat.

It is my first time on a date alone, away from the throbbing music and the camaraderie of the socials. I am just as nervous as the couple in front of me.

He takes her hand. 'I love her. Tell her I love her.'

'But you've only known her sixteen hours.'

'I don't pay you to think. I pay you to translate.'

I tell her. He expects her to be happy when she hears the words. She is anything but. In her eyes, I see that it is over.

Tuesday

He is fifty-three. She is twenty-two. He is divorced. She is divorced. He lives alone. She lives with her parents. At the Bondarenko restaurant, we each have a flute of champagne – he ordered the most expensive bottle on the menu. I sip. He gulps. She pretends to drink. She is sharp and wants to stay sharp. They sit next to each other. I sit across from her. She is stunning. So stunning that even I stare.

As time passes, he gets louder. The waiters look at me. I shrug.

They are lucky that they can't understand him. She is lucky that she can't understand him.

'The death penalty is the only answer,' he bellows.

I translate.

'I agree,' she murmurs, stroking his thigh.

'Some people don't deserve to live.' His words are slurred.

I translate.

'You're so smart,' she says. 'Let's go back to your hotel room.'

His jaw slackens in surprise, but he rallies and throws his arm around her shoulders. Her smile is tight, but he can't see it. I wonder if she is planning on marrying him or simply rolling him. Maybe her boyfriend is waiting for them outside. The man takes out a large roll of cash and throws some money at me. They leave arm in arm.

Wednesday

He is forty. She is twenty-four. He is a businessman looking for a blonde, she is a veterinarian looking for an animal lover. At the social the previous evening, I tried to tell him that it wouldn't be a good match. But alcohol and jet lag and lust dulled his common sense. Or perhaps because I told him no, he fought to prove me wrong and insisted this was the girl for him. Near the opera house, at the Bondarenko restaurant – lights soft, staff discreet – they sit next to each other, I sit across from her. They can't think of a single thing to say. Neither can I.

Before the second course comes, he tells me, 'It's not working. Get me another girl.'

'But you haven't given her a chance.'

'We aren't clicking.'

'Clicking?'

She looks at us, trying to understand the tense exchange.

'I paid three thousand dollars and only have a week. I don't want her.'

I look into her doe eyes and try to figure out what to say.

She doesn't need me to interpret. She's understood perfectly. She throws her *champagnskoye* in his face and walks out. The perfect Odessan exit.

He wipes his face and shirt with a linen napkin. Too bad it wasn't red wine.

I use the restaurant's phone to call Valentina, and she sends over another girl.

While we wait for her, he takes my hand and says, 'You're a very attractive lady.'

Thursday

He is fifty. She is twenty-eight. They both have sad eyes and gentle souls. Near the opera house, at the Bondarenko restaurant – food superb, décor elegant – they sit next to each other, I sit across from her.

He leads with, 'I was married for twenty-five years. Been divorced for three. I have two kids.'

'He has two children,' I translate.

It's her turn. 'I dated this guy for four years. Thought he was the one. Came home from work and found him in bed with my best friend.'

'She doesn't have children,' I tell him.

'I thought I'd be married for ever, you know?' he says. 'When she left, I thought I would die.'

'I thought I'd be married by now. You know, with kids, the whole deal. Why did I waste so much time with him?'

Friday

He is thirty-six. She is twenty-six. He is a poet and a professor at a community college. He is soft-spoken and asks good questions. She's a withdrawn Botticelli, which makes her seem mysterious, ethereal. Near the opera house, at the Bondarenko restaurant – we can hear the orchestra rehearsing in the courtyard behind the opera house – they sit next to each other, I sit across from her.

He does everything right. He listens. He doesn't press to hold her hand. He doesn't talk about his ex. He makes eye contact without staring. He doesn't complain about grasping American career women or tell off-color jokes.

She doesn't make eye contact. She is melancholy. I know her story: no degree, parents dead, works as a maid. Her hands are rough. She is rough. But he cares for her. He is patient enough that he thinks he can nurse her back to happiness.

'Look,' she tells me after he's paid the check. 'Tell him anything you want. I'm gonna go.'

She says goodbye and leaves. He looks bewildered. I tell him to wait and run after her. 'Have you thought of your future? He seems like a good guy. And believe me, I've seen plenty. Why not give him a chance?'

'It won't work,' she says. She shoves her hands in her pockets and goes.

I return to the table and break the news.

Saturday

On my birthday, my friends come at 4 p.m. In Odessa, you don't send invitations. Your real friends know who they are and they come. Boba has cooked all week. Valeria, Inna, Alla, Genia, Maria, and Yelena sit at our table. Varvara couldn't come, her son is ill.

'Has another year gone by so quickly?'

'I swear besides work, birthdays and the bazaar are the only occasions for me to get out of the flat!'

'And buying potatoes, beets, and onions is no fun. Birthday parties are the only time I can enjoy myself.'

'My little Dima runs me ragged. I wish I had half his energy!'

'Daria, you're so lucky to be free! Marriage isn't what I thought it was ... I spend more time in the kitchen than I do in the bedroom!'

Before the conversation turns ribald, Boba raises her glass. 'To Daria, happy birthday! May all your dreams come true!'

'To Daria, we wish you good health, success at work, and luck in love!'

Around the table they go, toast after toast, course after course. When we were school girls and then students, they stayed the whole weekend. We went for walks, dressed in each other's clothes, tried different hairstyles, and chatted all weekend long. But one by one they married and monthly long weekends became rare afternoons.

'Where's Olga? That slut never misses a chance for a free glass of *kognac*.'

'Didn't you hear she's got some new sugar daddy? A foreigner.'
'He'll go home and leave her in the dust. She'll never learn.'

Sunday

I sleep.

Chapter 10

Surely, one of the reasons that Olga wanted my job was the presents that I received from clients. Jewelry, chocolates, French perfume, figs and dates, thick envelopes. She probably thought I received them for looking good. Neither Harmon nor Olga knew what I did to receive such gestures of gratitude. But they were about to learn. In Odessa, nothing clears customs – coming or going – without goodwill, or what the custom agents call an 'expedite fee.' It could be anything, but what? Much depended on the agent and his mood. If the situation was handled improperly, or crudely, shipments rotted. The agents even had the power to put our containers back on the ships and send them back whence they came.

In Odessa, you couldn't just walk up to business associates and bribe them. This would be vulgar. You had to spend time with each to know which approach to use. The youngest agents wanted electronics. The middle-aged men didn't want their sons drafted and needed exemption letters from a doctor. Flattery worked best with the old-timers. All received a bottle and an envelope at the end of the year as an expression of gratitude for their great understanding and effort. It went without saying that I walked the most valuable shipments through customs myself. On those days, I packed a picnic basket of caviar (red and black), Black Sea sardines, a wide array of local cheeses, bread, and one of Boba's cheesecakes as a thank you. Of course, I expected my products to leave customs the same day that they arrived, in the same condition and with nothing missing. It took much time to learn what would make our shipments a priority. Our clients knew that without me their goods would never clear Odessa customs, even if Harmon and Olga did not.

It wasn't entirely clear what Harmon's position in the company had been before he arrived in Odessa. He'd told me that his grandfather had founded the firm and that he'd inherited the job whether he'd wanted it or not. Harmon never talked about his ex-wife, his friends back home, his other life. This was what Odessa did to a person – it erased the past and future.

To survive, you had to be in the present – to remark every nuance at work, to keep an eye on the unscrupulous vendors at the bazaar, to watch for pickpockets on the street. I kept my ears pricked; Vita and Vera had stopped talking about me. They mainly gossiped about Olga and repeated what their own bosses said about Harmon – that he was naïve and couldn't take a decision to save his life or the Odessa branch. When I was still Harmon's secretary, I had deflected this gossip, but it was hard because they were not wrong.

Harmon called Soviet Unions every day to ask how to refill the fax machine with paper, how to make a conference call – all the basic tasks that Olga was supposed to do. I smiled at the irony. When I was at the shipping company, I did his job and my own. Now it was his turn to do both. I always helped when he called. It took him ten days to realize that our shipments were stuck in customs. 'I don't know what Olga said, but she pissed off the agents. They keep asking for you. The meat and cheese will rot if we don't move them! What do they want?' he blubbered into the phone. 'What am I supposed to do? What did you tell them? What am I supposed to do?'

In one of Jane's American magazines for career women, I read that the secret to keeping any job was to become indispensable. To make sure that there was always one thing I could do that no one else could – a wildcard, they called it. Clearing customs was my wildcard. And I wasn't giving it up.

'I'd love to help, but I'm interviewing couples for our "Success Stories" page. Your new secretary will figure it out – in a year or two. The clients can scrape the maggots off the meat and cheese – if they ever clear customs.'

He made a strange choking sound.

Smiling broadly, I hung up the phone and went back to the

couple sitting in front of my desk. As usual, the woman was in her early twenties and wore a low-cut blouse, miniskirt, and heels, while the man was much older and wore tennis shoes and jeans. As usual, the man was entranced, the woman giddy. He clutched her small hand in his.

'So, Pete, you were telling me what you first noticed about Natasha.'

'Well, she sure was the prettiest girl at the social. It's true we don't speak the same language, but I still feel a connection with her.' Purdiest. That's how he said prettiest.

I jotted down his answer, then looked to Natasha and asked the same question in Russian, since she didn't speak English.

'He had kind eyes,' she said.

'Natasha said the first thing she noticed about you were your kind eyes,' I said.

'Aw, thanks, honey. Your eyes are pretty, too.' He kissed her on the lips. She looked at me and blushed.

'What brought you to Odessa?'

'American women – the ones I met, anyway – all seem to care more about money and their jobs than love. There's not a feminine bone in their bodies. I tried the social scene in Moscow, but it just didn't work out. There were too many girls, and they weren't as nice or pretty as the ones in Odessa.'

I'd have to tell that to Valentina, who prided herself on being better than Moscow.

'A buddy of mine found his lady in Odessa. He told me that it was a pretty city with the nicest people he'd ever met.' Odessa *is* a pretty city. This time, it was my turn to preen. I enjoyed hearing compliments about Odessa and translated his words for Natasha, who pulled on Pete's arm and nodded enthusiastically. '*Da*, *da*, *da*.' We Odessans love our city.

'Was our visa kit helpful concerning the paperwork for Natasha to return to America with you?'

'Absolutely. We filled out all the forms and I wrote my statement. Easy as pie.'

'Good. Do you feel that there is anything we could have done better to help you find the love of your life?' These were Valentina's questions, not mine.

He shook his head. 'No, I looked at the program and saw the girl I wanted, talked to her with the help of the interpreters, and that was that.' He squeezed her bare thigh. 'I liked the atmosphere of the socials – nice, clean fun. The hardest part was getting the visa to get into the Ukraine.'

The Grande Dame was working on that.

I took their photo for our success stories page. Her tight jaw was a contrast to his jowls.

'Well, good luck to both of you,' I said. 'Send us a wedding invitation!'

We'd put it on the website, too.

They left and I fixed myself a cup of tea, stirring in extra sugar to ease the bile in my throat. I was jealous. Jealous that she was moving to California. It was supposed to be me. I watched the girls go, one by one, or rather, two by two, while I remained. I longed to escape. To have a man whisk me away from the poverty and problems. A man like Tristan. He was younger than Pete and more handsome. I knew that he would be sincere and honest. He would be older (but not too old) and wiser. We would talk about literature, art, and philosophy. We would go to galleries and plays. He would be a good kisser with strong, sensual hands. I longed to meet him. Longed for what Natasha had found. Envy is a waste of time, my Boba would say, so I sipped my tea and concentrated on writing the success story.

The phone rang again. It had to be Harmon. I picked up the receiver and said, 'How are you going to last six whole weeks?'

He swore and slammed the phone down. His anger filled me with perverse pleasure.

Working only one job seemed like a vacation. It had been months since I'd dined with Boba. The evening was mild, so we decided to go for a walk. I loved this time of the year, when the humidity wrapped itself around my shoulders like a finely crocheted shawl.

I bent down to put on my sandals.

'Wear your other shoes,' Boba said. 'They're better for walking.'

I put on my flats, and she and I strolled arm in arm down the dusty street towards the beach. She gestured to the concrete apartment building on the corner. 'That's the place my mother, sister, and I lived before the war. When the Nazis attacked, we holed up in the catacombs outside the city. Weeks later, when we came out of hiding, our building was gone. But we were lucky – we had each other.'

I kissed her cheek. Boba's optimism never ceased to amaze me. The women in my family were so brave, so strong. Through famine, through war, through perestroika, they held everything together with no help from any man. My great-grandmother, grandmother, and mother each had a daughter but no husband. Could it be genetic? Or The Curse? Would this be my lot as well? Could people run from their fate or would it always catch up? Jane didn't believe in fate or curses. She believed in something called 'free will' in which people make their own choices and fortunes. I prayed that Jane was right, because I feared my destiny.

The next day I was happy to go to work. It was the first time that I would give the Americans a walking tour of the center. Of fifty clients, thirty came. 'Thank you for your interest in my native city. Odessa is Hero City, a designation given to only twelve cities for bravery during the Great Patriotic War.'

'Huh?'

'World War II,' replied the man next to him.

'Odessa is the former Soviet Union's sunniest and most social city. Conversation is our favorite pastime. People of all ages love to stroll in the park or lie on the beach and chat.' I stopped and pointed to one of my favorite men. 'Here we have a statue of the Duke de Richelieu. In 1803, Czar Alexander I made Richelieu the first mayor of Odessa.'

The Duke was clad in a toga, long out of style by the nineteenth century and despite the fact he was French, not Greek. Of course, Odessans don't think in terms of nationality. We think in terms of love. Catherine the Great, the passionate Russian czarina, founded Odessa. Our first mayors were French. A Dutchman laid out the city. Austrians designed the opera house. Italians sang there. How can we be reduced to one nationality? Everything that makes us who we are – fascinating, enticing, cosmopolitan – comes from this fusion.

It must be confusing to foreigners. Odessa is in Ukraine. We speak Russian. Who in Odessa doesn't have relatives in Russia? Who doesn't have chairs or towels or plates made there? Though the USSR was declared dead, the gray bones remain since much of our architecture is Soviet. Of course, the mentality of many politicians is still Soviet. In the years after perestroika, Odessans used the terms 'Russian,' 'Ukrainian' and 'Soviet' somewhat interchangeably. Things don't change while we sleep. Certainly New Amsterdam did not become New York overnight. Boba would say: *A man slashes a woman's face. The doctor sews up the wound. He later removes the stitches. But the scar remains. Moscow wielded the knife. Our souls bear the scars.*

Don't ask what nationality we are. We're Odessan.

The men looked at me, waiting.

'Directly to your right is Primorsky Boulevard.' I continued. 'The acacia trees that shade the stone walkway were imported from Vienna by the Duke. In front of us is the spectacular Potemkin Staircase, which has 192 granite steps that lead to the sea. The stairs were immortalized in one of the greatest films ever made, Sergei Eisenstein's *Battleship Potemkin*.

'When my friend Varvara's sister got engaged, she told her boyfriend, "I'll marry you on one condition – that you carry me up the steps." So early one sunny Sunday morning, we gathered to watch Igor carry Katya up the Potemkin Staircase. If any of you are looking for a way to prove your devotion …'

The men laughed and more than one said he needed to workout more before declaring his love. We criss-crossed the city, going from monument to monument – no city has more than Odessa – and ended our tour at a seaside café.

A few days later at quarter to five, Vlad stopped at the office to ask if I wanted to stroll on the beach, and then see *Carmen*. It had been so long since I had set foot in the opera house. I turned off the computer and grabbed my purse before I could talk myself out of going.

'I remember the first time I saw you,' he told me, my hand tucked between his, as we walked along the sea. 'You looked like a queen – regal posture, soulful eyes, golden skin. You smiled all the time.'

'I'd just returned from an internship in Kiev. I was relieved to be home.'

'So it wasn't hard for you to leave our fair capital?' He sat down on the sand and pulled me down beside him.

I bit my lip, not knowing whether to tell him the truth. Was Vlad interested in me as a person or as a challenge? At first, I'd assumed that I was the latter, but he'd sent his brother away because he'd insulted me, then seemed genuinely worried when he went to the shipping office and found I wasn't there. He'd offered to get my job back for me, and didn't insist when I said his help wasn't needed. I decided to tell him the truth. 'I couldn't wait to leave Odessa and be on my own, but I found the capital to be a cold place. I missed Boba and Odessa. I wanted only one thing: to come home.'

He brought my hand to his lips and kissed my fingers and palm. I stroked the planes of his face. He closed his eyes. For a moment, we listened to the sound of the waves hitting the sand.

'The hardest thing about coming back to Odessa was admitting I'd made a mistake in leaving. I was too proud and stayed there because I was afraid people would laugh at me for having failed. If I'd been smart, I would have returned immediately.'

'There's nothing wrong with being proud. Sometimes our pride is all we have.'

I drew my knees up and perched my chin on them. My fingers drew lines in the sand, my heart rejoiced at what I'd heard. Someone finally understood what I felt. 'What about you? How did you end up ...'

'Where I am?'

I nodded.

'When I left the Crimea and returned to Odessa, I got a job as a driver for a New Russian. I earned forty dollars that first month, twice my salary as a marine biologist.' He smiled sadly. 'Another mobster noticed that I kept the cars clean and my mouth shut, and he hired me to be his bodyguard and driver, tripling the salary. This happened again and again. I worked for all the greats. And they all conducted their business on phones in their cars. I absorbed everything. When Lev Tomashenko flew the coop to California, I took over his operation.'

'So you were at the right place at the right time?'

'I had two younger brothers to support. I did what I had to do.'

I nodded. We sat side by side, looking off in opposite directions. I thought of how Harmon had chased me, how I had run. How the office gossips had stung me. How I continued, no matter what.

Was Vlad thinking of what he had done to get where he was today?

He cleared his throat, which cleared the air. 'At the social, the men couldn't take their eyes off you, but you didn't seem interested in any of them.' He watched my face carefully. 'I thought all girls wanted to land a rich American husband.'

'So you think all women are the same?' I stood and wiped the sand from my skirt. 'I've had lots of marriage proposals. My Boba says any fool can get married. But I'm looking for love *and* friendship with a man I can count on, and I won't marry until I find it.'

He stood, too.

I added, 'Women at the social were interested in you. Does that mean you're going to date them?'

'I've been with girls like that. It's not what I want. Not anymore.'

'What do you want?' I asked.

'You mean after all this, it's still not clear? I want you.'

I looked away. My heart started to pound, as if to remind me it was still there, wanting to love and trust someone. My brain cried out, warning me not to trust any man, and certainly not him. I did everything I could to silence my heart: took deep breaths, thought of the people Vlad must have hurt, imagined Tristan in America.

We walked to the opera house, neither of us saying anything.

When I saw the magnificent theater, I broke the silence. 'I remember going to the opera with Boba and my mother. Mama wore a black beret, and Boba and I thought she looked French. They were on either side of me, holding my hands. The lights of the opera house gleamed like a lighthouse beacon. Snow flakes started to fall and I tried to catch them on my tongue. It made Mama and Boba laugh.'

He looked at me tenderly.

'That's one of my favorite memories,' I said shyly.

133

He kissed my hand and said, 'I hope that you and I will create many more together.'

At the box office, he asked where I wanted to sit and bought the tickets. We sat in a private loge in the mezzanine, my favorite section. I could see the musicians down in the pit, the singers on stage, and the men and women across from me. I leaned forward and rested my elbows on the edge, afraid to take my eyes off the stage for the entire first act. I felt Vlad's gaze, which did not move from my face. At intermission, he asked which ballets I wanted to see in the upcoming season. If I were a different kind of girl, he would have leaned over and asked in a low, sexy voice if I wanted to finish the performance at his place. As the lights dimmed, my eyes returned to the stage, and I acknowledged that sometimes I wanted to be that kind of girl.

I went to work early the next morning. Valentina had given me a key to the flat and tasks to accomplish – she was in Kiev. Because it was difficult and expensive for men to get a Ukrainian visa – an invitation was needed to receive one – Valentina had created a lobby group to ask (bribe) the politicians to waive visas for Americans and Western Europeans – she and her brethren wanted it to be easier for the men to come to Ukraine than to Russia for love.

I sat amongst the ferns and orchids, reading the questions we were often asked. Valentina wanted me to post her answers on our website.

1. Why do Russian and Ukrainian women want American husbands?

They long to create a stable family, which many men here can't provide because of financial reasons. (In the margin Valentina asked, 'Should we mention the high alcoholic rate of our men? Or their philandering?') The stress that results from limited housing, alcoholism, and unemployment contributes to the divorce rate, which is estimated to be 70 percent.

2. The photos on your site look too good to be true. Are the women real?

Absolutely. Our women strive to take care of themselves by walking and dancing and other physical activities. Also, a natural diet (Valentina continued, 'As opposed to the chemicals in the packets that American women cook with.' I made the executive decision to leave this out) contributes to thick, long hair and healthy, glowing skin.

3. What is the main difference between American and Ukrainian women?

Ukrainians are traditional women who love to sew, cook, and knit. Their priority will always be family. Being an excellent cook and housekeeper is a point of pride.

More and more, our first contact with American men was through the Internet, so it was in our best interests to have an easy-to-navigate site. To accomplish this, I researched other sites to analyze their approach. There were dozens – I had no idea that we had such competition. We charged more than the other sites – $3,000 for a week of socials. Leave it to Valentina to be the most expensive of the bunch.

When one agency praised itself for having the largest staff, I lauded ours for having an intimate, personalized service. When another bragged about parading the most women under the noses of clients, I stated our socials would not overwhelm. Many sites had scrambled translations. Some translated directly from Russian and dropped articles: 'Women want to go to United States and be good wife to honest man.' ('The,' 'a,' and 'an' don't exist in Russian.) Others applied Russian rules to the English language. 'My name – Tanya. I – twenty.' (The present tense of the verb 'to be' is not conjugated in Russian.) I underlined that our agency spoke English fluently. Countering every single conceivable argument, hitting back every ball, I felt like a lawyer with a tennis racket. On top of her form. On top of her game. In control. That is, until I turned to a page featuring a collage of a dozen young women. I was given a choice of three categories: 'ladies with a phone,' 'ladies with no kids' and 'forgotten ladies.' I chose the latter, which opened to a page of two by two-inch photos. I stared at the women, they stared back at me. I clicked on Marina, a chubby brunette. She'd tried to smile but couldn't manage it. According to the statistics next to her photo, she was twenty-three years old, a Pisces, and had had a child less than a year ago. Her strangely translated profile read, 'I like read, knit warm half-hoses and wonderful clothes. I am good cook, like rest at seaside, go to zoo and circus with daughter. I like to do half-finishes product, like family holidays and suppers. I – honest, modest, good mother and housewife. I seek man who loves children and dreams of family with traditional values. You can have family happiness, calmness, and cozy house with me (25–45 years old, without children, no Muslims).'

I stared at the screen, and her defeated eyes seemed to meet mine. I understood that we weren't helping women find love, find mates, or the thousand other things I had told myself so that I could go to work and do this job. We weren't selling romance, or opportunity, or love. We were selling women. Period.

When I closed the window, the original page appeared, and dozens of women stared out at me. I knew it was wrong, but continued to look anyway. The youngest was twenty and her name was Vera, which means 'faith' in Russian. She had gray eyes and weighed 112.2 pounds and was five foot four inches tall. Under languages, it was written: 'English (some forgotten knowledge from school).' To describe herself, she wrote, 'A calm, quiet and serious girl, who is always able to create a pleasant atmosphere in any given situation. I am a cheering and easy-going girl who enjoying communicating with different people and appreciates human friendship. I dream about the self-actualization in my life, but the most important for me is happiness in my family life. I want people close to me to be happy and for this I try to do everything. My right man is active, creative, caring, strong, kind, and clever. He must be a real man. If I find such a man, age 22 to 49, I know I can make him happy.'

The oldest woman – Galina – was fifty-five. She weighed 138.6 pounds and had blond hair and blue eyes. Under profession, she listed 'expert beautician.' She wrote, 'I am active woman, my heart is full of love. I have numerous friends, they love me but sadly I don't see That Man among them. I desire man who will love me and share my interest (literature and theatre, long romantic walks). His age unlimited, preferably tall, preferably European.'

I clicked onto another site. In the forty-five and over category, there were over sixty women; in the eighteen to twenty-five category, 127. I clicked on page after page and read the profiles. Each woman had one headshot and two photos revealing their bodies clad in short skirts and see-through lace tops. Fresh faces jumped out at me, as did their bosoms, bellies and bottoms. The women leaned back or forward to show their bosoms, and the site seemed more soft pornography than marriage minded. All the pictures had the same background. Was this matchmaking firm moonlighting as a photography center? How much had the women paid for these glamour shots? I read the profiles of Inna, Inga, Vika, Genia, Ksenia, Nadia, Tamara ... I was a voyeur looking into the lives of these fiscally challenged women. Economists, teachers, journalists – most divorced with a child – all attractive, university educated, and longing for stability.

One woman wrote: 'I don't believe that people are perfect, everyone has its ups and downs. I eager to build stable and long lasting family. Being brought in the Eastern family I can say that I know what men want and how I can give it to them.' Under these words, I could click on 'retrieve address,' 'send letter,' 'send gift or flowers,' or 'add lady to favorites.'

Going from page to page with the morbid curiosity of an onlooker at an accident site, I felt sick. But I could not stop. I landed on a forum for men who had married Eastern European women. 'Hey, men! Are you sick of demanding American bitches who nag, dont do any housework, and expect you to do everything? Russian ladies are the opposite of greedy Americans. They love to cook from scratch, will lovingly wash your clothes by hand *and* iron them (ever tried to get an American woman to iron your shirt?), *and* never ask for more money – they can stretch a nickel from Buffalo to Moscow. Russian ladies look gorgeous without wasting time at the gym or hairdresser. They stay home where they belong and take care of the house and kids. Hell, their just grateful to have a roof over their heads that they don't have to share with their parents. Do yourself a favor and get a Russian lady to love and pamper you.'

My God, was this what men really thought?

It was deplorable. We showed girls exactly as trainers exhibited thoroughbreds. Exactly as madams displayed prostitutes. Exactly as landowners counted serfs. Why hadn't I felt this horror as I helped women create their profiles or translated for couples?

Because I did what I had to do.

How many people before me had said these same words?

I paced the small office, remembering a scene, one of many, from a social. I'd stood with a group of women, waiting for the couple I'd been interpreting for to return from the dance floor. He escorted her back to us and said, 'I hope to see you later, Masha.'

She smiled shyly.

He sauntered over to his friends. What would he say about Masha, one of the sweetest girls at the social? I positioned myself between the circle of men behind me and the women in front of me.

'Masha, how can you date such a geezer?' one girl asked. 'You can barely see his eyes, his lids are so fleshy and droopy!'

'His throat looks like a turkey's.'

'Gobble, gobble!'

'I think it looks like a dried-up old scrotum!'

'Stop it!' Masha said. 'I want a man who's experienced and kind.' She gestured to her date. 'And family oriented.'

('Guys,' Masha's date began, 'I'm telling you. It's like buying a used car.')

'Who isn't going to play games.'

('A very nice *used* car.')

'Who really respects women.'

('I need to take her out for a test drive. Vroom, vroom.')

'Not like our men.'

('A test drive before I know which one I want.')

'Who are only interested in one thing.'

('Right now *I'm* looking at a room full of little hot Corvettes.')

'American men are serious, ready to settle down with one woman.'

('And I'll test drive every car here before I take one home and stick her in my garage.')

I'd justified my actions in a thousand ways: I was just doing my job; the women wanted to move to America and I was helping them; Boba and I needed the money; I was just following orders; I did what I had to do. How easy it was to judge others and see what they were doing was wrong. So much harder to step back and look at what I had done. It wasn't until I saw someone else doing the same thing that I clearly saw myself. I was despicable. There is nothing that women won't do to other women.

I sat down at the desk and put my face in my hands.

Day turned to dusk.

The phone rang. I expected it to be Harmon again, or perhaps Valentina calling from Kiev.

'Valentina Borisovna? Valentina Borisovna?' a woman shrieked into the phone.

'Not here,' I said. 'Can I take a message?'

'Daria, Daria? Is it you?'

'Who is this?'

'It's Katya. In California. I want to come home. He hurts me, he hurts me.' She started to cry.

The hairs on my body stood up. I didn't know what to do. I didn't know what to do.

'He accused me of flirting with his friends at his firm's party. When we got home, he punched me in the stomach. He knows where to hit so that no bruises appear, so that no one knows.'

'I'm so sorry.' My words sounded lame and ridiculous.

'He'll hurt me again when he sees I've made a long-distance call. Please help me, Daria. Please.'

'Can't your family help?' I asked.

'Where would they get a thousand dollars to fly me home? My father makes thirty-five dollars a month. And I bragged that I was going to America. I'm too ashamed to tell them the truth.'

What could I do? 'I have a friend in America. She can advise us. Give me your number and I'll call you back.'

Jane gave me two possibilities. Katya could go to a women's shelter if she wanted to stay in America. Jane had to explain the concept, because we did not have such places in Odessa. Or she could report herself to the INS as a woman who had married for a green card, in which case she would be deported. I relayed these possibilities to Katya. She said she wanted to come home.

Why hadn't I seen it earlier? Most of our clients seemed normal, but that lawyer had made my flesh crawl. When I read the bitter testimony like the one proclaiming that *Americankas* were all greedy and *Russkayas* submissive, I had to wonder about some of the men who used our services. Of course, I had made a point of telling our women that they had options and to wait until they felt a real connection – but how many had fallen in love with the idea of America, not the man who'd paid for their ticket? After the honeymoon, how many realized they'd made an enormous mistake but had too much pride and not enough money to rectify it?

I compared our photos with those of other sites. Many were group shots taken at the socials or afternoon teas, though some were glamour shots showing thighs, bellies, and breasts. The women's smiles were strained. The men – ten to thirty years older than the girls – looked nearly orgasmic, surrounded by our women. It was wrong. What I was doing was wrong, wrong, wrong. I thought of Mr. Harmon and hoped that he would take me back.

I turned off the computer and stood to leave. Just then, Vlad walked into the office. 'When are you going to find a rich *Americanka* to take care of me?' he joked.

When I didn't respond, he took my hands in his and asked, 'What's wrong?'

'I don't like myself.' I stared at the floor.

'Well, I like you.' He tipped my chin up so that I looked him in the eye.

'Let's get out of here.'

'Done,' he said. I handed him the keys and he locked all five dead bolts.

'Want to go for a drive?'

He opened the passenger door and I sank down into the leather seat and closed my eyes.

'Where's your driver?' I asked.

'I wanted a moment of privacy,' he replied. 'Where to?' he asked.

'I've never seen your place.'

We drove through the city center; the ride was so smooth that I didn't feel a single cobblestone. I looked at his hands on the wheel and wanted them on my body. I wanted what the girls at the socials joked about. I wanted to feel loved, if only for an evening. I wanted to feel what bound Mr. Harmon to Olga. We slowly made our way to the gated community where the New Russians had their mansions. Vlad waved at the security guard, who raised the barrier. He slowed down because the road was covered with craters. It was worse than those in town, which was saying a lot. One would think that the richest men of Odessa would band together to repave the street leading to the mansions bought with their ill-gotten gains.

'What are you thinking about?' he asked.

'The bumpy road.'

'Life has a way of surprising us,' he said slowly.

So true.

He opened my door and held my hand as I alighted from the car. It was a little windy and a tendril escaped my chignon. I moved to tuck it back into place, but Vlad said, 'Don't.' He took the lock between his fingers and kissed it. We stared at each other.

The spell was broken when the butler opened the door. Vlad placed his hand on the small of my back and guided me up the steps. His living room wasn't so different from Harmon's pre-Olga. Black leather couches, state-of-the art television and stereo. The butler placed a silver tray with chilled champagne and two flutes on the coffee table. Vlad opened the bottle with the ease of a Ukrainian man and poured two glasses. 'To you, Dasha. Thank you for gracing my home with your beautiful presence.'

We clinked glasses and sipped the Dom Perignon. He leaned in, until his cheek touched mine, then he ran his lips along my temple, cheek and neck. I breathed in deeply. He smelled of sandalwood. When he kissed me, I kissed him back, wishing I were someone else, someone passionate and smoldering. Someone who wasn't me. His arms brought my body closer to his, and I closed my eyes and ignored the voices of reason in my head, letting tingles and shivers of lust overcome me. He carried me up the stairs just like Igor carried Katya up the Potemkin Staircase and laid me gently on his bed. When he took off my shoes and skirt, I whispered, 'I'm not very good at this.' He took my hand and brought it to his lips. 'People are born to make love. If you think you're not good at it, someone must have been rough with you. We'll take our time. I have a feeling that in this, like everything, you'll come out on top.'

His words encouraged me. I felt a powerful attraction to him – his elegant hands, his strong shoulders and slim hips. I wanted him, wanted to forget, just for a moment. He caressed my back and kissed my breasts. He gazed at me; it seemed as though he worshipped my body. He held me reverently, like a Fabergé egg. I wanted him to move faster and tried to stir his hands into the frenzy that I felt. He refused. 'You've made me wait so long. So long that I even gave up thinking about this moment. Now that it's here, let me savor it. Let me savor you.'

His words thrilled me. No one had ever spoken to me like that. He grazed my neck with his breath. He sprinkled my belly with kisses as gentle as the warm spring sun. When I tried to sit up, he eased me back and continued down my body to my thighs, knees, ankles. He placed the sole of my foot along the length of his cheekbone, then turned and kissed the soft arch. I sighed.

No one had ever made love to me like this before. I'd dated two other men, but each had ripped off my panties, pulled his penis out and shoved it in. There was a moment of pain, then it was over. Each had blamed me, saying that I got him too hot, too fast.

'What are you thinking?' he asked. 'Why are you looking at me like that?'

'Like what?'

'Like you've just figured something out.'

'Until this moment, I thought that I hated sex,' I said. 'But with you, it's different.'

'Dasha. *Dushenka*,' he said, my little soul. He stroked my legs and belly until I found myself craving more. He caressed and coaxed me until I couldn't differentiate between his fingers or his lips, his tongue or teeth, his whiskers or whispers, until I couldn't differentiate between his body and mine.

When I woke up, I saw shades of gray: pale walls, mother of pearl satin sheets, a cloudy comforter. I looked for my watch and found it was 10 p.m. I dressed and flew down the stairs to the living room, so I could call Boba and tell her not to worry, that I was having a wonderful time.

'Wonderful?' I heard a voice behind me say.

I turned around and found Vlad with a small towel wrapped around his waist. Lust pounded through my body.

'Hungry?' Vlad asked.

I nodded and hung up the phone.

He took my hand and led me to the kitchen.

I watched him break seven eggs (odd numbers are lucky) and whisk them into a froth. He struck a match and lit a burner. He poured the eggs into a frying pan and put it on the flames. I stood and stared: an Odessan man who cooks is as rare as a man who gives birth. I didn't think either was scientifically possible.

We ate out of the pan, feeding and kissing each other.

Him: How long have we known one another?

Me: You've been extorting money from me for about a year and a half now.

Him: Not you personally! You think I make all the rounds myself? I went to the shipping firm because I liked you.

Me: How flattering!

Him: I watched you for months and couldn't believe you didn't have a boyfriend. Then when we spoke, and you talked back with that acerbic tongue of yours, I was hooked.

Me: Earlier, what did you mean about me coming out on top?

He laughed and grabbed my hand, pulling me back up the stairs.

Chapter 11

The next morning, I allowed myself a moment to luxuriate in the heat of Vlad's body, of our night together, then got up and dressed. I shook his shoulder and asked him to drive me home. 'Get the chauffeur to,' he mumbled.

I ran my fingernails along his ribcage and he jumped. 'I'm up, I'm up.'

He drove me home in silence. I felt a sort of doom in this stillness and hoped I was wrong. 'I'm not a morning person,' he finally said as he turned onto my street. 'I'll call you.'

His words gave me a small grain of hope. I got out of the car before he came to a complete stop, ran into the courtyard and up the stairs. I put my key in the lock, Boba turned the dead bolts.

'Dasha where were you? It's not like you to stay out all night.'

I hugged her. 'Boba, I had a marvelous time,' I said, thinking of the complicity between Vlad and me.

She pulled me into the kitchen and started to warm our breakfast. 'You must be starving. Who were you with? Why didn't you tell me you'd be gone? Were you out with a girlfriend or a date?'

I shoveled oatmeal into my mouth to give myself time to formulate an answer. 'I met a man. He's different from the others.'

'An American?' she asked hopefully.

'I'll tell you about him later, but now I have to get ready for work.'

I locked myself in the bathroom. Under the flowing water, I could still feel Vlad's stubble along my belly. Cupping my breasts, I imagined my hands were his. Tears flowed with the water – I was happy, but a little sad, too. Why was I so emotional?

Dressed and out the door before Boba could question me, I sped along the city sidewalk, as light as a stone skipping water.

When I arrived at Soviet Unions, the feelings of disgust and shame came flooding back. Men choosing women based on whether they were twenty or twenty-nine, five foot seven or five foot three, blonde or brunette. We used women to make money. We sent them off with strangers. It was frightening. *Shto delat?* What to do? There was nothing else to do. When Valentina returned from Kiev, I would resign. I would beg Mr. Harmon to take me back.

I hated the fact that I was a part of this ignoble traffic.

I hated that I looked at my watch every thirty seconds, wondering when Vlad would walk through the door.

Valentina had given me several tasks, but I didn't want to think up more tips for lonely men, didn't want to update our catalogs. She asked me to describe the city and to take photos for the website. For three days, I wrote an Ode to Odessa – highlighting the writers who'd visited, from Pushkin to Balzac to Mark Twain, and describing our cultural centers, from the '*mus-comed*,' the musical comedy theater, to the marine museum – all the time trying not to think about Vlad. For three long days, I stayed in the office, bent over my notebook, glancing at the door, looking out the window, waiting for him to come. I hoped the phone would ring. But it was as silent as a Sunday.

Was it working? I lifted the receiver. There was a dial tone. I tapped a number.

'What's this, little rabbit paw? You never call from work.'

'I just … I just missed you, that's all.' I choked back my tears. My stupid, ridiculous tears.

I left the office at five and took the long way home, through Park Shevchenko, past the sea, back into the city. I saw him everywhere: on the beach, in every black sedan that cruised by, in my bed before I closed my eyes.

I didn't sleep. I just lay awake, listening to Rachmaninoff's 'Vocalise' again and again. The languid tempo of the duet elegant and thoughtful. The melancholy throb of the piano. He sways over the piano as he strikes the keys. Eyes closed. Her fingers deftly move along the strings of the cello. A tendril of hair escapes as she plays. The music holds a tinge of regret. I desired him so much. My mouth hurt. It filled with saliva then suddenly went dry, my tongue and gums like bark. My head hurt. My soul hurt. I tried to think of anything but Vlad – my mother, tasks at work, Jane in America – but my mind always came back to him. *Vlad–Vlad–Vlad.* I imagined his hands on my hips, my lips on the hollow of his throat, his ribs floating on mine. I lay on my belly and grasped the pillow under my body until morning.

It had only been three days. He would come.

Four days.

Why hadn't he called?

Five days.

Had he been injured?

Six days.

He had so many rivals.

I started going mad. Stir crazy. I had to get out of the office. *His line of work wasn't the safest … How many before him had been shot down or trapped in a car that exploded? When there was an 'accident' all of Odessa's tongues wagged. I heard nothing.* I took Valentina's camera and walked along the leafy boulevard overlooking the sea. *Calm. Breathe.* I loved the rows of red roses, grown wild since gardeners were no longer paid to care for them; the breeze that made it seem as though the trees were whispering; the people out and about – young mothers pushing prams, girls giggling on the park benches, boys from the naval academy in their blue suits and hats, swaggering and hoping to catch a girl's eye. *Why hadn't he called?*

Since it was spring, Odessa was overrun by brides in white silks and satins. Wedding parties stood in line to have their portraits taken at the Potemkin Staircase and city hall with its stately white columns. This is the happiest day of a woman's life – all eyes on her, a bride deeply in love, girlish dreams of romance blending with a woman's desire for a home and family. Little girls rushed up to the fairy princesses come to life. The brides gave them candy and promised, 'If you're good, my darlings, someday you'll be beautiful like me and all your dreams will come true.' Who doesn't want to believe in love? Who doesn't want the moment to last? Brides are our fairy tales. *Why didn't he call?*

Brides are reckless and brave. They think with their hearts, they take a leap of faith (in this faithless society). The photographer moved the bride away from her wedding party. He didn't need to tell her to smile. She was radiant. Radiant. He fussed with her train, tilted her chin slightly to the left, then went back to his tripod. Red roses, another kind of satin, soft against her cheek as the photo is snapped. A picture of her alone, so later, when the dream collapses, she still has this one moment, this one portrait where she looks her best, to use in Valentina's matchmaking catalog.

How cynical I'd become. I watched the brides have their pictures taken for another hour, knowing how it would turn out, still wishing it were me.

He wasn't going to call.

That evening Boba and I sat on the sofa. The television was on, but we weren't watching it.

'Boba, remember that night I stayed away? I thought our time was special, but he didn't.'

She pulled my head into her lap and stroked my hair. 'This is often the case, my little rabbit paw, this is often the case. Men are like stray dogs, they go from house to house looking for a tender morsel. Once they get it, they move on to the next open door.'

I grabbed her around the waist and buried my face in her belly, weeping until my shoulders shook, until her housecoat was steeped in my tears. I promised myself that they would be the last I cried over Vladimir Stanislavski. I promised that every time he invaded my thoughts, I would push him gently but firmly out of my mind. I promised to be more careful in the future, never again to let my guard down. Promises I soon broke.

As I walked to work the next morning, I realized the city I used to love had begun to feel like a prison: I hurried along her streets, skirting the buildings, arms crossed to protect my fragile remains, gaze pressed to the ground. My body betrayed me: my stomach my throat my jaw clenched. I was as weepy as a war widow. I couldn't control a single thing. Not my love life, not my taste buds, not my thoughts, not my body, not my reactions. At work, I sat in front of the computer, pondering my life. Everything had changed. Before, I loved my job, now I felt trapped. The oatmeal I used to love now tasted like spackle. I'd wanted to see Vlad, but now I dreaded it: he would be talking to someone else, someone sexy and fun and free, and not even see me. Or worse, he would and there'd be that awful, awkward Hello yes yes we slept together goodbye.

When the bell over the door rang, I looked up, hoping to see Vlad, then hated myself for being so eager, so naïve, so stupid. It was Mr. Harmon. I wasn't disappointed – it had been three weeks since I'd seen him. He looked good. So very good. He'd lost a little weight and wore a navy suit with the red tie I had given him for New Year's. He stood in the doorway, unsure, holding a bouquet of pink roses. I went to him, hugging him as I only embraced Boba.

'I was going to come to you,' I said and started to cry.

He handed me a handkerchief. I blew my nose and cried even harder. It wasn't entirely about the job.

He patted my back awkwardly. 'There, there. You were right. I need you. Olga's ready to go home and be an artist again, if you'll return to the office. Please come back.'

'I thought you didn't need me anymore,' I sniffled.

'I was lost without you,' he admitted and handed me the flowers. Twelve! It wouldn't do.

'How many times do I have to tell you? Even numbers are for funerals!'

'I can't remember all your silly superstitions,' he retorted.

It wasn't silly, it was serious. Odd numbers are lucky. Everyone knows that. Even him. He did it on purpose, to get a rise out of me. I pulled a rose out of the bouquet, snapped the stem and put the bud in his buttonhole, then straightened his tie, stroked his lapel, and swept imaginary lint off his jacket shoulder and sleeve. I took a deep breath, smelling the sweet roses, happier than I'd been in days.

I scrawled a few words to Valentina, explaining that Harmon needed me.

'Let's swing by the port,' he said, opening the passenger door of his beat-up BMW. 'I should probably get a new car.'

'Don't,' I said, thinking of Vlad's. 'You don't want people thinking you're rich. It only brings trouble.'

When the customs agents saw me, they crowded around us. 'Dasha, where have you been? We missed you.'

They called me by my diminutive, a sign that they liked me. Or the money I brought them. All six said they weren't sure about our shipments. What kind of videocassettes were these? What kind of music? Would they contaminate the youth? Why these foreign meats and cheeses? Were ours not good enough? What of the pre-made food full of chemicals? Just add water and stir? There was nothing natural about this. Would it stop people from toiling in their gardens? The agents weren't sure they could let any of it into the country.

I smiled. 'All valid concerns, all valid concerns,' I said and offered samples to ease their apprehension.

Though he couldn't understand the transactions since we spoke Russian, Harmon grinned as he watched me. The negotiations took most of the afternoon. I was grateful for the work; it kept my mind off Vlad. For the most part.

Boba made my favorite desserts, which we ate for dinner. The best was her Napoleon cake, layers of cake and cream, cake and cream, which melted in my mouth.

Back at the shipping office where I belonged, things had changed. Olga's paintings and the photos had been taken down. The walls were painted my favorite color, a pale blue. Harmon must have had the laborers working all night. I felt a grudging respect for him. Finally, he understood how things were done in Odessa.

When I moved to sit at my station, Harmon insisted I take his office. 'You do most of the work,' he said wryly.

On the desk, there was a bouquet of red roses. Twenty-five. He'd got it right. I never expected this valorization of my work. I never expected this effort. I looked at him, almost expecting him to try something. Instead, he sat at the boardroom table and went over order forms from the Western-style supermarkets that had recently opened. I watched him for a moment. My esteem for him swelled. He'd done so much for me. And he didn't seem to expect anything in return. I stopping thinking of him as Harmon, and in my mind at least, I started to call him by his first name: David.

*   *   *

It had been over two weeks since I had seen Vlad. Naïvely, I kept telling myself that he would come, if only he knew where I was. I tried not to brood, and hated the way I'd become so sensitive, jumping when the phone rang, looking toward the hall when I heard footsteps. I was in danger of crossing the line from fragile to just plain pathetic. This thought made me straighten my spine and set my jaw. Why was I letting some man make me miserable?

Looking back, the clues were there, I just didn't see them. Chilled champagne, just in case. A king-size bed and satin sheets, for heaven's sake. He was a player. Just a player. And I was a record. He'd slipped me out of my jacket, laid me on the table and stuck the needle in. And I went round and round, thinking it was something special. Sex wasn't love, Boba had told me. How right she was.

To smooth things over with Valentina, I went to Soviet Unions with a bottle of cognac, an orchid, and a box of German chocolate. I didn't tell her why I'd quit suddenly, just that I was tired and the shipping job paid better – reasons she could relate to. 'I'll miss you,' she said. 'You're an honest, decent girl.'

'For all the good it does me,' I muttered.

She barked with laughter and hugged me to her bosoms.

She was in an excellent mood because she was close to getting the regulations changed so that Western Europeans and Americans – specifically, lonely men from these countries – could come to the Ukraine, hassle- and visa-free.

'Those fools in Moscow!' she crowed. 'They're making it harder to get in the country. Men will start coming to Ukraine because it's easier. I'll have more clients. In the Russian Duma there's even talk of stripping the girls of their nationality when they emigrate to the West, just like in Soviet times. Can you believe it? Russian politicians certainly don't believe in progress …'

Of course, when she said progress, she meant commerce.

I wanted to tell her about what happened with Vlad, but something held me back. Who wants to admit that they've been swindled? Instead, I relayed Katya's call. 'Valentina, what would you do if your husband beat you?'

'Isn't it obvious?' she asked, looking at me as though I had borscht for brains. 'You suggest a trip to the dacha where neighbors aren't so close, where you have an old wood burning stove at hand. You sit him down at the kitchen table and give him plenty of strong home-made vodka to drink.'

'I don't know how to make it.'

She took a sip of cognac. 'You modern girls! You don't know how to do anything! You should learn – home-made vodka is potent. Helpful in many situations. Ah, everything was better before perestroika – people did for themselves, and we didn't have all these problems with alcoholism and poverty. It's become a sad, sad world ...' Valentina looked out the window for a moment, as if she could see the better times of the Soviet Union on the street.

She came back to the present and continued, 'Anyway, when he passes out and slumps onto the table, you take a log and you beat him. Until the tendons in his back mesh with the cotton of his shirt. Until you can no longer lift the log. Then you throw it onto the fire. No evidence.

'Incidentally, dear, this is also a cure for alcoholism.'

I finally thought to check my inbox. There were twelve messages from Tristan, each more frantic than the last. It was embarrassing how easily I'd forgotten about him. I wrote immediately and explained that I had technical problems, because technically, I'd had problems. Tristan replied: *Enough writing. Let's meet. Soon.*

I thought of Vlad and let what I hoped were the last of the waves of hurt, anger, and disappointment move through my body before I typed my answer.

Yes.

As penance for having forgotten him, I mailed Tristan a bundle of photos of Odessa. He then sent some he'd taken in Yosemite National Park. He'd captured stunning sunsets, lonely stretches of road, and small plants that make you see the vastness of this world. Looking at his photos of sequoias, the largest living things, I could feel the damp bark against my skin.

He wrote long letters every day. He told me that his great-grandparents were Russian. I told him that I was half Odessan, half Hungarian. He said that he wanted to know more about his ancestors, and I said I did, too, though honestly, between school and work and life, I barely had time to think about Boba let alone my ancestors. Tristan suggested meeting in Budapest, and I readily agreed. It would be interesting to see where my father was from and where he'd run back to.

I gave Tristan my phone number, and he called on weekends. 'Dora? Hi, it's Tristan,' he said, a little self-consciously. The line was scratchy, and if we spoke at the same time, we cancelled each other out.

'Daria,' I corrected, then thought, perhaps Dora is a diminutive, like Dasha.

'What did you say?'

We both tried again. Nothing. Just a buzz that was louder than his voice.

'You go,' he said.

'I'm happy you called.'

'I'm glad you're –' And the phone went dead. It happened like this in Odessa sometimes.

Even if we could barely talk because of the poor quality phone lines, his effort and patience communicated everything I needed to know.

In the photo he sent of himself, Tristan wore a green scout uniform. He looked serious. Kind. Dependable. He loved children. He was ready for a family. For commitment. He wasn't the kind of man who would have champagne chilling just in case. He was a bit awkward, but this meant that he wasn't a user like Vlad, and it made me grateful for the awkward silences and his peculiar questions:

Do you have television?

Do you need nylons? Toilet paper?

Do people stand in lines for hours?

The strangest question was this: Do you have jeans in the Ukraine?

Didn't he know that jeans were invented in Odessa?

Tristan sent a plane ticket to Budapest. I could hardly wait to meet him and sight-see. My first trip to a foreign city. Each day I grew more and more excited, buzzing around the office like a spring bee drunk with pollen. When the city cut the electricity, I poured the last of the coffee into two cups, and David and I sat in the boardroom and talked. There was nothing else we could do, since the computers, printers, and fax machine were down. I was thankful he had not bought a generator. I had come to like these moments, when it was just the two of us in a darkened room.

'Why are you here?' I asked.

He laughed. 'I ask myself that very same question. I could say shipping is in my blood, since my grandfather started the company. But the truth is, I got into a bit of trouble and now I have to stay here for two years.'

Vita and Vera had been right? Odessa was his punishment? I must have said these words aloud because he replied, 'Not so much a punishment as a redemption of sorts.'

I waited for him to say more, but he was silent. After a long moment, he changed the subject. 'What about you? Why are you still here?'

'I love Odessa.'

'You've never seen anything else.'

'So you have to sleep with two hundred girls to know which one you want? You had to try fifty desserts to know chocolate is your favorite?'

'No,' he said. 'You're right. Sometimes you just know.'

'I don't know what I want. Boba says I should find an American man and leave Odessa. And sometimes that's what I want, too. I want to see the world, I want to travel, fall in love, meet people, speak English all the time, like we do in the office. But then I get scared about leaving everything I've ever known.'

'Odessa will always be here. Don't they call the city Odessa-Mama? She'll be right here, waiting for you if you want to come back. You're young, you should go, explore, live.'

The lights came on and broke the spell. Still we stayed in the boardroom. I thought about Budapest. I would go, explore, live. He got up and turned off the lights. I was glad.

'What are you so happy about?' he asked.

I didn't want to jinx it by telling anyone about my trip. 'Aren't you tired of Olga yet? I could find you a nice Odessan lady.'

'I was married to a nice lady,' he said. 'Now I want a wicked one.'

I blushed, content to fall into our old banter like nothing had happened, like nothing had changed. Though things had changed. My salary had doubled. That pawn Olga had been knocked off the board. Through strategic sacrifice, I had won.

He talked about their wedding plans. I wondered if I should warn him – she would turn on him as she had turned on me. But I didn't want to disturb the peace between us. I didn't want to hurt or disappoint him. What if he didn't believe me? Besides, everyone knows that in chess – and in Odessa – it's every man for himself.

'Your parents must be curious about where you work. Why don't you invite them here for lunch?'

I stared at him.

'What?' he said. 'Are you worried about the language barrier?'

I was worried about the dead barrier. How to explain one parent was dead and buried, the other dead to Boba and me? He was always complaining about his meddling, strict parents. He didn't know how lucky he was. And I didn't want him feeling sorry for me. I raised my chin a notch and said, 'I'll invite Boba, my grandmother.'

'You just did the thing.'

'What thing?'

'With your chin.'

'What are you talking about?'

'You have an inner conversation with yourself. I know because your mouth moves slightly and sometimes you even mutter. You resolve something, lift your chin, then announce whatever it is you decided.'

I scowled. Clearly, we spent too much time together. An offense is the only defense. That's what we say in Odessa.

'What about you?' I asked. 'You clear your throat about fifty times when you're nervous. You hide in your office when Vlad comes.'

'I don't hide. I'm busy.'

'Busy hiding.'

'Why should I deal with him when you're so much better at it?'

'You think a well-placed compliment will get you out of trouble.'

'The only person I ever compliment is you. You're just about the only good thing about this town.'

Infidel! 'Odessa is the best city in the world and don't you forget it!'

He put up his hands as if to ward off my blows. 'Don't hang me for treason. Just invite your grandmother to lunch tomorrow.'

Natalia Temofeevna. He tried to pronounce it five times before asking me to write it down. I did, but he stumbled so many times I said, 'Just call her Boba. Everyone does.'

Of course this wasn't true. We only let foreigners use the simplest version of our names.

Boba looked around our office just trying to find something wrong. She couldn't help it, it was her eagle eye. But there was no dust anywhere and the floors were immaculate. She nodded, which was quite a compliment.

'Is she your mother's mother or father's mother?'

'Mother's.'

He proffered his arm and Boba placed her hand in its curve. He escorted her to the boardroom, where she marveled at the feast. The last time I'd seen him make such an effort was when Mr. Kessler had come. Lobster from Maine. Caviar from the Danube. Champagne from France. Harmon had finally learned to drink like an Odessan. Maybe in France they choose white wine for this, red for that. In Odessa, the pop of the cork serves as the unofficial call to the table. *Champagnskoye* goes with everything – that's what we say in Odessa.

'Such an effort he's made for you,' Boba murmured.

'For you, Boba.'

'Such a handsome man …'

'Mixing work and pleasure is like mixing pickles and ice cream. Would you have dated your boss Anatoly Pavlovich?'

'I might have if he looked like that.'

Harmon looked down at his notebook where his Russian teacher had written some phrases phonetically. 'The weather is fine,' he said.

'Of course it is,' Boba responded. 'We're in Odessa.'

He raised an eyebrow and looked at me. 'I see where you get it.'

'Get what?' I asked.

He turned to Boba. 'Do you like the champagne?'

'Bitter.' *Gorko*. She frowned. Believe me, we Odessans are experts on bitterness. 'Next time, get Odessan *champagnskoye*. It's light and sweet.'

It seemed he couldn't do anything right. The butter was full of chemicals. Boba could taste them on her tongue. Get our all-natural butter from the bazaar, she advised him. How can you let him buy such things? she asked me. She told him the lobster was bland, the vegetables undercooked.

Harmon and I took the plates to the kitchen and waited for the coffee to brew.

'She hates everything,' he whispered glumly.

'No,' I corrected. 'She loves it. And she likes you. She wouldn't bother to pick everything apart if she didn't. It's when she's polite that you have to worry. She thinks you've spent too much money on her. She just wants you to be less decadent next time.'

'Really?'

'*Absolutno!* The more critical we are, the more we like you. Watch out for people who are too nice – they're not being sincere.' I thought of Olga and hoped he picked up on my subtle warning.

'You might be the most sincere person I know,' he said dryly.

After coffee, Boba stood and said, 'I'd better let you two get back to work. Thank you for such a fine meal.'

Harmon escorted her to the door and I followed behind them. Boba squinted in the sunlight.

'It was such a pleasure to meet you. Next time, bring your daughter,' he said in hesitant Russian.

Boba glanced at me. I shook my head, but she told him anyway. 'Daughter – dead.'

His jaw dropped. Boba patted his cheek sympathetically and walked down Soviet Army Street.

'When?'

'When I was ten.'

'Why didn't you tell me?'

My chin jutted out. 'Not your business.'

He sighed. 'Why don't you go home?' He dismissed me as

effectively as I had him. Then he softened the blow. 'Wouldn't you like to spend the rest of the afternoon with Boba?'

'I'll clean up the boardroom.'

'Suit yourself,' he replied.

'I always do.'

'Cheeky girl.'

He turned to walk down the hall.

I grabbed his arm. 'Wait. Thank you. For everything you did ... for Boba.'

He looked at my hand on his sleeve. 'Pleasure,' he said automatically. 'Anything ... for Boba.'

Three days before I was supposed to meet Tristan, Jane phoned and I told her about my plan. A big mistake. You should never tell anyone anything.

'Are you nuts?' I heard a scream so loud that everyone from Montana to Odessa must have heard it, too. 'He could be a sex fiend or an axe murderer! He could be a serial inviter of girls to foreign hotels! He could be a pedophile! He could be married! What do you know about this guy?'

'He's a teacher.'

'Whatever!' she shrieked. 'Get out of it! Get out of it now!'

Jane never reacted like this. Usually, she was level-headed and full of good humor. But perhaps she was right. She was two years older than me and she had traveled. More than that, she was American and knew American men. Perhaps he preyed on innocent foreign women. Perhaps he was like Milla in Donetsk and had written to ten girls simultaneously. I couldn't decide to go to, or not to go. But I couldn't bring myself to call Tristan to tell him no. So I didn't call at all. Like the days after my encounter with Vlad, like a slow leak, days dripped by.

Splut.

Splut.

Splut.

Shut-shut-shut. Since I'd already asked for the vacation days, I stayed home. When I felt regret about not seeing Budapest, I replayed Jane's words. Axe murder. Serial inviter of girls to hotels. Pedophile. Married. I ripped the ticket into pieces until it resembled sad confetti. He'd seemed so sincere, how could I have been so wrong? I looked at my watch. If I'd gone, we would have been having dinner. Talking and laughing about my jitters. He would have taken my hand and reassured me. I would have smiled shyly. His gaze would have caressed mine ...

But Jane was right. Tristan, if indeed that was his name, was surely a slick con man who used dumb girls like me for sex.

It hurt to think this – he'd seemed genuine. But then, so had Vlad. Tristan had never been my boyfriend. Like Will from Albuquerque. I had never seen him or touched him. He wasn't real. Then why did it hurt so much? Perhaps I was still tender from my experience with Vlad. I thought about how I'd allowed myself to be duped. Again. How could I have considered flying off to a foreign country to meet some man I didn't know? Only a fool would do such a thing. Hadn't I learned?

The ringing phone cut through my contemplation. 'Allo,' I answered.

In the softest, saddest voice I had ever heard, Tristan asked, 'Where are you? Why didn't you come?'

I knew then that he was a decent guy, a bit awkward, a bit rough around the edges, just looking for love. I sat down in the black easy chair David had given me when he'd remodeled his apartment.

'Why did you change your mind?'

How could I tell him the truth – that my friend had convinced me that he was a sex fiend? That I'd ripped up the ticket? I couldn't bear to hurt him more than I already had.

'Tristan,' I croaked into the phone. 'My grandmother is ill. Terribly ill. I can't leave her. I tried to call, but you'd already left.'

I waited for him to answer, but I only heard static.

'You believe me, don't you?' I asked. There was a little Siren in me, too.

I heard a sniffle.

'I don't know what to think,' he finally answered in a voice as small as a grain of sand.

'I wanted to come. You believe me, don't you?'

'Of course I do,' he sniffled again. 'I'm just so relieved. Not that your grandma's sick, but I thought you changed your mind.'

'Never,' I said with conviction. We spoke for a few more minutes and I told him that tomorrow I would call him from the office. Too late, I realized it was incongruous to go from my grandmother's death bed back to work in the space of a day. Luckily, my limitless effrontery was met with limitless gullibility. Sometimes we want so desperately to believe that we swallow lies without chewing them over. Boba had often told me that my father wanted to see me. I never questioned her; I wanted to believe.

Afterward, I sat near the phone in a daze, feeling horrible about what I'd done. I tried to blame Jane for talking me out of meeting Tristan, but could not bring myself to be angry with her. She'd tried to protect me. I had only myself to blame. How could I let a man fly to Europe then stand him up? The following day, I called and apologized repeatedly. He told me 'not to sweat it,' that he would come directly to Odessa next time. He spoke with conviction and sounded happy with this decision, but I was frightened.

Boba started planning what she would cook, a sure sign she was looking forward to his visit. I had conflicted feelings. I wanted to see him, but worried, too. What if I got all excited again and then he just disappeared like Will? What if he used me and disappeared like Vlad? What if he didn't like me and disappeared like my father? I wanted to ask Jane's advice but feared she would talk me out of meeting him again.

Jane was skeptical of Russian–American joint ventures. To earn money for college, she'd translated letters for a fifty-year-old farmer addicted to Moscow women. He corresponded with a dozen Muscovites, met a few, then returned home with a young bride. The first one told Jane she couldn't stand the wide-open space of the stark Montanan steppe. When she returned to Russia, the farmer mourned for two months, then got right back on the horse and rode it straight to Moscow. It is true that we'd already had a few return customers at our socials. Valentina told me she'd thought of a new ad campaign – if your first marriage with a girl doesn't work out, the second one is free.

Both Valentina and Boba pushed me towards Tristan. (Foreign is better.)

I hoped that things would work out with him, that he would love me, that he would want me to go to California, the Golden State, that we would have a family and be happy. But in my life, how many things had turned out as I had hoped?

Chapter 12

Tristan flew home early. He said he couldn't enjoy Budapest without me. He confessed that it was the first time he had ever taken a plane, the first time he had ever visited a foreign country. I felt even worse about standing him up. I knew I'd have to learn to trust him.

'I am so sorry.' I typed out the words twenty times.

'Please don't feel bad. Your grandma was sick. It wasn't your fault. I wish I could of come to visit you. I could of helped take care of her. Is she feeling better? Are you?'

'Much better,' I wrote. This was true. I was confident that he was a good man and that our meeting was fate.

Three weeks later, on the day of his arrival, I did something I'd never done before. I called David and pleaded sick. He told me to get some rest. It's true I had been so nervous that I hadn't slept for two days. *Choose-chose-chosen.*

I stood in front of the mirror and pulled my hair into a chignon as I did for work. Spinster. I took the pins out and brushed my hair. *Become-became-become.* In my black suit, I looked like I was going to a business meeting. I put on a short skirt, and a gauzy peasant blouse. My hand trembled as I put on my mascara and I covered my lids with specks of black. I had never been so nervous in my entire life. *Begin-began-begun.*

What if things didn't work out?

What if they did?

'Dasha, Dasha,' my Boba said. 'There's no reason to be worried. He's just one man. There are millions. You'll find the right one.'

I nodded and walked past the wishing well, past the wisps of wisteria that clung to the building, out onto the street. Rather than taking the bus, I hailed what we Odessans call an 'informal taxi' and negotiated a fair fare to and from the airport. When the driver asked, 'Picking someone up?' I told the fib I'd prepared for David, in case he saw me with Tristan. 'An American cousin who wants to get in touch with his roots.'

'They want to visit, but they never want to stay,' he said bitterly.

I regretted the lie. There's something about taxi drivers, these men and women who know everything about the city, who see you at your best – on the way to a wedding or the opera, and at your worst – after a disastrous date, that makes you want to confide in them. The silence left me alone, uncomfortable with my thoughts and fears, so I asked, 'What's your other job?'

'I'm a surgeon.'

Doctors make a pittance. Everyone has to moonlight – the main trade and the spare – to keep our noses above water as the tide of poverty sweeps Ukraine. Why else would I be thinking of marrying a total stranger? I longed for stability. Although I earned a good salary today, I could be unemployed tomorrow – without the dole or redundancy packages offered in the West. The firm I worked for was under constant scrutiny from the government, who wanted more taxes. Despite the 'rent' we paid, in the last six months alone, there had been three acts of anti-Semitism. And no arrests or investigation since no one had been hurt. Of course, the real reason was that we were an Israeli firm and no one in Odessa cared about Jews. If I'd been the branch manager, I would have pulled out. I didn't know why David stayed. Even I wanted to go. That's why I was on the way to the airport. Tristan was my ticket out.

While the driver parked, I went to see if the flight was on time. And waited for the man who'd flown halfway around the world to walk through the door. As people filed out, I stood on my toes and tried to catch a glimpse of his brown hair and blue eyes. When I saw him, I noticed strands of white hair. Clearly, the photos he'd sent of himself had been taken ten years ago, maybe more. I knew he'd be tired from such long flights. I knew his age. I just didn't expect him to look so … old. And he wore tennis shoes and jeans.

I hadn't imagined him in a tuxedo, but assumed he'd make an effort for our first meeting.

If I went by Tristan's reaction when he saw me, I stunned. 'Glad. To meet you. Dora. Wow. To finally see you. Wow. To be here. Wow. You sure are pretty.'

'Daria. It's nice to meet you.' I was disappointed. I knew he was older, but he wasn't what I expected ... Boba would have urged me to look for something positive. He had soft blue eyes and a tentative smile. He flew all the way from America to be with me. He's a real man. A decent man. Not a player.

Tristan stared at me, seemingly at a loss for words. I didn't know what to say either. We'd written so many letters, but now that we were standing face to face, we were speechless. It was easier to face a computer screen than a real person. I should have rehearsed for this moment. *Swim-swam-swum. Dive-dove ... doven? Do-did-done.*

The driver said, 'I better grab this guy's luggage. He's so taken with you, he's liable to forget it.'

Tristan couldn't stop gaping. On the way to the car, his hand came towards me, as though he wanted to hold mine or place his palm on the small of my back. It wavered near my body for a minute, then returned inertly to his side. When the driver opened the boot of the Lada, he said, 'The American doesn't look at you like he's your cousin.'

I smiled. 'We're a very close family.'

The driver chuckled. Odessans are used to being lied to. But we appreciate it when the liar takes the time to make up a story. I worried that Tristan would find it odd to ride with a stranger, so I introduced the driver as my uncle. He laughed, slapped his thigh and said, 'Uncle Vadim!' We were unofficial passengers in an unofficial taxi. So the police wouldn't suspect we were paying customers, I sat in the front and put Tristan in the back.

The airport was close to Odessa, so we went from the country to the city in ten minutes. We sped around gigantic pot holes, down cobblestone streets, past the concrete Soviet high rises of the modern section, to the heart of the city. I asked Tristan what he thought of the city as we drove through Odessa.

'It's like nothing I've ever seen. I didn't know there were, uh, so many fancy buildings. I mean, I know you sent me all those beautiful photos. Uh. You know, what I'm trying to say is that it's even better in person …'

I smiled, encouraged by his words; he continued to tell me his impressions. It was interesting to listen to a native speaker. His pronunciation was so novel. Nothing became 'nuthin'. The sound 'uh' was sprinkled onto sentences like cinnamon flecks on Boba's apple tart.

When the driver opened the boot to get Tristan's luggage, he handed me a piece of paper with his number and the word *takci* on it. 'Don't be shy about calling Uncle Vadim if you need a lift. And I expect an invite to the wedding,' he said in Russian. I blushed. 'Goodbye and good luck,' he said to Tristan in English.

'You have a nice family,' Tristan said.

'Thank you. Welcome to our home.'

When Boba heard my voice, she came down the steps into the courtyard. Her hands were clasped in front of her heart. She looked from me to Tristan and I had never seen such naked joy on her face. 'What a fine-looking man. And he came all this way for you,' she said. Boba was so wise. 'Tell him I say hello and welcome to sunny Odessa.'

I translated, and Tristan turned to her and said, 'HELLO. NICE TO MEET YOU.'

We escorted him up the stairs, through the entryway into the living room, where we had covered the kitchen table with an embroidered tablecloth and my favorite foods: a beet dish so bright it was guaranteed to cheer up any sad winter day; a potato salad so delicious no one ever left without begging Boba for the recipe; small open-faced sandwiches; aubergine caviar that tasted better than the real thing; fish that Boba had de-boned by hand (which left her gnarled hands covered with hundreds of paper-cut-like nicks); black bread still warm from the bakery. Boba and I were both vegetarians, but she had prepared a rabbit for Tristan. (In the old days, when food was scarce, unscrupulous vendors sold skinned cats as rabbits; now they're sold and served with their furry paws and buck teeth intact to prove that everything is on the up and up.)

'Dasha, invite the gentleman to be seated,' my grandmother said, wringing her hands nervously.

'Won't you sit down?' I asked and filled his plate with Boba's delicacies. As I reached for an Odessan favorite, a slice of bread topped with a thick layer of butter and lovely sardines, Tristan whispered, 'I'm not hungry.'

'Please don't refuse, you'll offend my grandmother.'

'I'm a little sick to my stomach,' he whispered. 'I see you went to a lot of trouble, but maybe I could wait until later to eat.'

Poor Boba couldn't understand. When I repeated his words in Russian, she still didn't understand. 'I've never seen a man turn down a meal,' she said between clenched lips. In Odessa, food isn't just nourishment, it is love and respect. When we invite you to our table, it's covered with home-made dishes prepared with the guest in mind. When we invite you to our home, we invite you to be our friend.

'Tristan, please understand, refusing food in Odessa is like refusing to shake someone's hand.'

He looked at Boba's stony face and picked up the open-faced sandwich. 'Do I eat the heads and tails?'

I nodded.

He bit down and chewed slowly. I saw not only that he wasn't hungry, but that he didn't like sardines. He tried to hide it by taking a drink of Boba's home-made compote between each bite. But he finished the sandwich without a word. Then he started to cut the meat. He smiled at me. I nodded encouragingly. It was important to have my grandmother's blessing.

Boba and I hadn't eaten for two days, we were both so nervous. After Tristan started to eat, we did, too. I could see that Tristan didn't like rabbit, but after he tried the potato salad, he exclaimed, 'My God, it's incredible. I can die happy now.'

I didn't need to translate his words. Everyone said the same thing about Boba's potato salad. Before we could serve the cake, Tristan's eyes started to close slowly, then fly open. I showed him to my bedroom, the guest room during his stay.

Boba and I ate dessert, just the two of us, as we had so many times in the past. Some things would never change. I raised my glass of *champagnskoye*, 'To the lovely hostess and her golden hands!'

'To my beautiful granddaughter!' Boba toasted. 'May she be lucky in love!'

I kissed her quickly three times on the lips, as is our custom.

Boba stroked my hair and said, 'A man promised, "Darling, when we get married, I'll be there to share the trouble and sorrows." His fiancée said, "But I don't have any …" The man replied, "I said, when we get married …"'

I giggled.

'He certainly liked the potato salad,' Boba said.

'Of course he did.'

'What do you think of your young man?'

I shrugged. How could I tell my grandmother that he didn't make my heart gladden? 'He's all right. It's too soon to tell.'

'Too early to tell?' She threw her hands out and looked up at the ceiling. 'He's American. He came all this way. He was polite, so polite that he ate food he didn't like so he wouldn't offend. You said he doesn't live with his parents and he has a steady job. What are you waiting for? A message from God signed by all twelve apostles?'

My mouth fell open. Who was this woman? Never had Boba tried to force me to date. She always told me to take my time and to make a wise choice. That the choice of life partner was the most important one that a woman would ever make.

'What are you saying?'

'Stop moping about Vladimir Stanislavski. He's not the one for you. Give *this* man a chance. I'm not saying you have to get married tomorrow. Just be open. Try to get to know him. Let him get to know you. Don't you want a family? Don't you want children?'

'You know I do, Boba. More than anything.' Of its own accord, my bottom lip started to quiver. Why was Boba attacking me like this? I was so far over Vladimir Stanislavski that he was just a speck. I could barely see him. How could she think I was moping?

'Don't be offended, granddaughter.' She stroked my face. 'If you want a family, if you want to break The Curse, you'll have to open your heart and look past appearances. Handsome devils are just that – devils. They won't make you happy. Not in the long run. Your mama and I both figured that much out.'

It seemed that everything had been said. Wordlessly, we rose from the table and started to take the dishes from the dining room table into the kitchen. As I was covering the beet dish with a plate so that it wouldn't dry out in the refrigerator, Boba said, 'When I was a young woman, my neighbor Alla asked me to make my potato salad for the evening she invited her boyfriend Arcady to dinner. Of course I did, and of course she passed the dish off as her own. He proposed that very night. I'm sure it was the potato salad that cinched the deal.'

'I'm sure it was, too.' She told me this story every time she made potato salad. I'd heard all her stories at least one hundred times each.

'One evening, years later, when he was a little tipsy, he told me he married the wrong woman. He found out only after the wedding that I had made the famous potatoes. Men! They'll do anything for my salad.'

That night as I lay in bed I stared at the ceiling and thought about what had Boba said. I was judgmental. And hard on people. I needed to be softer.

The next morning, Tristan stepped out of the bathroom after a long shower. His hair was wet, and his eyes shone. He looked better than he had the day before. Or maybe after Boba's strong words, I saw him differently.

'Did you sleep well, Tristan?'

'I love it when you say my name. It sounds so sexy.'

I blushed and was pleased that I pleased him.

Boba smiled as she watched him devour the cheese *vareniki*, or ravioli, that she had made for breakfast.

'Ah, the appetite of the young,' she said contentedly.

'This is awesome,' he said. 'You guys are spoiling me rotten.'

His voice sounded raspy. I hoped he hadn't left the bedroom window open last night. That was a sure way to catch a cough.

'Would you like to go out and explore the city?' I asked, already apprehensive about running into acquaintances.

'Do you mind if we stay in? I think I've got a cold.'

Boba roasted a chicken and made mashed potatoes, then went to visit people in the old neighborhood so Tristan and I could be alone. If she and I still lived in the sleeping district, our neighbors would have invented excuses to borrow a glass of flour so that they could come in and meet our visitor. In our former building, the old women knew about things before they even happened. Luckily, our new neighbors – young foreigners – did not care about us.

In our tranquil blue living room, Tristan and I sat in David's chairs.

'You have such a nice apartment,' he said. 'Small. Cozy. When I was in college, I lived in a dorm, but I was sure glad to get back into a house.'

'In the city, we can only dream of having a private house. I've always lived in a flat. What is it about living in a house that you like so much?'

'Mainly, it's the yard I like. And growing fruits and vegetables. Nothing makes me happier than being in nature. I love working in the garden, on my knees with my hands in the dirt. It probably sounds weird, but I feel connected to something bigger than me.' He glanced at me, as if worried that I didn't think he was manly.

'That's exactly how I feel when I walk along the sea.'

'It's a great feeling, isn't it?'

'The best.'

'I love my roses. My mom grew them, too, and when I see them blossom, I think of her.' His voice was low as he said this, and he looked at me almost sheepishly, as if he were ashamed.

'Our parents always inhabit us, don't they?'

'Thank God,' he replied.

We sat in awkward silence for a moment. Perhaps we were each thinking about our families, our past, and what the future might hold. I was looking for something to say. A way to lighten the mood, which had grown too somber. Finally, I settled on, 'What do you like best about teaching?'

He smiled. 'I love working with young people. The money's not the best, but I love knowing that I'm helping kids. Like this one little guy, Adam. He's in fourth grade – nine years old – and his head goes back and forth like a bobble head because his old man used to shake him. Every day, he brings me a drawing of an airplane. You just feel bad for these kids and want them to have some kind of future. He barely knows the alphabet, but man can he draw! He's in my scout troop. If I can help these kids, help them have a few good memories of childhood... Besides, I want kids of my own and figure it's good practice ... What about you? What do you like best about your job?'

The unbidden answer was sitting in the darkened boardroom with David, drinking cold coffee and talking about literature. 'Giving tours. I love to introduce my native city to people.'

'Maybe we can go out later.' He rubbed his jaw and neck.

'Does your throat hurt?'

He nodded.

'Black tea with raspberry jam will soothe it.' I went into the kitchen to make him some. He followed me and got the cups out of the cupboard. This surprised me – most Odessan men would sit at the table and wait to be served. I put three large spoonfuls of Boba's home-made jam in each cup and three small spoonfuls of tea leaves in the pot. When the tea was ready, I poured it into the cups and opened a tin of Boba's cookies and encouraged Tristan to try them.

He took his tea and the tin of cookies and left the kitchen.

'Where are you going?'

'Back to the living room.'

'Usually we have tea here.' The kitchen is the coziest room in the house.

'The chairs in the other room are more comfortable. Come on.'

He was right.

Back in the living room, he looked at me and said, 'I'm so glad we're finally here together, face to face. It was so frustrating to call you and not be able to talk.'

'I know. My boss hates the phone lines in Odessa, too. Once, he got so mad he threw his phone across the room.'

'What a jerk. Sounds like he needs an anger management class.'

'He's not so bad.'

As we spoke, Tristan held my hand. I felt his appreciative glances. I, too, was interested in him, a foreigner from California, and hoped this curiosity would grow into something more. Little sparks can create a roaring fire, that's what we say in Odessa. True, he wasn't as cultured as some clients at the socials, but unlike them, he'd come for me. Me. He didn't carry a clipboard to compare and grade the women he met.

Yelena	25	waitress	no kids	good English	B
Vika	22	dancer	1 kid	no English	C
Anya	29	lawyer	divorced – no kids	English OK	A

'This tea is awesome,' he said. Jane used that word all the time, too. It must be an Americanism. 'I've never had anyone take care of me like this …'

'You're in Odessa now. The most hospitable city in the world.'

'In the galaxy,' he seconded. 'It seems like a beautiful place.'

'It is. I love Odessa. I love it here. But …'

'But?'

Odessa will always be here. Don't they call the city Odessa-Mama? She'll be right here, waiting for you if you want to come back. You're young, you should go, explore, live.

'I'm wondering if there isn't more.'

'More?'

'I want … I want …' I couldn't articulate the things I desired. I looked down at my hands.

'It's okay,' he said. 'Sometimes I have trouble finding words, too.'

I smiled gratefully.

'*Ti – krasivaya.*' You're beautiful. Then he said, hello and thank you in Russian.

'You're very welcome,' I replied. 'How?'

'I wanted to be able to say a few words of your language so I've been listening to tapes in my truck. I should have said hello in Russian to your grandma yesterday, but I was too nervous.'

'Thank you,' I said. 'What a lovely, unexpected gift.'

There was something in the air suddenly. Something charged and fragile. He leaned towards me. I leaned towards him. Our lips connected. He tasted like warm raspberries.

After a moment, he pulled back, 'I don't want you to catch my cold.'

I smiled shyly. 'I wouldn't mind.'

We chatted all afternoon. I was surprised at how much we had in common. For example, we both liked the Beatles. We both wanted two children. We both dreamed of going to Paris. We both loved the sea. He loved looking at my pictures, and I loved having my picture taken. Neither of us understood why people thought football was so interesting. If given the choice between happy or rich, we both chose happy.

And twenty years wasn't so much, was it? Boba and I were dear friends. As were Valentina and I, despite a gap of thirty years. Most women married older men. After all, as we learned in health class, girls mature faster than boys. Tristan's years meant additional experience, which was a good thing, wasn't it?

For dinner, I served Tristan a large scoop of Boba's mashed potatoes and a succulent thigh.

'You don't have to wait on me,' he said. 'You should dish up. Ladies first.'

No Odessan man would ever think like this let alone say such a thing.

'You're a good cook,' he said.

I should have admitted that I couldn't bear to touch a chicken carcass let alone roast it to perfection as Boba had. But I wanted him to think the best of me. So I said, '*Spacibo*.'

'You're welcome,' he replied in Russian. *Nechevo*.

'It feels good to sit here with you. Usually I'm so busy with work that I never get home before seven. My friends think that I do too much. That I want too much.'

'Well, we wouldn't be sitting here if you weren't such a hard worker, if you hadn't taken that second job. Nothing wrong with having dreams. In America we say, "Shoot for the moon. Even if you miss, you'll still be among the stars."'

'In Odessa we say keep your feet on the ground and your head out of the clouds.'

'That's a downer. You gotta try, don't you? I mean if I hadn't signed up at Soviet Unions, I'd be sitting alone in Emerson instead of with you in this awesome city.'

Two evenings later, Tristan proclaimed himself 'over jetlag,' and we explored the city.

'This place is a little run down, but pretty,' he said. 'It smells like diesel.'

I couldn't concentrate on what he was saying. I looked over my shoulder, worried about crossing paths with a friend or colleague.

Catch-caught-caught. I hadn't told anyone about him – I didn't want to jinx things. So much could go wrong. He could simply disappear just as Will had. Vita and Vera could try to steal him away, or worse, tell David. I glanced behind me again. And again. Odessa is like a village. I'd never walked more than two blocks without running into an acquaintance. Still, tonight my luck was holding.

'Nothing's written in English.'

'Well, you're in Odessa,' I said tartly. 'How many signs written in Russian do you have in San Francisco?'

'We have a whole Russian Hill,' he said.

I wanted more than anything to see it, my earlier irritation forgotten. I was dying to see America, and Tristan could make that happen. So he complained that the city smelled. Things weren't perfect here – that's why so many people wanted to leave.

As we crossed onto Pushkinskaya Street, he stopped and stared at the golden cobblestones, which made the street seem as if it had been paved in gold. 'Why, it's a real yellow brick road!' he exclaimed. 'How can that be?'

Finally something in my native city impressed him. I recited the information from my guide book: 'They're made from clay and remain in the furnace until vitrified.'

He took my hand and exclaimed, 'A real yellow brick road! We're a long way from Kansas, Dorothy!'

Sometimes he said things I couldn't understand. Like my first American film years ago – Woody Allen's *Manhattan*. I'd bought my ticket weeks in advance and carried it with me everywhere. I couldn't wait to hear real native speakers and went alone so that no one would distract me with comments or jokes. In the movie theater, the lights dimmed and I stared at the screen and fidgeted in my seat, ready for a life-changing moment. I sat in the dark and stayed in the dark. I understood all the words and none of their meaning. It was deeply frustrating to understand everything and nothing. Why was Tristan talking about Kansas? Why did he call me Dorothy?

I gave him the same tour as the other Soviet Unions clients, then took him to a modest discotheque on the beach. The bar served our vodka, *kognac*, and *champagnskoye*, as opposed to the foreign drinks (and foreign prices) of clubs like the Crazy Horse. The sliding glass doors of the disco were opened to the night. Half the club was a dance floor, the other half a restaurant with tables covered with white floor-length tablecloths. The doorman took one look at Tristan's jeans and T-shirt and shook his head. I slipped him a few bills and explained, 'My friend is a foreigner.' He frowned, but let us pass. Tristan looked at the young people dancing. 'They're perfect. Perfect skin, perfect hair, perfect bodies.'

I looked at them, but didn't see anything unusual. He was more interested in the youth than he was in the architecture. He asked how old they were, how much it cost to come to a club like this. Why was he so amazed? This place wasn't unusual. There were dozens of them in Odessa.

'In the States, we have a problem with obesity,' he explained. 'Plus lots of teenagers fight acne. I did. You'll see when you get to America.'

America. He sounded so confident when he said this. I just hoped he wouldn't disappear. Like Will. Like Vlad.

'Everyone looks so ... good,' he continued. 'They're wearing nice, even fancy clothes.' He sounded surprised. He looked at the young men in dress shirts and trousers dancing with slender girls in gauzy summer dresses, which showed off their tanned legs.

'Why is that so hard to believe?' I asked, interested in his observations. Did he expect us to be dressed in rags? We had our pride. Looking good was our way of saying we may be poor, but we're not downtrodden.

'I guess ... and this is going to sound bad, but us Americans always think we're the best and that we know best, but I'm looking at these kids, and I'm thinking they know how to live.'

I still didn't know what he meant. He ran his finger over my furled brow and tried to explain his thoughts and his culture. 'In America, when kids go out ...' I must have looked confused because he started again. 'When young adults go out, it's to see how much they can drink and how fast they can get drunk.'

'Strange,' I said.

'But here, I see kids dancing and having a good time in moderation. They aren't binge drinking, they're eating a meal

173

and visiting and dancing. This is good. At their age, I was getting drunk under a bridge in my truck with my buddy.'

Why would anyone do that?

A slow song came on and he asked me to dance. I rested my hands lightly on his shoulders. He stroked my back, almost to my bottom. The guys on the dance floor looked at me. Their expression said, 'Why are you with this geezer?'

To escape judgment, I closed my eyes and rested my chin on Tristan's shoulder. He took this as a good sign and pulled me closer. I heard Vlad say, 'In this, as in all things, you'll come out on top.' I imagined it was Vlad who kissed my temple, Vlad who held me tight, Vlad who wanted me.

When the song ended, I opened my eyes and was surprised to see Tristan. I moved away and glanced down at the floor, dismayed. When I looked up again, I saw his eyes glowed with the same passion I'd felt only a moment before.

A fast song came on and I moved my hips and stretched my arms up above my head. The tension left my body and I closed my eyes, this time staying in the moment with Tristan. When I opened them, he was staring at me. I smiled. He kissed me. It felt like the white down of a dandelion tickling my lips. Soft. Silky.

I kissed him back.

'Say my name,' he whispered.

'Tristan.'

'Tree-stahn,' he repeated softly.

On Monday morning, I went to work and worried. What if Tristan left the flat and got lost? He couldn't even read the street signs. There was no color in my cheeks and I was as damp as a bottle of vodka taken out of the icebox. I couldn't help fidgeting. David endured me for two hours before he said, 'What's wrong with you? If you're still sick, go home. I don't want to catch whatever it is you have.'

It was hard to say what I had. As I walked home, I tried to sort it all out in my mind. I was nervous. And confused. Before meeting Tristan, I'd had this image in my head of a romantic teacher. I fell a little in love with an illusion I'd created. I pored over his letters, reading whatever I wanted into them. The photos he'd sent of himself were a decade old, so I'd imagined a young, virile man.

Now that he was here, I had to admit that the reality was quite different to what I'd imagined.

In Odessa, men are either lovers or acquaintances. When a woman says, 'He's my friend,' it's assumed she means 'he's my boyfriend.' When the romance ends, so does the relationship. Love or nothing. I'd spent time with Jane and her boyfriend Cole. Even after they broke up, he was cordial and looked after her. They talked and laughed like friends. This was what I wanted: lasting love and friendship.

When Boba opened the door, I said hello and she shushed me. 'He's resting.'

It seems I had worried for nothing. He was here, safe. Boba pulled me into the kitchen and sat me down.

'Did you think about what I said?' she asked.

'Yes, Boba,' I said meekly.

'He talks to you and treats you like an equal,' she said. 'And he paid so much for a plane ticket. He's better than any man you'll find here.'

Maybe she was right.

Tristan was ready to settle down and start a family. So was I. Tristan was a serious person who longed for love and companionship. So was I. Tristan had a steady job. I couldn't say that about Vlad or any of the other men I'd dated. Tristan had phoned and written faithfully, despite the great expense; Vlad promised to call, but hadn't – and local telephone calls were free. Tristan had crossed an ocean to see me; Vlad couldn't be bothered to cross town. Tristan was a gentleman and had not even hinted that he expected anything. I wanted someone who would love and honor me. Someone faithful and serious. Someone ready to have a family. Looking back on all my male classmates, co-workers, neighbors, dates, the only one who hadn't disappointed me was Tristan. And he promised a golden future in California. It wasn't hard to make the choice. America the beautiful, or Ukraine in the dark, long shadow of Russia. Tristan: steady, mature, kind. Vlad: fickle, immature, callous. It was true that I did not feel a current, an electricity with Tristan as I had with Vlad. But this was a good thing. Those sparks had singed me, and I was still sore. I didn't want to be hurt again. Tristan was the intelligent choice.

He came out of the bedroom, rubbing his eyes. His legs were not quite steady and he stumbled. He placed his palm on the wall to steady himself. He looked at us, watching him, shyly, self-consciously. He looked vulnerable and somehow more attractive to me.

'The poor thing needs something to eat,' Boba clucked and stroked his arm, pulling him towards the kitchen.

After he ate, I suddenly wanted to be alone with him and asked if he wanted to go for a stroll. Of course, in Odessa, all roads lead to the sea. He nodded and smiled.

'So you're an only child,' he said as we walked along the beach. 'Did you ever want brothers and sisters?'

'Yes.' I thought of Olga's baby Ivan. 'A little brother would have been heavenly.'

'I'd have liked to have a little sister. I grew up in a house of guys. My mother died when I was four, so it was only Dad, my big brother Hal, and me. Maybe that's why I've never been comfortable with ladies ... I've just never known what to say or how to say it. That's why I liked dating online. I could think about what to say and take my time. I wasn't all nervous and tongue-tied. I was in my living room, not at some fancy restaurant trying to make a good impression, but using the wrong fork and spilling food on my shirt.'

He was so sweet. I didn't know men worried about such things.

'Am I making a total idiot of myself here?' he asked.

'No, no. Of course not! I was listening. I appreciated what you said. I get nervous on dates, too.'

'Why? I mean, you're gorgeous.'

I thought of Vlad. 'Some guys here pretend they're serious ...' Boba was right. I had to stop moping about him. 'I mean, some guys my age just want to have fun. They're not thinking about marriage or starting a family. I am.'

He took my hand. 'Me, too.'

I just hope your uterus hasn't shriveled up. Instinctively, my arm curled around my belly. 'You don't think I'm too old, do you?'

He looked at me like I was crazy.

'This ... girl I used to know said ... that I was too old ... and that no man would ever want me.'

'She sounds seriously fucked up. My God, who wouldn't want

you? You're hard working, intelligent, and beautiful. If anyone around here's too old, it's me.'

'No!' I stopped walking. We stood facing each other. 'No. I want a man who is mature. Who knows what he wants.'

'Are you sure?' He looked away. 'I feel like a cradle robber.'

'This feels right.' And as I said the words, I realized it did. I wasn't nervous with him like I'd been with Vlad. He didn't ask anything of me. He didn't pressure me in any way like the other men I'd known. 'I'm ready to ...'

'Start a family.'

His lips were cool on mine and seemed to ask for the love that I longed to give.

But I had to be sure and decided to test him one last time. I told him about the socials, the flowing *champagnskoye*, the fact that there were four gorgeous girls for each guy. Technically, he'd paid the money to be a member of Soviet Unions. Did he want to go to a social just to see?

No, he replied, he was with me now.

Chapter 13

The evening before he left, Tristan asked me to take him back to the beach.

'I don't want to go home,' he said. 'I just want to stay in Odessa with you.'

'Farther from the eye, closer to the heart,' I quipped, though I too felt sad when I thought about him leaving.

On the warm sand, he knelt in front of me and took my hands in his. 'You are the most beautiful woman I have ever met – beautiful inside and out. I'm in love with you and want to marry you. Come to Emerson with me.'

All I could think was *California*. And that he had chosen me.

'I'd love to.'

We kissed. A slow, sweet kiss. Pleasant, but not hot. I reminded myself that hot only gets you burned. Passion was dangerous. What I felt for Tristan was safer.

Back at the flat, he went to his room and returned with a box wrapped in silver paper, a gift from America. He sat beside me on the sofa and placed it on my lap.

'What is it?'

'Open it,' he said gently.

I removed the paper slowly then opened the box, which held a portable computer. 'This is too much,' I whispered.

'It's not enough,' he said. 'Now you can e-mail me from home.'

Tristan followed the phone line to the wall, only to find that there was no way to connect because there was no jack – the line disappeared directly into the wall. We couldn't plug the computer in because the electrical outlets were different in Europe. I wouldn't be able to use his gift right away, but that didn't matter. The computer had already served its purpose. It showed that Tristan was a generous man who wouldn't be churlish with money. He must be rich.

'Thank you,' I said.

'Say it with a kiss.'

I placed my hands on his shoulders and touched my lips to his. He moaned. I couldn't believe that an American was interested in me. That he had come all this way and that I would have the chance to live in California. All my dreams were coming true. He pulled me on to his lap. I ran my hands through his hair.

'God, you feel so good,' he said, grinding his hips to mine.

'You feel good, too.' I heard the locks turn and tried to disentangle myself from him before my grandmother walked in. 'Do you think that Boba could come live with us?'

'Anything you want,' he groaned and pulled me tighter. 'Anything you want ...'

Before he left, Tristan handed me a one-way plane ticket. I was leaving in a month's time, right after my appointment at the American consulate. We were lucky to get an appointment so quickly. I knew that the wait was usually closer to two months. At least my work at Soviet Unions had prepared me for the daunting bureaucracy that was to come.

Boba and I danced around the kitchen, hugging each other and singing, 'America, America, California, California.' At night, I couldn't sleep. I just stared at the ceiling and thought about how marvelous everything would be. I'd have a car. A house. A yard. We'd get married and have two children. A girl named Nadezhda, a boy named Ivan. No, a boy named Alan.

I didn't dare tell anyone I was leaving. Neither did Boba. We didn't want to jinx it. We kept the secret to ourselves. Even when it felt like we would burst with the news. I couldn't concentrate on anything work-related. I sat at my desk and imagined my new apartment in San Francisco. It would be a Victorian for sure. I'd have a bay window. On sunny days I would walk on the beach. On rainy days I would curl up on the window seat and read. I'd have friends who were intelligent, funny, and well traveled. I'd have a car. And a huge paycheck. An American Express credit card. Free time to drink a coffee at a sidewalk café. I'd go to galleries and plays and restaurants. I'd shop in exclusive boutiques. I'd spend hours in bookshops filled with novels and magazines in English.

Then, just when I thought life couldn't get any better, it did. Jane called to say that she and her friend were arriving by train in two weeks. She was keeping her promise, and I was thrilled. All I could think about was seeing my old friend and starting my new life. But I couldn't tell her anything. Not a thing! She would talk me out of going and I would be stuck here.

'You look gorgeous! Positively glowing!' Jane gushed when she saw me on the platform.

I handed her a bouquet of roses, the typical gift Odessans give to visiting friends. She hugged me and spun me around. 'You look so different. Blissed out. What's new?'

'I'm just so happy to see you.' And it was the truth, but not the whole truth.

She'd cut her mane of red hair and in its place was a bob. Her hazel eyes sparkled behind tortoise-framed spectacles, and she was rosy and plump.

She introduced me to Tans, who was old enough to be her grandfather.

'Tans?' I asked.

'Edward Tansley III,' he said. 'Everyone calls me Tans.'

He was shorter than she and had wavy silver hair and a black mustache. He was always touching her – caressing her arm, her shoulders, her nape. I longed to talk to Jane, just Jane, about Tristan, about California, about the future. At moments, I feared my news would burst from my lips like a trumpet blast. It was for the best that Tans was there to confirm my silence. I only asked peripheral questions like, 'What are rednecks?' since Tristan considered himself a reformed redneck. Jane gasped. When I asked about Emerson (which I had not been able to find on any map), Tans said he wasn't sure, but thought it could be close to Sonoma, the wine country. Jane looked at me shrewdly and asked, 'What are these questions really about?'

I changed the subject and asked Jane how she'd felt when she'd come to Odessa to teach.

'Nervous, but excited. I didn't know what to expect, what to bring, how to act.'

'What do you mean?'

'When I came here, I didn't stop to observe how things were done. I just charged right in like a demented general. A spoiled rotten twenty-three-year-old general. I didn't respect the hierarchy and unwritten rules. I thought that my co-workers should follow my lead and respect my feelings and ideas. I alienated my boss immediately because I reacted before looking at things from her point of view. If I'd been a little older, a little wiser, things would have been different.'

I nodded. Remember that, I said to myself. Observe. Be ready to adapt. Don't be rash. Don't assume. Wait. Listen. Think.

Jane sighed, as if she was reliving painful moments.

'Darling,' Tans embraced her. 'How could anyone not love you? You're so honest, so true. That's what I love about you. You're the exception. Rare. Beautiful.'

'I don't know about that. You're right about one thing. I am different. It was obvious I wasn't Ukrainian. Most of the time I didn't mind standing out. But there were days it was hard.'

Compared to Odessan girls, Jane had not looked polished. Her clothes were wrinkled – she'd said she couldn't be bothered to iron. Her Birkenstocks hit the pavement hard, and when it rained, mud splattered from the hem of her cream-colored trousers all the way up the backs of her thighs.

'If you're planning a long trip, take the books and photos you really love,' she said, which made me think she could read my thoughts. She looked at me, even when I looked away. I was helpless under her gaze. Jane knew me well enough to know I was hiding something, but like a true Odessan, she also knew not to pry.

They stayed for a week. We met every day, walking along the sea in the evening. We even went out with her Ukrainian ex-boyfriend, Misha. As Jane talked to him, Tans sat up taller and sucked in his stomach. Misha was slightly younger than Jane and of course his stomach was as flat as Boba's ironing board. His gray eyes lingered on Jane, and her lips curled into a shy smile.

Misha tried to pay for our drinks but Tans wouldn't let him.

The next evening, when Jane and Tans boarded the night train to Kiev, Misha brought a bottle of *champagnskoye*. We clinked glasses and wished them bon voyage. I secretly wished myself bon voyage as well.

After we drank the last drops, I hugged Jane and whispered, 'I'll be in America before you.'

'What?'

I smiled and quickly said, 'Nothing. Just a joke.'

She wanted to say more, but the whistle blew, and Misha and I had to leave the train. He hailed a car for me and paid the driver in advance. I turned to look at him, and as he disappeared from view, I found myself wondering if I hadn't shortchanged Odessan men. In Misha, Jane had found someone who was attentive, strong, and loving. She told me she'd asked him to go to America with her; he'd said he wanted to but couldn't abandon his recently widowed mother.

As the time drew near for me to go to Kiev to get my American visa, I went from friend to friend, including Valentina. Not to say goodbye. I just wanted to see them one more time.

On my last day in the shipping office, my eyes started to water. I would miss Odessa and my job here. I would even miss David. I dabbed at my eyes and he asked, 'What's wrong? Do you need help? Are you having money problems?'

His solicitude only made me sadder.

I'd told him I was taking a leave of absence to take care of an aunt in Kiev. 'I wrote out a list of instructions for your next secretary –' He opened his mouth and I added, 'Including instructions for how to proceed at the port, so that it will be smooth sailing for everyone involved.'

He pulled five crisp hundred-dollar bills out of his wallet, saying, 'Take this. Health care bribes in this country are insane.'

I couldn't believe the trajectory of our relationship. We had moved from hardcore hunter and jumpy prey, to an awkward cold war after the incident, to adversaries during the beginning of the Olga phase, and finally to a bond of friendship. I would miss him. I missed him already.

I looked at the money, offered out of love, with no strings attached. I hugged him very hard. 'Thank you, David. Thank you.'

He kissed my hair and said, 'Hurry back. I need you.'

I refused the money – I wouldn't need it in America. But at home, I found he had tucked the bills into my purse.

I hugged Boba constantly, asking her again and again if I was doing the right thing. 'Of course! Who are you going to find here?' she asked. 'I didn't raise you so that you could hand-wash some man's socks and wait on him hand and foot. Go to America! They have things we don't, their lives are easy in a way ours will never be. Look at my hands, Dasha.' The nails were short, the skin dry and tight; veins had popped up like mountain ranges, brown spots dotted the landscape. 'These hands have spent a lifetime washing sheets, clothes, nappies, and menstrual rags by plunging them into pails of scalding water. I don't want that for you. I want you to be free. Free from menial labor; free to get a good-paying job because you're qualified, not because the boss wants to take advantage; free to live your life without having to worry about shortages, or how you are going to pay the bills.'

I hugged her tight. 'I don't want you to be alone.'

'I don't mind. I've endured long periods of solitude. I don't know if this man is the love of your life, but he has kind eyes and is polite. He didn't smoke or get drunk while he was here. You'll be better off with him than with a Ukrainian. Better off there than here. God Himself is helping you. Now go.'

As I knelt in front of my enormous suitcase, Boba flitted from the living room to my room, bringing books and photos. I packed my finest clothes so that I would fit in in America. I didn't want anyone thinking I was poor. I started to worry. Would Americans accept me? Would I experience culture shock? Probably not – everything was perfect there. I would follow Jane's advice and quietly observe. I wouldn't judge and I would adapt. My head was deep in my suitcase and deep in thought when I heard heavy footsteps behind me. 'I'll take all the photos you want, but I can't fit another book in! Babel, Pushkin, Akhmatova, and Tolstoy will do!' I said.

'I didn't bring any books,' a deep voice said behind me.

I closed my eyes. How many weeks had I waited to see Vlad? I didn't even allow myself to think about him anymore. I'd locked him out of my heart and mind. Yet at the sound of his voice, my treacherous heart opened to receive him. I didn't turn around. I continued to rearrange my shoes and books.

'It's okay if you don't want to look at me,' Vlad said from the doorway. 'I don't want to look at myself either. I'm ashamed.'

I didn't move.

'I have a confession – that morning after our night together, I was awake. In fact, I hadn't slept. I was terrified, feeling emotions I'd never felt before, desiring things – a wife, a family – that I hadn't known I'd wanted a day earlier. I want to spend my life with you. I want to marry you.'

I righted myself and faced him. His cheekbones were what I noticed first – he'd lost weight. He took off his sunglasses. The dark circles under his eyes were almost purple. His cheeks and chin were dotted with stubble. His lips were sensual.

'I, I, I. All you care about is you and what you think and feel. You're just like every other guy I've ever dated: selfish, unreliable, and fickle. Where was all this months ago? Where were you?'

'In Irkutsk to see my brother and check on business there. At first, I told myself I had to stay there until I felt nothing more for you. After three months, I realized my feelings would never go away. That's why I'm here.'

How long had I waited to hear these words? How long had I waited to see him? Even if I wanted to throw myself into his arms and accept, my pride wouldn't allow it. Instead, I rolled my eyes and sneered, 'You make me sound like some kind of disease. Do you really think I just sat around and moped? I've moved on.'

He gestured to the clothes strewn around the room. 'What's all this? Where are you going?'

How I wanted to brag that I was going to the American embassy to get my visa, then flying to San Francisco the following day. I only said, 'To Kiev.' I was afraid that he had ways of making me stay. And, worse, that I would be happy to.

'Let me drive you.' He crossed the room to stand before me.

'I don't need you. Please go.' I looked out the window. I didn't want to look at him. Didn't want to weaken.

'Why are you taking so many books and clothes?' he asked,

184

taking my hand. I jerked it away and walked to the doorway. 'Just how long are you planning to stay?'

'I've taken a leave of absence from work … to take care of my frail aunt. I don't know how long I'll be there.'

'You don't have any family aside from your grandmother.'

'This woman was … a friend of my mother's. I've always called her "auntie." I need to finish packing. Please leave.' But I stood blocking the door. A part of me didn't want him to go. No, not just a part. All of me.

He got down on his knees and inched towards me with a green leather box in his hand. 'I'm prostrate before you, my beauty. I'm holding out my hand, I'm holding out my heart, I'm holding out a seven-carat diamond ring.'

I smiled down at him. My tears fell onto his cheeks. 'My little soul,' he murmured as he slipped his ring onto my finger. I held up my hand; the stone sparkled. His hands rested on my hips, and my body remembered the sensations of pleasure and satiation that I'd shut out of my mind. He kissed my stomach reverently; I held his face to my belly and ran my hands through his hair. He sighed and wrapped his arms around my waist.

Finally, he stood and took me in his arms. A gentle wisp of air blew in through the window. Just as he bent to kiss me, my nose twitched.

Vodka.

I took a step back. My eyes narrowed, my resolve returned. 'Have you been drinking?'

'The boys wanted to celebrate my return to Odessa and my engagement. I was nervous about coming over here, so I had more than usual.'

I don't know which made me more furious – the fact that he assumed I would fall into his arms and accept his proposal or that he needed a drink (quite a few from the smell of it) to bolster his courage. My mother had loved an alcoholic who'd run off at the first sign of trouble. That wasn't going to be me. Vlad would be a horrible husband and an even worse father. If I married him, I'd be stuck. The breeze had sent a sign that I'd have been a fool to ignore. I pulled off the ring, put it back in its box, and shut the lid on all my naïve fantasies.

I held out the box. 'Leave. Just leave.'

He refused to take it. 'What's wrong?'

I crossed my arms and looked away.

'You're angry because I went away?'

I didn't say anything.

'I understand you feel betrayed. I'll let you go to Kiev. I love you; I can wait. I don't blame you for being proud, or for wanting to make me walk through the hell I put you through.'

Let me go to Kiev? He was so arrogant, thinking I was just waiting for him to come back so that my world would continue to spin again. He thought I'd just give in and fall into his arms and his king-size bed. He tried to hand me the box, but I didn't uncross my arms. He placed it in my suitcase and turned to me. He put his hands on my shoulders and gave them a gentle squeeze. I pulled out of his grasp. I hated that I'd fallen for his lines yet again.

'I want you to be mine. I want you to wear my ring. Dasha, swear that the minute you get back to Odessa, we'll talk.'

I almost laughed, so I bit my lip, then looked into his eyes and said, 'You have my solemn word. When I return to Odessa, we'll talk.'

I was so happy to make this promise that I also made myself one – I'd never come back. Never. Not even if I was miserable. Then I let myself laugh, great barks of mirth. Who could be miserable in America?

Vlad smiled back, as though my laughter somehow concerned him. He was so vain. How could I ever have cared for him? He tried to kiss me, but I countered his move so quickly that all he got was a mouthful of hair. He took my hand and kissed it. And walked out the door.

After he left, Boba returned to the bedroom and asked, 'Was that ... ?'

When I nodded, she sneered, 'Gangster. You're better off without him!'; made the sign of the cross the Russian Orthodox way, tapping her forehead, chest, right shoulder, left shoulder; then spit three times. I handed Boba Vlad's gift and asked her to return it to him.

I called Uncle Vadim and asked him to take us to the train station. He loaded my suitcases in the boot. 'You're going to see your American cousin. I'm right. Tell me I'm right!'

'She's just going to Kiev for a while,' Boba said, ending his speculation.

As we pulled away from the curb, I saw a black sedan do the same. Uncle Vadim said, 'You have an admirer. Is he the reason you're going to ... Amer–, uh Kiev?'

'One of the reasons,' I admitted.

When we arrived at the train station, I could feel Vlad's gaze as the Mercedes floated by. Uncle Vadim took my luggage and the three of us made our way to my compartment. Boba pulled a bottle of *champagnskoye* and plastic goblets from her purse. We clinked glasses and they both wished me luck. Uncle Vadim left to give us a moment of privacy. Boba took the green leather box out of her purse and pressed it to my palm. 'Take it, Dasha. If you ever want to come home, you can sell it.'

I didn't want to tell her I wasn't coming back, didn't want my last moment with my Boba to be an argument, so I took the ring and slid it onto the silver chain that David had given me to celebrate our first month together, then tucked it back underneath my shirt. The diamond was worth enough that if the wrong people saw it, I would be in danger.

'If you married Vlad, you'd need a bodyguard to protect that ring,' Boba pointed out. 'I'll miss you. I'll miss you so very much, my little rabbit paw, but you're making a wise decision.'

'I love you, Boba.' Tears streamed down my face. I hugged her hard, pressed my cheek to hers. Our tears melted together. They were bitter and salty, like the Black Sea.

Chapter 14

To be in the sky, to fly through the clouds is a miracle. A miracle of man. We can do so many marvelous things when we try. I traveled twenty-four hours to arrive in San Francisco. From Kiev to Warsaw, from Warsaw to Atlanta, Atlanta to San Francisco. The obstacle course through the airports was nothing compared to the day of standing outside the embassy gate, waiting to receive a visa.

Odessa is a friendly town with many cafés and colorful architecture in the city center. Strangers grumble together while waiting for the trolley bus. It's easy to meet people because Odessans are curious and open. Like America, Odessa recently celebrated its bicentennial. On the other hand, Kiev is over a thousand years old. People are polite rather than friendly. The capital is gray and reserved, its formal architecture meant to impress and even intimidate. Unfortunately, I didn't have time to explore the stately avenues and rich museums. I had an appointment at the American Embassy.

Once there, I waited outside the tall fence with dozens of other people. We'd been given appointments for the day but not the time, so we stood along the wall for hours until our names were called. Then we stood inside the embassy for hours. There wasn't a single chair, not even for the pensioners. Also, there wasn't a bathroom. I feared I would explode, but didn't dare run to a restaurant down the block to use the ladies' room. The official said that if we weren't there when our names were called we'd have to make another appointment – and they were backlogged for weeks.

I had waited so long, I feared that they'd forgotten me. But all the girls said that. You wait and wait. *Stand-stood-stood.* I remembered Irina, a girl with a lovely sense of humor. She'd been denied a fiancé visa because of a little joke she'd made during her interview. When the official asked her about marrying John, and she replied, 'If I like his house, I'll marry him.'

The girls said that American officials had no sense of humor and no amount of goodwill could sway them. I practiced my answers to the questions they had told me they'd been asked. What day did you meet? Do your parents approve of the match? What do the two of you have in common? Where did you go for dates?

When it was my turn, I handed over the file with the visa application, color photos, his tax information, my passport, and proof that Tristan and I knew each other: pictures of us together, copies of his phone bill to prove that he called often, and a stack of e-mails. I was led to a small room and an official gestured for me to sit.

'When did you become engaged?' she asked.

For some reason this question fazed me. Until that moment, I hadn't thought of myself as engaged. It seemed like a big step, somehow bigger than going to America. I was thinking in terms of months, not in terms of a lifetime. 'We're not exactly engaged. I mean ... he asked, but I told him I'd have to think about it. It's a big step.'

She wrote furiously. *Write-wrote-written.* What did I say?

'So you're here to apply for a *fiancé visa* but you're not engaged?' She sounded skeptical.

I gestured to the papers she had in front of her. 'We've been corresponding for some time. It's just that we only met for the first time a month ago when he came to Odessa. I want to get to know him more before I make a lifelong commitment.' I continued to babble, talking more to myself than to her. Engaged. A new life. An irreversible step. What was the right thing to do? As I spoke, she smiled cynically. I could read every thought that passed through her beady little brain. *And you want to get to know him better in America. Or maybe even find someone better while you're there.*

The woman looked at the photos of Tristan and me together and asked, 'Are you really interested in this guy or do you just want a green card?' Under her breath she muttered, 'Goddamn e-mail order brides.'

But she granted the visa.

The Warsaw airport was nothing special, but Atlanta's was like a dream. I hadn't realized how hazy my life in Odessa was until I entered a building where it seemed as though no one had ever smoked. Everything was so pristine and dazzling – the walls, the windows, the carpet. It was day, but the lights were on. There was art on the walls, as if it were a museum. No one pushed or shoved or grumbled. I took in the waves of English, the smiling people, the restaurants, the boutiques. I was in America now. Yes, this is what I want.

Yes.

I boarded the next and last plane to San Francisco.

Though I was tired, I bounded off the plane to start my new life. While waiting for my luggage, I went to the bathroom and closed the stall door. Stall was the right word – like a horse in a barn, anyone could see me. There was an inch between the partition and the door! Also, the door didn't go down to the floor. How odd! When I finished, I swear I heard the roar of a large jet taking off behind me. But when I turned, it was the clean water rushing into the porcelain bowl. I thought of the public toilets in Odessa. Even in the opera house, they were just porcelain footprints around a hole. In their finery, women had to squat like dogs.

I moved to the sink to wash my hands, but couldn't see how to turn on the water. I watched the woman next to me. She ran her hands under the silver faucet; water poured out. I looked at myself in the mirror. My hair was starting to come out of its chignon, so I brushed it out and put it back up. A little girl looked up at me and said shyly, 'You're a pretty lady.' I thanked her and handed her a sweet. She stared at it, but didn't take it. No matter. As I ran my hands under the dryer, I couldn't believe that I was finally here. Land of the Free, Home of the Brave. Perhaps one day I would be an American citizen.

As I waited at the luggage carousel, I looked at the people. Tall, short, thin, plump, completely natural, totally plastic. Such a variety of faces and features. The fashion surprised me. There were a few businessmen and women in suits, but nearly everyone else wore faded jeans and scuffed tennis shoes or flip-flops. The young people wore their jeans low on their hips – underpants and folds of flesh visible. How odd that in the richest country in the world, people looked so poor and wore such ill-fitting clothing. In my black suit and heels I felt overdressed.

I collected my suitcases and made my way out the door. Tristan was the first person I saw. I smiled tremulously, he grinned and came forward. He looked much better than when he arrived in Odessa, he was tanned and his cheeks were rosy. I was the pale, tired one. He hugged me. His hands roamed my back, my arms, my hair. *Hold-held-held. Run-ran-run.*

'How are you?' he asked. 'You look tired. I hope the flights weren't too long.' He seemed to vibrate with excitement. I, too, was thrilled to have come so far.

Tristan led me to his vehicle, a dusty truck. He opened the passenger door for me. 'Do you want to stop and eat something?'

I shook my head, embarrassed at how we'd force-fed him when he arrived in Odessa. I didn't realize that a person felt nauseous after a long flight, as if they had a belly full of helium.

'We'll head straight home then.'

On the freeway, I looked at the cars. So many colors and sizes. Everyone drove so fast, like it was a race. In the distance, I could see the high rises of San Francisco. Tristan was talking to me, and I tried to listen, but my ears seem to close as my eyelids did.

He squeezed my thigh. 'We can explore when you're not so sleepy.'

The road was smooth. Although I was excited to be in America, the hum of the motor lulled me to sleep. When we pulled into the driveway, Tristan shook my shoulder. He pressed a button and the garage door went up. Unbelievable! An automatic toilet, automatic faucet, automatic door opener. Automatic everything. When he saw my delight, he said, 'Here, press the button.' I did and the door crawled back down. It was silly to be enchanted by such small things, but they truly did underline the differences between my old world and the new one.

Tristan took my hand and led me to his house. The dark wood went well with the surrounding plants and trees. There were pink

191

roses near the front door. The windows were large and didn't have any bars. It must be a safe neighborhood. I noticed a chimney – was there a fireplace, just like in the movies? He surprised me by lifting me up and carrying me across the threshold. *Bite-bit-bit. Sweep-swept-swept.* Clearly, he already considered me his bride. Back on the ground, I felt touched by his romantic gesture. Surely Tristan wouldn't sleep with me only to disappear.

'Here we are,' he said, looking at me expectantly.

'Indeed,' I replied, feeling awkward. I didn't know how to behave with him or what he expected. In my experience, men always wanted something. He held his hand out as if encouraging me to look. The whole house felt as if it were bathed in light. White walls, beige carpet. Framed posters of Yosemite National Park. Photos of smiling children on the refrigerator. Did he have kids? My mind raced. He said he'd never married. Had he lied? Or were they illegitimate? I shook my head to empty it of these horrible thoughts. I had to learn to trust him. This wasn't Odessa, where I always had to be on guard. This was America, this was Tristan, my gentle schoolteacher. He'd gone to Odessa to meet me, asked me to marry him, and paid for my ticket to San Francisco. Clearly, he was a decent man with good intentions.

I walked from the entryway into the living room, through the kitchen, into the dining room. It was all one open space. No barriers between rooms, only light. I loved it, especially the brick fireplace.

'Your home is *lovely*. So light, so airy.'

'I designed it myself,' he said, looking proud and happy. I was happy, too.

He showed me the bedroom, office, and bathrooms which were down the hall from the entryway. I had just started to relax when Tristan put my things in his bedroom. Surprise robbed me of my speech, but only for a moment. 'We're not married yet,' I reminded him stiffly. 'I'd be happy to sleep on the sofa.' Boba said men don't buy the chicken when they get the eggs for free. I'd learned it was true with Vlad and wouldn't make the same mistake again.

Tristan said he respected my feelings and moved my things into the office. We made the sofa there into a bed. Although it was only 8 p.m., I went straight to sleep. I didn't even wash my face.

I awoke at 6 a.m. like I always did at home. Jane had once told me that jetlag was terrible, but it didn't seem to affect me. I lay in bed and listened. No cars honking, no babies crying, no neighbors yelling, no one stomping overhead. It was so calm. If it hadn't been for the birds chirping, I would have feared I'd gone deaf.

I got up and made coffee. Tristan's machine wasn't as sophisticated as the one David had given me. While it brewed, I looked out of every window which looked out onto trees. It seemed more like the country than a suburb. Where was I?

Tristan came out of his bedroom already dressed in jeans and a T-shirt. 'Sorry to leave you on your own today, but I don't have any vacation days left since I used them up in Budapest.' Was his tone reproving?

'And Odessa, where we met, where you enjoyed my Boba's hospitality,' I reminded him. 'Do teachers in America work in the summer?'

He looked surprised by my question.

'Do they work in the summer?' I asked again. 'Do you have to clean your classroom? In Odessa, teachers are responsible for their own rooms and must do all maintenance before September the first. My teacher friends painted their own walls and one even laid linoleum to hide the cement floors.'

'No,' he said. 'Teachers don't have to do anything like that in America. We have summer school.'

'Summer school?' I asked skeptically. I'd never heard of summer school.

'For kids who need extra help.'

'Maybe I could come with you today. It would be interesting to see where you work.'

'No!'

My eyes widened at his instant refusal.

'No, you should rest up. Take it easy on your first day here. Besides, the kids are shy.'

I supposed that if they didn't do well in school, it made sense they wouldn't want to be observed.

He opened a cupboard, took out a large box and poured its contents into a bowl, then added milk. He sat at the counter and crunched down on the dry bits. It reminded me of a recent arrival in Odessa – commercial pet food. Our foreign neighbor bought it for her cat.

'Want some?' he asked.

I shook my head. 'What is it?'

'Cereal. It's good for you.'

He slid the box over the counter to me and I read the ingredients and couldn't pronounce most of them. I asked for oatmeal, which is what Boba always made for me. I asked to call Boba to tell her that I'd arrived. He mumbled, 'Hit speed dial one.'

'What?'

'I'm sorry, sweetie. I'm a bear in the morning.' He hugged me.

I thought of how Vlad had been the morning after and asked, 'Are you sorry you invited me?'

'No! God, no.' He dialed the number and gave me a peck on the lips. 'I gotta go to work. Talk to your grandma. I'll be home at five.'

'Allo? Boba, Boba, it's me. You wouldn't believe it here. Just like on television. It's so beautiful. His house is so big. We're not in the city, though. We're in the suburbs.'

'You made the right decision,' she said.

Her voice crackled on the line. She was so far away. I sat down in a daze and touched the fuzzy surface of the white couch and looked at the white walls. I imagined Boba, sitting at our kitchen table staring at nothing. She'd pushed me so hard to leave Odessa that she convinced me that I was right to leave her behind. Yet when the train had pulled away from the station and I saw her face in an unguarded moment – the bleakness, the desolation – I realized her adamancy was just a cover. Oh, Boba.

Finally, curiosity got the better of morosity and I explored my new surroundings, hoping to get an impression of Tristan's life, his personality. I went into his bedroom first, wondering if it would be like Vlad's.

Tristan had a large bed with a plaid, flannel comforter. No books on the nightstand, just a phone and digital clock. When I turned around I saw the wall was covered with all the photos I'd ever sent him. Me on the beach. Boba and me on the sofa. Me at the office. (I'd cut David out of the photo but his hand still rested on my hip.)

The phone rang. I picked it up.

'Hi, sweetie. Miss you already.'

He was so thoughtful.

In the kitchen, I looked at the dishwasher, the appliance my grandmother most coveted. Walking in front of the large, shiny refrigerator I heard a noise and opened the door. Ice cubes dropped into a plastic box. Boba wouldn't believe it! In the cupboard where Tristan kept his cereal were cans of pre-made soup and boxes of Stovetop Stuffing and Rice-a-Roni the San Francisco Treat. In the dining room, I found shelves of books. Tomes of photography such as *A Day in the Life of the Soviet Union*, a set of encyclopedias, and ten books on the Civil War. He didn't have many novels, but he did have the most important one ever written: *Anna Karenina*. This was a reassuring sign.

Moving to the living room, I glanced through his collection of CDs (sixties music) and videocassettes (action films). I walked down the white hall to a small room with a washing machine and dryer. Outside on the back porch, I listened to the quiet and inhaled the fresh air, which smelled of moss and sunshine. I wrapped my arms around my body.

I thought that there would be more noise in the suburbs.

'Hello!' a woman called out.

She was in the house. I ran back in. The intruder had flushed cheeks and frizzy hair, and her eyes were big as they looked at me. I looked at her, too. In Odessa, no one just entered. We kept the door locked at all times.

'Golly, you must be Dora. So nice to meet you.' She put a plate of cookies on the counter and hugged me. 'Nice to meet you. I'm Molly.'

'Daria. I'm happy to meet one of Tristan's friends.'

'Goodness, yes. I've known him ever since I started dating my Toby – he and Tristan were best friends in high school, and that's been twenty some years now. Those are my little ones on the fridge.'

I looked at photos of the two blond darlings. I would have to learn to trust him. It's just that I was used to people lying – bazaar vendors said they had the freshest fruit, then when you got it home, it was spoiled; the government lied – after the accident at Chernobyl, Gorbachev said nothing serious had happened; all the time Olga and I spent together was a lie. Things would be different here.

'Hon, I just stopped by to see if you need anything and to invite you to a barbecue tomorrow.'

I thanked her for thinking of me. And looked forward to my first American party. What kind of food would she serve? Jane told me about Christmas and Thanksgiving, when her mother made pies, mashed potatoes, turkey, stuffing, and cranberry sauce. What were Molly's specialties?

When Tristan came home, he kissed me and said, 'What should we have for dinner?'

My head shot up. He expected me to prepare a meal? 'I don't know how to cook,' I admitted.

His brow furrowed. 'But on the dating site it said all the ladies could cook, sew, knit, wash clothes by hand, and iron. And you cooked me dinner in Odessa ...'

Lie-lay-lain. Lie-lied-lied. 'Actually,' I looked down at the beige carpet, 'it was my Boba who cooked all the meals. I never learned how. She said my career would be more important than learning to make borscht. But those sites are right, these are skills that our women have.'

He was silent a long moment. 'So you don't know how to cook at all? You lied?'

'I'm sorry.' I gnawed at my bottom lip, waiting for him to say something, but he just looked at me. What if he sent me home because I couldn't cook? 'Are you sorry you chose me?'

'No,' he took me in his arms. 'I bet you have other skills.'

There was a gleam in his eye.

'I bet I do,' I confirmed, thinking of my ability to hold off men with words.

'We can cook together. I can teach you to cook.'

'I'd like that.'

He hugged me. 'Anyway, I didn't mean you should cook. It's

196

your first day here. Let's relax. Hang out. I meant what should we order? Pizza? Tacos? Burgers? They deliver.'

Food delivered right to the door?

We decided on pizza, half cheese, half supreme. 'See,' he said as he hung up the phone. 'You don't need to know how to cook or clean – you're in America. Just tell me what you want and it's yours.'

I looked at the fireplace. 'I would love to have a fire, but I guess it will have to wait until it's cold outside …'

'Hell, no,' he said. 'I'll just crank up the air-conditioning and then build one.'

We sat on the sofa eating pizza on paper plates and watching the fire roar. After dinner, we threw the plates and the box on the flames. I'd never lived like this before.

Knowing we would have a feast at Molly's, I didn't eat anything for breakfast or lunch. I was excited to meet Tristan's friends and wore my midnight blue dress which caressed my calves when I walked. When Tristan came out of his bedroom wearing jeans, I was surprised but didn't say anything. He, on the other hand, said, 'Why all the black? You always look like you're headed to a funeral, sweetheart.' I looked down at my dress and went from feeling beautiful to feeling like an overdressed crow. In Odessa, like most cities, people wore dark clothes. I didn't have spare money for casual attire – everything I bought had to be suitable for work. When I got home from the office, I changed into a housecoat Boba had sewn for me.

We drove to Molly's, though Tristan said it was only a fifteen-minute walk. I asked if we could buy her a bouquet, but he insisted it wasn't necessary. I felt uncomfortable about visiting someone empty handed. In Odessa, only the rudest, most uncultured swine would not bring a gift to a hostess.

A banner over the door proclaimed, 'Welcome, Dora!' I smiled. They'd almost got it right. I wanted to ring the doorbell, but Tristan said we were family and walked in. The interior looked just like Tristan's – white walls and beige carpet. Phrases from several conversations came to me. Tristan advanced, but I wanted to stop and listen, to savor the moment. To be surrounded by

English. My former teacher Maria Pavlovna would be so thrilled to hear these words.

'I was just like holy smokes.'

'He's mulching. He's never mulched before.'

'She shouldn't push it.'

'The bump on his forehead stuck out an inch. He was on the flimsy ladder, not the good one. It's so hard to keep him off the roof!'

This was what I wanted. English all around me, all the time. People laughing and chatting. It felt fabulous.

When we entered the living room, the talk stopped. Tristan grinned and clamped his arm around my shoulder. People stared. I was not offended. Odessan women are striking.

'This is my new fiancée.'

New fiancée? That made it sound like he'd had another one. No! Quit being so suspicious!

They were silent a moment longer, until a man came forward, grabbed my hand, and shook it vigorously. 'So you're the little Russian gal Tristan saved.'

Saved?

A woman Tristan's age handed me a pile of worn children's books. '*The Three Little Pigs*,' I read aloud. 'Thank you.'

'They're to help you learn English,' she said loudly and slowly.

'Thank you.'

'Bet yer thankful ta be outta there,' another said. 'You sure are a purdy thing.'

'Aren't you glad to be in America, honey? Bet it was rough in Russia.'

'Actually, I'm from Ukraine.'

'Boy, that communism. That's a toughie,' a man said as he stroked his beard.

The others greeted me in the same fashion. Interesting that they perceived me as some sort of refugee. 'I come from Odessa, a port city on the Black Sea. We have the third most beautiful opera house in the world. The weather is mild and people come from all over the world, especially Moscow, Kiev, and St. Petersburg, to spend time at our beaches. Odessa is in Ukraine. Ukraine and Russia are separate and distinct.'

Was it just me, or had their eyes glazed over? They didn't say anything or ask any questions. Perhaps I should have used Valentina's ample example ... Once, at a social, she'd drunk much too much vodka and I heard her explain the former Soviet Union to an American, who luckily had also had too much to drink. 'You see, my dear man, the USSR is like a breast,' she said in her deep voice as she ran her hands over her large bosoms for emphasis. 'Think of Russia as the pale fleshy part. It is large but who really focuses on it? No one. Everyone stares at the nipples – smaller, but more colorful and more interesting. The part that nourishes the world. The nipple is Ukraine, the breadbasket of the former Soviet Union.'

I smiled at the memory, at the kind people in front of me.

'She just loves it here,' Tristan said. 'The first thing she did was play with the garage door opener. Up and down, up and down. Isn't that right, sweetheart?' He mimicked me – eyes wide, mouth agape. 'Hell, the minute I leave for work, she's probably out there hitting the button and watching the damn thing go up and down.'

People laughed. I felt like an idiot and vowed never to be caught off guard again.

'She's blushing,' a woman said. 'You shouldn't embarrass her.'

Tristan hugged me. 'I'm sorry, sweetie. I'm just teasing.'

Eventually, the laughter subsided and the focus turned to other things, notably the junior high football team.

Molly came into the living room and said, 'Please God, don't let Peter break any bones. I can't believe I let him play. That kid will be the death of me.' She pulled me away from Tristan and led me into the kitchen. 'We're so glad Tristan found you. Help yourself. Don't be shy.'

I looked at the table and read the bright labels on the large bags: Doritos, Cheetos, Fritos. There were also store-bought dips, pickles, ketchup, cans of cola and beer, a bucket of potato salad, and a tray of tomato, lettuce, and onion. I was disappointed. In Odessa, the time and effort put into planning a meal is a gauge of the importance of the guest.

A man opened the sliding glass door and asked, 'Who wants a weenie?'

Molly whispered something in his ear. He looked at me and said, 'You must be Dora. I'm Toby. We're so glad to meet you.'

He hugged me. It would take time for me to adapt to this effusive greeting. Looking me up and down, he slapped Tristan on the back and said, 'You done good, bro!'

My stomach roared; I coughed to camouflage the noise. Molly gave me a paper plate on which I put tomato, lettuce, onion, and pickles. People piled food on their plates and we sat at a picnic table. As he watched me devour the vegetables, Toby said, 'For a skinny thing, you sure can eat a lot. Don't you want a hot dog?'

Before I could tell him that I was a vegetarian, Tristan said, 'Russians are so poor, they don't ever get to eat meat, so she doesn't like it. Probably doesn't know what it tastes like.'

People nodded, as though Tristan was an authority because he'd been there once for five days. I bit back a scathing comment and said, 'Actually, many Russians *and Ukrainians* enjoy eating meat, but I'm a vegetarian.' When I was thirteen, my class spent a week taking care of animals on a communal farm. It was the first time I had come face to face with my dinner. How could I eat something with eyes? With a soul? After that, Boba and I never ate meat again.

'Nothing wrong with being a vegetarian,' Molly said kindly. 'My niece who goes to Berkeley is one.'

People ate and spoke under the warm sun. I sipped the tart cola and listened. The woman who'd given me the children's books said, 'I just don't know about that Rita. Brownie needs hip replacement surgery and she won't spring for it. When she wouldn't pay the two thousand dollars, well, I knew exactly what kind of person she was ... I said I wouldn't talk to her again unless she treated that dog right.'

When I understood that the two thousand dollars was for a surgery for a dog, the Coke came flying out of my mouth. I started coughing and Tristan whacked me on the back.

'All right, babe?' he asked.

He and Toby went to get another beer. The alarms in my head went off. I didn't leave Ukraine to avoid our problem men only to find myself with an American alcoholic. I had to be careful. My three-month visa would give me time to get to know him.

'What do you think of Emerson?' the woman sitting on my left asked. She was wearing a tie-dyed shirt and skirt, and her hair was so long that she could practically sit on it. The sky was blue and we were sitting in a garden. It was just as idyllic as the scenes I'd seen on American television shows. I pinched myself and responded, 'I still can't believe that I'm here. It's only been two days, but so far I've enjoyed the calm. How long have you been here?'

'Ten years now. I moved to get away from L.A. I have my own store in Paloma, a town just down the road. I make scented candles and soaps.'

'I'd love to see your shop.' What an accomplished woman: an artist *and* a businesswoman. It seemed everything was possible in America.

A small diamond twinkled on her left hand. Instinctively, my hand went to my chest to feel my own ring, tucked away from prying eyes. 'Would it be impolite to ask if you're engaged?'

She laughed. 'Not at all. Yes, I've been engaged for eight years now.' She paused to let the surprise sink in. 'See, my fiancé and I came here from different directions, and the first thing we each did was build a home. For my log cabin, I did everything from dig the hole, pour the cement, and cut and stack the logs. Jason put as much effort into his geodesic dome. But now neither one of us wants to move. So we spend half the week at my place and the other half at his.'

People here had such different problems. In Odessa there wasn't enough housing. Young, and not so young, couples often had to live with their parents. Americans had so much they couldn't decide where to live.

'How do you know Tristan?' I asked.

'I don't know him very well. Molly invited me because I'm her best friend. I'm Serenity, by the way.'

She stuck out her hand. I shook it. 'Daria.'

'I didn't think *Dora* sounded Ukrainian,' she said with a laugh.

Molly cut a chocolate cake and asked who wanted some. People said, 'Me! Me!' But I didn't say anything.

'Would you like a piece?' Molly asked, her eyes warm and friendly, a blond twin wrapped around each of her bare legs. The knife blade was covered in frosting. The air smelled like chocolate. My mouth felt dry and empty like a desert. How I wanted a slice of the moist, sinful cake.

'No, thank you,' I said politely. And waited. She didn't insist. Instead, she turned to Serenity, who said, 'You don't have to ask me twice.'

Molly gave her my slice.

In Odessa, a hostess politely offers and the guest politely declines. You see, after the Great Patriotic War, when food was scarce, a hostess didn't always have extra. And guests certainly didn't want to take food if there wasn't enough. So a system was devised. A hostess offers, a guest declines. This way no one loses face. If she is earnest, the hostess will offer again and again, insisting that the guest partake. Only then may the guest accept. Today, I learned an important lesson. In America, people don't ask twice.

If you want something, you'd better take it.

On Saturday, I woke up early and waited for Tristan. He was clearly not a morning person. He walked arms out like a zombie to the kitchen and poured cereal into his bowl.

'Maybe we could go to San Francisco today,' I said.

He laughed. 'Sweetie, the city is half a day away. Too far for a daytrip. How 'bout we go for a hike?'

'The drive from the airport didn't seem that far.'

'You fell asleep after fifteen minutes. It's a four-hour trip.'

'But you said you lived near San Francisco. That's what you said.'

'Relatively speaking, we do live close to San Fran. We could live in Miami – now that would be far!' He laughed again.

Thoughts swept into my mind like gusts of wind. Was he telling the truth? Where were we? My throat constricted and I felt the wide open space of Emerson, no longer anchored by the buildings and museums and hotels and restaurants and theaters and traffic – elements that had been constants for me. I sank down on the couch and hacked, trying to get my throat to reopen.

'Come on, honey,' he said blithely. 'Let's get out into nature, that'll help you breathe better.'

He pulled me up and we went for a walk in the woods. I followed him through the trees. Neither of us said much. I couldn't help but feel that he had lied. He'd told me he lived near San Francisco.

That's what he said. Four hours. An eternity. I tried to make the best of things as Boba always told me to do. I took a deep breath and looked at the silent beauty of the woods. (It was so very quiet. I found it disquieting …) I looked at the flowers near the trail and asked, 'What's the name of that flower?'

'The pink one? That's Liza Jane.'

I couldn't help it. I laughed.

'The white one is Russell,' he added.

'And that tree?' I pointed to the tall pine.

'That's Melissa,' he replied.

'Nice to meet you, Melissa,' I said. We both laughed.

He held out his hand and I entwined my fingers through his.

That evening I called Jane in Montana. She couldn't believe I was in America. 'Obviously you are, though,' she said. 'The phone line is so clear.' We calculated that I'd arrived in the States only hours before she had. 'So you weren't kidding when you said you'd be here before me. And that's why you asked so many questions about California … and rednecks.' She asked who I was with. I said nothing. 'Tell me in Russian,' she urged. How could she know that Tristan was in the background pretending not to listen?

'He lied. He said he lived near San Francisco,' I told her quickly in Russian. 'But he lives four hours away.'

'Actually, that isn't a lie,' she responded in Russian. 'My sister lives five hours from my parents, and we consider that close. It's in the same state and it's not a bad drive. Maybe a person from New York City or Odessa would have a different perception of distance.'

Different perceptions. An interesting notion.

'What is he like?' she asked.

'Gentle. Patient. His house is big. He gave me a computer. He has nice friends.'

'When I visit Tans, we can meet in San Francisco for a weekend.'

When I hung up the phone, Tristan asked, 'Why were you speaking in Russian?'

'It's my native language.'

'I know a few words. Maybe you could teach me some more.' His lips brushed against mine. 'How do you say "kiss"?'

'I kiss you. *Tseluyou.*'

'*Slyouyou,*' he said.

He sounded like the drunken sailors on our ships.

'*Slyouyou, slyouyou,*' he said, leaning towards me. He wrapped his arms around me and kissed me again. 'Marry me.'

I kissed him back to avoid answering.

Chapter 15

Our letters never start with the paltry 'dear.' Salutations – in the true Odessan style – are two lines long. And no comma either – only an exclamation point will do for a proper greeting.

Hello, my dear Boba!
Greetings from the American Dream!

Everything here is wonderful and automatic – you don't even have to flush the toilet in America! Unbelievable! The road from the airport to Tristan's home was as smooth as rails. As excited as I was, I actually fell asleep, can you believe it?

Tristan said it would be easy for me to get a job as an engineer. He said that he could really talk to me. I worried that he'd be upset when he learned that I couldn't cook. But he said that he liked to cook, that he wants us to cook together. He said he can teach me. And in the meantime, he can call the restaurant and tell them what we want to eat, and they deliver it! Just like in the movies!

Tristan's house is huge! He has a fireplace, and we sit and talk in front of a roaring fire. In America, they have air-conditioning. Cool air circulates through vents so you don't get too warm. Tristan and his friends have it. So does the supermarket. Remember our old flat and how hot it got in summer? How we joked that we'd already gone to hell?

He said that he didn't make much money as a teacher, but clearly he was being modest. He must be rich. Not only does he not live with his parents, he has his own house – everyone has their own home and their own yards. There is not one single apartment in this whole suburb – can you believe it?

He said he wants children with me. He said we could be a real
family.
 All my love,
 Dasha

In Yosemite National Park, exactly three weeks after my arrival,
surrounded by sequoias and ferns, Tristan got down on one knee
and presented me with a ring. My hand flew to my chest, where
I felt another engagement ring warm against my body. *Give-gave-
given.*

'I haven't even been here a month. There's so much we don't
know about each other ...'

'I know I want to marry you. You're so beautiful,' he said, sliding
the ring onto my finger. 'I want everyone to see that you belong to
me. I love you.' He stood and hugged me tight. *Find-found-found.*

I stared at the ring. 'You don't have to give me an answer. Just
think about it. You and me happy in America.'

In the evenings, we continued to chat on the sofa. He told me
about his older brother Haliburt, a minister everyone called Hal,
who lived near Seattle. 'After Mom died, our dad just disappeared,
man. He was there, but he wasn't, you know what I mean? I owe
Hal so much. He kept everything together. Made sure we had food
on the table, made sure I went to school. I was always pushing it,
but Hal pushed back and made sure I did the right thing.' Tristan
shook his head. 'He's still bailing me out. When I told him how I
felt about you, he paid for your plane ticket since my credit cards
were maxed out.'

I wasn't sure what he meant. Maxed out?

He kissed me gently, rubbed my back, and ran his fingers
through my hair. His hands inched lower and lower. I don't know
why his hand on my breast made me stiffen, why his body on
mine made me more rigid than Boba's ironing board. After a few
minutes, I pushed him away. I told myself my reaction was normal
and that this time I wouldn't forget the most famous Odessan
proverb: Not all who make love make a marriage. I wouldn't be
had again.

Tristan untangled himself from me and said, 'Thank you
for saving yourself for me. Of course, I respect you.' I didn't

correct him, grateful that he'd invented himself a reason for my involuntary refusal of an otherwise mostly perfect union.

Jane and I decided to meet in San Francisco for a long weekend. I was so looking forward to seeing her. In Tristan's truck, I couldn't sit still. My toes tapped with excitement.

'Your friend lives on Snob Hill,' Tristan said snidely.

'You'll love Jane.' I just wasn't sure she would love him. Something strange had happened: in the miles from Emerson to San Francisco, he'd grown surly.

As the truck climbed higher and higher, I saw the Victorian homes featured in photos and movies. Between city blocks, I caught glimpses of the bay. What a breathtaking city!

We parked behind a Jaguar. Jane came running out of the house followed by Tans. My eyes started to water when I saw her. It had been weeks since I'd seen a familiar face. She took me in her arms and crooned all the words I needed to hear. She said them all in Russian, 'You're so brave, so pretty, so smart. Everything will be fine, you'll be fine.' Eyeing the ring on my finger, she added, 'Just don't rush into anything. Time will show.'

When I stepped away, I ran my fingers through her hair, which was as unruly as ever. I was so happy to see my Jane that I couldn't stop touching her. I stroked her face, her arms. I brushed away imaginary wrinkles from her white blouse. I tucked a stray lock of hair behind her ear, then twisted my arms around hers. Touching her felt like touching my native city again, like I was holding a piece of home in my hands.

Tans gave me an enthusiastic hug and kissed my cheeks, chin, and forehead, tickling my face with his mustache. Tristan looked at them warily. Tans noticed Tristan's sour face and greeted him man to man, with a strong handshake and a phrase indicating that they should give us women time together. Tans walked Tristan up the steps of the elegant four-story Victorian and ushered him in. He shot Jane a look that said *He's not one of us*.

The flat was spacious and dark. The blinds were down. Perhaps because Tans knew he looked better in soft light. He seemed aware of things like that. We walked down the darkened hall to the kitchen, the heart of the home, which was full of friends – Jane said Tans hated to be alone, so at any given time, there were at least ten people at his flat. The table was a scarred hunk of wood surrounded by mismatched chairs. I touched the fat spider burners of the massive stove and felt nostalgic for Boba and Odessa.

Jane introduced me to Zora and Gambino – accountants by day, musicians by night. Lea, a woman with no angles, only curves, sang with Zora. When she looked at me a little too intently, Jane told me in Russian that the woman was 'pink.' (In Odessan slang, it means lesbian.) Tans's best friend Jonothan wore a bright silk shirt and was young enough to be Tans's son. In Russian, we would call him *smooglie*, swarthy. We would also call him well built, for his shoulders and upper arms were muscled like Vlad's. He stared at Jane, who carefully ignored him. Jono's sister, a lanky stockbroker, was so proud of her G-string decorated with a sparkly butterfly that she lowered her trousers to show everyone.

'Come meet my friend Daria,' Jane said.

She pulled up her trousers, asked, 'Is that an engagement ring, *ma chérie?*' and took my hands in hers. She squinted at the diamond and said, 'Darling! That speck of dust isn't a reason to get married! It's a reason to get divorced.'

Tristan turned red. Jane glared at her. My hand flew to my chest.

'Behave!' Jono warned. 'Or you can spend your nights in a rented conference room at the Sheraton with the other low-life sharks.'

She shuddered at the threat.

'Size doesn't matter,' I told her, taking Tristan's hand. 'Intentions do. Tristan called faithfully, wrote every day, and traveled to Odessa, Ukraine. No other man I know would have put in so much time, effort and money.'

Tristan looked at me gratefully and Tans's friends looked at me with interest. I thought of Vlad, who would have defended himself. Then I remembered how he'd given me jewels and vanished after he'd got what he wanted.

Perhaps to erase the awkwardness, Tans swept Jane into his arms and said, 'Let's dance, darling.' Jane laughed but she didn't say no. They swayed together. I smiled; they were such an unlikely couple. Jane was four inches taller and three decades younger. Tans met my gaze. I looked into his eyes and saw something disturbing in them. Then he smiled, and I saw that I was being ridiculous. Why did I have to be so suspicious? Why couldn't I relax and enjoy myself, instead of sizing everything and everyone up?

When the song faded away, Tans told everyone I was from Odessa. He described the gracious people and the gorgeous architecture. Gambino asked if the staircase was as majestic in real life as it was in the film *Battleship Potemkin*. Jono recommended a book about the Black Sea. Zora said her great-grandparents had lived a thirty-minute wagon ride from Odessa. They emigrated in 1910 after a pogrom had left many homes in their village charred.

They were so kind that I nearly cried in relief. No one assumed that because I was from Ukraine (Yes, they'd actually heard of the Ukraine!) I was destitute, or that Tristan had 'saved' me. In fact, they thought that I saved him! Jane and Tans and their friends saw me for who I really was.

Tans's personal library was richer than the Emerson bookmobile, which came only once a week, Fridays from nine to noon. In the dining room, lined with shelves of leather-bound books, there was a constant buffet on a formal table. Freshly squeezed orange juice. Coffee so rich, it could have been served in Turkey. And the food. Oh, the food! Hummus so creamy. A potato salad so light and golden it rivaled my Boba's. Dolmas wrapped by hand. Not since I had been home with Boba had my stomach so rejoiced. Food – how it feeds the soul, feeds the memory, feeds the needs we don't even know we have. More than one person watched me devour the bundles of rice wrapped in grape leaves.

Jane and I sat across from Tans and told him how wonderful it all was. He basked in our praise, his mustache twitching with pleasure. Tristan slumped down beside me, 'What am I supposed to eat? This's all different.' Diffrnt.

'Would you like to try the potato salad?' Jane asked. 'It's delicious. Almost as good as Boba's. Let me get you a plate.'

In Odessa, women serve the men. Jane told me that in America women didn't serve anyone. So I knew this was a big gesture on her part and was grateful.

He perked up when she put the plate in front of him. 'Boba did make the best, didn't she?'

Tans protested good-naturedly that his was the best.

'Maybe in San Francisco,' Jane said.

'Let's give him California,' Tristan said.

'But Boba has the title for the universe,' I concluded.

I was thrilled that they were getting along. That everyone was making an effort. How I wanted Jane to like him.

There was a constant coming and going of artists and singers and intellectuals. *This* was what I expected when Tristan had told me he lived near San Francisco. *This* was what I wanted. I felt at home with these people. They were witty and clever and amusing. Several took me aside and said, 'When you decide to leave that putz, I'll help. Call me.' The women slipped me fifty dollars so I wouldn't be completely dependent on him. I tried to refuse, but they insisted that I could pay them back. Although I appreciated their kindness, I felt embarrassed for Tristan, and hurt for him that he'd been rejected. But I could also understand why.

Tans, Jane, and their friends weren't seeing him at his best, in his Emerson aquarium surrounded by familiar greenery.

As usual, I woke up at 6 a.m. Some of Tans's guests were just leaving. I sat at the kitchen table with a burning-hot glass full of coffee in my hands and savored the moment. I liked to get up early, to have the world to myself. When Jane joined me, we spoke Russian for hours. We had the kitchen to ourselves and no one was there to be offended by our escape into another language. Tans seemed to understand how important it was that Jane and I had time together. He tried to occupy Tristan. For most of the day, she and I moved from room to room. With Tans's running interference, Tristan was always a room behind.

I asked Jane to tell me about Montana, about life with Tans. I was too embarrassed to talk about my life. How could I explain? How could I tell Jane things I didn't understand myself? How I'd fallen in love with Tristan before I met him. How here and now I wasn't sure that I still loved him. How could I tell her when I could barely admit it to myself?

After lunch, Tristan thoughtfully offered to take Jane and me on a tour of San Francisco. He drove us to the Fisherman's Wharf, which was packed solid with tourists, but I appreciated the gesture nonetheless and bought some postcards for Boba. Then we went to a park, where families picnicked, children played, friends threw Frisbees, couples cuddled on the grass. In Emerson, people walked or jogged exactly thirty minutes for exercise, or not at all. They drove to the store, even if they lived only three blocks away. I marveled at these throngs of people who, like me, were happy to spend a glorious day out of doors.

Tristan offered to buy us tea at the Japanese Garden. Jane and I found a table and he went to order. I felt proud that he had given us such a *lovely* day. I wanted Jane to like him.

He returned with a tray. 'Can you believe it? Eleven dollars for tea?'

Shame washed over me. Jane had paid for her plane ticket to San Francisco, and he complained about spending a few dollars. I could barely meet her gaze. An Odessan man would never talk about the price. It's uncultured.

'They forgot to give us napkins.' He went back to the counter.

In her distinctive Russian (Jane sounded like an old Odessan lady because her vocabulary and inflection were learned from her neighbor, a lavender-haired pensioner with an attitude), she said, 'Eleven dollars for tea?'

We giggled.

'Seriously,' she continued, 'Tans and his friends can be intimidating. It's probably not easy for Tristan. It was nice of him to take us around today.'

'It was,' I agreed, happy that she appreciated him, at least a little. 'Men just like to grumble so that we acknowledge them.'

'Sound the horn and praise him,' she said as he returned with a handful of napkins.

'Beeeep!' I squealed out like a schoolgirl.

My eyes met Jane's, and I burst out laughing. So did she.

'What's so funny?' Tristan asked.

How could I tell him that *he* was what we found amusing?

I loved America. I loved the wide, clean streets. I loved the spacious wood homes set on invincible green lawns. I loved the choices at the supermarket – from the pre-made food to the cleaning products. I loved living in a place where no one stole light bulbs in hallways, where no one pissed in the elevator, where dust didn't cover my shoes, the streets, the sidewalks, the buildings. I loved the light that filtered through Tristan's home. I loved the distance between houses. Privacy. What a wonderful concept. I loved the calm. No bottles clanging together, no one stomping on the ceiling, no family fights seeping through the walls, no babies wailing, no babushkas complaining, no televisions blaring. It was as though someone had pressed the mute button on the soundtrack of my life.

I loved living in a house – not waking up to the smell of a neighbor's burned toast in the morning, not falling asleep to another's techno music at night. I didn't miss the domestic disputes of the Sebova household – the missus screaming that the mister was an alcoholic, the mister shouting back that if he was it was because of her. I didn't miss Petr Ivanovich's incessant hammering.

In America, the houses were unique. So were the people. Everything was so personal. Even license plates held messages – from *Go Packers!* on a Jeep to *Thanx Dad* on a red convertible. If there was a child in the car, there was a 'Baby on Board' sign. I couldn't say Americans wore their hearts on their sleeve, but they did wear their logos on their chest. Nike. Coke. Pepsi. The flag was everywhere – on sweaters, on cars, hung outside people's homes as well as at businesses. In Odessa, no one wore a Ukrainian flag on their chest, I could tell you that. In Odessa, the bakery sign read *Hleb*, or bread; here, it was Mama's Little Bakery. Here it's not just 'restaurant,' it's Ruby's Café or Aunt Sarah's Pancake House.

Above all, I loved listening to the language, to all the contractions and contradictions that my English teacher Maria Pavlovna never taught us: gimme, gotta, gonna, wanna. Perhaps she didn't know they existed. I wrote down new words in my notebook. Spiffy. Snarl. Stuck up. Dead meat. Dude. Even if I didn't recognize them, often I could tell their meaning by the person's expression.

I loved America. I loved that drivers let me cross the street instead of trying to mow me down. I loved the post office personnel, so cheerful when I sent letters to Boba. I loved the way total strangers talked to me. When I went to the doctor's office for a blood test, the nurse came out wearing all white, looking like a shiny star, and said in a beautiful voice, 'Daria Kirilenko, we're waiting for you.' I felt like a princess. At the supermarket, a teen put my purchases in bags. In the stores, the saleswomen asked if I was looking for anything in particular. In the café, the waitress brought a glass of ice water with the menu and said, 'Take your time.' Everyone said, 'Hi, how ya doin'?' These small courtesies filled me with gratitude. No strangers were nice like this in Odessa unless they wanted something.

Sometimes, I looked around in wonder. But the Americans didn't seem to notice the thoughtfulness surrounding them. How they took things for granted. Everything was easy here. Everything worked all the time – no shortages, no blackouts. Everything was perfect.

My visa would be up in six weeks. I was passionate about America, but not about Tristan. Maybe I'd learn to love him, like oatmeal. Like the way I grew to appreciate David. I didn't know what to do. I could call Jane, who would tell me I shouldn't marry him. Or I could call Boba, who would say I should.

I dialed and said, 'I'm not sure what to do.'

'You went to America to get married.'

'I don't think I love him,' I said in a small voice.

'Does he love you?' Boba asked.

'*Da.*'

'My little sparrow, give him a chance. There's nothing for you here. You looked for an engineering job for six months and ended up a secretary. Think about your friend Maria, who graduated first in her class at the conservatory and has a voice like an angel. And in Odessa, she's a waitress. It's not right. It's just not right. But that's the way it is. Don't come home. There is nothing for you here. Remember how lucky you are to be in America. Passion fades. Love grows. Security is the most important thing.'

She was right. I should marry Tristan. That's why I'd come. He wanted to marry me, wanted children with me. He was honest, decent, and dependable, unlike Vlad. He'd been a perfect gentleman. And he was American.

And if I married him, I could stay in America.

Part II

Three things in this world he loved:
Evensong, white peacocks
And worn maps of America.

He didn't like crying children,
Tea with raspberry jam
Or hysterical women.

And I was his wife.

– Anna Akhmatova

Chapter 16

My Darling Boba, the best Grandmother in the world!
Greetings and love from Emerson!

Waiting impatiently for a letter from you. Please do write! It would make me so happy.

You'd be surprised by so many things here. People have yards, but no gardens. They buy their fruits and vegetables at the supermarket. They don't can at all, can you believe it? Tristan's friend Molly says she has enough to do without worrying about that. She wrote down the names of the best brands so that I wouldn't be confused about which ones to choose. There are over one hundred kinds of shampoo and toothpaste. There are so many different brands of jams and jellies. The best raspberry jam here isn't half as tasty as yours … Next year, I am planning on growing my own tomatoes, potatoes, and strawberries. What else do you think I should plant?

The sparrows are plump and happy here. People are open and friendly. You can get exactly what you want. In a café in Odessa, we are lucky to get real coffee rather than instant. We are lucky if it comes to the table warm. In San Francisco, when Jane and I went for a coffee, she ordered a 'half caff skinny extra hot latte easy on the foam with a shot of vanilla.' When it was my turn to order, I didn't know what to say! Can you imagine the look the waitress would shoot you if you tried such a thing in Odessa?

I miss your voice, your jokes, your stories. Won't you consider coming to visit? When he was in Odessa, Tristan said you could come and live with us. I do hope you'll think about it. I want you to see this paradise for yourself.

All my love,
Dasha

Freeze-froze-frozen. Ring-rang-rung. I put on the velvet dress that Boba had sewn for me. Tristan looked handsome in his khaki trousers and blue button-down shirt I'd spent an hour ironing. He held my hand tight. His palms were sweaty. So were mine. He kept pushing wisps of hair behind my ear, I kept untucking them – I'd left them down on purpose. Little by little, everyone arrived. *Everyone.* Everyone was no one I knew. Forty people – the women in dresses, the men in jeans, the boisterous children climbing on furniture and knocking down lamps – clogged the dining room. I gave the little ones sweets and told them that they would soon grow up and all their dreams would come true. Harried mothers handed me casseroles. I accepted their offerings with the smile and kind words Boba had instilled in me.

Boba.

I felt a pang. If only she could have come. Or my mother. Or even Jane. Then I remembered: I wasn't talking to Jane. Not after what she said to me. She still called, begging me to open up, but I only spoke about the weather until she tired and hung up.

Hal, an older, jowly version of Tristan, squeezed me in a grip that felt like the jaws of life. Hal was a minister and his wife Noreen, whose pinched expression gave the impression that her heels were two sizes too small, was holier-than-thou.

'You're a very lucky girl to go from rags to riches,' she said. 'Every woman in your country dreams of coming to the U.S. of A. You should be grateful for all this family has done for you. That other girl wasn't grateful at all.'

'What other girl?' I asked.

Noreen looked to Hal.

'One of Tristan's ex-girlfriends,' Hal said. 'You have to forgive Noreen, she doesn't think anyone is good enough for Tristan.' His tone was as cold as a Siberian winter and he held Noreen's arm so tightly she winced.

Behind them Molly rolled her eyes then winked. Noreen and Hal moved on, and I stood watching all these strangers. As people talked around me and over me, but not to me, I was reminded of the buzzing of a thousand flies.

And to think, this was my wedding day.

I laid my hand on my chest. Of course I thought of him. And of what our wedding in Odessa would have been like. An intimate ceremony, certainly, followed by a feast prepared by Boba and me. Well, mostly Boba, but I would have helped. Glasses raised to me, the beautiful bride; a toast to the groom, lucky in love; another to Boba for raising such a granddaughter; a final word of praise for his mother, so courageous in bringing up three strong sons. Vlad and I would feed each other a piece of braided bread so that we never go hungry, dipped in salt so that life always has flavor. He would smile tenderly. I'd lick the salt from his fingers ... No. I shook my head. That gangster was not welcome at this celebration.

Everyone got in their cars and drove to a patch of forest. Tristan declared that since I hadn't gone to service in the time I'd been in the States that I was like him: 'not churchy.' I thought of telling him about the synagogues in Odessa that had been destroyed, the rampant anti-Semitism. I wanted to remind him that religion had been forbidden in the Soviet Empire. After perestroika, people were leery about returning. Many like me didn't know how to return.

But I remained silent, fearing that he would get it wrong again, like when he said I didn't eat meat because there was none. He clearly had problems with interpretation.

Plus, he'd said, after spending so much 'dough' to get me to America, we didn't have much left for 'frivolous things like weddings.' He decided that we would have ours as God intended, in a wooded area outside of Emerson. We exchanged our rings solemnly. The only sound was the birds chirping. It seemed like a good omen.

We returned to Tristan's house for the 'potluck.' No use wasting good money to pay a caterer, he'd said, and asked his friends to supply the food. To me, our reception didn't feel like a celebration at all, just a huge bring-your-own picnic with dishes and paper plates perched on a card table on its last legs. In Odessa, no woman ever asked guests to cook their own dinner. In Odessa, women created feasts, and this effort showed how much they cared. I tried to smile. In America, I'd noticed that people smiled when they were happy, but also when they were nervous or uncertain. No one noticed that my smile was of the melancholy variety. They hugged me and called me hon. They wished me well and asked if I was happy. I smiled.

It had all happened so fast. Tristan and I went hiking on Sunday afternoon a week after we returned from San Francisco. He'd been nervous all morning, stuttering and losing his train of thought. We sat on a faded blanket and ate cheese sandwiches. After lunch he got on his knees and pulled me to mine. Holding my hands in his, he looked into my eyes and asked, 'Will you make me the happiest man in the world? Will you marry me?'

Tenderness spread through my body as I understood how difficult it had been for him to work up the courage to propose. No vodka necessary.

'This will be the last time I ask,' he said and squeezed my hand. 'I know what I want. But this has to be what you want, too.'

I thought about what I wanted: security. A home. A child. A real family. An end to the family curse. This was what Boba wanted for me. Tristan had proven himself, unlike Vlad. I looked into Tristan's eyes and saw gentle simplicity. I could trust him. He loved me. We wanted the same things. Why wait? I threw my arms around his neck. 'Yes!'

He kissed me and kissed me and hugged me tight. It felt pleasant. I was thrilled to know I'd be staying in America with a dependable man. He would never just disappear. He would always be there.

'We should get married right away,' he said when we got home.

I nodded, dazed by the conviction of his voice, by the haste of our engagement. But wasn't that why I'd come to America?

'I don't want you changing your mind,' he joked. Then he speaker-phoned Molly. I heard her cry, 'Oh my God! Congratulations!', call Toby, then shout, 'Oh my God!' again. Tristan asked if she thought we could have the wedding in a week. She said she would organize everything: invitations, caterer, hall. He replied that we had 'a budget,' a word that means no money, and suggested we have the reception at home.

I called Jane and asked her to be my maid of honor.

'Oh my God! Of course!'

I noticed that God is always on Americans' lips, on their minds, on their money.

'The ceremony is Friday.'

'This Friday?' she shrieked.

'What's the matter?'

'It's so sudden. You have a three-month visa. Don't you want to use the time to get to know him better?'

'I know all I need to; we want the same things. Why wait?'

She said she had to ask for the time off and check ticket prices. She called back an hour later. 'The last-minute fare is over one thousand dollars. Why Friday? Why a weekday? Why so soon?'

She already knew the answers. She just wanted me to say them. *He doesn't want Jane or Boba to come. He wants us tied together as soon as possible. He doesn't want to give me time to think.* These thoughts were somewhere in my brain. I'm not stupid. But knowing and admitting are two different things.

'He's so much older. And you haven't known him very long. Do you love him?'

The only defense is an offense, that's what we say in Odessa. 'What about you? That Tans is practically a pensioner! Do you love him?'

'Yeah, I love him. And no, I'm not going to marry him.'

'You have that luxury. You're American. I'm here on a visa.'

'Do you love him?' she repeated.

I wanted to.

'Please, please wait,' she pleaded. 'There's no rush. You'll have your whole lives together.'

I heard the frantic notes in her voice: worry, concern, and fear. But I hadn't asked her opinion. I didn't want to hear that I was being hasty or that I was wrong.

'When you gave me advice in Odessa, I always listened to you,' she said. 'I always trusted you. And you were always right. Please trust me now. Don't do this. Don't. Let's try to find another solution. Maybe you can get a work visa. Or find someone else.'

I wanted to hear I was making the right decision. She'd been wrong about Budapest. I could have trusted Tristan. I should have gone. She was wrong about this. And perversely, the way she said no made me want to say yes. She didn't understand Tristan the way I did. She didn't know how kind and thoughtful he could be. And she was practically an old maid anyway. What did she know about marriage? I pulled away from Jane, the voice of reason.

'I have to go. I need to talk to Boba.'

So it wasn't my dream wedding. I was still lucky. I was in America. I would have my own family. I would make new friends. I looked at Molly, who'd greeted, cleaned, and organized the entire day. She had even cooked *vareniki* for the reception. I was touched by her kindness and put three potato ravioli on my plate. God loves three, that's what we say in Odessa.

'I hope they taste all right,' Molly said.

I took a bite and nodded. 'My Boba always says the first time is good, the second time even better. Thank you for bringing a piece of Odessa to Emerson.'

'My pleasure. I made the dough from scratch, just like the recipe said. You Ukrainian gals sure don't do things the easy way.'

So true.

I looked down at my bouquet and touched the red petals. Last night, Molly's husband Toby had come to Tristan's. Looking sheepish, he said he'd been ordered to invite Tristan over for a beer. 'A laid-back bachelor party,' he explained.

Tristan didn't want to leave, but Toby proved to be persuasive. 'Come on, man. When have you ever said no to a brewski?'

'Brewski! Ha! Didn't know you spoke Russian.'

And off they went. I drew a bath, intending to try to relax and reflect on my new life. Reality – the fact that I would be tied to this man for life – was seeping in. I grew more and more nervous. Was Jane right? Should I wait? Now that the date was set, was it too late to have doubts? I stepped into the water. I steeped in the water, thinking thoughts that got as dark as Boba's favorite black tea.

Here is the one thing all Odessan women know: men stray; men leave. They go to sea, they go to see. They go off to war, off to seek their fortune, off with their drinking buddies. But women, women stay. We wait, we wonder. Penelope was the original *Odessitka*. She waited for Odysseus to come home. She waited, she cried, she wondered, maybe she even prayed. What a paragon.

(What an idiot! Jane said.) Women don't leave. Women don't file for divorce. Women endure. We learn in health class that girls mature more quickly, that women are stronger, live longer, can bear children, can bear more, *do* bear more, period. Ask any *Odessitka*. She'll tell you that our men went off to war after war, that Stalin killed our men, and that now there are more women than men. And you don't have to be a capitalist to understand the concept of supply and demand.

Odessitki are taught to be cultured, well bred, feminine, clever, to work hard, to solve problems, to bear the brunt, to accept that some day, we may be alone ... We have staying power. Patience. The man is the king of the castle, even if his castle is a *communalka*. No provision is made for his wife. Sometimes I wonder: when sailors go back to sea, are their wives relieved?

Just as I stepped out of the tepid water, the doorbell rang. I dressed quickly and opened the door. Molly and Serenity grabbed my hands and insisted on whisking me away. They were giggly and fidgety and looked happy. Happy. I went with them. We drove to a bar with neon lights, which looked magical to me. The Step On Inn. Five women waited for us at a table topped with boxes swathed in shiny paper and bows. Introductions were made.

'We wanted to throw you a bridal shower slash bachelorette party!' Serenity exclaimed.

'Thank you. Thank you so much,' I murmured, touched by this unexpected attention.

The barman, who Molly referred to as hunky, came to take our orders.

'Bud Light, please,' Molly said.

'Michelob Light.'

'Diet Coke and rum.'

I had no idea what American women drank, so when the barman turned to me, I replied, 'A cognac, please.'

'Oooh! That's so classy!' Molly said. 'I changed my mind. I'll have one of those.'

'So will I.'

'So will I.'

I was pleased that they wanted what I wanted. The cognac warmed my belly and loosened the tightness in my chest. I felt relaxed, truly relaxed, for the first time since my arrival. We talked and laughed. How I had missed this camaraderie. I thought of Boba, of Valentina, of Jane. I even thought of David and how we sat in the darkened boardroom, drinking cold coffee and talking.

'Open your presents!' Serenity exclaimed, bringing me back to the present.

Gently lifting the paper from the cardboard so I could use it as stationery to write to Boba, I opened the box and pulled out a snippet of silk. When I realized what it was, I blushed and stuffed it back in.

'Show us what you got!' Molly yelled. Her eyes were as wild as her auburn hair.

'A guaranteed wedding night pleaser.'

'And teaser.'

'Open another!'

Frilly undergarments, finer than I had ever had before. Scented candles. Massage oil.

They whooped and whistled. As the barman served another round, Molly whispered something to him and he returned with a bouquet of red roses and white freesia. I caressed the velvety leaves that surrounded the flowers. I couldn't believe that I'd forgotten to order a bouquet and felt such gratitude.

'I hope I'm making the right decision ...' The cognac had loosened my tongue.

'You'll be able to stay if you marry him, right?' Serenity asked.

I nodded.

'You have to stay, we want you to stay,' Molly said.

'That's what I want, too. I'm just not sure ...'

No one said anything for a long moment. They just looked at me. I felt their care and their concern. The bachelorette party seemed suddenly separate from the wedding, from the marriage to come. Finally, Molly said, 'He's a good provider.'

'He's a good provider.'

'A good provider.'

'Good provider,' they echoed.

I buried my nose in the bouquet and inhaled deeply. Molly squeezed my hand. Then Serenity put her arm around my shoulders. We sat like this for the rest of the evening.

* * *

The longer the wedding reception, the longer the marriage, that's what we say in Odessa. Our celebration was over by 9 p.m. On the porch, Toby thumped guests on the back as they passed him on the way to their cars. Molly went through the house with an enormous black garbage bag, clearing away the paper plates and plastic cups. She put two pieces of cake in the freezer for us to eat on our anniversary and discreetly left. Tristan and I stared at each other. Tonight I was moving from the office to the bedroom. I knew what he wanted, and I was curious, too. What would it be like? I liked his hugs and kisses – it felt safe in his arms.

At least, thanks to Vlad, I knew that making love could be wonderful. Spectacular. Hot. Why was I thinking of him? I felt disloyal suddenly. Tristan touched my arms, my back, my hair with the tips of his fingers, as though my body were Braille. I waited to feel a burst of passion, a frisson of lust. His caresses weren't disagreeable.

'Should I use protection?'

I shook my head, since we both wanted children right away. He took off my dress and lay me down on the bed. 'Wow!' he exclaimed as he looked at my breasts. 'Wow!'

Just when I started to relax, he stopped and pulled off his clothes. He pounced, wet kissing me everywhere. *Ride-rode-ridden. Sow-sowed-sewn. Go-went-gone. Grind-ground-ground.* His frenzied movements made me tense. I wrapped my arms around his shoulders and kissed him hard, willing myself to feel desire. I shoved my tongue in his mouth. He groaned and ground his pelvis to mine. I arched my body towards his, hoping our hip bones would strike together and ignite a spark that would grow into something more.

Greeting Boba, from a very happy bride!

Yesterday, Tristan and I were married. How we both wished that you could have been here to celebrate our joy! I wore the dress you made me and so many people came to wish us well! Tristan has so many friends and it was lovely that his brother and sister-in-law could attend. In fact Hal is a holy man! It was so special to have family not only there, but to perform the ceremony! Soon you will be a great-grandmother! I kiss you, Dasha

*   *   *

I mailed the letter in a package with the all beautiful cards we had received, and we left for our honeymoon. Although I had never camped ('roughing it' – going without water and electricity – never sounds like much fun to people who have done so for a portion of their lives), I was thrilled to go to the Pacific. There is nothing like the sea. The sound of the waves hitting the sand. The constancy of the tide. The rhythm of a mother rocking a child to sleep. The sand and the water as old as time itself. The smell of the salt and mist. The mystery of it all as you look out at the horizon and see the blue-gray sea meet the gray-blue sky and you have the impression that heaven does meet the earth. At least somewhere.

'As a scout leader, I know all the good sites,' he said as he unloaded the food from the truck. He dug a shallow hole and built a fire. We sat side by side, holding hands, looking out at the waves.

He went back into the trees and came back with two slim branches. With his knife, he scraped away the bark at the tip.

'What's it for?' I asked when he handed me one.

'You'll see.'

He reached into the food box and grabbed a plastic bag. He tore it open and pulled out a white spongy confection. I watched him pierce it with a stick and hold it over the fire. 'Go ahead, take a marshmallow,' he encouraged, handing them to me.

When his was golden and bubbly, he pulled it off the stick and put it on a bar of chocolate which he slid between two crackers. I did the same.

'Isn't this the best?' he asked after he finished his. 'Want some more? Get it? They're called S'mores.'

I nodded.

'I have so much to teach you,' he said.

He was kind and gentle. I'd made the right choice. It was fate.

So why did I constantly touch my palm to my chest to feel the diamond ring, safely tucked underneath my blouse? I put the necklace on after Tristan went to work and took it off before he got home. I don't know why I still wore it. At first, it was so that no one would find it, on the train to Kiev, then at the airport ...

I should have been able to take it off for good. That part of my life was over. I wouldn't take any steps backward. I would only go forward.

But lately, I forgot to take it off before he arrived. Lately, I left it on until bedtime. It comforted me. I saw Boba hand it to me, heard her say, 'It could save you.' I saw Vlad before me on his knees.

Before bed one evening, Tristan took off my blouse and froze when he saw the ring. He choked out the word, 'Who?'

I froze. *Tell-told-told.*

'Who gave you that?' he asked.

'What did you say?' I made him repeat himself – an old Odessan trick – to give myself ten extra seconds to think of a suitable reply.

'Who gave you that ring?' he asked, his voice hard.

'Boba did ... right before she said goodbye.'

I bit my lip. In Odessa, we say a half-truth is better than no truth at all.

He smiled indulgently and exhaled in relief. 'Do you think it was hers?'

'Whose else could it be?' I asked, using the famous Odessan technique of answering a question with a question.

'Your mom's. Hal got our mother's wedding ring.'

I nodded. Of course.

'It's sexy in your cleavage,' he said. His fingers traced a line down my breast bone. 'It looks expensive.'

'It's worthless,' I responded, surprised by the bitterness in my voice.

At first, I didn't know what to do with myself. Time moved quickly. I sat and watched it fly by. I remembered what Jane said about observing and adapting. I didn't want people to think I was stupid, like when Tristan told them how I was agog at the garage door opener. In general, Americans were so warm, and so friendly. I loved to listen to them talk as I waited in line at the post, as I walked through the aisles of the supermarket, as I watched them on television. TV. People here call it TV. They had a channel for every subject. Golf. Weather. Decorating. Sex. I watched the cooking channel to learn how to make real American dishes for Tristan.

In Odessa, I never had time to just sit and do nothing. I studied, worked at the shipping company and Soviet Unions, I beat rugs with Boba, went to the bazaar, carried pails of water from the stove to the bathtub to wash our clothes and sheets. It was pleasant to have days to read books, to watch TV, to look at the Internet, to talk to Molly on the phone, though she could never talk for long – she was always chasing after her twins. Still, I wished there were an engineering firm in Emerson.

My first two months in America had been a cocoon. Tristan and I ate pizza, lit fires, rented movies at the convenience store on dollar night, and cuddled on the couch. We never talked about the future. We didn't spend time with other people, which hadn't bothered me – I had wanted to get to know him. But now that we were married, I was ready to beat my wings and break out of the cocoon.

When he came home from work, I suggested, 'Why don't we go out? Or we could invite Molly and Toby over. Or go see Serenity.'

'Aw, sweetie. I just got home. I wanna kick back with you.'

'I've been here by myself all day with nothing to do. I want to go out, see people.' I smiled and stroked his arm.

'Well, if you feel that way, why don't you get a job? Or learn to cook? I'm getting tired of pizza. Besides, we can't afford takeout all the time.'

Feel-felt-felt. My smile faded. I'd wanted to look for a job right away, but Tristan said there'd be plenty of time later. Of course, he'd also told me he lived near San Francisco. I assumed I'd find a job in my field – finally. Instead, I was surrounded by fields in the middle of nowhere. 'There are no engineering firms here.'

'You could apply down at the café or the grocery store. Things are expensive here. Most wives work.'

'I'd love to. Why don't we move to a bigger city so I can get an engineering job?'

He didn't reply, he just went to the kitchen and got a beer. He emptied the can in one long swig, then said, 'You knew I lived here when you married me. We're not moving. This is my house. My money. My rules.'

I knew what Valentina would say about him and his rules. Give a man a centimeter and he'll think he's a ruler. Let him think that he's the head of the household, you and I know who's the brains.

Life in America was so ... calm. There was always water and electricity. The computer always worked. Building façades and windows were immaculate. When the orange and red leaves started falling to the ground, a man in a cosmonaut suit blew them into piles with a large apparatus, then a truck picked them up. I missed talking to Boba every day; I missed old Volodya puttering around above us, his heavy steps reminding me that I wasn't alone; I missed the scent of Maria Denilovna's cookies wafting in through the window; I missed the sound of cars racing down the cobblestone streets. Sometimes it felt dead here, as though I was living in a cemetery.

He insisted we have sex every night so I would get pregnant faster. I wanted a baby, too. Still, some nights when he was huffing and puffing on me I wished he would just run out of sperm.

In Odessa, women are excellent cooks and hostesses. Wives fuss over their men, serving their husbands the best slices of meat before sitting down and serving themselves. Tristan certainly loved it when I waited on him. I expected to feel more satisfaction. Adapting wasn't easy. *I'm worse off here than I was in Odessa.* This thought invaded often. I pushed it away. I was lucky! I was lucky. I was. I was trying to make the best of the situation and to do my best, but nothing I did was right. Like tonight. I peeled some potatoes, which took an hour because I'd never done it before coming to America – Boba always prepared our meals. Then, I put the slices in the frying pan with some oil. Potatoes were my comfort food. I loved hearing them sizzle, I loved the salty smell. They reminded me of Boba, of home.

'Look at that! You put like a gallon of oil in there. What, are you trying to kill us?'

'How are potatoes going to kill us?'

'On the death certificate they'll write, "cause of death: clogged arteries." '

I cooked the same way my Boba did. Her potatoes were always so tender and crispy. Odessans are the best cooks in the world.

Everybody knows that. Ask anyone in Moscow or Tbilisi. They'll tell you.

Tristan pulled the pan off the burner and dumped the potatoes into a strainer. He rinsed them off and put them back in the pan.

'They'll burn,' I warned him as the potatoes started to cook. I smirked. I didn't know much, but I knew that.

'You really have a lot to learn,' he said. 'This is a non-stick frying pan. And I have a secret weapon. You're going to love this.'

He took an aerosol can out of the cupboard and started to spray the potatoes.

'What are you doing?' I yelled. 'Why are you spraying chemicals on our food?'

'This is Pam. Zero fat,' he said slowly, as if he were talking to an idiot.

I ate the potatoes because wasting food is a sin. But they did not taste good.

That weekend, when I called Boba and told her of our argument, I expected a little sympathy, but she said, 'Nu, child, men always think they know better. Let him continue to think so, what harm will it do? All people disagree, it doesn't mean anything. He loves you. He's trying to help you adapt to his ways. How many times have we heard Americans cook with chemicals? Now you know it's true.'

'But, you don't understand, Boba –'

'And now you're arguing with me? What kind of girl did I raise? Marriage is like the sea – rarely calm, rarely stormy, but somewhere in between. Living together takes patience, compromise, and wisdom.'

Tristan brought home a recipe book he borrowed from Molly, Low Fat and Lovin' It. It suggested cooking vegetables in plain water. I tried this and the potatoes tasted bland, but Tristan liked them. Or I thought he did, until he a month later, he asked, 'What's with all the potatoes? Haven't you ever heard of rice or spaghetti?'

I was proud of the way I cleaned his house. In Odessa, I hadn't so much as wiped the table after a meal – Boba always insisted she wanted to do it. In Odessa, products came in boring brown packaging and were called names like 'industrial cleaner.' Not very alluring. But Comet? Or Fantastik? Maybe I used more than necessary, but they smelled so good and I wanted to have clean, shiny surfaces. And I didn't know what else to do with myself. Emerson didn't have a real library or book shop. It had only taken me a half a day to explore the town. I'd read my novels several times and had explored nearly every inch of cyberspace. I didn't know what to do, but wanted to be helpful, so I scrubbed. And maybe it was a form of penance. Atonement for my wayward thoughts.

When he came home from work, Tristan opened the windows and said, 'What? Are you trying to asphyxiate me?'

But then he would hug me and say, 'It's okay, you don't know any better.'

I frowned. And bit back scathing remarks, Jane's words about offending others and expecting them to change firmly in my mind. I shouldn't expect Tristan to change. I was the one who should adapt ...

He worked part-time, so when I tried to read a book and listen to music in the living room, he was there, too. Only he turned on the television to watch his ball game and the commentator drowned out my beautiful Bach. Suddenly, the open floor plan I'd loved seemed very limiting.

I turned off the stereo and went into the office to read. He followed me and played computer games. The bleating machine guns made it impossible to concentrate, but I knew that if I went back to the living room or into the bedroom, he would just follow. There was no place to hide. No little nook or cranny.

'Could you turn the sound down?' I asked.

He looked at me, his sour gaze lingering on my ebony blouse and trousers. 'Sweetie, do you have to dress up all the time? Let's go shopping and out to dinner.'

It would be pleasant to get out of the village. A change.

He took me to a store called Wal-mart and chose some clothes for me. When I came out of the dressing room, wearing baggy jeans and a bright T-shirt, he nodded approvingly, 'Now you fit in.'

Odessans would rather stand out than fit in.

I looked around at the other shoppers. He was right. I looked just like them.

'Thank you, Pygmalion,' I said, only a little sarcastically.

'Did you just call me a male pig?'

'No, no. It was a reference to a play by George Bernard Shaw. He was well liked in the former Soviet Union. All school children read his books.'

I stared at myself in the full-length mirror. I didn't look bad. But I didn't look great. And Odessan girls like to look fabulous. Plus I hated to waste money on something I wouldn't wear. What to do?

A man may be the head of the household, Valentina would say, but the woman is the neck. She can turn the man's attention at will. Turn on the Odessan charm. But your eyelashes – that's why mascara was invented, for God's sake. Smile. Speak softly. It's more effective than a rock between the eyes. He won't know what hit him.

'Tristan,' I took his hand in mine. 'The clothes you chose are lovely, but I was thinking more along the lines of something …' Speak his language. 'Sexier. Maybe a blouse? Or a little sweater?'

'Sure … yeah, anything you want.'

He really did look stunned, as if someone had hit him. We scanned the racks until I found something suitable, but I felt guilty, as if I had used a weapon against an unarmed man.

I was lucky to be in America. Lucky to live in such a big house. So how could I protest when Tristan upbraided me? How could I complain when he told me how he wanted his food cooked and house kept? The more one is scolded, the more deeply one is loved. He wasn't finding fault, he just wanted me to adapt to the American way. To fit in. And I tried. But it was hard. Especially when I couldn't defend myself.

Like the time Tristan came out of the bathroom with my tube of denture cream. 'Sweetie,' he laughed, 'you have to learn how to read. This isn't toothpaste, this is Polident. It's for senior citizens who don't have any teeth. I'm old, but I'm not that old, ha, ha!'

What could I possibly say? Self-conscious, I put my hand over my mouth like I used to.

He hugged me and said, 'You're so cute.'

Of course that really meant, You're an idiot.

Life in America was quiet. No signs of life wafting through Tristan's windows, which were closed all the time – if it was warm, he turned on the air-conditioning. No one grumbled, no one complained. Everyone smiled. People in the village drove large Fords and Chevrolets. No Mercedes with blacked-out windows anywhere. It was a relief is what it was. Really.

The euphoria of my arrival had worn off. The days in which I marveled at a smooth stretch of road, the garage opener, the microwave were over. I felt as though I was being submerged, covered little by little by white gauze, caught like a spider in her own web. I didn't know anything about culture shock or homesickness. Who could tell me about it in the former Soviet Union? Most people lived and died in the same place. Those that left, left for good.

One crisp Saturday morning Tristan suggested a hike. He grabbed the rolls of toilet paper off the passenger seat and threw them into the back. I followed their trajectory and saw a mop and metal bucket. The cab smelled like bleach.

I sat down and he closed the door behind me. What kind of teacher carried toilet paper? Don't judge, I reminded myself. I opened my window and breathed in deep. The smell of the pine, moss, and sunshine was calming. He whistled as he drove. I thought of how Jane said that everyone in America had a car, that cars were freedom. Suddenly I wanted this freedom. 'Can you teach me?' I asked, gesturing to the steering wheel.

He smiled. An easy, relaxed smile. He was happiest in nature, just as I was happiest lost in a city. 'You bet. Just pucker up, like this.'

'Excuse me?'

'If you want to whistle, you have to put your lips like this.' He looked like he was going to kiss me, lips tense and pursed together.

I realized that he'd misunderstood, though he would surely say that I had not been clear. I wanted him to teach me to drive, he wanted to teach me to whistle. I sighed.

He frowned. 'Can't we just go out and have a nice day? One minute you're smiling, the next you're sulking. I don't understand you. God, I hate it when you sigh like that. You sound like my raft when I let the air out.'

I certainly felt deflated. Misunderstanding after misunderstanding. Was it my fault? Was my English flawed? This thought made me feel reticent to say anything more. I turned to look out the window.

'Don't pout,' he said.

I looked at him. Unbidden, a line of Sergey Yesenin's poetry came to mind, Мне осталось одна забава: Пальцы в рот – и весёлый свист. There is only one joy left, to put my fingers in my mouth and whistle a pretty tune. Yesenin was a great Russian poet, though westerners would know him in a different context, as the husband of dance pioneer Isadora Duncan. They divorced of course, and later, it is rumored that he slit his wrists and wrote his last poem in his own blood. Мне осталось одна забава . . .

Yesenin's sadness and difficulties were so much greater than my own. Here I was in this magnificent country and all I could do was feel sorry for myself. I was lucky! Lucky. I put my fingers in my mouth and tried to whistle. Only air came out. I tried again.

'Don't use your fingers. Just pucker up and blow.'

Nothing.

'Try touching your tongue to your teeth and blow.'

A quiet sound came out.

'There you go! Just keep practicing.'

He parked and we walked off the lot into the woods.

'We're going to have to get you some decent shoes,' he said, looking at my ballerina flats.

We walked and walked. Whistled and whistled. Birds chirped and little animals, perhaps squirrels or lizards, rustled in the plants near the trail. 'What is this flower?' I asked, pointing to the delicate pink petals.

'That's Liza Jane.'

I smiled. 'Seriously, what's the name?'

'I don't know,' he admitted.

A few minutes later, we came across another plant I'd never seen. 'What's this one called?'

'I'm not sure.'

'Just tell me its Latin name then.'

'I don't know.'

'But you're a teacher. And a scout leader.'

He looked at the ground.

'In Odessa, all school children learn the flora and fauna of Ukraine. It's part of being a cultivated citizen. How can you not know?'

He didn't look up.

'I just don't know.'

'Why do you carry toilet paper in your truck?'

'I'm a scout – always prepared,' he tried to joke. His expression was nervous, tense.

Something wasn't right.

'Let's keep going.' He started walking.

I grabbed his arm. 'No. Not until you tell me the truth.'

We stood there for a long moment – him looking like he wanted to escape, me digging in for an answer. Odessans can stare down anyone. The technique is this: we cock our chin like a gun, raise one eyebrow, and glare until the person capitulates. Success guaranteed.

'I'm a maintenance supervisor,' he finally said.

'What does that mean? Are you a teacher or not?'

'I clean and take care of the school.'

I gasped. We were hours from San Francisco, I lived in a village and had married a cleaning man. What else was he hiding? What had I done? How could I have come to a foreign country to marry a complete stranger?

He tried to take my hand, but I pulled it away. 'I'm sorry,' he said. 'I didn't think you would want me if you knew the truth.'

'No one appreciates being lied to,' I said, hating myself for being taken in.

'I didn't lie exactly. I *do* work at school. And I do lead a scout troop.'

'Why don't you teach?'

'I never finished college.'

'Well, how long would it take you to get your teaching degree?' Maybe he had just a semester of university left and could finish, then look for a teaching job.

'Three and a half years,' he admitted.

'You only completed one semester of college?' I yelled.

He nodded. 'Without the degree, I couldn't get a job as a

teacher, so I took the only one I could get. I work in the school. I help kids. I *feel* like a teacher.'

I felt like a fool. I remembered how he said he taught summer school. How he didn't want me to go to the school. I should have known right then and there. He'd lied to me for all this time. He stood there, looking pathetic. His eyes downcast, his hands trembling. I didn't yell or scream or cry. I didn't say anything. I blamed myself. Let the buyer be wary. Marry in haste, repent forever. I trudged back to the pickup. He followed in silence.

Chapter 17

Boba, my dear and darling grandmother,
Greetings from San Francisco!

You were right to encourage me to come to America. Tristan takes
such good care of me. Just last week, he bought me two new outfits.
He is a good provider. Life is so much better here. Everything is of the
finest quality. People are cultured. The sparrows are plump. Only a
fool would not be happy in this paradise.

Tristan must be a caring teacher because when he and I stroll in the
early evening, children run up to him to chat. When did I ever want to
see my teachers outside the classroom? He will be a wonderful father.
And I can't wait to be a mother.

I got a job at an engineering firm. It feels so good to be able to use
my knowledge. And the salary! It's even better than at the shipping
firm ...

I would be so much happier if you were here, Boba. Sometimes I feel
so blue because I miss you so much. I feel lost without you. It's silly but
sometimes even deciding what to cook for dinner can be overwhelming.
Won't you please consider coming? It would make me so very happy.

I love and miss you,
Dasha

Our marriage wasn't fate – it was a huge mistake.

The worst was that I couldn't talk to anyone. I couldn't tell
Boba the truth. How devastated she would be. She'd start her
talk about us being cursed, and I would begin to believe that she
was right. As for my friends back home, they'd be offended that I

hadn't confided in them about coming to California, and they'd be jealous. If I dared to complain, then I imagined they'd snap, 'Poor princess in America.' I couldn't blame them, even I'd have reacted this way. From a distance, life in America looks perfect. Molly and I spoke often, but she was Tristan's friend and I feared she would take his side. I wanted to confide in Jane, but was too embarrassed – after all, she'd tried to warn me. I didn't want anyone to know that I'd been duped.

Jane and I met on her very first day in Odessa and knew that we were destined to be best friends. The American missionaries I'd met before her whined about how hard life was in Odessa and I vowed to help Jane. I phoned every evening and often invited her home. When I asked how things were, she only said it was difficult to learn Russian. Now, I saw she had a lot to complain about: blackouts, poverty, no heat in the winter, no washer or dryer, a telephone that was an antique compared to those in America.

She called me now as I had once called her. She spoke my language, she urged, 'Talk to me. Tell me in Russian. I know it can't be easy for you with him.'

But I remained silent. Even in Russian, I couldn't find the words.

I was offended he had started our marriage off with a lie. More than that, I lost respect for him. Not because he lied – everyone lies. But because he wasn't smart enough or didn't care enough to hide his lack of knowledge. After our first walk in nature, any Odessan would have been clever enough to buy a book on flora and fauna. Any Odessan would have covered their tracks. That's what we did. If something went missing, we replaced it before anyone noticed. If a recipe called for an ingredient we didn't have, we improvised. If we didn't know the answer, we learned it – and fast. We think on our feet because we live on the edge. Ukraine, *Ukraina*, means on the edge. On the edge of Russia. On the edge of poverty. On edge from living and loving in close quarters. We needed any edge, any advantage we could get. And Tristan, sadly, did not have this drive. He was happy to be a part-time custodian and a full-time redneck in a village that wasn't even on the map driving a truck that was older than me. Was this why he'd gone to Odessa to find a wife? Was this why no *Americanka* would have him? Was I wrong to feel this way?

Boba wrote her letters to me on the only stationery we had in Odessa – rough gray paper that people here would think suitable only for geometry homework, since instead of lines the paper had small squares. Boba didn't believe in waste and filled the page front and back with no margins. She did not sign her name – leftover paranoia from the former Soviet Union.

Dashinka, my darling favorite girl,
Hello from sunny Odessa!

Little rabbit paw, the paper you wrote on was so beautiful. If everything there is of such fine quality, surely I was right to push you to leave Odessa.

Thank you for the money you sent. You didn't need to do that – and you shouldn't do it again. You know perfectly well that nine times out of ten the postman opens letters. And anyway, I manage just fine with the money you left me.

Yesterday, I came home from the bazaar to find your boss standing in the courtyard entry looking flustered. What he was doing there, I never did find out because I lit into him. I told him to stop sending me the fancy food, to stop wasting his money. He just laughed. I had the money you sent me in my purse and I tried to get him to take it, but he just blushed and backed away. Since he was there, I went ahead and fed him. He's as skinny as a matchstick and he ate my potato salad like a wolf. His Russian isn't as bad as you said it was.

I hadn't realized that he still sent Boba food. She was right to tell him to stop. I should tell him to stop. And what was he doing there anyway? Skinny as a matchstick. Why wasn't he looking after himself? Of course, if he depended on Olga for meals, it was no wonder that he was emaciated.

It felt strange to think of him. Certainly, I'd never seen him blush. I'd imagined that everything would stay exactly the same in Odessa, like a scene in a snow globe. But life moved on, whether I was there to observe it or not.

*   *   *

While doing the grocery shopping for the week, I saw a tall blonde stocking the shelves. Something told me that like me, she was a foreigner. Maybe it was her rosy cheeks or her clunky shoes or her handmade sweater.

She looked at me and said, 'You must be Daria.'

'How did you know?'

'Small town. I've been meaning to stop by your house to say hi. So you're Russian?'

'Ukrainian. *Odessitka.*'

'*Odessitkaaa,*' she repeated, the word sounding like a sigh of rapture on her lips. 'So lucky,' she said. 'The beaches, the cafés, the monuments. I was there once and loved it.'

Of course I immediately liked her for loving Odessa. She introduced herself. Name: Anna. Rank: married to an American doctor. Profession: Polish teacher. She, too, had had trouble finding a job in Emerson. Some people here wanted to learn Spanish, but most didn't seem to want to learn any foreign languages.

'I can't complain,' she said. 'This job allows me to send money home to my parents in Krakow.' She never stopped smiling, she looked like she couldn't believe her luck. Maybe I had looked that same way when I first arrived in America.

'Come to my house for tea.'

I went the very next day. Anna kissed my cheek and pulled me inside. I took off my shoes and she pulled out a pair of slippers for me. 'Come in and meet my husband Steve. Steeeve!' She yelled down the corridor. A lanky man with merry eyes walked towards us.

He shook my hand and said, 'So nice to meet you. I'm just on my way out the door.' To Anna, he said, 'I promised Father William that I'd give him a hand.'

Anna giggled. 'Give him all the hands he needs.'

He chuckled and kissed her. I didn't know why they were laughing, but I laughed too.

'Enjoy your visit,' he said. What a cultured man.

Anna took my hand and led me to the kitchen, where the table had been set with a white tablecloth (I touched it, such quality!) with embroidered red flowers on each corner.

'My mother made it. Her wedding gift to us.'

'How long have you been in the States?'

240

'Three years total. Two married to Steve. Two months in Emerson. Before we got married, I was a nanny in Sacramento. It goes by fast, doesn't it?'

For me, the days seemed to drag, but I didn't tell her so. I just nodded.

She put the tea leaves in the pot and said, 'It's real English china. So are the cups. His parents were so generous when we got married. They thought Steve would never settle down.'

'Why not?'

'He was a playboy when we met. He and my boss were colleagues and he came to their house. They had pool parties all the time. Steve asked me out, but I always said no. I didn't want to waste my time with someone who wasn't serious.'

'Then how did you end up married?'

'My visa was about to expire, and I was looking forward to seeing my family again. It had been a year and talking on the phone just isn't the same.'

'I know exactly what you mean,' I said.

'Then he asked me to marry him. I laughed, figuring that he wasn't serious, that he wasn't capable of it. But he convinced me, and now here we are, crazy in love.'

'A great story.' I was happy for her, yet her fairy tale made me jealous. It was exactly what I had wanted for myself. I stared down at the cup, trying to hide my poisonous feelings. 'Such fine craftsmanship.'

'I never use them,' she said. 'People here want their cheap mugs. They prefer Made in China. I prefer china.'

'They're just afraid to break your nice things.'

She'd made brownies and Polish sugar cookies. I took one of each and said, 'Thank you for going to so much trouble.'

'No trouble,' she smiled. 'Only pleasure.'

'How are things ... really?' I asked. Surely her smiles hid something. A problem with her in-laws, dissatisfaction at work, tension with her husband ...

'I love Steve, I love it here. I'm so glad we moved to the country. Life is great! How are things for you?'

Since she lied, I did, too. 'Great. Just great.'

*   *   *

Tristan watched me carefully for weeks. I tried to smile, but couldn't manage it. I tried to laugh, but it came out as a sigh. In bed at night, I wrapped my arms around a pillow, turned my back to him and curled into the fetal position. He was patient. He did the dishes every night. (Well, he put them in the dishwasher.) He vacuumed. He ordered cheese pizza. He asked if I wanted him to light a fire. I shrugged. He asked if I wanted to practice whistling. I told him I didn't feel like whistling.

Each week I called Boba and talked for five minutes. I didn't want her to know how sad I was. Didn't want her to worry. And anyway, I couldn't explain what I felt.

When he came home, I looked up from the book I wasn't reading. He was grinning and asked me to come onto the front step. I followed him and saw a small white car in the driveway. 'It's for you,' he explained. 'It's an automatic, so it'll be easy for you to learn how to drive.'

'Wow!' I exclaimed, using a word I'd learned from him. I embraced him. The first spontaneous hug in a long time. Usually he was the one grabbing me.

'The car's ten years old,' he said apologetically, 'but Toyotas never die. Want to go for a spin?'

He showed me how to turn the key, step on the brake, and move the lever into reverse. Then roll back, pivot turn, and go. We drove for an hour. I knew it wasn't a gift, it was goodwill. A bribe. Still, I hadn't felt so wonderful, so free in months.

Jane still called. She asked how I was doing, if I'd made any friends. I said yes, but the truth was that I'd been in Emerson for months and spent most of my time alone or with Tristan. When I arrived, Tristan practically swaggered as we walked down main street where he introduced me to Phil, the bar owner and organizer of the village's baseball team; Joseph at the fire station; Louise, a retired secretary. He bragged to everyone that I 'stopped traffic.' The villagers brought food to welcome me, to congratulate Tristan. But after that, we never saw them again. I waited for people to come until I realized it was up to me to reach out.

I invited Molly and Serenity over for coffee on Sunday. Tristan was supposed to watch the game at Toby's. That was the plan.

'You can't know how I long for adult conversation,' Molly said. 'Not that it isn't great to raise a family.' She smiled and pointed to her frizzy hair and pale face. 'I haven't had time to put on make-up in about ten years.'

We laughed, but a part of her was serious. It was true that despite the modern machines to make life easier, she ran and ran, taking her kids from football to soccer to play practice. Her son Farley was in school only half a day, her small twins always toddled off in different directions. Not to mention the house and yard she had to tend. Whenever I called, I heard the clanging of cutlery. I pictured the phone wedged between her ear and shoulder as she used both hands to empty the dishwasher then refill it with the dishes from the last supper. I hoped to offer her a moment of respite.

We sat at the dining room table, which I had set with the linen napkins I'd brought from home. They were embroidered with blue and yellow thread, the colors of Ukraine. Yellow stood for our wheat fields. We were, after all, the bread basket of the former Soviet Union. Blue stood for the sky above us. I served Boba's pound cake, white and creamy, while Molly poured the coffee, dark and rich. I listened to my new friends unravel the small mysteries of who had bought the Johnson house, who got a new refrigerator, who was planning a move to Las Vegas, recognising, if not the exact phrases, then the cadence of the words. I rejoiced at having found the reassuring realm of women. I started to relax. These women didn't want anything from me. Their eyes were welcoming, understanding. Their bodies were plump and soft and lovely. There were no sharp edges or sharp criticism. I wanted to curl my arms around theirs, to lay my head on their shoulders like I would have with Boba. I wanted to ask them about my relationship with Tristan (Was it normal that he called three times a day? That he needed to be with me all the time when he wasn't working?), but Molly was his friend, so instead, I pulled out photos of my Boba, the Black Sea, Odessa's opera house, and the *philharmonia* (our world-renowned orchestra had an American conductor, Hobart Earle). I told them that we had the most beautiful beaches in the world. Golden sand caressed by warm water. The sea changes color the way a kaleidoscope changes its pattern – blue, green, silver – depending on the sun.

'Why did you leave such a gorgeous place?' Serenity asked, looking at the waves.

I didn't know what to say. Suddenly, my mind raced with questions that had no answers. Should I explain about the weak economy? Should I tell them how difficult it had been to find a good-paying job? That our Hobart, the great conductor, only received fifty dollars per month? Could they – women from the land of plenty – understand? Was it fate? Or free will? Had I been pushed? Had I been pulled? Was I running from my fate or running towards it?

'She fell in love,' Molly replied for me. She wisely didn't say if I fell in love with Tristan or America. 'You're so lucky,' she continued. 'In the beginning, it's all flowers and kisses. It feels like every year gets harder. And Toby doesn't make it any easier. The other day Farley refused to brush his teeth. When I asked Toby to help, he told Farley if he brushed five days in a row, Toby would buy him a hamster. Now I have to clean the rodent's cage. Pretty soon we'll be bribing the kid to do his homework.'

Serenity was the next to open up. She spoke of her feelings of doubt. She did want to live with her boyfriend, but didn't want to leave her cabin. Something was holding her back. I, too, had had this feeling. What was it? Nervousness? Or self-preservation?

I never found out. The front door slammed. *Cling-clang-clung.* Tristan had returned after only thirty minutes. I wanted to howl. Unfair! Unfair! Not even an hour to myself. I hoped that he came to get something and would go back, or at least that he would go to the office and stay put. But no. He stood at the head of the table and said, 'Ooh, cake!' in a manic tone of voice (he'd eaten a slice before he left) and sat down as though he hadn't noticed the awkward silence.

'You weren't enjoying the game?' Molly asked. 'You usually stay all afternoon.'

'I'm not a bachelor anymore. Just wanted to see what you gals were up to.'

'Girl talk,' Molly said, 'Just girl talk.'

She sounded disappointed.

I got a plate and served him. I turned to Serenity, hoping she would tell us more, but the moment had passed.

'You wouldn't believe the week I had,' Tristan said. 'Kids decided the new fun thing is to shake Coke cans and open them in the school halls. Pop everywhere – on the ceiling, on the walls, all over the floor. I'm not fast enough to catch them red-handed and I've mopped ten times in four days. Man!' On and on he went. Louder and faster.

The three of us just stared at him, stunned. Maybe he didn't realize how we had looked forward to chatting. Maybe he didn't realize he was monopolizing the conversation. He means well, I told myself. Molly and Serenity excused themselves from the table. 'He just likes to be with me all the time,' I said apologetically to them as we moved towards Serenity's Subaru. They smiled brightly. Too brightly. I worried they wouldn't ever come back.

Molly turned to me and whispered, 'I feel like I should tell you –'

'What's that, Molly?' Tristan asked, with an edge to his voice I'd never heard before. I felt his fingers dig into my shoulder as he pulled me to him.

She looked at me and swallowed. 'I just wanted to tell Daria thank you.'

What had she tried to tell me?

'It was lovely to talk to you,' I said. 'Please come back again. Please.'

They nodded and got in the car.

'Well that was nice,' Tristan said. 'Nice ladies. Glad you're making friends.'

'It was nice until you came home and ruined everything. Why can't I have just one afternoon to myself with my new girlfriends?'

'But I, I …'

'Did you see how quickly they left? You didn't let them say a word.'

'But sweetie, I just want to be with you.'

Molly invited us for dinner a few days later. I met her older children, Ashley and Peter, who were in junior high. Peter talked about his band – they couldn't decide if they wanted to play grunge or country, and they couldn't decide if they should call themselves cue-ball or eight-ball. Ashley, who had braces and talked with a gentle lisp, told us that all the other girls could watch R-rated movies, wear make-up, and date. Her mother replied quite firmly that Ashley would never be just 'another girl.' Farley took his hamster Clementine with him everywhere. Her cage was tucked under his chair; she ran on her squeaky wheel the entire meal.

'Clem gets in about four hours of cardio a day,' Molly joked as she fed the toddlers in their highchairs.

This is what I wanted. A happy family life. Delighted parents – a mother *and* a father – proudly listening to the stories of their children, light tension diffused with love. It wasn't until later that I realized Molly and Toby had not interacted at all.

After dinner, we moved to the easy chairs in the living room. Watching Farley with Clementine was better than watching TV. He coaxed her to the side of the cage with the promise of a potato chip and delighted in how she kept the morsel in her cheek, which was so swollen it looked like she had the mumps. I offered to baby-sit any time – their children were so darling. Tristan and I each held a toddler as they drifted off to sleep. This bundle of love, so warm and soft, felt like heaven in my arms. Tristan's eyes met mine and he smiled tenderly. I smiled back shyly. Things could be so simple and bring such happiness – a good meal with friends, a child who smelled of milk and honey slumbering in your arms, a moment of complicity.

That night, when Tristan climbed on me, I prayed that this time I would conceive. When he finished, he rolled off me and kissed my cheek. Two minutes later, he was snoring. I stared at the ceiling.

I was marooned in the country.

We didn't live anywhere near San Francisco.

My husband was not who he'd claimed to be.

He gave me no privacy unless I was in the bathroom.

I didn't have the great job in the city that I had hoped for.

After this series of disappointments, perhaps a child would mean even more.

The car gave me a goal: to get the real American ID card – a driver's license. I studied for the exam. I smiled for the photo – a bright, happy grin. I had my own car, I was in the driver's seat. When my license arrived in the mail, I felt American, free, proud and capable. How long would it take to get my green card? We'd filled out the papers right after our honeymoon. Soon. Let it be soon, I thought to myself, though I knew that it would take two years.

I rolled down the window and blasted my music, shouting out the words. Jane was so right: a car is freedom. For the first time, I didn't miss the sea, I didn't mind being landlocked. For the first time, I could imagine myself living here. I saw the landscape in a different way. Not as a wall, but as a window to this great country. In my car, I didn't feel frustrated. I felt free.

The first place I drove was to Serenity's shop in Emerson. She congratulated me and offered me her newest creation: a candle called Black Sea, inspired by me! It looked like a sculpture of the waves coming together and rising up. On the bottom, it was ebony but became progressively lighter until the tops of the waves were silver-gray.

'It's silly,' she said. 'I mean, I know that the Black Sea isn't black.'

'No, no! It's not silly at all. The Black Sea can be azure and it can be black. All depends on the sun. When there's a storm brewing, this is exactly what the sea looks like. Thank you. It feels like I'm holding a piece of home in my hands.'

The candle smelled of salt and mist and mystery.

I loved her shop, filled with her fine handmade candles and soaps. It felt like a finishing line. A fragrant reward for passing a test. People here cared about me. I was making real progress instead of just rotting away in that house. As customers moved about, we chatted and I touched every single candle with wonder. Luscious lemon. Fir tree. Night. Black Sea.

Over dinner – it was Wednesday, so we were having cheese pizza and Diet Coke – Tristan said, 'I called you three times today.'

'I went for a drive. I wanted to see Serenity's shop.'

'Tell me when you go someplace so I don't worry.'

I nodded.

'I have a surprise for you,' Tristan said. 'I talked to this guy at the gas station a while back, and he married a Russian, too.'

'What's the surprise?' I asked.

'Well, when we found out that we were both married to Russian ladies, we decided we should get together. Double date. I called yesterday to set it up.'

I smiled, pleased at the thought of meeting a *Russkaya*. Apparently, this couple lived in Modesto, a city near Emerson.

At the steak house, Jerry, a beefy truck driver in his fifties, explained that he and Oksana had met at a social. I could see why he had chosen her. Men at the socials liked the busty petite blondes best. Jerry bragged that he'd 'bagged' a much younger woman – she was only thirty.

'Yep, those socials were like a butcher shop – tons of raw meat.' Shocked, I looked to Oksana. She didn't react to his words.

'Yep,' he continued. 'Choice cuts.'

He threw his arm around her shoulders and pulled her to him. Lifelessly, bonelessly, she moved toward him, as though he had grabbed her like this a hundred times, as if she were used to it. She smiled, a bitter twist of her lips, a ferocious look in her dark eyes. Then I realized that she didn't move lifelessly. She moved like water. Like a gentle wave against a rock. The sea seems calm, but it can break rocks in a storm, and it can wear the largest stones down to nothing, one grain of sand at a time.

'How did you find Moscow?' I asked, trying to make polite conversation.

'Damn cold,' he said. 'Prit near froze my nuts off.' He looked at Oksana and, 'Lucky for you it didn't.'

I was scandalized by his comment but Oksana's expression remained detached. The realization hit me: she didn't understand him. She didn't understand English.

Since the restaurant was non-smoking, Jerry went out to smoke and Tristan accompanied him.

'How did you meet him?' I asked Oksana in Russian.

'Through the Lovely Russian Ladies catalog. As a joke, my colleagues at the medical institute paid to have my photo put in it. I didn't find out about it until American men started writing to me. Jerry saw my photo and wrote nearly every day.'

'That takes effort,' I said, revising my earlier opinion of him. Perhaps I'd been wrong to judge so hastily.

'The most beautiful letters. I think the person he hired to

248

translate them to Russian just made stuff up. Now I see that Jerry had nothing to do with the letters.'

'*Nyet* . . .' What a cruel joke.

'Then he started to call.'

'Did you understand him?'

'No, but I pretended to. Whenever there was a pause, I said "yes" or "Jerry." He seemed satisfied with that.'

'Do you speak any English at all?'

She shook her head. 'I learned German at school. He doesn't want me to work, so I sit home and watch soaps – the story lines are so simple that even if I don't know every word, I understand. I repeat the lines to help my pronunciation.' She looked at me intensely, took my hand, and said in perfect English, 'Nikki, you're the only woman I've ever loved.'

We giggled. I, too, had watched a few episodes of *The Young and the Restless*.

Her smile faded. 'Jerry doesn't articulate and he's certainly not articulate. Now that I understand English better and comprehend a little of what he says, I regret knowing. He's so. . . crude.'

I nodded sympathetically. 'There must have been other men. Why him?'

'I'd paid for a flight from Vladivostok and was staying in a hotel in Moscow. I had to make a match before my money ran out. Jerry seemed so intent on me, it was flattering. When I got home, other men wrote, but he called every day.'

'That's nice.'

'*Nyet*. Not nice. Control,' she said quickly, her eyes widening when she saw the men return. 'Control. Control.'

We ate our salads as if everything was normal. She smiled brightly. The waitress cleared the plates away and Jerry went out for another cigarette. Tristan followed. He rarely left me alone, but he seemed to crave Jerry's approval.

I turned to Oksana; she continued as if we hadn't been interrupted. 'He asked what time I finished work, and always called thirty minutes later. I found it touching until the day I was late getting home – it wasn't even six o'clock. He went into a black rage and accused me of cheating.'

'What did you do?' I asked.

'I hung up. But then he wrote and convinced me that his feelings were strong because he loved me so much. And he explained why he went nuts. Now I realize he isn't jealous – he's insecure.'

Insecure. This word described Tristan. 'Why?'

'You'll never believe it,' she said. 'It's like a science fiction movie. Or a porn flick.'

'Tell.' I leaned in.

'His wife was a prison guard. And she fell in love with another guard.'

'That doesn't sound so bad. These things happen at work.'

'The other guard was a woman.'

'*Kino!*' I said, the word we use in Odessa to say 'unbelievable.' It comes from German and means movie. In Russian, it refers to something that could only happen in a film.

'*Da*. She came home one day, after twenty-five years of marriage, and said, 'I never loved you. Never liked you. And I'm a lesbian.'

'She's pink?'

'Like a rose.'

'Where does that leave you?' I asked. But she had that frozen grin on her face. Our husbands had returned.

The waiter arrived with their steaks and my eggplant. Jerry talked loudly whether his mouth was full or not. I kept my eyes on Oksana, who sat so straight, who ate as though we were at the Kremlin rather than the Chow Wagon, and wondered what she was going to do. How could a smart, pretty girl like her be with a guy like that? I pitied her. When she met my gaze, she tilted her head, and a horrifying realization hit me: she was sitting across the table, thinking the same thing – about me.

After the meal, Jerry stepped out again. Tristan trailed.

'His three kids hate me. I'm not a doctor here. I'm nothing. I didn't expect that. And of everything,' she gestured to the door, where our husbands stood, 'that hurts the worst. In Vladivostok, I was always someone – the top of my class, the youngest doctor at the hospital, a specialist sought after for interviews. But here, I'm nobody.'

I could only nod glumly. She had given voice to my exact feelings. There were no engineering firms in Emerson. I sat at home all day, dependent on Tristan. At least he didn't have children who hated me. I was lucky.

'How long have you been married?' I asked.

'Almost a year and a half. It seems like more. Sometimes I think of leaving him. He must know, because he tells me every day that if I ever divorce him, he'll have me deported.'

We sat in morose silence, each thinking about what we'd left behind, each thinking about what we'd have to give up if we went back.

'What's your story?' she asked.

I pulled out the diamond ring and showed it to her. 'A guy gave me this right before I left Odessa. Asked me to marry him.'

'*Kino!* What did you say?'

'I was packing to leave for America, but I didn't tell him that. He thought I was going to Kiev for a few weeks and that I would come right back to marry him.'

'Why didn't you?'

'He was a mobster.' I tucked the necklace beneath my sweater. She nodded.

The men came back. Jerry left a dollar on the table and said, 'Let's scoot.'

They walked towards the door, we followed.

'He's so much older than me,' she whispered in Russian. I nodded.

'But, you know, maybe things will turn out.' Her tone sounded so hopeful. I knew exactly how she felt. And there were brief moments it felt possible. Then she added, 'Maybe he'll just die.'

Chapter 18

Greetings from the great state of California!
To my Boba, the loveliest grandmother in Odessa!

Can you believe that Tristan and I just celebrated our fourth month
wedding anniversary? Time flies faster than a jet. He is sitting at the
kitchen table right now, correcting the last of his pupils' homework. He
is so conscientious and caring.

Tristan's family has been kind. His brother and sister-in-law arrived
two days ago. She is so gracious and welcoming. She said I was the best
thing that had ever happened to Tristan. They have come to spend
Thanksgiving with us. The holiday season in America begins at the end
of November. I will be cooking a grand feast! How I wish you were here
to help me! Of course, sitting around the table with Tristan's family
inevitably reminds me of you and I become terribly glum. I know that
the holidays just won't be the same without you. In my heart there is
a plate set for you.

I kiss you,
Your Dasha

Each time my period came, I cried. A woman who can't have
children might as well be a man. Worthless. Tristan knew about
'that time of the month' and let me be. When he heard me
sniffling, he assumed it was because of 'women problems' and
asked if I wanted Midol or the heating pad and made me a bowl
of Campbell's tomato soup.

I never thought I'd be like this. Weepy. Touchy. Tender. In
Odessa, I'd noticed little children playing on the beach, and

mothers pushing babies in prams. What woman doesn't? I loved babysitting for Olga. I liked children. But now ... I was desperate. It was as if getting pregnant was the key to my happiness. I was an engineer. In fact, I graduated at the top of my class. I'd mastered foreign languages and got myself to America. No small feats. And yet I found myself unable to perform the most basic human function. I felt like a ... loser, as Americans would say.

Winter was coming. Each day was shorter than the last, the sky was gray, and Tristan's brother and sister-in-law were here for Thanksgiving. I made turkey, gravy, mashed potatoes, corn, and pumpkin pie. It was a lot of work, but I was proud to be following the tradition in my new country. Hal brought three bottles of wine. I remembered my last glass of Chablis with David. We sat in the darkened boardroom discussing Gogol. I'd sipped slowly, savoring the 'bouquet' as he called it. Today, I gulped – Noreen would drive anyone to alcoholism. As she talked about her latest purchases and which room she was going to remodel next, I started to think of Boba.

'What's wrong?' Noreen pinched my leg under the table. 'You have so much to be grateful for. You're in America now. Your husband is a good provider. You have a beautiful house and a car. What more do you want?'

'I just miss my grandmother.'

'Have your own family. Then you'd miss her less. I don't know why Tristan puts up with you, Miss Moody. Lena was never moody like you.'

The three of them froze.

'Who's Lena?' I asked.

'Tristan dated her before he met you,' Hal said and shot Noreen a look.

'You should be grateful,' she repeated. 'Today of all days. When I think of how much Tristan paid to go to Budapest to *not* meet you, then more money to go to Odessa, then he had to borrow money from *us* to pay for *your* ticket to America. It makes me sick. You know, if you're another one of those scammers, all it would take is one word to Immigration to get you deported.'

Deported? Was what she said true?

'Noreen,' Hal warned. He turned to me and said, 'She didn't mean that.'

Oh yes she did.

I glanced over to the brewing coffee and then back at Noreen. No, I could never throw hot coffee on the sow. An *Odessitka* never uses the same trick twice. I'd dealt with the likes of Olga and Vita and Vera – Noreen was nothing next to them. Why was I letting her get to me?

I put my palm on my chest and excused myself from the table. In close quarters, sometimes a strategic withdrawal is best, that's what we say in Odessa. Of course, the end of the phrase is: but if that doesn't work, show her who's boss. I paced the porch. What was wrong with me? I was surely the only unhappy person in America. I dabbed at my eyes with a Kleenex. The wine had made me weepy. It didn't matter that I had given up my life and my Boba to come here. He'd always be superior because he had more money. It was his house, his furniture, his car, his friends, his family. Nothing was ours. I had nothing.

'You have me,' a quiet voice behind me said.

Had I said these words aloud?

'You have me,' he repeated.

I had no one.

He pulled me into his arms. 'Want me to tell you a secret? It'll make you feel better. You know my brother Hal, the great preacher? The one who took ten minutes to bless our turkey dinner? He's an atheist.'

Kino! 'Does Noreen know?'

He shook his head. 'It would kill her. Her whole life's about being the minister's wife.' Then he chuckled and said, 'I'm always tempted to tell her.'

And just like that, I felt a little complicity with him, like we could be a family. I clung to these moments, knowing they wouldn't last, knowing he would wreck the fragile foundation that had been built.

It happened three days later. He'd been touchy and I didn't know why. I went to visit Anna in the morning and helped Serenity at her shop in the afternoon. Why did he care if I wasn't home? Neither was he.

254

I still did the cooking and cleaning, taking care to open the windows after I scoured the sink so the smell of the cleaning products would not offend him. I prepared a variety of bland food with no fat. We were at the dining table, me eating rice pilaf, him a chicken breast I had cooked. We were talking like normal people when all of a sudden he burst out, 'You're never home when I call. Why did I get married? So I can have a wife who runs around on me? And another thing, I'm so goddamn sick of hearing about how things are done in Odessa. You live here now. Deal with it. And my name is Tristan. Not Trees, not Treestahn. You have to learn how to pronounce my name. Learn how to talk right. You're so stupid. God.'

My cheeks burned as though they'd been singed by an iron. I covered them with my hands so if he looked, he would not see that he'd scored a point. Was I stupid? A voice answered: Yes. Stupid for having left Odessa.

No one had ever said anything negative about my English. Not my superiors at the shipping company. Not my teachers. Why, Jane told me I spoke better than some native speakers! I took courage at this thought.

Was my English flawed? It was true I didn't speak like Tristan or the other citizens of Emerson. I never criticized – Boba said truly intelligent people put others at ease rather than pointing out their sad lack of knowledge – but he mistook prepositions for verbs! While we corresponded, he wrote, 'I should of called you earlier.' Not only that, he had no knowledge of the third group of irregular verbs. For example, he said, 'He could of went with her.' And everyone in Emerson disregarded the existence of adverbs. It was always 'Drive safe!' or 'I'm doing good.' More than that, pronouns were wantonly strewn together as in 'that's between him and I.' I wasn't the only one who made mistakes. How dare he insult my English! He could criticize my cooking and my clothes, but my English was sacred. It was all that I'd had. Other girls played with dolls, I played with idioms. Other girls had shiny bangles on their wrists and gold earrings, I had a collection of irregular verbs. I wound and rewound the tapes of English songs to learn the lyrics. I befriended American missionaries and endured their lectures just to hear the way they spoke. I even read the Bible and religious pamphlets they gave me to expand my vocabulary.

I didn't know what to say. Or rather I had plenty to say.

Though I hadn't called her since she begged me to wait to marry, after dinner, I took the phone into the bathroom, locked the door, and reached out to Jane, a certified teacher, for help. I explained what had happened and this is how she replied: 'That asshole. Your English is fine. But we can do an exercise right now to fine-tune your pronunciation. Really focus on the "i" sound and repeat after me: Prick, idiot, shit head, Tristan.'

I repeated her list, over and over. We laughed together and I felt better.

Then she asked, 'Did it ever occur to you that your name is Daria, but he calls you Dora?'

My dear granddaughter, my darling little rabbit paw,
Greetings from the Pearl of the Black Sea!

Received your letter and had even started worrying since I had not got one in so long. It took three weeks for this one to arrive. It's not your fault, but if you're not too busy with work, perhaps you could write more often. Don't phone! It's too expensive. I don't even want to think about the cost. Save your money for your little family – and remember, God loves three.

Since you've been gone, a friend from the old neighborhood, Boris Mikhailovich, has come calling. Says he worries about me now that I am alone. He helps me with the heavy lifting – ten kilo bags of onions and potatoes from the bazaar, etc. etc., so I cook lunch for him. He brings me flowers. I don't want to accept them – so expensive, so unnecessary! – but he insists. Says that he does the bazaar for me only twice a week whilst I cook for him nearly every day.

I love you, my darling girl. I think of you every day, and I am so proud that a woman in our family has finally broken the curse, that your life is full of contentment, and that you have a good home with a decent man. Soon you will have a child and you will know true bliss. I hug you very tightly. I kiss you.

In Odessa, I almost never remembered my dreams, though I always wished a trace of these sweet moments would remain, the way the taste of dark chocolate lingers in the mouth a moment after you swallow. But no. The slightest impression rarely remained. Perhaps because I studied so hard, then worked so hard that I slept like the dead. Perhaps because my longing during the day was so great it overshadowed the dreams that came at night.

But now that I was well rested, even too rested, the dreams came and stayed with me until morning. In them, I was back in the shipping firm. My teeth were gone; my lips curled around my gums. David came out of his office with my dentures and cackled, 'I'll always have a piece of you.'

My eyes opened. Even though I had been asleep, my hand covered my mouth.

Perhaps you would expect that I felt horrible during those weeks in which the dentist pulled my teeth and fitted me for dentures. But I didn't. Though self-conscious, I knew I'd soon look better. I felt lucky that David gave me teeth as fine as porcelain. No other man had ever given me so dear a present. During this period of discomfort, I sensed the solace of the end. I could see the port lights. It's easy to get through a term at school with a severe teacher or an evening with a churlish date. You just do your best to navigate the rough water. The lights of the port signal the end of the journey, knowing land is near helps you traverse the difficult moments. But my situation with Tristan was different – neither lights nor land were visible. I could barely keep my head above water.

As time went on, my dreams began to mirror my reality. I was no longer with David. I was with Tristan. He told me I was stupid, that I couldn't cook, that I couldn't talk right, that he didn't understand me, that no one understood me. In these dreams, I constantly covered my mouth. I had no teeth and no voice. I was ashamed. I awoke from these nightmares thirsty and scared, my fingers already at my lips. I looked over at Tristan and whispered, 'God help me.'

Chapter 19

Dear Boba,

All is well in the big city. I'm sorry that I haven't written in a few weeks. Here at the engineering firm, we raced to complete a big proposal, and luckily we were awarded the contract! My boss gave me another raise. The newspaper featured me in the 'Movers and Shakers' section.

Tristan is so cultured. I am the luckiest of wives. In the evening, we sit in the living room and he reads me Anna Karenina. His voice is low and tender, and it is so interesting to hear the master's words rendered in English.

We never go out. Of course this disappointed me at first – you know how much I love the philharmonic. Remember the 8th of March concert last year when our Hobart triumphed with his orchestra? Had we ever heard Tchaikovsky played so well?

But Tristan is right. We need to save money. It doesn't grow in the garden. He said it would cost ten thousand dollars to have a baby. Can you imagine? How can something so small cost so much?

Yesterday, we bought a crib and the softest sheets. To think, I slept in a drawer for the first months of my life. We didn't buy a baby blanket. I was hoping that you would crochet one for the baby and bring it when you come. We both want you to visit with all our hearts. I want you to come help me with the baby. I want you to come period.

Love,
Dasha

In Emerson, decorations for Christmas had gone up right after Thanksgiving. The strings of lights kept the darkness at bay. I loved looking at the reindeer and sleigh or inflatable snowmen on people's lawns. Tristan put up a tree. The whole house smelled of pine. This time I wasn't stupid enough to show how entranced I was. I didn't want people to mock me. Anyone looking at me would think that I had seen beautiful displays like this year-round. In fact, this was my first Christmas. In Odessa, under the Soviet Union and even afterwards, we celebrated the New Year, when Grandfather Frost delivered candy and oranges.

Christmas morning, we opened our presents. I gave him three button-down shirts and a blue silk tie; he got me another pair of jeans, T-shirts, and hiking boots. Though the gifts weren't my style, I was grateful. One feature of this perverse social experiment called the Soviet Union: It kept us thankful for every mouthful of food, every garment, every drop of water, every light bulb that brightened our dark days. Every time the furnace came on in Tristan's home, I said a little word of thanks. We'd lived too many winters with no heat. When provisions, clothes, and opportunities are scarce, you learn to appreciate every little scrap. I kept trying to remind myself: even if he's not my soul mate, even if he doesn't understand me, life here is better than at home.

I hoped that next year we'd have a baby to share Christmas with. Holidays were for children. All days were for children. For family. I decided to call Boba. Each time I dialed her number, I prayed that the line would be clear so that we could talk. In America people pick up the receiver and say, 'Hello.' In Odessa, as you know, we say, 'I'm listening.' But each and every time I called Boba, she answered, 'Dasha?'

'It's me, Boba.'

'How's my little *Americanka?*'

'Oh, Boba.'

'What is it, my little rabbit paw?'

'Nothing ... I'm just happy to hear your voice.'

'I miss you.'

'And I you, sunshine.'

I was afraid that if I said another word, I would start to cry, so I bit my lip and batted my eyelashes, trying to control my tears.

'How do you double the value of a Lada?' Boba asked. She knew her jokes always cheered me.

'I don't know?'

'Fill its gas tank.'

I laughed.

'Boris Mikhailovich told me that one. He keeps me in stitches.'

'Boris Mikhailovich?' At least she wasn't calling him simply Boris. That meant there was still a certain formality in their relationship.

'He checks on me from time to time. Last night he brought over some fish that he caught and cooked it himself. You know how I hate to clean fish.'

I heard the rumble of a man's voice in the background.

'Is he still there?' I asked.

Kino. Boba had a boyfriend.

At Wal-Mart, while Tristan looked at tires, I bought a white baby dress and knit booties. I topped my purchases with feminine hygiene products so he wouldn't pry. When we got home, I felt ridiculous and shoved the plastic sack under the bed. But when he was at work, I pulled the dress out and stroked it. The cotton was so soft.

How could I not be pregnant when I wanted it so much? At least Tristan didn't seem angry about it. He just grinned and said, 'Well, guess we'll have to keep trying.' I begged him to take me to visit Oksana and Jerry, so that she could examine me. But he said, 'Sweetie, don't nag me. When I get home from work, I just want to wash up and kick back in my BarcaLounger.'

Three things in this world he loved: computer games, his recliner and the national parks of America. He didn't like fussy clothes, potatoes all the time or ungrateful women.

… And I was his wife.

Jane was flying to San Francisco after New Year's and invited me to join her. He'll never want to go, I told her. She said, Who cares what he wants? Take the bus. If you need money, I'll send you some.

'I'm not going,' Tristan said.

'Fine, I'll go alone.' I could use some of the money David had given me to buy a bus ticket. I was thrilled at the idea of going on my own.

Tristan smirked. 'How will you get there? You don't have enough experience to drive in the city and you don't have any money.'

'I'll hitchhike,' I said, feeling like myself again – impudent and just a little perverse. It felt good.

He pouted for a solid week, slamming the cupboard doors, sighing, and shooting me malevolent looks across the dinner table. *Fight-fought-fought.* I held my breath and tiptoed around the house, trying to hide my joy at traveling on my own. Sadly, at the last moment, he decided to go and grabbed the keys from my hand. I couldn't wait to see Jane, but hated the tension between Tristan and me in 'my' car.

'I guess your friends are more important than me,' he moaned. 'I guess what I want doesn't count.'

Prick, idiot, shit head, Tristan, I repeated to myself, really focusing on getting the 'i' sound just right.

When we pulled up in front of the Victorian, Tans and Jane came out to greet us. She wore an expensive cream-colored pantsuit, he his usual blue blazer. I noticed an emerald ring on her finger. Was it a gift from Tans? He put his arm around Jane, she pressed herself to his side. Somehow, when he stood next to her, he looked younger. I imagined he knew that. He greeted us – a kiss for me, a handshake for Tristan – and said apologetically that he had too many guests at the house so he'd reserved us a room at a nearby hotel. Tristan's lips tightened – he didn't want to pay for accommodation. I whispered that it would be like a honeymoon. He grumbled that our honeymoon hadn't cost $100 a night.

In a sulk, Tristan took our luggage to the hotel. I was grateful for this moment of respite, grateful to be back in San Francisco – the noise of the passing cars, the throngs of people on the sidewalk, the possibilities, the marvelous possibilities of the city. Tans's house was filled with people eating in the kitchen, talking in the hallway, and dancing in the living room. As time went on, more and more arrived. Doctors, lawyers, heiresses, writers, gays, mothers against drunk drivers, swindlers, actors, refugees – there was one of everyone at Tans's parties. Jane and I stood near the entryway and watched guests in evening clothes stream by. She gestured to the group down the hall. 'Jono brought cocaine – that's why they're loitering in front of the office. He sets up shop

there. He's also a bookie for the daftest bets. They're interesting,'
she nodded to Mia, the stockbroker; Marco, the upstairs neighbor
who owned a Jaguar dealership; and Destiny, a top model. 'But
they have too much time and money on their hands. Last month,
they bet on which of them would get pulled over by the police
first, then they drove like maniacs to win the wager. I wouldn't be
surprised if they bet on when Tans and I will break up.'

'Does that bother you?' I asked.

'The bet? No. I know it has to end, even if I don't want it to.
Coming here on the weekend is fabulous, so different from life
in Montana. Tans is great. There's no future, he and I both know
that. God knows the betting pool knows it. But for now what we
have works.'

She grabbed us each a flute of champagne from a waiter
circulating through the strands of guests. Jane and I touched the
rims together, recited a silly Odessan toast, 'To the best people in
the world, to us!' and laughed.

She had opened up, somehow that made it easier for me. I tried
to apologize for not talking to her for all this time.

'Ne nada,' she said. There's no need. 'I understand. I shouldn't
have opened my big mouth about your getting married. You have
to do what you have to do ...'

I downed my champagne and wrapped my arm around hers and
put my head on her shoulder. She stroked my hair and murmured
in Russian, 'You're a smart girl, you'll manage, everything will be
fine. I have confidence in you.'

Her words made me feel strong, fortified, happy. Happy to
be with a dear friend, happy to be in the city. Happy to listen
to musicians and to receive energy from the notes. We accepted
another glass and then another. My mind spun so quickly my
thoughts were jumbled. She saw me stumble and pulled me
towards the plush sofa in the living room. In front of us, Zora
played the violin (which Jane called a fiddle), Gambino the guitar.
It was like an evening at home when we gathered at our friend
Sasha's because he had a piano, and we sang and laughed and
danced. Zora began to sing a folk song. It was so magical that
I could almost forget that Tristan had returned and was sulking
beside me.

'I don't trust Jono,' Jane whispered as more people made their way down the hall to the office. She gestured to his red silk shirt. 'Look at him, dressed like a Las Vegas lounge singer. Who does he think he is? Sammy Davis, Jr.?'

I had no idea who that was.

'I don't know why he has to bring that stuff here,' she continued.

Tans approached us. 'Tristan, a beer?'

'Huh? I can't hear with all this racket.'

'A beer?' he repeated. 'Let me show you where we keep them.'

Tans raised his eyebrow as if to say, See? I'm not so bad. I'm taking Tristan for a walk so you girls can chat.

When they'd gone, I turned to Jane. 'Tell me about the ring. It's so beautiful.' And it was. Curved gold flowers held the emerald in place. What a pity that goldsmiths had gone the way of blacksmiths. I looked at my wedding ring. Today's jewelers plop a diamond on a circle of gold. No talent is needed for that.

'Tans gave it to me for Christmas. Said it was his mother's.'

'You don't sound convinced.'

'He's fifty-five years old and never been married. He could have given his mother's ring to anyone by now. The thing is,' she nodded to the young man who was smiling widely, whose eyes were too bright, 'Jono sells estate jewelry. That means when someone dies, he buys the jewels cheaply and resells them.'

'But Tans said –'

'I know what he said. I also know what his best friend does for a living.'

'He loves you.'

'That doesn't mean I trust him,' she said. 'Everyone here is a liar. It's the only thing they have in common.'

'Are you going to keep the ring?' I handed it back to her.

'Of course.'

I nodded approvingly. In some ways, Jane had become a real Odessan. I put my hand to my chest. I wondered if I could bear to part with my ring. I wondered how much Jonothan could get for it. And what I could do with the money.

As if to make up for being stingy about the hotel, Tristan asked if Jane and I would like to see *Phantom of the Opera*. I was thrilled to be going to the theater and proud of Tristan's thoughtfulness. Jane hadn't seen him in the best light. No one in Tans's crowd thought much of him. But he was showing that he could be considerate. It was important to me that he and Jane get along, and that she see she'd been wrong. An usher escorted us to our seats – in the very last row. I muttered that we could hardly see. Tristan countered that tickets were seventy dollars each, right in front of Jane. *Die-died-died*. That's what I wanted to do. Earth, swallow me now. I could take dozens of small humiliations and attacks on my dignity. But to have Jane bear witness was more than I could take. She squeezed my hand and whispered, *Everything will be fine*.

'Thank you for inviting me. It was so kind of you,' Jane said to him.

'When I asked you to go, I didn't think the tickets would be so much.'

I gasped. I couldn't believe it. No man in Odessa would ever be so uncultured. What kind of person invites another then hints at being reimbursed? Jane pulled some bills out of her purse. He looked at them, then at me. I glared so ferociously that he didn't dare accept the money. Jane tried to mollify me, but I was mortified. I could swallow my pride in Emerson, where no one could see, but in front of Jane, it stuck in my throat.

I couldn't stand to look at him and turned my head. Jane squeezed my hand again and repeated *Everything will be fine*. I heard a tinge of pity in her voice and it made me want to weep. I looked away so she wouldn't see my tears. I needed to get out of there, but Tristan was blocking my way.

'Execute me,' I whispered, wishing someone would lop off my head.

'What?' Tristan asked.

'Excuse me,' I said.

'It's about to start,' he said.

'The curtain will rise whether I'm here or not.'

I wandered the halls until they emptied. Until I was blinded by my tears. I knew I should be grateful. At least I was at the theater, right? I was lucky. Tears glided down my cheeks and I blew my nose hard, half hoping the gray ropes of my brain would come out as well. As I walked and muttered to myself, I crossed the path of an older gentleman, who asked what was wrong. 'I went from a box seat – the best seat in the house – to the very last row.'

He handed me a handkerchief. 'Well, that's a problem I can solve. Join my wife and me.'

We entered the black box. I focused on the stage and forgot everything. When the lights came on for intermission, the man asked what I did for a living. This is always the first question they ask in America. I was ashamed to admit that I was unemployed, so I said, 'I used to work at ARGONAUT, a shipping company.'

'Here in San Francisco?'

'I didn't realize there was a branch here …'

'Our son works there,' the woman said.

'What's your degree in?' the man asked.

'Mechanical engineering.'

'Smart girl.' He took out a business card. 'I'm writing my son's number on the back. Call him.'

And just like that I had a lead. I tucked the card into my purse as the curtain rose to a new era of my life. Maybe Tristan could find a job in San Francisco as well. Or maybe I could rent a room for the week and return to Emerson on the weekend.

At the end of the performance, I thanked the couple warmly. People in America were so kind and helpful and open. I couldn't believe my luck. I waited at the entrance for Tristan and Jane. I couldn't wait to tell them my news. When Tristan saw me, he charged like a rabid bull and grabbed my shoulders. 'Where were you?' He shook me. 'I spent two hours searching the halls! I've never been so scared in my entire life!'

'I told him not to worry …' Jane said as she tried to loosen his grip. 'That you could take care of yourself …'

'What's the matter with you?' He shook me again, until my dentures clattered together. 'I plan a fun evening and even invite your friend and this is how you repay me?'

'Of course, I'm grateful.' I tried to placate him. 'I'm so grateful.'

'You know how much I paid for those tickets. What a waste! Where were you anyway?'

Money. It always came down to money. I decided not to tell him my news. And then I thought, What news? He would never let me work in San Francisco. And if I left him, what would I do? I didn't have a green card, everything depended on my marriage to him. I was trapped. The happiness I felt just an hour before slipped away, as though it had never existed.

Jane came with us to Emerson. We sat in the back seat, ignoring Tristan when he grumbled about being the chauffeur. *Drive-drove-driven.* 'In America, a man and wife sit together.'

'Well, in Odessa a man is chivalrous.' Odessan men were sensitive to a woman's pride. How I'd taken that for granted …

He smirked. 'Not so chivalrous if you had to leave the country to find a decent guy like me.'

I snorted. And didn't reply because Jane looked most uncomfortable.

Tristan wasn't himself in front of other people. He crowed to Jane about introducing me to jeans and T-shirts, as if I were totally ignorant about style. He could not have been prouder of introducing a great chef to fast food. He snickered at the way I prepared borscht saying I was crazy for wasting time boiling beets when I could just buy canned ones. We're in America, he said, there's no reason to do all this work. But I liked cooking for Jane. I liked spoiling guests. For the first time, I noticed that when he laughed, he brayed like a donkey.

'Of course, she does things in her own way,' Jane said, 'but it's not wrong, just different. It would be a boring world if we were all the same.'

When I wanted to take a walk, he said it was easier to drive. When I made coffee – measured the beans, ground them, prepared the cups by warming them with hot water so that the coffee would stay hotter longer – he opened a can of beer and said his way was faster. His way was always more practical, faster, easier, cheaper, better.

This was why I loved Jane. There were times I said or did something – I don't know what exactly – and Tristan would give Jane a conspiratorial smirk as if to say, 'She's just a dumb foreigner. What do you expect?'

Jane never smiled back.

When I first arrived in Emerson, Boba and I spoke for only a few minutes, though Tristan encouraged me to talk longer. Since it was expensive, I phoned once a week just to say that I was fine. I was so happy to be in America that I didn't miss Odessa and I didn't miss her. It was only as time went on that I started to realize I'd taken Boba for granted. Each week, without really noticing it, we talked more and more. It grew harder and harder for me to hang up the phone.

Often, when we finished speaking, plump tears rolled down my cheeks, a bitter cocktail of love, longing, and frustration. More and more, I felt guilty for leaving her. She had done everything for me, and now when it was my turn to help her, I had abandoned her. The horrible truth was that I hadn't truly appreciated her and all that she had done for me until I left Odessa. She had been the peg on which I hung my jacket when I arrived home from work.

After my mother died, our life revolved around me. What I did at school. Who my best friend was that week. What I should study. What I would like for dinner. Me, me, me. I didn't know anything about her. It wasn't until I was in America that I started to ask questions. Now that I couldn't see her anymore, I longed to know everything about her.

It wasn't easy. The phone lines in Ukraine were so bad, I could barely hear her. Sometimes, because of crossed wires or the party-line system in Odessa, Boba and I could hear other people conversing. Their voices were louder than my Boba's.

'Whoever you are, hang up, please; I'm trying to talk to my babushka.'

'You hang up,' the woman replied.

'Please, I'm calling long-distance from America.'

'Oy, from Ameeeericca,' she sneered. 'Then you should be the one to call back. I'm the one still stuck in this hole.' She and her friend cackled and continued to shout.

When dealing with crazies, you have to be crazier. That's what we say in Odessa. I screamed until those cows got off the line.

Tristan gestured for me to put the phone down. 'What is wrong with you? Hang up!'

I turned my back on him. 'Tell me something interesting, Boba.'

'Your Mr. Harmon came to visit.'

'What?' I screeched. 'Why didn't you say something?'

'He brought mangoes.'

'Mangoes? What was he even doing there?'

'He comes from time to time. Says he wants to make sure I'm doing all right. Sat at the table and peeled the mangoes like a pro.' She sounded impressed. 'The most delicious food I've ever eaten.'

For some reason, this news made me want to cry. Not this kindness, but the fact that someone else was giving treats and attention to Boba. I should have been there. It should have been me bringing home mangoes.

'What did he say?' I asked.

'His Russian isn't bad.'

'Boba,' I warned.

'He just asked if I needed – kkkkkkkk' Static.

'What?'

'He just asked where you – kkkkkkkk' Static.

'What?'

'He wanted the same thing he always wants – your number in Kiev.'

I knew she would never give him any information about me, though I appreciated that he'd tried.

She spoke again, but her words were swallowed by static.

'What did you say?'

'I haven't received a phone bill since you left. Isn't that strange?'

'Boba, I can barely hear you. Are you all right?'

Each week, it seemed like Boba's voice grew softer and softer. 'Don't worry about me, little rabbit paw,' she said, but I knew that she must be tired. To bathe, we heated water on the stove in a large metal pail then carried it to the bathroom and dumped it in the tub. I knew she couldn't lift it. And the shopping. Boba couldn't lift the large sacks of onions and potatoes on her own. It was good that she had Boris Mikhailovich, but I still wanted it to be me helping her. I never should have left her. How selfish I'd been. She was elderly and she needed me. And more than anything or anyone, I needed her.

Chapter 20

My Darling Grandmother Boba,
Greetings from the Golden State!

Today is Valentine's Day, the day of love in America. Tristan bought
me a red heart-shaped box of chocolates. He took me to the fanciest
restaurant in town and told me to order anything I wanted.

After dinner, we went to a concert. The children at his school have
a small orchestra and play well, considering that they have only played
instruments for two years.

My English improves every day. I must say, the English we learn in
school has nothing to do with the way people speak. I scribble madly,
filling my notebooks with slang and notes on pronunciation.

Of course it's a struggle, but a rewarding one. Of course, happiness does
not just curl up on one's lap. One must pursue it, no matter how elusive.

I miss you, miss home. I even miss the walls of our apartment and
long to press my forehead, my palms against them. Everything will be
fine. I will be fine. But please won't you consider coming to California?
We have a spare bedroom. Don't you miss me?

Love,
Your Dasha

Tristan and I spent our six-month anniversary at the clinic where
the doctor informed us that a couple is not considered infertile
until they try to conceive for a year. 'Just keep going,' he advised.
'If there are no results, come back in six months.' He explained
about ovulation and cervical mucus and gave me the business to
find out the peak time of the month.

Here we'd been having sex every night when in fact there was a propitious window of twenty-four hours. Only one day. There was so much I didn't know. But how could I? Boba never talked about sex. Even if she had, I would have been mortified. I doubted that she knew about cervical mucus. My classmates barely knew more than I. In grade school, many of them slept in the same room as their parents. They described the fumbling and moaning in the night, but their stories sounded just as implausible as Grandfather Frost bringing presents on New Year's Eve. As teens, some of my girlfriends were curious about sex, but they were nervous without an envelope for the letter. We'd heard about the miracles in the West. A woman could urinate on a twig to find out if she was with child or take a pill to avoid pregnancy. We also heard the pill contained male hormones and that women who took it grew beards. Anyway, it was difficult to find a place to have a private moment – when three generations lived in the same flat, someone was always home. My first time happened in a deserted basement in the position called 'the lookout.' The man lifts his partner's skirt and penetrates her from behind – if someone approaches, the couple can hide. It was nothing special. If anything, the preliminaries – a bouquet, soft words, the opera – were better.

But it would be worth the discomfort to have a child. A little girl to share my joy of being in America. A little girl to share my impressions with. I wanted someone – my own flesh – so I wouldn't feel so isolated and alone. Someone who would always love me. Boba, Mama and I had formed a trinity – God loves three. And now it was time for me to create my own. I wanted my daughter to have something I never had: a papa.

Tristan wasn't my dream husband, but he would be a caring father. He had deep roots. A house, a job, a future. He would be there every step of the way. Like me, he wanted children immediately. A little voice in my head said it was because he didn't want to lose me, and a baby would be the cement that would keep us – two mismatched bricks – together. He said he didn't want to be too old, like his mother and father when they'd had him. I sensed he was still angry with them. He never spoke of his parents except to say he felt removed from them. I'd been very close to my mother. It had always been just us girls. I remember sitting on Mama's lap in the kitchen where it was always five degrees warmer than the rest of the flat while we pored over Western fashion magazines together. How she loved *Vogue*! She smelled of vanilla. When we walked down the leafy boulevards of Odessa she held my hand. She read to me at night. Her voice was the last thing I heard as I fell asleep. I'd always wanted a little sister, but my father was long gone, then Mama became sick. Boba and I took care of her until she died. And Boba became my everything – my grandmother, my mother, my older sister, my confidante. And now that I was alone, more than ever I wanted someone with whom I could share her wisdom, her courage, her life. A child to pass our stories on to.

Tristan would never run off the way Vlad had. No child of his would ever wonder.

How many times had I asked my mother, 'Who do I look like?' When I was small, she replied, 'You look like a fairy princess, come to earth to bless Boba and me.' The answer charmed me but it didn't satisfy. Later, I felt my fine arch and looked at her thick brow. At her wiry hair, her broad shoulders, her large hands. She was my mother; she was my opposite. Again and again, I asked, *Who do I look like? Who? Who?* I yearned for one small piece of my own history. Why couldn't I know? What had I done? Who? Who? *You,* she answered. *You look like you.*

End of discussion.

I wanted my child to know where she came from.

The doctor's words had soothed me. I touched my belly often, wistfully thinking: *Soon.* I pulled the baby dress out from under the bed and marveled at how something so small could bring such joy. Tristan and I moved the computer out of the office into the living room to make room for the crib. He took my hand in his. My daughter would have a father. A *real* family. God loves three. We kept trying.

Sometimes, I pretended it was all happening to someone else. The distance helped. It wasn't me who was frustrated. It wasn't me who was disappointed. It was someone else. *He rolls off her. Naked, she goes to the bathroom to wash. She imagines that if she loved him, she would pull on one of his old T-shirts, the faded cotton soft to the touch.*

271

Instead, she pulls on pajamas that her grandmother has sewn for her and returns to bed.

Groggily, he takes her in his arms and kisses her temple. Patiently, she waits for him to fall asleep before she disentangles her legs from his and moves to the cool edge of the bed.

You can't have everything, she thinks to herself.

You can have one thing, a voice replies.

She looks at her husband, his face softened in sleep.

He's a good provider, she hears Boba say.

He's a good provider, she hears Molly say.

He snores gently. If she loved him, this soft sound would remind her of the constancy of the sea.

She is unsatisfied. She wants release. Release from the days and nights of longing.

I want, I want, she thinks.

Give yourself this one thing, the voice says again. It is a man's voice. She craves its caress. She runs her hand down the plane of her stomach to her hip bone. She pauses.

Yes, yes, he says.

Yes, yes, she says.

Her back arches, her hand travels lower, she closes her eyes, she gives herself this one thing.

Another barren month passed. Tristan turned forty-one, the same age his dad was when he was born. 'I'm going to be an old father. An old man. It's your fault.'

'You shouldn't have left it so long,' I shot back. 'You could have had a dozen children by now. You should have been like me. Married at twenty-four.'

'I didn't want to marry someone I didn't love.'

And you think I did?

I didn't say it. But God was I tempted.

I begged the clinic secretary to schedule another appointment for us, even though the year wasn't up. As usual, things were easier for a man. Tristan's exam consisted of a plastic cup and a *Playboy*. His sperm count was below average but 'far from catastrophic.'

The doctor stuck a gloved finger into me and groped my lower abdomen, looking for any kind of deficiency. I wondered if he found it. After the examination, Tristan and I sat across from the doctor. The Verdict: He felt I didn't have enough stores of fat and mentioned it could help if I gained weight. Tristan told him I'd grown up in Russia and had suffered as a child. I rolled my eyes.

'Well, she's been in America for a while, and she's still slim. I'd guess it's more about healthy choices than any kind of suppression.'

I looked at him gratefully.

'She's a vegetarian,' Tristan blurted out.

'There are lots of vegetarian moms out there,' the doctor assured him. 'Let's not assign blame here.'

Back in the waiting room, Tristan wrote out a check for the appointment and tests. I couldn't believe how much it cost. And we hadn't even been there an hour! Seeing my shock, the receptionist soothed, 'The insurance should cover most of it.'

'What insurance?' Tristan asked bleakly.

The ride home was tense. Dinner was tense. I was tense. *Bind-bound-bound.* When the phone rang, I flinched. It rang so rarely and when it did, it was usually a telemarketer. Tristan always seemed to relish the fight. 'New windows? Why don't you give me your home number so I can call and interrupt your dinner? Huh? Huh?' he yelled, then slammed the phone down. 'I showed them.'

'They're just doing their job.'

'If their job is to piss me off, mission accomplished.'

I shrugged.

'No one likes telemarketers,' he said.

I rushed to the phone to avoid another shouting match.

'Hello, beauty,' Oksana said. 'Good news. I may be a doctor again.'

'What do you mean?'

'Let me start from the beginning. In Russia. When Jerry said he didn't want me to work, I thought that meant he wanted to spoil me – and I was all for it. You wouldn't believe the fantasies I had. Mansions. Dollar bills growing on rose bushes. A fabulous husband.'

We both laughed. I remembered how I'd thought Tristan was wealthy because he'd given me a laptop. I'd imagined myself living in a Victorian house in the smartest district of San Francisco. I thought we'd be so happy. I knew all about fantasies.

'Now I realize he didn't want me to have friends, colleagues, or my own money. I'm so isolated. It feels like I'm going mad in this big house. Two months ago, I applied for a job at the hospital as a doctor.'

'*Molodets!*' Good for you!

'It's not so easy. They want my transcript. My mother sent it to a translation agency in Los Angeles. I was supposed to pay by check or credit card, but I don't have either. Jerry doesn't give me any cash except for groceries. Holding back a little here and a little there, I saved enough for a money order.'

'He's so cheap?' I asked.

'You can't even ask him for snow in winter,' she replied.

'Who's on the phone?' Tristan yelled.

'Oksana.'

'Speak English!' he said.

'He's just like Jerry.' Oksana said.

'He's not that bad,' I said weakly.

'I'll need to take an exam – in English. Will you help me?'

'I'd love to. But maybe you should ask a native speaker,' I said, worried that Tristan was right, that my English wasn't good enough.

'No one here is as rigorous as a Russian or Ukrainian.'

'That's the truth,' I seconded.

'How are things?'

I sighed.

'I know. He says he'll get me deported if I leave him. Do you think he can?'

'I don't know.'

'Everything's in his name: the car, the house, the bank account. It's like I'm a ghost. I don't exist. Americans are always talking about their rights. "It's my right," they say. What about us? What are *our* rights?'

'I don't know.'

'I'm totally dependent on Jerry – for everything. He says I'll be penniless if we divorce.'

'Are you thinking about it?'

'I wasn't. But as time goes by, I realize he'll never trust anyone again. He's waiting for the bomb to drop. It's almost like he wants it to, so he can say "I knew I shouldn't have trusted you." '

Tristan was glaring at me. 'It's rude to leave the table in the middle of a meal.'

Oh, great. Now he was giving me etiquette lessons.

'I came here for security,' Oksana said. 'I knew I'd never be in love with him, but I thought that we could build a life together, as partners. But he controls everything. It feels like I have less security here than I did at home. What would you do if you were me?' she asked.

I looked over at Tristan, who was shoveling rice into his mouth. 'I am you.'

The nurse called to say the tests revealed there was nothing wrong. She advised me to check for peak days and have intercourse then. After all those tests and all that money, this was all she could say? I was starting to lose faith in Western medicine. It worked about as well as the fertility goddess statues that David had in his apartment pre-Olga.

I asked Oksana to examine me. She said if I'd consulted an American doctor, there wasn't much more she could add, but she did suggest that I see an acquaintance of hers, a white witch who'd worked as a midwife. We decided on a Sunday. Tristan moaned, but he drove me to Jerry's. Oksana and the white witch stood on the front porch, waiting. I felt immediately welcomed. She was short and plump with dark eyes and raven black hair. It was silly, but she reminded me of my mother. I felt a surge of hope. Maybe she could help me.

Tristan started to follow us women down the corridor, but Jerry said, 'Don't be a pussy. Get in here and watch the game.' He gestured to the gigantic television.

In the kitchen, Oksana pointed to the dark cabinets and brocade wallpaper. 'I call it the "ex-wife kitchen." I wanted to lighten it up, but Jerry forbade any changes. He said he wants his kids to feel at home. But they never come.'

Tears filled her eyes. 'Everything will be fine,' I clucked like a mother hen, putting my wing around her dejected shoulders. The white witch put the kettle on. Over tea, she and Oksana shared gory hospital stories until finally Oksana started to feel better.

The white witch took my pulse, my temperature, and asked the same questions as the fertility specialist. I had been embarrassed to talk about such things with the American doctor, but in my own language, with another woman, I felt at ease. After taking my medical history, she asked a question that the American doctor had not. 'How are things with your husband?'

I glanced at Oksana.

'Your life can't be any worse than mine,' she said.

'Difficult,' I whispered, not looking at them, not wanting to admit anything aloud. 'He monitors my calls. I had friends at first, but he ran them off. I thought he was just awkward, but now I think he does it on purpose, to isolate me ... He told me he was a teacher, but he's a custodian. I didn't think he was a millionaire, but I didn't know he was broke. Nothing I do is right – not the way I dress, cook, or talk.'

The white witch nodded. 'Stress and an unhealthy home atmosphere. I'll give you some incense to get rid of the negative energy.'

It would take a lot more than incense to help me.

She pulled a stethoscope from her purse and asked me to take off my shirt.

I looked at Oksana. 'Can we lock the door?'

'You can't even lock the bathroom in this house.'

'*Koshmar!*' I said. What a nightmare!

'He wants access at any time.'

The white witch put the cold disk on my chest and told me to breathe deeply. 'What's this?' she asked, pointing to the diamond ring.

'It's complicated,' I said, looking at Oksana.

Oksana told her the story. Girl meets mobster. Falls for mobster. Flees mobster. Keeps souvenir. 'Get rid of it,' the white witch said. 'It's not doing you any good.' She placed the disk on my back. 'I am listening and listening and your heart tells an interesting story.'

She put the stethoscope away and stood behind me. I was just about to turn around when I felt her hands on my shoulders. Her fingers worked their way towards my neck. '*Nu. Nu,*' she muttered. Well, well. She lit a cone of incense in a small metal locket. Rosemary and thyme. Walking around me, she swirled the incense around my head and watched the thin trail billow and disappear. 'My child,' she said after a long moment of looking at the smoke

276

that was no longer there. 'The reason you can't conceive is because you don't want a child. Not with this man.'

I put my face in my hands.

'That can't be it,' Oksana sputtered. 'If a woman could choose when to get pregnant or not there would be no need for birth control.'

'She is so tight,' the wise woman said. She tried to loosen my shoulders, but they would not soften. 'When a woman is this tense, the body closes up. The mind and the body are linked. The body obeys the mind.'

It was painful to hear aloud what I already knew in my heart.

Chapter 21

My Dear Boba
Greetings From Sunny California!

America is all that I thought it would be and more. I have a wonderful job. Tristan is the perfect husband. Life in the country is like already living in heaven – quiet and peaceful.

Despite my avid happiness, I miss you. I miss you terribly. I miss Odessa. I miss our cozy apartment. I miss my job. I miss feeling smart. And important. I even miss David. More than anything, I want to go home. I've realized that true happiness comes from being with the people you love. All the things I thought would make me happy – food delivered right to the door, a driver's license, a house – don't mean much if

I pulled out another sheet of stationery and recopied the first paragraph then signed, *Love and miss you, Dasha.* I had joined the ranks of struggling immigrants who write home about American streets paved in gold. Lenin said everything that glitters is not gold. How right he was.

The more I wanted to tell Boba the truth the more I lied. And here is the worst Odessan sin: I wasn't even original – I stole details from letters written by Soviet Unions clients. He's the perfect husband. Life in the country is like already living in heaven. Why hadn't I read between the lines of what our girls had written? How could I have been so blind? Maybe I could talk to some of them here in America.

'What are our rights? What about us?' Oksana's words haunted me. What are our rights? I called some of girls I'd helped and they told me their experiences. Some were happy, some were not, but they said the same things. One had even put a document together called *Getting the Love You Deserve: Finding and Marrying a Russian Woman*, available on the Internet for only $49.99. She sent me a copy as a thank you for having interpreted for her. I sped through the pages – preparation of documents, waiting, fingerprinting, waiting, interview, waiting, adjustment of status, waiting, green card. She didn't cover rights or deportation. The bottom line: Couples have to be married for two years before a foreign bride receives a permanent green card. Oksana was thrilled to learn that she was close to becoming a permanent resident, with or without Jerry. I realized I wasn't even halfway there.

I continued to fight the static and party lines to talk to Boba every Sunday. Unfortunately, Tristan had become one more thing I fought. He stood in front of me and pointed to his watch. More and more, I fantasized about going home, even for a visit. I wanted to see Boba. But there was only one way I could afford a ticket. The ring. My hand flew to my chest.

Maybe the white witch was right.

After I hung up, Tristan took my hand. 'I'm not trying to hurt you,' he said. 'I'm just telling you that we can't afford it. Money's pretty tight. I didn't tell you, but that San Francisco trip cost over 500 bucks. A ten-minute call to Ukraine costs forty dollars. Can you please try to talk less? We're really in trouble here, money-wise.'

'I can try,' I said. 'I just miss my Boba.'

'I know you do.' He took me in his arms and kissed my temple.

Monday morning, the second he drove off, I dialed my old number. I needed this connection. I needed to hear Boba's voice.

For once, the line was clear.

'Tell me about your mother, Boba.'

'Mama was a beauty, but after she was widowed, she never remarried. That meant we were poor because we only had one salary. I went to work at the factory when I was sixteen. Life was hard then. We were always struggling, always hungry. My sister Stasia and I fished with string and a bit of wire for the hook. We were always proud when we caught something.' Boba and I spoke for hours, like when I was back home, in our kitchen. Only this time, she talked, and I listened.

'Boba, one thing I never understood, about religion …' I didn't know what I was asking exactly. Perhaps how she had gone from a Jew to a Ukrainian in Odessa. Perhaps I was asking why. Perhaps I was asking who she was. Perhaps I was asking who I was.

She sighed. 'Where to start, my little rabbit paw? My neighbor Izya and I entered the factory on the same day. We worked near each other, the only Jews in the whole place. He fell in love with a girl named Inna. His parents weren't happy about it, but it was right after the war. Everyone had lost someone, everyone was hungry, everyone was suffering. They allowed him to marry his *Ukrainka*. Weddings were small in those days – families couldn't afford to feed many guests. He married on Saturday and came back to work on Tuesday. Only Izya was now Igor and he'd taken his wife's surname.

'He wasn't the only one. This is how I knew it was possible to have documents changed. Izya and I worked together all our lives. He was heartsick my brilliant daughter didn't have the right to go to college because she was a Jew. He heard me brag about how smart you were and suggested that I have my papers changed, so you'd stand a chance of going to university. His wife's cousin, the one who'd altered his documents, was retiring in a week. She would do the deed for a thousand rubles; Izya offered to pay half. I didn't have time to think. You were still young, but I wanted you to have opportunities. Maybe I was wrong. I don't know. But you did go to university and you did get a degree.'

'But do you believe, Boba? What do you believe?'

'Believe?'

Silence.

Did she hear my question? Or did she not want to answer? Should I just let it go?

'What was it like, growing up a Jew?' I tried again.

'My sister and I didn't have any religious education. Neither did our girlfriends. Maybe if we'd been boys it would have been different. Growing up, I didn't think about religion or faith. It wasn't something we ever discussed. Mama was reserved, and Stasia and I could only respect her feelings.'

'And you, Boba? What about you?'

'Maybe in America it's different,' she said, her voice low, almost a growl. 'Perhaps there you're an American first and a Jew second. Here you are not a Jew *and* a Ukrainian, you are either or. I was born here, yet not considered Ukrainian, not considered a citizen. Not until I changed our papers. That's what I think. That's why I wanted you to leave this insane asylum for good. I don't want you surrounded by people like Olga, who smile to your face, then stab you between the shoulder blades the moment you turn your back.'

'What about the icons? Why do you have so many?' I pressed. I didn't want to think about Olga ever again.

'Ah, the icons,' she said, her voice hardening. 'I didn't tell anyone I'd had our papers altered. But people found out. Odessa is like a village. One evening, when I got home from work, there was a small package lying in front of the door. I picked it up and took it inside. It was an icon, a small wooden square with a saint painted on it. Her face was so calm and peaceful. There were words of old Slavonic painted on the bottom left-hand corner. The person put it on the landing in the same way one would hang garlic on Dracula's door. As a warning or a reproach, as if to say, *I know all about you.* But that's not how I took it. I looked at the cool beauty of the saint and thought, she knows something about suffering, about loss, and I put her in a prominent place on our bookshelf. Another, then another arrived, usually with a message. *Liar. Hypocrite. Fraud.* Who left them I don't know. I only know looking at these faces soothed me. And now they remind me of why I wanted you to leave this place.'

How could I tell Boba that I wanted to come home?

A month later, when he received the phone bill, Tristan slammed it on the kitchen counter. *Hide-hid-hidden.* 'How could you?' he yelled. 'I tell you we don't have any money, and you go behind my back and call even more? A four-hundred-dollar phone bill! That's double the usual. Man! You're crazy. Or stupid. I don't know which one. I don't get it.' *Leave-left-left.*

He slammed paper after paper onto the counter. Bank statements. All in the red. Phone bills from when he courted me. Credit card bills. 'Calls to Ukraine. Plane tickets to Budapest –

mine and yours, restaurants, and the hotel there. The laptop and fare to Odessa. Your ticket from Odessa to San Francisco.'

He'd spent thousands. Before we even met. Of course, I knew he'd paid a lot for me, but to see my debt in black and white … I stood there, stunned and sick with the realization that I could never pay back all that I owed.

'You cleaned me out. I had to borrow money from Hal after I maxed out my credit cards. There's no more money to pay for your fucking phone bills. Or your five-hundred-dollar visits to San Fran. Hotels cost money. Gas costs money. We're broke. Do you know what that means?'

I nodded.

'I gave up a lot to get you here, now it's your turn to sacrifice. I know it's not anyone's idea of a dream job, but they need nurses' aides up in Paloma. They're always looking for help at the café. If we're going to have a family, we'll need a nest egg.'

He tugged on my chin. 'No more phone calls, right?'

When he left for work the next morning, I called David on his direct line. *Tell-told-told.* I don't know why I did it. Maybe I *was* crazy.

'I'm listening,' David answered briskly like an Odessan. One word. *Slushiyou.* That surprised me. I felt a moment of pride. He was adapting. He liked our language.

'*Slushiyou,*' he repeated.

I didn't say anything. I was listening, too.

'Who is this? How did you get my number?' he barked in English.

I sighed. 'David.' I couldn't help it; I missed him.

'Daria,' he whispered. 'Is it you?' Tears streamed down my cheeks. 'Daria, wherever you are, come home.'

I sobbed.

'Do you need money? I can get it to you, if you'll just tell me where you are. Come home. I miss you. I need you.'

Home. I miss you. I need you. I hung up, afraid that if I didn't, I'd repeat his words. Tristan was right – I needed a job, something to do before I went even crazier. I left the house, knowing that if I stayed near the phone, I would dial his number again and tell him everything.

I couldn't stay at home any longer. I'd cleaned every surface of the house, including the windows, several times. I'd cooked every recipe in the *Low Fat and Lovin' It* cookbook. I'd watched all his movies (*Die Hard* I, II, III; *Star Wars* I,II, III; *Indiana Jones* I, II, III; *Rambo* I, II, III, *Rocky* I, II, III, IV), I read my books dozens of times. I paced. I wrote *Dear Jane, Forgive me for my silence. You were so right and I so wrong, and I simply did not want to admit it.* Then I ripped up the letter and threw it into the fireplace and watched it burn.

Jane had written to the closest universities for information on master's classes; I looked through catalogs from Berkeley and Stanford, touching the smooth, shiny pages of happy students. But if we couldn't afford to pay the phone bill, how could we pay for schooling? Even if I could get loans and grants like Jane said, he would never let me out of his sight.

I walked to the town's only café before I made any other insane phone calls.

It was a dark place. Dark paneling and carpet, and it smelled as if the cook had fried chicken for thirty solid years. The man behind the cash register wore chewed-up jeans and a T-shirt and had long hair and a handlebar mustache. When he smiled, I noticed he had more tattoos than teeth. I asked him who I should contact for a job.

'I'm the owner,' he said. 'Name's Skeet.'

Americans often asked impertinent questions. I loved this. I longed to do it. 'What is Skeet short for?'

'George.' He guffawed and handed me an application.

I filled it out, requesting evening shifts. As defeat spilled over me, I did what Boba would have instructed – I looked for the positive: the job would give me room to breathe, it would give me my own income. I didn't let myself resent the small town. Didn't remind myself that there was a reason I hadn't been able to find Emerson on a map, that only a fool doesn't look before she leaps. I went to the bathroom to put on the brown sweat-stained uniform Skeet handed me. And felt my childhood dreams die. Buck up, I told my reflection. A job is a job. Money is money. You're in America. That's what you wanted.

Skeet taught me to take orders and how to carry five plates at the same time. 'This's a tough job. Ya have to be strong.'

I was strong. I could do it.

I went home and told Tristan my news.

Waitressing wasn't so bad. I enjoyed talking and joking with the customers. I grew accustomed to the job and even looked forward to it. It got me out of the house. Of course, after the first time, I never ate at the restaurant. Never. The bagged salad tasted like formaldehyde. The potatoes were bought already peeled and boiled. Where? And by whom? The cooks soaked the steaks in large tubs of mayonnaise to tenderize them. They prepared a large pan of lasagna and kept it in the refrigerator for weeks. And I saw Skeet drop a slice of buttered toast on the floor, pick it up, and put it back on the plate.

The cook's name was Raymond. He worked double shifts because his wife was sick and they didn't have insurance to cover her 'meds.' The evening dishwasher was a high-school student named Rocky. He loved his truck, shop class, and a girl named Pamela Anderson.

I loved this feeling when I was with Americans. They would say anything, absolutely anything. Even intimate details about their lives. On a slow night at the restaurant, I talked to Pam, another waitress. She wore the same uniform as me, a knee-length polyester dress with a large white collar. Right away, she told me she'd gone through a bad divorce (which made me wonder if there was such a thing as a good divorce) and needed a place to 'recoup.' She was about thirty and had eyes with watery whites that were actually pink – she scared me a little because she looked so sad, I thought she would burst into tears.

'So where'd you come from? You talk all funny.'

I failed to see what was humorous, but answered, 'Russia,' because no one here knew or cared about Ukraine. I continued to ladle the ranch dressing from the white bucket into the plastic squeeze bottles. She refilled the salt shakers.

'Well, you sound prissy.'

I shrugged. I couldn't help how I sounded.

She looked at my hands. 'So you're married?'

I nodded.

'Got kids?'

I shook my head.

'I got two,' she said. 'It just happened. Don't know what I was thinking. I should've been like you and waited.'

It seemed she was seriously telling me she regretted having children.

'So how long you been married?' she asked.

'Nine months.'

'I heard he comes around.'

'Yep,' I said, trying out a new word I heard people use all around me. I'd had a week of freedom at work in the evening. Then he came in 'just to see how things were going.' He asked for a Coke, so I served him and he sat there for an hour, just watching me. He came in the next night and the next and the next and glowered at anyone who talked to me. In these moments, I hated him.

'Think he'll come in tonight?' she asked. She started filling the pepper shakers.

How I wished I had the courage to say, 'God I hope not.' But I remained silent.

She nudged me and winked. 'So how's your sex life?'

I wanted to talk 'casual' like a real American, to use phrases like 'you don't know shit' or 'she works her butt off.' More than that, I wanted to be honest and forthright like Americans. I wanted to tell her what I was unable to tell Jane, to tell myself. I closed my eyes and screwed up the courage to be honest about just one thing, then looked her straight in the eye and said, 'It sucks. It really sucks.'

I had a job and money and paid the phone bill, but when I called anyone, even Molly, he turned up the television volume so I could barely hear. He hated to hear me speak Russian with Boba because he couldn't understand. Paranoid, he thought we were talking about him. As if. We talked about everything but him. Boba described the borscht she made that week, or the amber-colored honey she bought at the bazaar. My mouth watered as I imagined these tastes of home. She said she still hadn't received a single phone bill. When she called the telecom office, the clerk insisted it was paid. How could that be? She said, 'For once, they made a mistake in my favor, I won't question it.'

'Are you still on the phone?' he growled.

Shrink-shrank-shrunk.

'Why is he always grumbling?' Boba asked. 'He was so nice in Odessa. Was that just a façade?'

Oh, Boba, you have no idea. I put my hand over the mouthpiece, and said, 'Will you please let me talk to my grandmother?'

'You've been talking for twenty minutes, eighty dollars. That's enough.' He grabbed the receiver and slammed it down.

'You, you monster!' I sputtered. 'I have my own money, I can do what I want.'

He stood there, as if stunned.

'S-sorry,' he said.

The phone rang. And rang. We just stared at it. Finally, I picked it up. It was Boba. I'd given her the number in case of an emergency but never expected her to use it – calling from Ukraine was horribly expensive. A minute cost one-fifth of her monthly pension.

'We must have been cut off. You know how the phone lines are.'

'I know how the phone lines are,' she repeated in a tone of voice that told me she knew exactly what had happened. 'Little rabbit paw, maybe you should come home. Maybe I was wrong to tell you to go to America …'

'I'm fine, Boba. Wouldn't I tell you if I were suffering? This is costing so much. Let's say goodbye until next week.' I hung up the phone.

'I'm sorry,' Tristan sniveled. 'Sorry, sorry. I love you. I love you.'

'Would you just leave me the fuck alone?' I yelled, speaking my mind like a real American woman. I grabbed my copy of *Anna Karenina* and took refuge in the bathroom – the only room with a lock. I stayed there the whole afternoon, lying on a towel in the tub, reading. As always, Tolstoy spoke directly to me from the first page. '… there was no sense in their living together and that people who meet accidentally at any inn have more connection with each other than they …' What to do? Like poor Oblonsky, I again pictured all the details of my quarrel with Tristan, all the hopelessness of my position and, the most painful of all, my own guilt.

And yet … How dare he hang up on my grandmother? Boba was right. He'd been so nice. That was then. And now … Now I didn't want to look at him. I didn't want to touch him, not even accidentally while asleep. I would sleep in another room. And it would be a relief. I hated the way his milky sperm oozed out of my body, how most nights I went to sleep with a pad between my legs to sop up his mess.

I made up the bed in the office and lay there, next to the empty crib. At midnight, he threw open the door and turned on the light.

'Are you coming to bed?'

I squinted up at him. 'I am in bed.'

He slammed the door.

At work the next day, I asked the guys at work to put a deadlock on the office door. Tristan brought home six limp roses as a peace offering. I stuffed them down the garbage disposal. Never was I happier to have a modern appliance.

True to earlier Soviet-American cold war relations, we did not fight, we did not yell. We simply did not talk. After six nights of sleeping in the office, the door locked, Tristan came to me as I stood at the kitchen counter making a rump roast for him, apple compote for me. I bristled with anger and he slunk towards me like a dog that has displeased his master. He laid his latest peace offering on the counter. *Men are from Mars, Women are from Venus.* He'd chosen the right gesture. Books always pleased me. Dinner was a somber affair in which we did not speak, the only sound was him chewing and the scrape of cutlery on his plate as he dissected his meat. After dinner I took the book and began to read. Men are different. They have different needs. Different desires. *Nu, da.* Well, duh. Between the last page and the back cover, I found a letter.

Dearest Daria,

We haven't wrote to each other since you came to California. I miss your letters. They told me exactly what you felt. And when I wrote, I thought of what I was going to say a head of time. Now, I say and do things without thinking of how it will effect you. Maybe I should go back to writing letters.

I have made many mistakes since you got here. I'm so sorry for hanging up on your grandma. It is the worse thing I have ever done. I should of understood how important talking to her is. I should of been more understanding. You and her should be able to talk as much as you want, whenever you want. I will work more hours so that you can talk to her more.

I hope that you can forgive me for being such a jerk. I love you more than anything more than anyone with all my heart and all my soul and more than anything want to live with you as husband and wife, to start a family, to be a real family with you. You are the most beautiful woman in the world and when I am with you, I finally feel like I am someone.

Your loving husband, Tristan

I opened the office door. When he took me in his arms, I felt only pity and exhaustion. But these emotions are just as binding as love. He steered me to the bedroom. His eyes were solemn and he wanted to talk about it all over again. I had no desire to. As he opened his mouth to apologize again, I asked, 'How did you find me?'

He looked at me, tears floating in his eyes. 'It all started at my twenty-year high school reunion. A buddy there had a Filipina wife. She was real pretty and young. She didn't speak a word of English and looked up at him like an adoring puppy. She'd arrived the month before. We all thought he didn't want to be single for the reunion, so he got himself a wife.

'I asked him about it and he told me that it was easy, that there are dozens of dating sites and thousands of women looking for a decent guy. When he read what Amelia wrote and looked at her picture, he decided she was the one.'

'Amelia doesn't sound like an Asian name,' I said.

'Actually, she changed it. Her real name was unpronounceable.'

A little like Daria, I thought to myself. 'What did she look like? What did she say?'

'She was short and cute. On her profile, she wrote – well, someone translated what she said, because she hardly speaks two words of English – that she was a traditional lady who wanted a home, a husband and children. She didn't need a lot of money, she just wanted kindness and respect. He went and got her. Well, that gave me the idea. If he could do it, why couldn't I? He's just an ordinary guy like me, but he has a sexy wife twenty years younger than him. I thought I'd have more in common with a European woman, so I looked at the Russian sites. Some had over eight hundred ladies. It was overwhelming. I looked at the ones my age and they looked ten years older than me ...'

It's true that our women have so much work and so many worries that they age quickly.

'So I looked at younger ones. Ladies so beautiful that I could never have scored with them in America. It was, like, whoa –'

'Whoa?'

'Because it just didn't seem right. Looking at those pictures. I thought it made me desperate and crazy. So I stopped.'

This reassured me. He felt the same way I had. I took his hand in mine.

'But then winter rolled around and I was so lonesome that I thought I was gonna die, so I started looking again. There're no single women in Emerson. It seemed like every girl has a guy, you know? Everybody my age is married and anyone younger leaves this town for bigger and better things. So I started looking on the net again and planned a trip to St. Petersburg.'

'You went to Russia?' Bells went off. He told me he'd never traveled before. Was that a lie, too?

'No, no,' he said quickly. 'I chickened out.'

'Chickened out?'

'Wimped out. Got scared.'

'Oh.'

'Then I saw the Soviet Unions site. You were in photos at the socials, but not in the profiles section, so I figured you worked there. The way you smiled ... you just glowed. I wanted to be happy like that. It probably sounds stupid, but it just seemed like you were looking at me. Like your eyes met mine. Like there was a connection. Like you wanted to meet me, so I gave my credit card number and created a profile on the website like the girls did. I hoped you'd see it, that you would feel the same connection and contact me. Is that what happened?'

'My boss asked me to correspond with someone. I chose you.'
I felt a pang. I missed Valentina and her forthright, shrewd way. Why had I cut myself off from everyone? If I told her about my situation, I wondered what she would advise. *Take him camping, where neighbors aren't so close and you have a large piece of wood at hand...*

'You chose me?' His voice was awed, as though he'd never been first choice. 'Why?'

I couldn't tell him I'd been annoyed and didn't want anyone, so Valentina had chosen. I stole a common phrase from the couples at our socials. 'You had the kindest eyes.'

'Awww.' His hand reached over and kneaded my hip like it was tough dough. I felt no chemistry, no spark. I cursed Vlad. If I'd never been with him, perhaps I would have been content with Tristan's wet kisses and his awkward attempts at lovemaking. I told myself that it was a blessing that Tristan wasn't a gifted lover – it meant that he wasn't a player. That good sex didn't mean anything. But I didn't believe my own words. I wanted strong, sensual hands. I'd tried to show Tristan what I wanted, but as usual, he continued his own litany of moves. I closed my eyes tight and prepared for the onslaught. Every time was the same. His tongue spun in my mouth like a pinwheel. Then he whispered, 'I love you.' The effect was ruined when his tongue went back into my ear, as if to block the words from crawling out. I tried to inch away, but he pulled me tighter to him. This time, I spun around so that my breasts were squished against the mattress, my head twisted away from him. My legs were tangled in the flannel sheets and my bottom was raised slightly as I tried to shuffle forward and away like an inchworm.

'So that's the way you want to play it,' he said and thrust inside me. I looked at the pine headboard and started to count. It was over by number eight.

Chapter 22

Dear Boba,
I hope that you are well. I am

The phone rang; I hadn't even finished the word hello when I heard, 'Daria, is it you? Have I finally found you? You're in America, but where? I don't recognize the area code.'

Tears welled in my eyes. I didn't want to tell him. And anyway, it seemed ridiculous. Lost. In America.

'Do you need help? Are you ever coming home?'

I tried not to cry.

'I miss you. We need you here. Vlad is breathing down my neck, the rates keep going up at the port, and Vita and Vera have made life hell for your replacement. If you were here, I know those bastard inspectors wouldn't have dared raise their "fees." You could rein in Vita and Vera. You could get Vlad off my back.'

It had been so long since I'd had any reminder of who I'd been: an audacious, clever girl. I couldn't respond to a single thing he said. Bile and mucus and blood pounded together. My throat constricted. My jaw quivered. I fought to regain control.

'How did you get to America?'

Hiccough.

'Please don't tell me you married one of those losers from your socials.'

Hiccough. Sniffle.

'You did. I can't believe it.' He sighed. 'Didn't I tell you that they were all pathetic freaks who couldn't get a wife in their own countries? Why didn't you listen to me?'

I sobbed. And sobbed. It felt good that someone knew the truth. That I didn't have to say a word. If he would have shown any sympathy at all, I would have died. Instead, and rightly, he pretended that nothing was wrong, that I wasn't bawling my eyes out on the end of the line. He started talking about Odessa: the weather (perfect, of course. It was, after all, Odessa), the opera he'd seen the evening before, the monuments going up in the city center. These details, the sound of his voice calmed me and I could finally respond with a sniffle, 'No city in the world has more monuments than Odessa.'

'I know,' he said. 'You've told me ten times. You also told me Odessa's opera house is the third most beautiful in the world after Sydney's and Timbuktu's.'

I laughed. 'What can I say? We Odessans are proud of our city.'

It was so easy to talk about Odessa. I was mortified that he knew, relieved I didn't have to explain. He didn't talk about his life either. As he spoke, my tears dried and I felt happy for the first time in months. Finally, I worked up the courage to ask, 'How did you get this number?'

'How do you think? I stole it.'

I smiled. He really was an Odessan.

'I knew your grandmother would call you. I've been stealing her phone bill for months, hoping. And she finally did.' He sounded very proud of his intrepid self.

'I'm glad you didn't give up.'

'I was about to. I felt ridiculous loitering around the entryway of the courtyard, waiting for the postwoman to pass, avoiding nosy neighbors, then prying your grandmother's mailbox open with a penknife. But after your call, I knew you needed a friend.'

'More than ever.'

'No one knows where you are. Why didn't you tell anyone you were leaving for good? Why not write to Valentina and some of your other friends?'

'You're right. I don't know what I was thinking. Afraid to jinx everything, I guess.'

'You Odessans with your superstitions.'

'We can't help ourselves.'

'You sound so unhappy. Isn't there anything I can do?'

I sighed. *Move back time. Get me a green card so I can get a job in San Francisco. Offer me my old job in Odessa. Find someone to put Tristan down.*

'Can you really hear that I'm unhappy?' I hated that I sounded pathetic. That he could actually hear I was miserable.

'Only because I know you. Hasn't your Boba said anything?'

'No, but I hide everything from her.'

'What do you mean "hide everything"?'

'With Vita and Vera, you have to stand up for yourself. Tell your new girl that. Tell her to shout that they're nothing but a two-headed, one-brained pink monster any time they start in on her. If she makes a scandal in front of co-workers, they'll back off.'

'What are you hiding?'

'Threaten one port inspector. Say that if the company lodges enough complaints, he'll be fired. Remind him dozens are lined up in his shadow, just waiting for a shot at his goods-paying job.'

'What did you mean?'

'Tell Vlad you can't concentrate on earning money and running a business with him breathing down your neck. Tell him if you have the space you need, he'll see results.'

'Won't you tell me?'

'Don't make me say,' I whispered. 'Everything you imagine is true.'

'Why won't you let me help you?'

I didn't say anything.

'Tell me what to do and I'll do it,' he said, his voice hoarse. 'Tell me what you need and I'll get it to you. You know I'd do anything for you.'

I closed my eyes. I wanted help. Needed help. But didn't want any more debt. 'I have to go.' I started to put down the phone.

'Wait!' I heard him yell. 'Vlad still asks about you. He's here all the time. He thinks I know where you are. He tore up all of Odessa and Kiev looking for you. I heard he has someone tailing your Boba. You should throw him a bone.'

I imagined Vlad emaciated with love for me, destitute after spending his millions looking for me, riddled with self-anger, no, self-hatred, at having let the best thing in his life escape. I imagined him on his knees before me again.

'Why do I care about Vlad?' I asked. 'Besides, I'm married.'

'So?'

Just so.

I folded down the first page of the marine biology section in the University of California catalog, put it in a manila envelope and sent it to Vlad with no note, no return address – just the postmark from Emerson. This simple act gave me such perverse pleasure. I imagined it was somehow cheating on Tristan and torturing Vlad.

How was I to know a month later, I would go to work only to find a black Mercedes with blacked-out windows parked in front of the café? There was a ticket on the windshield, since the car was parked in a handicapped zone. Perhaps the driver was a wealthy oligarch who didn't care about other people. Or perhaps he was from a country that didn't have handicapped zones or priority cashier lanes for pregnant ladies. Vlad? No, it couldn't be. Could it? I smoothed down my hair, just in case. No, it couldn't be. But how I hoped it was him.

Comme la vie est lente
Et comme l'Espérance est violente.

Yes, life is slow, and hope is violent. It couldn't be him. I put my hand to my ring – his ring, to my heart. *Beat-beat-beaten*. I entered the café. Vlad was sitting on one of the metal chairs facing the door. *Shake-shook-shaken*. He stood when he saw me. Instead of his all-black uniform he was wearing jeans and an Oxford shirt. He'd come. All this way. Surely that meant something, I meant something to him. Hope tore through my body. *Sing-sang-sung*. He stared at me, taking in my face, my brown polyester uniform, my white socks and tennis shoes. All he said was, '*Nyet.*'

He was here. My heart rejoiced as my pride wallowed.

'*Da.*' I looked down at my sneakers. In Odessa, I'd had so many fine high heels. In Odessa, I'd been someone important. Here, I was no one. My only solace had been that nobody had witnessed my descent. Now the one person I didn't want to see me like this was here. Here! He was here! I bit my lip. Emotions flurried together like snowflakes coming down in a winter storm over the streets of Odessa. Shy hopeful scared flattered thrilled ashamed.

Everything would be fine. Everything would be fine. *Fling-flung-flung.* I tucked a lock of hair behind my ear. And couldn't think of a single thing to say.

'When the man at the grocery store said you worked here, I assumed you were the bookkeeper.'

My chin shot up and he laughed. 'Don't be offended, my darling. It doesn't matter to me what your profession is.'

'Really?'

'You're beautiful, like a melon in a field of scarecrows.'

I smiled shyly and took a step towards him.

'What's that?' he asked, looking at my left hand.

And he did not take his eyes,
Staring blankly, from my ring.

'What do you think it is? How do you think I got here?' I responded, suddenly angry.

He walked around me and out the door.

I sat down and stared at the wall.

'Jesus he was a handsome man,' Pam said. She'd walked out of the kitchen and stood in front of me. 'Look,' she held up a twenty. 'This is what he gave me for a tip.'

'He's a very rich man. He can buy whatever he wants,' I said bitterly.

'You know him?'

I looked up at her. 'He's a guy from home I dated right before I came here.'

She sat down. 'You married Tristan instead of him? Why?'

A bitter bark of laughter escaped my lips. 'I'm having a really hard time remembering why.'

She tucked the twenty in her pocket. 'He must really love you. Do you still love him?'

My lips twisted into a sour little smile. Love. What was love? I still didn't know. 'What kind of guy flies all the way to America to see a girl and break her heart all over again?'

'Maybe you made the right choice.'

'Maybe I should have gone with choice c: none of the above.'

She put her hand over mine. 'Aw, hon.'

'Please don't tell anyone I said that,' I said.

'Your secret's safe with me.'

And I knew it was. She was like a lot of women in Odessa. One look at their faces and you could tell they'd endured a lifetime of crap. All the things I couldn't admit to Boba, couldn't divulge to Jane, Pam knew them. Why can we tell things to strangers, things we can't tell our closest friends?

'Thank you, Pam.'

She pulled me to my feet. 'It's like there was just a shooting star and we're the only two people to see it.' She looked around the café. Vlad had been the only customer. Skeet wasn't there and the guys were in the back doing prep work.

I smiled sadly. 'More like a mirage.'

'Do you think he'll be back?' she asked as she put paper placemats on the table.

I shrugged.

'Why didn't you follow him? I definitely would have.'

I laid the silverware on top of the placemat. 'It wouldn't have made a difference.' If you run after a man, he'll just run faster. That's what we say in Odessa. Wasn't it the same in America?

I tried to find some small thing to be thankful for. Tristan hadn't come in for once. At least he hadn't seen Vlad, thanks to Monday night football. Or was it baseball?

It was a slow night, so Pam told me to go home early. I trudged down Main Street, conscious of the smell of grease that permeated my skin, the perspiration that clung to my body, the hollow ache in my ribcage. Why hadn't I hidden my ring? Why hadn't I grabbed his arm when he strode past? No. I should have punched him when I'd had the chance. I looked at my reflection in a darkened store window. I saw a tired, miserable fool with dead eyes and defeated shoulders. A fool who'd deserted her grandmother, cut herself off from friends, left Odessa, and for what? She still loved Vlad. She still didn't love her husband.

I stared at the glass until I saw Vlad's reflection beside mine. Another mirage.

'What's that?' I mimicked, holding up my left hand. 'Nothing compared to this.' I pulled out the diamond that I kept so close to my heart. His expression, for the first time unguarded, was one of tenderness, of understanding. His mouth softened, his dark eyes shone.

'*Dushenka*,' he whispered. My little soul. 'You wear my ring. I'm sorry. I should have known. I had no right to be angry. You did what you had to do. No one understands that more than I.'

'What are you doing here?' Chin up. Defenses up. I was still an Odessan. Emotion scares us.

'I thought you sent for me. Wasn't that university catalog a love letter?'

He was still an Odessan, taking refuge in sarcasm. Make a gigantic gesture, then make it seem like it doesn't matter. Did I really expect him to say, 'I missed you. I wanted to see if there was a chance we could be together.'?

'Fuck you,' I said.

'I noticed that wasn't "fuck off." Do I still have a chance?'

Instinctively, my hand crept to my chest and I cradled his ring in my fingers.

'I ripped Odessa apart looking for you. Hell, I even went to Kiev. My eyes and ears searched for you in Moscow and St Petersburg. The minute I got your "love letter," I applied for a visa and bought a damn map of California. Do I still have a chance?'

'For what? I'm married. And it's your fault.'

'What?' he yelled. 'How could it possibly be my fault?'

'You left. For three months.'

'I came back.'

'Too late.' I wrapped my arms around my body as if to shore myself up. 'Look at you in the restaurant. I say something you don't like and you walk out.'

'I came back. I'll keep coming back.' He took a step towards me. I stood my ground. Let him come.

He held out his hand, palm up. 'I don't want to force you. It has to be your decision.'

I stared at him. The anger left my body. Pride, resentment, frustration, loneliness, and desire remained. Which emotion would win? A year ago, he could have wriggled his finger and I would have come running. I'd grown up since then. I'd changed. I wouldn't go to him. I couldn't go to him.

Or could I?

A mysterious exchange occurred within me. Pull. Push. Yes. No. Why? Why not? Give yourself this one pleasure. Forget Tristan. Forget everything. Just this once.

I grabbed his hand and pulled him off the deserted main street. Five minutes later we stood in the trees, staring at each other. He nuzzled my neck, my hair. I sighed.

'You smell good,' he growled.

'I smell like grease,' I protested and pushed him away, embarrassed.

He pulled me to him. 'Exactly. Like fried potatoes. It makes me want to devour you.' He took my right hand and kissed my fingers, my palm, my wrist. 'I missed you so much. Missed talking to you. Hell, I even missed your sharp tongue.'

I didn't want to talk. I tugged at my uniform and kicked off my tennis shoes. 'Want. You. Here. Now.'

'Not here,' he protested, but I knew this was one of the times that no meant yes, right now.

I pulled him down with me onto the leaves and grass and warm earth. Pulled his body onto mine. My fingers dug into his flesh, my lips hot on his neck. I wanted his body to pound mine. Again and again until I was sated.

'You don't have to go back,' I told him afterwards. 'You could stay here. Buy your citizenship.'

'You ran a shipping company in Odessa. You dealt with the port officials, the tax men, and me. The smartest girl in all of Odessa is a waitress here. A waitress. America hasn't done you any good. At home I'm the king. What would I be here? A guy you fuck after a hard night at work before you go home to your husband?'

I ignored the anger in his voice. 'You could be a marine biologist.'

'A single marine biologist,' he countered. 'Pining after a married lady. Come back to Odessa. I can give you anything you want. Forget you were ever here. Come home.'

His words brought me crashing back down to my little life. Part of me wanted to return to Odessa. To see Boba, to take her in my arms. David would take me back, I was sure of it. No one ever laughed at me in Odessa. I was strong there. If Vlad was king, I would be queen. But would going back be a step back? And could

I leave Tristan after all he'd done for me? *You have a job. You could reimburse him. Go home with Vlad. Don't you want to see Boba?* The voice was tempting. It came from deep inside me and knew exactly what I wanted. But how could I leave America for Vlad, who was as undependable as he was handsome?

'How can I trust you?' I pulled the twigs and leaves from my hair.

He brushed the dirt from my nape and back. A moment ago his touch had been sensuous. Now it was matter-of-fact, almost angry. 'Well, God knows you've been nothing but honest and straightforward.' Typical Odessan. Attack. Attack. Attack.

'What did you expect?' I asked, my arms akimbo, my chin thrust out. 'That I'd drop everything for you? I like it here.'

I expected him to strike again, but instead he placed a calling card in my palm and took my hand in his. 'I miss you. That's why I came all this way. To see you, to see if we could work things out. Come to me. I have a suite at the Beresford in San Francisco. I'll stay there forty-eight hours to give you time to pack your things and say your goodbyes.'

I stared at him.

'Come to me,' he whispered. 'I love you.'

We dressed in silence and stepped out of the woods, and back to our respective worlds.

I walked to Tristan's alone, chewing on my bottom lip, chewing over the possibilities. How wonderful it would be to see Boba. To see Odessa. To be able to trust Vlad. But if I went to him, it would mean leaving America for good.

Before opening the front door, I made sure I'd pulled the last of the leaves from my hair. Tristan met me in the entryway. I bristled at the sight of him.

'You know,' he said, 'you're making pretty good money down at the café. Maybe we could start splitting the cost of things.'

I looked at him and wondered what the hell I'd been thinking when I married him. 'Send me the bill.'

I thought about driving to San Francisco. I thought about taking the bus. I thought about leaving Tristan, leaving everything behind. I thought about Vlad non-stop. I stared the card with the Beresford address and phone number. His room number was scrawled on the back. I picked up the phone and dialed the number, then hung up. I picked up the phone and dialed the number, then hung up. I picked up the phone and dialed the number, then hung up. I stared at the clock and let the hours pass me by. If only I were brave. If only I weren't such a coward.

Three weeks after the deadline lapsed, a UPS truck stopped in front of the house. (When these brown trucks first arrived in Odessa, some people were convinced that the initials stood for Ukrainian Postal Service.) And indeed, the package, marked fragile, was from Odessa. It wasn't Boba's handwriting on the label. And only one other person knew exactly where I was.

I sat and stared at the box. What could it be? I thought of him, thinking of me. Was he angry? Could he understand? When I opened it, I found a glass snow globe with Odessa's opera house inside. He remembered. I shook the globe gently until the snow swirled.

In Odessa, there are no western souvenirs. No T-shirts, no key chains, no shot glasses. This gift had been custom made. There was no letter, no card, no signature. Just the program from our evening at the opera.

On the anniversary of my arrival in Emerson, Molly brought over the cassette her cousin had shot of our wedding. I looked at myself in the dress that Boba made.

'You're beautiful,' Molly said, her eyes never leaving the big screen.

The ceremony in the woods was solemn. My eyes shone with hope. I watched myself take Tristan's hand and slip on the silver ring I'd brought from Odessa. At the time, the fact it fit perfectly seemed like an omen.

At the reception, the videographer asked people, 'Any advice for the newlyweds?'

'If he wants to go fishin', let him go fishin'!' Toby exclaimed and the people around him laughed.

'Love each other,' a pensioner said. 'And don't go to bed angry.'

'Yeah,' the woman next to her said. 'Stay up and fight.'

Then the camera turned to Molly. 'You know those things that you really loved about him at first? Well those will be the things that really start to drive you nuts.' She smiled nervously and continued, 'But try to remember what first attracted you to him. That might help.'

The video continued, but I stopped watching. Molly was right. I'd been flattered by Tristan's interest in me. He seemed so loyal, so intent on me. When I offered to take him to a social in Odessa, he said, 'No, I'm with you now.' Proof that he was ready to settle down – unlike Vlad. But I never suspected that I would become his whole life. His intensity hadn't changed; my feelings had changed, or rather my interpretation had. Before, I'd felt flattered, now I felt suffocated.

Anna invited me for tea nearly every morning. Tristan grumbled, but I didn't care. She was so cheerful, one couldn't help but be happy in her presence. She was like a firefly or a snowdrop, a kind of good omen. Serenity's business was booming and she opened a second shop. Every week, David called to encourage me to 'reach out' and to 'move on.' But I was too embarrassed to talk to Jane or Valentina. Of course, I didn't need to say anything to Pam, she was a silent witness. I still saw Molly, but with her children and non-stop schedule, even when we were together, she was barely there.

We sat in her backyard watching the twins play. She looked pensive and I wasn't sure if she was watching the twins at the far end of the yard or if she looked off towards something I couldn't see.

'What's wrong?' I asked.

She took a deep breath. 'I'm thinking about leaving Toby.'

I didn't say anything for a long moment. I just looked at her. I didn't understand. They seemed so happy. Seeing she was waiting for a response, I grabbed her hand and said, 'I'm so sorry.' Clearly, I had not looked beyond the façade. Clearly, something was going on. 'Did he cheat on you? Does he ... hurt you?' I looked at her neck and arms for signs of 'violets,' Odessan slang for bruises.

She looked appalled and said, 'God, no. We just grew apart.'

I didn't understand. In Odessa, couples got divorced because the husband beat his wife or because he was an alcoholic, because of the tension of having to live with in-laws, or because a spouse cheated repeatedly (usually, once was not motive enough). No one in Ukraine got divorced because they grew apart. Growing apart, as near as I could tell, was just part of marriage.

At the café, Rocky, Raymond, Pam, and I met twenty minutes before our shift began. I'd never gone to work early in Odessa, but here, I was glad to get out of the house, away from Tristan. I must admit, there was something comforting about sitting at the lunch counter and having coffee with co-workers. It reminded me of sitting in the boardroom with David in Odessa. Raymond teased Rocky about his love for Pamela Anderson. Rocky told us about the progress he was making at school: he'd almost finished the engine for his Ford. Pam proudly told us her daughter was on the Honor Roll again. She asked if I'd heard from anyone back home, surely meaning Vlad. 'Just my grandmother,' I replied. She looked disappointed.

I was so grateful that he had come. Grateful for our moment together. But I didn't know what to do. Should I contact him? How could I trust him not to leave me again? What if he'd already replaced me? What if I gave up my life in America only to have him disappear?

'Get your green card yet?' Raymond asked.

'Nope. It takes two years.'

'Two years? I thought foreigners were supposed to get one when they married an American.'

'You and me both,' I said, liking the way the casual phrase rolled off my tongue.

'It'll be good when you have it. Then you can stay, no matter what.'

I smiled, touched by their concern. They'd become like a family to me. I enjoyed the time we had together in the evenings, even if we spent it serving and cleaning up after strangers. They worked so hard. I wished that life were easier for them. I looked from Pam, who was skittish, to Ray, the strain around his gray eyes permanent, to Rocky, who was becoming a man in front of our eyes, and I realized this was an America that we never see on TV. There, everything looked so perfect and bright, all Beverly Hills and Santa Barbara. Here in Emerson were the real workers, the real Americans. Why didn't the television show them?

Ray constantly worried about his wife. Even double shifts didn't cover the medical bills. When he worked, she was on her own in their trailer house. Pam's ex made threatening calls and she was afraid for herself and her children. She said the police couldn't do anything about the ex until he actually did 'something.' And they didn't consider death threats 'something.' Rocky didn't say much, he just fiddled with the straw in his extra-large Coke. Though he was in high school, he was already part of this adult world. He understood Ray and Pam's suffering. We knew that he wanted out of the house. Of course, I didn't have to tell them about my problem: he came in almost every evening.

Tonight I served him a cola, as usual. He watched every move I made, as usual. When Rocky came out for a break to do his homework, he smiled at me when I brought him a plate of fries.

'Quit staring at my wife!' Tristan yelled.

The whole restaurant – six people – looked at him. Ray came out of the kitchen to make sure everything was okay.

Mortified, I went to his table and hissed, 'What's wrong with you? He's a kid. A nice kid who works a shit job to escape his asshole stepfather. Leave him alone.'

'I'm sorry,' he said to me. 'Sorry,' he said to Rocky.

Pam's eyes met mine and I knew she understood. One more thing I couldn't tell Jane, couldn't tell Boba or Valentina, yet Pam knew. I wasn't shy or proud with her.

'He doesn't treat you right. Have you ever thought of divorcing him?' she whispered to me when we went to get orders in the kitchen.

I'd been thinking of it more and more.

'He's mental,' she said.

'Mental? You mean insecure?'

'It's more than that. Something's wrong with him. It's like he's stalking you. Maybe I should call Skeet, ask him to have a talk with your hubby.'

I nodded.

'How are you ever going to last two years?' she asked.

I shrugged.

'Sorry,' she said. 'I shouldn't have said that.'

He was angry all the time; so unlike the gentle man I thought I'd married. I didn't have a father or grandfather or uncle to compare his behavior to. He didn't behave so differently from my old boyfriends. Even Vlad had followed me around town in his sedan ...

To celebrate the arrival of summer, I invited friends over for a real Odessan meal. I cooked and baked for days – all of Boba's best recipes. A bright beet salad that melts in your mouth and brightens any day. And borscht because Molly wanted to taste it. Boba never put eggs in the *vareniki* dough – she was used to the hard times of the Soviet Union, but I decided to be decadent and added one. For the *pelmeni*, I rolled the meat into small balls and wrapped them delicately in the dough, creating a fan shape, then threw them into boiling water. When they rose to the surface, I fished them out and put them in a serving dish with a little butter so they wouldn't stick together. I had a good cry when I cut the onions. While they sizzled in the olive oil, I peeled and boiled the potatoes. Before mashing them, I drizzled the onion-flavored oil onto them. It tasted heavenly. I didn't understand Tristan's pathological hatred of oil (which he called fat). I read that in countries like Italy and Spain, olive oil is revered.

I made a Napoleon cake (I'd read in France it was called a *mille-feuille*, or a thousand leaves), stacking the layers of cake and cream just like Boba did. I also baked Molly's chocolate cake and pecan sandies (in Odessa we make them with walnuts). I invited Oksana and Jerry, Molly and Toby and their little ones. Anna and Steve, Rocky, Pam, Raymond and his wife. Tristan was in his comfort zone – at home, drinking beer and laughing with Toby and Jerry.

We sat at the dining table, so close our elbows touched. It was cozy and wonderful. Anna and Steve held hands and fed each other little bites. He whispered in her ear and she blushed and smiled a secret little smile at him. Maybe she'd told the truth when she'd said things were great. They had such complicity. Seeing it at my table made me happy for them and yet sad for myself.

I turned to watch Oksana eat. Her eyes were closed and she chewed slowly, savoring every bite. 'It tastes like home,' she said. 'Delicious.'

Everyone agreed.

Oksana raised her wine glass and said, 'To the hostess and her lovely hands.' Her English had improved in just a few months thanks to our lessons over the phone.

After dinner, everyone admired Farley's hamster. He opened the door to her cage, but she stayed on her wheel. 'Come on, girl. Come on, Clementine,' he encouraged.

Her nose twitched nervously.

'Leave her alone, buddy,' Toby said. 'She doesn't want to come out. She feels more comfy in her cage.'

Just like me in my Emerson cage. The door was open. I just had to work up the courage to escape.

After the guests left, I asked, 'Are you happy with the way things are between us?'

He opened the refrigerator and grabbed a beer. 'Yeah.'

Trailing him from the kitchen to the living room, I said, 'But you seem angry all the time.'

He turned on the TV and flipped through the stations.

'How would you feel?' he asked, his eyes focused on the screen. 'I done everything for you and you're not grateful.'

'I *am* grateful. Is that what you're angry about? That I don't seem grateful enough?'

'You don't do what I say. *That* makes me angry.' He turned the volume up.

'So your moods are my fault?'

'What are you getting at?' he asked sharply, suddenly turning on me.

Swing-swung-swung. He seemed poised to jump at me, his body tense, his teeth bared. No. This was my gentle schoolteacher. Only he wasn't a teacher. Still, he wouldn't. Would he? I squeezed my eyes shut. If only I were brave. If only I were honest. If only I could tell him that we shouldn't have ever married. If only I could find a way to tell him I wanted out ...

Perhaps I could propose a half measure just to test the water.

'Maybe we should spend some time apart.'

'Are you telling me you want a divorce?' His breathing sped up and he stared at me intently.

So intently it scared me. I changed my tactic.

'Well, you want a child and I don't seem able to conceive. Maybe you should consider finding someone else.' I looked down at the beige carpet. Waiting for his verdict. Would he accept this form of plea bargain?

'I don't want anyone else. And you're crazy if you think you can find anyone who will love you like I do. Who else would put up with your shit? Man.'

'You're right. You deserve someone better than me.'

'Is there someone else?' he asked. 'That dishwasher down at the café. I've seen how he looks at you. How they all look at you.'

'This is about us,' I tried to sound calm.

'I'll kill myself if you leave. I'll kill myself. I'LL KILL MYSELF. Who put this separation idea in your head? Was it Oksana?'

I shook my head. He stood. I took a step back.

'Was it Anna? You're there every day. I don't like her.'

I shook my head. 'No one put the idea in my head. It just seems we've ... grown apart.'

'Did Molly tell you about Lena? Or was it that bitch Serenity?' He stepped towards me.

I took another step back. 'Who's Lena? What are you talking about?'

'Nobody. Nothing.' He ran his hand through his thinning hair and muttered, 'You haven't given us time to grow together. Every marriage has its ups and downs. After all I did for you and now you just want to give up? Well, I won't let you.' He grabbed my shoulders and shook me. Hard. When he released me, I was so shaken that I fell back onto the sofa.

A good wife makes a good husband. That's what we say in Odessa. If a husband cheats or beats or drinks, then his wife is clearly doing something wrong. Her cutlets aren't tender, she doesn't serve him as she should. Perhaps she nags him when clearly, she should just let him be.

I took more and more baths when he was at home. I just wanted to lock myself away from him. I turned off the light and sat in the tub until the water became tepid, reciting Akhmatova, the grocery list of foods I didn't buy, *counting the empty days* – anything to avoid thinking about the inevitable. I had imagined divorces happened like this: a couple sits at the kitchen table – tense, terse, certainly, but making a joint decision. Now I realized that this was just as naïve as the image I'd had of conceiving a child when I was little. The papa hugs the mama very tightly and a baby starts to grow in her belly. No mess, no effort.

('Sweetie, what's for dinner?' Tristan called out.)

Now I realized that when it comes to divorce, one person knows first. It is a terrible knowledge.

I forgot the clothes in the dryer. When I finally took them out, they smelled singed. I didn't want to see friends. I didn't want to talk to Boba. It was so sunny outside and so dark in the temple of my heart. I just wanted to hide in the water. *I hate the light of monotonous stars.*

A terrible knowledge to walk through the door knowing that soon everything will change. That your home is no longer your home. Knowing that you will break the promise you made in front of friends, in front of God himself. Knowing that you will break a heart. *So let the snow flow down like tears.*

It is easier to be abandoned – sniveling and wailing, 'Why did you go? What did I do wrong? Why don't you love me anymore?' The decision is made for you. It hurts, but the burden is off you. You are not accountable. You did not make it happen. It happened to you.

('Do you want to make something?')

I imagined deep down a person *knew* that a divorce was the right step. This was not my case. Every time I decided to leave him, another part of me would say, You owe him, give it time, he'll be a wonderful father, he can change, you can change, be patient, what if you leave and you end up on the street? Odessans' worst fear is change, because what if we make a change and our situation gets worse?

I remembered the way he spoke about children so passionately. I remembered how he loved Molly's children. Giving Farley endless piggyback rides. Helping Ashley with her math homework. Going to every single one of Peter's football games, cheering louder than anyone. He would be a good father.

Roots. Wasn't that what I wanted? Stability. A home. In America. How was it that I got exactly what I wanted, yet it wasn't at all what I wanted?

('Why isn't there any food in the fridge? Didn't you do the shopping? I guess I'll order pizza. Man.')

In the same minute, I could be scared, thrilled, sad, resigned, happy – all depending on which way my decision swung. Yes, no, maybe, definitely, impossible. To divorce or not to divorce, that was my question. And I found that there was no easy answer.

('Half cheese for you, half supreme for me. How's that?')

Chapter 23

My Darling and Dear Granddaughter!
Greetings from the Pearl of the Black Sea!

Dasha, Dasha, I haven't had a letter from you in so long! What are you
doing with yourself? Don't you have time to write to your grandmother?
Or has something happened to you? I'm worried. You work so hard.
Are you eating enough? Getting sufficient rest? Everything will be fine,
everything will be fine. That's what I tell myself. I think of you every
moment of every day. God protect and keep you.

I felt horrible that I'd made Boba worry so. It was just that I didn't
know what to do, and as usual, when I didn't know what to do, I
did nothing.

Thank God you left this rat-infested country. Prices at the bazaar
doubled then tripled. Someone broke into the downstairs neighbor's
flat. Obviously young hooligans – they stole her CD player and
television. The poor young woman, a foreigner who doesn't know what
to think of this city. I made her some blini and compote. Some solace.
  Boris Mikhailovich comes by more than ever. Says I'm not safe on
my own, wants to protect me. Changed the light bulb in my entryway
and paces there like a sentry, waiting for, hoping for, an invasion. I
told him I didn't need a man 'You don't need one,' he said, 'but do you
want one?' He even proposed. Imagine the gall!

What Odessan flair! Over sixty and she still had it! Even as I
was angry that she didn't tell me her response, I admired her

panache. Maybe he was why she never replied when I asked her to consider coming to America. Had Boba found love? Another thought invaded: had she had love all along, but put it on hold for me?

I was dying to call, but knew she'd never say anything. Even on paper, I couldn't tell if she was annoyed by him or merely pretending. It is nearly impossible to get a straight answer out of an Odessan. Paper will endure anything – that's what we say in Odessa. A letter does not blush.

> *Dear Boba,*
> *Tell me everything! Immediately! What on earth did you answer?*
> *All is well here. I'm just trying to figure things out …*

I couldn't be angry at her for keeping things from me – after all, I, too, had my secrets. There are some things you can't tell a grandmother, some things you can only tell a real friend.

'He said he'd kill himself if I leave,' I told David during his weekly call.

'Good. You'll be rid of him and inherit his house.'

'You're horrible,' I said with affection.

'Maybe. But I've never threatened suicide to keep a woman. Anyway, guys like him never do it. He's pathetic. He just wants attention. I can just see him, sawing away at his wrist with the sharp edge of a sheet of paper.'

I laughed.

'You shouldn't be with someone like him …'

His words felt open-ended, and I was suddenly breathless. I wanted him to finish his sentence. 'Who should I be with?'

'Someone who can hold his own with you, that's for damn sure.'

I waited for him to say something. He didn't. We just sat there, each on our end, waiting. I broke the silence. 'How's Olga?'

'I wouldn't know,' he said stiffly.

'What happened?'

'My Russian improved. I heard her refer to me as the dirty old Jew to someone on the phone.'

'Which part offended you?'

'I'm not old,' he said.

'I'm sorry,' I said in a serious tone of voice so that he would know what I meant.

'Did you know?'

'Not until she started dating you. That's when she stopped hiding her true feelings from me.'

'You could have said something.'

'You wouldn't have believed me.'

'Perhaps,' he said. 'What are you going to do?'

'I don't know.'

'The Daria I knew always had an escape plan. She was always three steps ahead of everyone else. What would she do?'

'It's different. I'm married now. For better or for worse.'

'Has it ever been better?'

I didn't answer.

'So stay. Stay in America, but dump him.'

'He paid all this money to bring me here.'

'So get a divorce and write him a check.'

'With what money? I'm a waitress.'

'A waitress!' he roared. I pulled the phone away from my ear so I didn't hear the obscenities. 'Where are you?'

'In a village four hours from San Francisco.'

'In the country?' he asked, appalled. 'Go to a city. Get a real job. There's a branch of ARGONAUT in San Francisco.'

'I know.'

'Then why haven't you contacted them? Kessler can make sure you get a job there.'

'I've thought about it, believe me.'

'What's holding you back?'

'It's complicated.'

'No, it's not. You're the one making it complicated. You've put in the time, it's not working out. Cut your losses. You're young and a year seems like a lot, but it's nothing compared to a lifetime. Get out now before you have kids.'

'You don't understand. I owe him.'

'So he did a nice thing for you. Are you going to pay for the rest of your life? He had a hot wife for a year. That's payment enough. Ciao!'

'I told you, he threatened to kill himself . . .'

311

'Then find him someone before you leave. God knows you're an expert.'

That stung so hard I flinched. 'I'm through with matchmaking.'

'Do you have any money?'

'Money, no,' I fingered the diamond. 'But Vlad gave me a ring.'

'Sell it.'

'I've been considering that.'

'Why haven't you done anything?'

'I don't know ...'

'You've changed. You're probably depressed.'

'I'm in America. How could I possibly be depressed?'

'It can happen anywhere. Leave him before you turn into a total wimp.'

I felt my spine straighten and my chin lift. 'How dare you, you presumptuous –'

He laughed. 'And she's back.'

I subscribed to the *San Francisco Chronicle*, paying by check from my own account. Each morning, I scoured the housing and employment pages. Could I live on my own? I'd never been alone, not even for a weekend. Was I brave enough? Was the city safe? How much would an apartment cost? How much could I earn? Would it be enough?

Caressing Vlad's gift, I remembered the emerald Tans had given to Jane. I thought about Jonothan, who bought and sold jewelry. I wondered how much he could get for my ring. Perhaps if it was enough, I could ...

Escape. And start over. The diamond was large and bright, and everyone I knew said that Soviet gold was the best in the world. But then the people who had said that were all Soviets. And they had also said the Soviet system was the best in the world. Maybe the ring wasn't worth much after all. I called Jane, who gave me Jonothan's number and warned me to be careful. After I described the ring, he volunteered to drive up and appraise it the following day.

We met at the café, while Tristan was at work. I unhooked the dainty silver chain and let the ring slide off of the necklace onto Jonothan's palm. He held it between his thumb and index finger, turned it around slowly, taking it in from all angles. When he pulled out a jeweler's magnifying glass from his shirt pocket and fitted it into his eye socket, he went from looking like an easy-going party animal to a hard-nosed diamond merchant. The change startled me.

'I can get ten thousand for it,' he said authoritatively.

'Dollars?' I exclaimed. Of course he wasn't talking about grivna or rubles. Finding out it was worth so much made me hesitant, and I fought the urge to snatch it back. Common sense and greed warred within me. Jane had told me that he was a 'cokehead.' What if he used the proceeds from my ring to buy drugs? I would be a fool to trust him. But what other choice did I have? I needed money, and he had connections. He held the ring in the palm of his hand, silently offering to give it back to me. Pam walked up and said, 'My gawd, is that thing for real?'

'Sure is,' he said. 'I'm proposing to my girlfriend next week and wanted to show Daria the ring.'

'Isn't that sweet?' she said, her eyes fixed on the glittering diamond. 'Who would say no to you?'

'Ninety percent of the girls in the Bay area.'

'All it takes is one.' Her head lilted to one side and she sighed. 'I'll never have anything so beautiful,' she said, then made her way back to the kitchen to answer the bell and deliver her order.

I looked at the ring. The white witch said to get rid of it, that it wasn't doing me any good. But Vlad's gift had been with me all this time. A talisman, a solace, a reminder. Do you want to look backwards or forward? I asked myself sternly. Do you want out? This is the only way. Jonothan held my gaze. I nodded. He put the ring in the pocket of his green silk shirt. I felt nervous when it disappeared from sight and sat on my hands so that I would not grab it back. It hadn't been out of my possession since Vlad – since Boba – had given it to me.

'How much time do you need?'

'Depends on how long it takes to find a buyer. My commission is ten percent. I'll return it if I haven't sold it in six months.'

Six months. An eternity.

*   *   *

The minute Jonothan left, I regretted trusting him. *Take-took-taken.* What had I done? No Odessan would ever trust a total stranger. I'd gone soft in the head. I'd given my ring to a known drug man. *Fall-fell-fallen.* In Odessa, I never would have done that. David was right. I was different. I hadn't noticed because the change had been so gradual. In Odessa, you fight for everything: a seat on the bus, an education, a fair price at the market, a good-paying job … Things there were uncertain – even the flow of water through the city pipes, heat in the winter, electricity. You always had to be prepared, steeled against adversity and problems.

In comparison, life in America was easy. People were open and friendly. The supermarket was full of tasty food. You turned on the faucet – hot water flowed. In nearly a year, the power was cut only once. And I'll never forget this: the electric company wrote a letter apologizing for any inconvenience they may have caused. No one in Odessa apologized for anything. In Emerson, I made more in a week as a waitress than I had in a month as a secretary. I had a car, just as Jane had said I would. I'd been lulled to complacency. And I'd just given my diamond away thinking everything would be fine. Fool!

Please, Jono, please. I felt every second pass like I was back in the classroom listening to that vile metronome, waiting for my turn. Tick-tock. Tick-tock. Ticktocktick. *Bite-bit-bitten.* It seemed like months since I'd heard from Jonothan, but it had only been six days. I left the house so that I didn't call him, parked at the lunch counter at work trying not to think of what I'd done. He said it could take up to six months. Six months! Jane's warning about him being a 'cokehead' echoed in my mind. I veered from hopeful to hopeless, from joy that I would be leaving to fear that I was stuck for good. *Please, please, please.* My stomach churned like the butter makers at the bazaar. Pimples dotted my face and back. I couldn't sleep. Yes, no, stay, go. *The rain in Spain stays mainly in the Plain.* I drank Raymond's Pepto Bismal straight from the bottle. Pam fed me soda crackers.

'What's wrong?' she asked.

I couldn't say. I didn't want to tell her how foolish I'd been. Jane, of course, heard from Tans. She rang immediately and didn't even say hello.

'You just handed him the ring?' Jane yelled. 'Why didn't you let him take a picture of it and see if there was any interest before handing it over? You must know you can't trust him.'

'You're right, I wasn't thinking ... I just want to leave so much ...'

'I'm sorry, Dasha. I'm the one who's not thinking clearly. I didn't mean to shout. I'm just scared for you, that's all. Jono is Jono ... He's charming, but he's into a lot of bad stuff ... You're an Odessan. I thought you could take care of yourself. But you know what? I'm probably worrying for nothing. Everything will be fine.'

'Everything will be fine,' I repeated, hoping that for once the mantra would work.

When I got home from work, from the grocery store, from Molly's, from Anna's, I checked the answering machine. There were never any messages. I picked up the receiver to make sure the phone line worked. I checked my e-mail every three minutes. I longed for comfort and tried to make compote like Boba used to, just for a small taste of home. But I got distracted and burned the apples. At night, I stared at the ceiling until Tristan fell asleep, then I paced the house, going from room to room like a ghost.

On my day off, I went to visit Serenity at her shop. When she saw me, she hugged me and made us a pot of herbal tea. *Please, Jono, please.* I tried to follow what she was saying, but was so distracted that she had to repeat herself several times.

'What's bothering you?' she asked.

I shrugged.

'You like to keep things to yourself. That's okay. But you know you can talk to me, right?'

I nodded.

'Sometimes it helps to keep busy,' she said and put me to work dusting the shelves. I was glad to have something to do with my hands, other than wringing them. Her presence comforted me. Whenever I glanced at her, she was looking at me, smiling gently. At five o'clock, when it was time for her to close the shop, I drove to Tristan's with all four windows down, listening to my music.

When I got there, he was waiting. He'd moved his BarcaLounger out onto the front lawn and was sitting there with his arms crossed. The grass around him was littered with beer cans. *Sink-sank-sunk*. Thank God my neighbors in Odessa couldn't see my crazy husband. My crazy life. I cut the engine and unbuckled my seatbelt. I was afraid to get out of the car. *Hit-hit-hit*.

'Where the hell have you been?' he yelled. 'I called ten times today! You never answered.'

'I went for a drive!' I shouted the obvious.

'You need to tell me if you go somewhere!'

'You've been drinking!'

He strode to the car. *Hide-hid-hidden*. *Hide-hid-hidden*. *Hide-hid-hidden*. He flung open the door and pulled me out. 'The speedometer shows you drove twenty-nine miles today. Where did you go?'

I rubbed my arm where he'd grabbed me.

'Tell me where you were. And who you were with.'

My chin shot up and the only thing that would have unlocked my jaw was a tetanus shot.

I didn't stop talking to him on purpose. I just found that there was very little to say. I pulled out my clothes from the closet and my suitcase from under the bed and moved into the office, like before we were married. Only this time, there was a deadlock on the door and a crib in the corner.

Finally, *finally*, Jonothan called.

'Did you sell it?'

'I'm this close.'

'This close? What does that mean?'

'It means I'm holding my thumb and finger an inch apart. That's close.'

I was this close to going mad.

Ten days later, he called to say he'd made the sale and would deliver the money. Thank God. I spit three times, like Boba did. It couldn't hurt. When the Jaguar pulled into the driveway, relief turned my knees wobbly. His arrival was my deliverance. When he opened the car door, I told him it was better if he didn't get out, better if Tristan didn't see him. He nodded. I blushed at this curt acknowledgement of what my life had become.

'I told the buyer that the ring had belonged to a czarina,' he said. 'You don't have any other jewelry, do you?'

I smiled and shook my head.

He reached into the glove compartment and grabbed the money. I counted it – $12,000 in one-hundred-dollar bills – and handed him back $1,200.

'If you decide to leave what's-his-name, you can stay at my place. Just call and give me heads up.' He peeled out of the driveway, and I went into the house and sat on the couch with $10,800 on my lap. This amount seemed like a fortune, although according to the ads for apartments in the *Chronicle*, it wasn't even a year of rent money. I stroked the bills and wondered if I was making the right decision. When I heard Tristan's pickup door slam, I ran into the office and pulled my suitcase out of the closet. When I opened it, I saw the white booties and dress. I bit my lip so hard that tears pricked my eyes. Some dreams just aren't meant to come true, that's what they say in Odessa. I hid the money with the baby clothes and shoved the suitcase back in the closet. I turned the deadlock and disassembled the crib, throwing the wooden limbs to the floor.

Tristan knocked on the door. 'Sweetie, are you okay in there?'

'I'm fine.'

'Can I get you anything?'

I sat on the floor, staring at the pile of wood in the corner. Night crept into the room. I crawled onto the bed and curled into the fetal position.

I gave two weeks' notice at the café before I gave it at home.

Pam hugged me. Raymond said that they would miss me.

'Does this mean you got another job in town?' Rocky asked.

I shook my head.

'She's got to think of herself,' Raymond explained. 'Got to move on. This isn't where she belongs.'

'You're leaving us?' Rocky sounded shocked. 'Leaving Emerson?'

Raymond put a hand on his shoulder. 'It's better this way.'

'I still haven't told him.'

Pam squeezed my hand. Raymond patted my back awkwardly. The look in their eyes told me that the hardest was yet to come. When I thought about how he would react, my stomach clenched until I felt ill. I ran to the bathroom.

When I returned, Raymond said, 'You're white as a ghost. Looks like you might have the stomach flu. It's going round. You should go home, rest up.'

I thought of Tristan sprawled in his recliner with a beer can in his hand and crumbs on his chest and said I'd rather work. Pam served me a glass of 7-Up with more soda crackers. As the evening progressed, I felt worse and worse. Was it the flu or was it something else? Had I worried myself sick? I sat down, hoping that my head would stop spinning. Just the smell of meat made me nauseous and I ran to the bathroom again.

All week, I couldn't keep anything solid down and had a bit of a fever. And I was so tired that I could barely pull myself out of bed. I put it down to nerves. I was losing weight and felt horrible. Tristan served me Campbell's Tomato Soup. I didn't have the heart to tell him that I threw it up minutes later. I needed to see a doctor, so I talked Tristan into going to Jerry and Oksana's. I could have gone on my own, but he would have seen the mileage. I wanted to avoid another scene. I simply didn't have the strength.

'Look at you!' Oksana said when she saw me. 'You don't look good. Circles underneath your eyes. Wan complexion. My God, you're trembling.'

'I haven't slept in days.'

She put her arm around my waist and sat me down at the kitchen table. As she took my pulse and listened to my heart, she peppered me with questions: 'What are you eating? Are you sleeping well? Is the sickness more pronounced at a certain time of day? Are you coughing? Do you have a runny nose? Are your breasts tender?'

I answered, then asked, 'What do my breasts have to do with anything?'

She took my hand in hers and said, '*Ribochka*,' my sweet little fish. 'The symptoms you're describing don't sound like the flu. They sound like morning sickness. Or, in your case, all-day sickness. Your wish came true. You're having a baby.'

'A baby!' I jumped up and hugged her.

'I'm so happy for you.' She held me in her arms.

For a moment, I felt so light, so happy. I couldn't wait to tell Boba.

Tristan. The realization that this would change everything hit me.

I sat down, buried my face in my hands, and started to cry.

'I thought you'd be happy,' she said. 'Maybe I'm wrong ...'

She was right. Even without years of medical school, our women have a way of knowing these things.

Oksana stroked my convulsing shoulders. When I stopped crying and started to hiccough, she dried my tears with a handkerchief. My head spun. Pregnant. Pregnant. It couldn't be. I couldn't be. I lowered my hand to my belly. A baby.

'What's wrong?'

'I'd just decided to leave him,' I whispered. 'What am I going to do?'

'You don't have to decide anything now,' she said. 'You have time.'

My eyes widened when I realized that maybe Vlad had left me with another gift. I buried my face in my hands again. 'Oh, God.'

'What?'

'I was with someone else.'

'Does he suspect?'

I met her gaze. 'No. On both counts.'

'That makes it easier.' The way she looked at me. The concern in her eyes. 'A pregnant woman has over 150 times the normal level of hormones in her body. You'll be feeling a lot of ups and downs. Don't decide anything right away.'

I tried to stand, but had to sit back down. What was I going to do?

Before returning to Emerson, I asked Tristan if we could go to a bookstore. As we sat in the car, I watched the trees rush past and felt the blood pound in my veins. Felt the thoughts swirl in my brain. Felt the baby grow in my belly. *A baby. What if it's Vlad's? What if Tristan finds out? What had I done? What would I do? Could I really leave now?*

319

At the entrance of the store, he said, 'I'm not into all that literature. Come get me in the magazine aisle when you're done.'

The minute he turned his back, I ran to the self-help section. (In Ukraine, we weren't big on self-help. People depended on fate or the State to help them.) Americans were very much into self-serve, self-medication, and self-help: the ultimate do-it-yourselfers. Americans were all part-time pharmacists. They knew exactly which medication to take for any ailment. They found answers in books. Look at Tristan. *Men are from Mars, Women are from Venus* had clearly helped him. I found titles like *Closing the Deal; The Rules; Men are like Waffles, Women are like Spaghetti*, and then I found a book entitled *Ten Stupid Things Women Do To Mess Up Their Lives*. I looked at the table of contents and found that I had committed a completely different ten. So many books were aimed at getting a man. What I needed was a book entitled *Catch and Release: Put Him Back in the Sea Painlessly and Effortlessly*. No such luck. I went to the maternity section and looked for books, then worried that if I bought one, it would be like announcing my pregnancy. So I stood in the aisle and read the first chapter of *What to Expect When You Are Expecting*.

What to expect? What to do? What is in my best interest? The best interest of the child?

A baby.

For days, I felt like a spectator watching a tennis match, the sun glaring down until blisters broke out all over my body. Should I stay or should I go? The ball went from one side of the court to the other. What I wanted versus the right thing to do. The right thing for him versus the right thing for me. What would be better for the child? Pros, cons. Backhand, lob. Maybe I should give him another chance. No. Yes. I don't know. Yes, a divorce. No, don't give up. Run. Run as fast as you can. Stay. Don't be a coward. Don't be a quitter. Yes, be a quitter. Tristan's refrain pounded in my head. You're stupid. You're crazy. No one will love you like I do. Forty, love. Would the score ever be even? No. He would always win. He had home court advantage. But a baby would make things bearable.

* * *

Though it was warm outside, Tristan lit a fire to please me. After he went to work, I pulled my suitcase from the closet, took my money, and sat on the white couch with the stacks on my lap. I stared into the blaze. The human eye is drawn to fire. The flames jumped and I wished they would give me some kind of answer.

I'd missed having a father in my life. I never had a goodnight kiss from him. He never told me he loved me. A baby. I was so happy, and yet so terribly sad. Sad for me if I stayed with Tristan for the sake of the infant. Sad for the infant if I left Tristan to save myself. How could I take a child away from its father? In my family, we women had a tradition of raising a baby alone, but that was because the men deserted us. I thought about my dream of being a real family – a mother and father raising a child together. I thought of spending the rest of my life with Tristan.

It felt like a prison sentence.

I thought of my time with Vlad. Seeing him again. Lust stronger than sense. Skin on skin. How I'd opened to him. I imagined telling him. Imagined his voice hardening, demanding that I return to Odessa. I imagined telling him. Imagined his gaze softening, imagined him dropping to his knees and kissing my belly. Imagined him saying *Dushenka*, my little soul.

My hand automatically moved to my chest and felt around for his ring, seeking the strange comfort. But my talisman was gone. Oh, God. I'd moved on. The white witch was right, wasn't she? It had been smart to get rid of the ring, of the past. Did she mean I should stay with Tristan? What if I wanted someone else? The more I thought, the faster my heart beat. *Stop thinking*, I told myself. *Just for a minute.*

I stroked the money. It felt good between my fingers. I hadn't had so much cash in my hands since Boba and I had sold our old apartment and bought the new one. I knew what I had to do. I had to try to work things out with Tristan. I could depend on him. He had roots. I needed to make sure that my child had a real family. I needed to make sure that I wouldn't just take the easy way out. I threw a hundred-dollar bill into the blaze. The flames swallowed the paper. I wanted to throw it all into the fire, to see the money burn. To see it disappear. To watch it catch fire, to burn down to almost nothing, until the flames coughed up little pieces of paper only to swallow them again. I wanted to get rid of every piece of Vlad. I'd sold his ring, now I had to get rid of his money. Perhaps then I would be free. I threw another hundred-dollar bill onto the logs, then another, then another, and watched the fire devour them. Mesmerizing. Another. Another.

My hand went to my belly. It was no use. I would always have a part of him. *Don't do anything rash.* Oskana's words came back to me and I tried to collect myself. Tried to rein in this crazy desire to watch my future burn before my eyes. I threw another bill on the fire, then another.

I had to call someone. I picked up the phone.

Boba would tell me to stay. Jane would tell me to go. David would tell me to get the hell out. Vlad would tell me to come home. Valentina would tell me to stay put. Molly would say Tristan is a good provider. This was my call. My life. My choice. I put the phone down.

Chapter 24

Dear Tristan,
I

How fitting that my relationship with Tristan would end the way it began – with a letter. It was cowardly, but I decided to leave Emerson the same way I'd left Odessa – by a strategic exit. This time I didn't even tell Boba.

My suitcase was in the entryway. He was at work, and I had no intention of waiting for him to come back to say goodbye. I was blowing my chance for a green card by marriage, but I couldn't take another day. There had to be another way and I would find it. I stood at the kitchen counter, mulling over what to write: *Dear Tristan, I tried.* God knows I tried. *You tried, too. I know that. We're just too different. We want different things.* I could have continued with a post-mortem of our relationship, but didn't want him to think there was a chance to patch things up. *Dear Tristan, I'm sorry.* No. I was sick of apologizing and ripped up the paper. *Dear Tristan, You suck.* Too direct. *Dear Tristan, I come from Odessa, you come from the country.* Too self-help. *Tristan, Things didn't work out. I'm outta here.* Too American. Yet perfect. I let it stand. I thought about all the money he'd spent, took out enough to cover my plane ticket and phone bill, and laid it on the counter next to my note and wedding ring. I didn't like to owe anyone.

In the bus to San Francisco, I felt. After feeling numb for so long, I felt. Relieved. Relieved that I was escaping. Relieved that I wouldn't see him anymore. Relieved that I would be where I belonged – back in the world. Relieved that I had finally made a decision. Excited. Excited about my new life. Excited about all the possibilities before me – a new job, a new apartment, a new life, a new freedom. Excited to be in a city again, with the theaters, galleries, book shops, museums, libraries, and thousands of people. Happy. Happy. And yet... I felt apprehensive. I was scared that he would find a way to ruin it all. That he would come after me. It was as if I'd received a fifty-year sentence, but had escaped after only one. He could hunt me down. He could turn me in.

When I got off the bus, I looked around furtively, almost expecting him to be there to snatch me back. Instead Jonothan was waiting and drove me to his apartment on Russian Hill. (There was nothing Russian about it.) He cooked dinner for us. As I set the table, he came up behind me and ran his fingers through my hair. 'You're beautiful,' he said and took my earlobe in his mouth.

'I'm pregnant.'

He spit my earlobe out and jumped back three feet. I laughed until he grinned ruefully. Men had been coming on to me for ages. If I'd known what an effective deterrent pregnancy was, I would have used it much, much earlier.

At first, I was afraid to leave the apartment, afraid he would find me and drag me back. I was as much his prisoner in San Francisco as in Emerson. I peeked out the window, wondering if it was safe, wondering if he was out there.

'Don't be a chicken,' Jono said. 'Let's go get a bite to eat.'

But I wouldn't budge.

He held up a gruesome Halloween mask. 'Come on. You can wear this.'

'He's not just going to let me go. And he has guns.'

Jono dropped the mask and ordered Chinese.

I continued to pore over the *Chronicle* for a job and apartment, wondering if there was any way I could get a job at ARGONAUT. I called Boba just like I always did from Tristan's – Saturday morning for me, Saturday evening for her. Ten time zones, two continents, and an ocean separated us. The truth felt like another chasm that separated us – bigger and darker than the ocean. I didn't want to tell her about my precarious situation. Pregnant. Soon to be divorced. Unemployed. No green card.

'Dasha?' she answered.

In her voice, in this one word, I heard these notes of hope, worry, and love that made up the symphony of her voice.

'*Da*, Boba. It's me.'

'What's wrong, little rabbit paw?'

Could she hear the tension and reticence I felt? I forced myself to smile, hoping that this would lighten the tone of my voice. 'Nothing, Boba.'

'Has he hurt you? Maybe you should come home like that Katya did. She said America was terrible.'

I remembered her anguished, hysterical call to Soviet Unions and was relieved to hear she was safe. 'It wasn't America, it was the man. I promise, things are fine.'

I wrote to Jane and Valentina to explain my distance from them. Jane phoned immediately. 'I knew you'd gone. Last Thursday Tristan showed up on Tans's doorstep – drunk out of his mind – at three in the morning.'

I was mortified. She laughed it off and told me I wasn't responsible for his asinine behavior.

'What if he finds me?'

'He doesn't even know for sure you're in San Francisco. And even if he did, where would he begin to look in a city of a million? Tans's was his only lead, and he saw it was a dead end. You're safe.'

'I'm just worried ... and scared. And nervous.' *You have a fragile soul, Dasha. That's why you're more sensitive than other people. Maybe I should have raised you differently ...* Oh, Boba. I miss you.

'You were smart to leave,' Jane said. 'He wasn't the right person for you.'

'I know I did the right thing ...'

'Did you tell him?'

'About what?'

'You know.'

My hand went to my belly. I glared at Jono. He shrugged. Why do women have a reputation for gossiping when it's a scientific fact that men have bigger mouths? 'No. It's not his concern.'

325

'Oh.' She understood immediately. 'Whose concern is it?'

I didn't have the courage to tell her. Jane was like my grandmother: overprotective. And overreactionary. And Vladimir Stanislavski was a legend. 'You don't know him.'

'Will he be in the picture?'

'I'm not sure,' I whispered.

Jane was right. Tristan wouldn't find me. I roamed the city streets, my fingers caressing the buildings. My ears rejoiced at finding the staccato of the city – horns bleating, people yelling, sirens blaring, jackhammers jumping. I haunted the bookstores, reading their novels and drinking my skinny decaf latte. In the parks, I watched families picnic and play and thought, I'm one of you now, with my own little world. I sat on the beach for hours, watching the ocean. You know you're home when you see the waves come forth to welcome you. At the Legion of Honor museum, I marveled at the hallowed halls of beauty. I stood in front of Rodin's bust of Camille Claudel and wept.

I applied for several jobs, including a position at ARGONAUT. Although I hated to do it, I e-mailed David and Mr. Kessler and asked for help. I don't like to owe anyone.

Mr. Kessler wrote: 'Lovely to hear from you. If there is a position available in the San Francisco office, we will be happy to consider you.'

David wrote: 'Go to ARGONAUT immediately. I'll take care of everything.'

I called the next day. When I said my name, the woman from human resources told me to hold. And then I found myself speaking to the director of the San Francisco office who suggested I meet with him the following Monday.

New city. New hopes. New life. Things seemed to move so quickly. Perhaps because I'd remained still for so long. I found an apartment. It was the size of a shoe box, but it was my shoe box.

When I moved out, I tried to give Jonothan some rent money, but he refused it. 'You've already repaid me. We had a betting pool going at Tans's – which week you were going to leave that hick.

When you called to tell me you were coming, I placed a bet and won the pot – five hundred bucks.'

'Shouldn't I be embarrassed that everyone saw the divorce coming before I did?'

'Don't feel bad. Think of us as wagering on when you'd come to your senses.'

I spent the weekend cleaning my studio, scrubbing surfaces, pretending I was Boba waging war on in-coming dust and bacteria. I even washed the windows, keeping my back carefully turned to the telephone, as if I could ignore the fact that I had to come clean with Boba.

She didn't even know where I was.

To my shame, I'd already put off the conversation for three weeks, hoping the right words would come to me. They never did.

I dialed the number slowly, still not sure of what to say. The family curse had worked its dark magic. Maybe I had worked the dark magic. I needed to confess that everything I'd told her had been a lie.

The words came pouring out before she could even say hello.

'Boba, Boba, I'm so sorry, I've told you so many lies.'

'What are you talking about, my little rabbit paw?'

'I never should have left Odessa, never should have left you.'

'What's this?'

'I never had a job as an engineer.'

'Never an engineer? How can that be? You wrote so many letters about how you loved your job …'

'I was a waitress.'

'A waitress … ?'

I closed my eyes and forced myself to continue. 'I never lived in San Francisco, I lived in a village.'

She gasped. It is true that Odessans consider life in the country hell.

'And that's not all. After we married, he changed. He chased away my new friends. He said it was his house and his rules. He …'

'Shh. Shh. Everything will be fine. Everything will be fine,' she said. 'Don't say anything more. You'll just upset yourself. You just have to find a way to leave him.'

'I already did.' I started to cry, perhaps from relief.

'What's all this emotion, then? You surely did the right thing. You've always been a smart girl. You know your own mind.'

'I thought you'd be disappointed. In me.'

'Never! Bad doesn't get better. Bad gets worse. You were right to leave.' She paused. 'That's why your mother left your father.'

'Mama left him?' I didn't understand anything. He left us. 'But … I thought that the curse was being left.'

'Maybe I should tell you …'

'Tell me what?' I couldn't breathe. *Strike-struck-struck.* It felt as if ninety-nine clocks were striking the hour in the cavity of my ribcage. I scratched at the skin at my sternum, trying to get to the source. 'Tell me what?'

'When you assumed that Dmitri left us, we didn't correct you. We thought the less we talked about him, the sooner you'd forget. Like a nightmare. You wake up in the morning and your night fears are swept away by daylight. It didn't help that your Mama – so proud – refused to discuss it. And then …' There was a catch in her voice. 'And then she was gone. And for so long I felt guilty.'

'About what?' I leaned against the counter and waited for the worst. Odessan secrets are never good. 'Tell me, Boba. Please.'

'Guilty that I'd been so blind. Your father was a handsome, charismatic sailor. No one could tell a joke like Dmitri.' High praise in Odessa. 'He was also a brutal drunk. Your mama didn't realize at first. And I found out far too late. They'd moved to the Crimea, away from her friends, away from me. When I think of what that man did.' She sighed, one of those hoarse, soul-wrenching sighs. The kind that makes you think it could be a person's final breath. 'My girl. My baby girl. How he bloodied her nose and cracked her ribs. What else he did, I don't know. But when she bundled you up and stole away from Yalta in the dead of the night, she came to me, and I saw the bruises, the burns.'

She started to sob. So did I. Poor Mama. Poor Boba. Why hadn't we had this conversation years ago in our kitchen so she could clasp me to her breast, so I could throw my arms around her waist?

It felt as if the foundation of my whole life had crumbled underneath my legs. I thought men left. My father left. Will left. Vlad left. I expected any guy I ever dated to leave. I never even gave them a chance. Never gave myself a chance, except with Vlad, for a moment, to let my guard down. But the shields went right back up.

'Perhaps the real curse is not finding love,' Boba said. 'Perhaps I was wrong to steer you away from our men. Whenever you brought one home I remembered what happened to your mother, and I got so scared. Then when that Vladimir Stanislavski came nosing around ... I knew I had to push you out of harm's way.'

I closed my eyes. Vlad. How could I tell her?

How could I not?

'I haven't told you everything, Boba.'

'What is it, my little rabbit paw?'

'I'm pregnant.'

'A baby!' I heard the tears in her voice. 'Does he know?'

'No.' I took a deep breath. 'And that's not the worst.'

'Dasha?'

'The worst is that the baby might not be his.'

'*Gospodee.*' Oh my God. I pictured her making the sign of the cross and spitting three times. 'Dasha?'

'It might be Vlad's.'

'Not Vladimir Stanislavski's! How can that be?'

'He came, we talked ...'

'Talked! What are you going to do now? Alone. In a foreign country.'

'You were right to insist I take his ring, Boba. I sold it. Everything will be fine.' I repeated her mantra, only this time I believed it.

Surprisingly it was the director who came to the lobby to greet me. We made small talk in the elevator.

'David said he was very impressed with you. I've never heard him speak so highly of anyone.'

'Such kind words,' I said. 'How long have you and he been colleagues?'

'We went to college together,' he said. 'When we graduated, he got me a job here.'

The director and I walked down a long hall with bland art – thankfully, no stiletto heels or splatters of paint. I crossed my fingers – *please let me get the job. And if I get the job, please let there be a door and walls. And no bars.* He showed me to a small desk in a large entryway. Perhaps human resources was on the other side.

'Is this where you're going to interview me?' I handed him my résumé and steeled myself for the interview.

'No need. You've been transferred.'

'Wonderful ...' I said, stunned. It was a relief to have a job. And only a little disappointed that I didn't have a door or walls. Boba would tell me to look on the bright side. No bars. There are no bars. I sat down at the desk and thanked him for the escort. He looked at me strangely, then opened the door to a corner office with a fantastic view of the fog. 'This is your office.'

Apparently, thanks to strong recommendations, I was made a senior account manager – the youngest in the whole company! It seemed daunting at first, but after a week, I realized it was essentially the same work I'd done in Odessa, only there were fewer bribes and less paperwork – just one set of books to fill out. I even had my own personal assistant, Cyndi. Of course, some things don't change – offices are offices and there will always be gossip, whether you are in Odessa or Vladivostok. But the talk about me was quite nice. Somehow, sections of a letter of recommendation that David had written circulated around the workplace.

> *I cannot emphasize enough how challenging business in the Ukraine is. Sane businessmen would take one look at the government demands and mafia threats and run. Even armed with my business degree, I would not have lasted forty-eight hours in Odessa without Daria. She cut through red tape with a machete. She knew every single customs agent, tax man, and mobster. Each had a price and Daria was the only one with an index. She not only has a head for business, she has a nose for trouble and eyes that see things most people don't. She has impeccable work and personal standards. She is not only an astute business partner, she is a wise, intuitive young woman. She speaks English, Russian, and Hebrew ...*

I was stunned. I could not have been more moved if his recommendation had been a love letter. Perhaps, after all, it was of sorts, a declaration of love.

*   *   *

My hand went to my belly the same way it had once moved to Vlad's ring. Instinctively. Tenderly. This new life filled me with such love, such hope. I thought of the little soul growing inside me. I needed to nurture and protect my baby. My baby. I was so happy. And yet there were moments I was petrified. Would Tristan's sister-in-law denounce me? Would he? Would the government throw me away because I'd left my husband? I didn't want to be tense all the time – it wasn't good for me and it certainly wasn't good for the baby. Before, I would have paced the apartment, I would have stewed and hesitated. But I had to take action, I needed concrete answers. It wasn't just me any longer.

I called Molly.

'My God, where are you?' she asked. 'Are you okay? I've been worried sick!'

'I'm sorry, I should have told you … I was just afraid.'

'Afraid?'

'Afraid of him, afraid to tell people – friends – that I was leaving. Afraid to trust …' I babbled.

'I'll keep your secrets,' she said.

'I'm in San Francisco.'

She said she wanted to see me. I hesitated to tell her my address.

'We could meet at a café,' she offered. I decided to trust her.

Two days later, on Saturday morning, I stood on the sidewalk in front of my building, waiting. She came right on time. She was wearing a mint green blouse and a pair of slacks instead of an extra large T-shirt and baggy jeans. I noticed she'd done her make-up and pulled her auburn hair into a smart ponytail at the base of her neck. She looked relaxed and happy. I wondered at the change.

When she saw me, she hugged me. 'Thank God you're okay. When you disappeared, I didn't know what to think.'

'I just couldn't take it anymore.'

She put her arm around my shoulders. 'I should have helped you.'

I covered her hand with my own. 'You did.'

She looked around at the buildings and the busy street. 'It feels good to be in the city. Toby and I used to come once a month, but then … well, I guess life happens.'

'You're here now. Thank you for coming all this way.'

We walked up four flights of stairs.

'No elevator,' I apologized.

'I needed to stretch my legs. It's a long drive.' She started to giggle like a schoolgirl. 'No one knows I'm here. Not even Toby.'

'He'll find out,' I warned her. 'He'll look at your mileage.'

She laughed. 'It wouldn't occur to him to look at my gas gauge, oil level, or mileage. He's no mechanic – I'm on my own.'

She looked at my face. My expression must have said something my silence did not, because she stilled.

'My God. He did that to you, didn't he?'

Tears filled my eyes. I don't know why. Perhaps in gratitude that someone understood a small part of what I had lived. I put the key in the door and opened all three locks. Boba was not on the other side.

Molly looked at the books on my shelves while I turned on the electric kettle.

We sat at the kitchen table in front of the small window.

'You look fabulous,' I told her.

'I realized I'd become worn down and even depressed. Toby and I are in marriage counseling. He's chipping in more around the house, and I realized that I need to start doing things for myself. I'm going to come visit you, gal.'

'Brava, brava!'

'This is where you belong.' She gestured out to the city. 'You were right to leave. You're very brave. I'm proud of you.'

'Thank you.' I put two spoonfuls of raspberry jam in my tea and stirred viciously, trying to work up the courage to ask what would happen next. 'Do you think he'll try to find me?'

'No. I think he's got his mind on other things ...' After a long pause, she said, 'I should have told you this, but he made us promise not to. You're not the first girl he brought over.'

Kino.

'I'm sorry,' she said. 'I almost told you once, but he stopped me ... I should have tried harder. Her name was Lena. She didn't last as long as you.'

I opened my mouth, but no words came out.

'Please don't be mad.'

'I'm not.'

'Are you okay?' she asked.

I nodded. 'Where was she from?'

'St Petersburg.'

'How long did she stay?'

'Three months.'

'Did he go there?'

'Yes, he went to several "socials," as he called them.'

'He told me he'd considered it, but "chickened out" at the last moment. Everything was a lie. He told me he was a teacher. He told me he'd never gone to Russia. I was such a fool!'

'Don't blame yourself, hon.'

'Who else can I blame? I should have seen it. The worst is that my life is in his hands ...'

'What do you mean?' she asked.

'Women like me have to stay married to guys like him for two years before we're granted permanent status. If I don't fulfill the bargain, all he has to do is notify Immigration. They'll think I married him for a green card, and I'll be deported.'

'That's horrible! No one should have to stay married ...'

Pity crept into her voice.

'That's just the way it is,' I said briskly. I didn't want her feeling sorry for me. Odessans know that even if the deck is stacked against us, we must continue to play. 'Do you think he'll turn me in?'

'I don't know.' She bit her lip.

'Oh, God.' I pressed my hand to my chest. The ring was gone, but in its place was something more, something of infinite value. My hand traveled down my body to my belly.

'Don't feel bad. Anyone could see that ... I don't want to say you're too good for him. But we could all see that you didn't belong there. He was the only one that didn't see it.'

'Oh, Molly. Part of me feels guilty for leaving him. Is that crazy?'

'No, hon. But you don't have to worry about him. When you left he was drunk for about a week, just like when Lena took off. But he's moved on. You won't believe it, but he's already looking for another bride. He said he was going to try the Philippines this time. He said he heard the women there are more docile.'

I laughed. And laughed. Odessans laugh at the most perverse things. Molly joined me.

'It is pretty funny,' she admitted. Then she started to cry. 'I hope you don't hate me.'

I started to cry, too. 'Truly, I'm not angry. You were such a good friend to me. I'll never forget all you did. The lovely bachelorette party you organized. The bouquet for my wedding. The kindness you, Serenity, and Anna showed me made me want to stay. Made me fall in love with America. Your friendship has been the best part of this journey. I hope we can still be friends and that you'll visit me again.'

She nodded. 'Didn't I just say I would? Are you sure you're not mad at me?'

'I'm not mad. I'm relieved.'

And it was true. That chapter of my life was over. I wanted to concentrate on the future. I was free. I could talk to Boba and Jane for hours, eat potatoes three times a day, and cover myself in black if I so desired. I wrote to Anna and Serenity. I made blini for my neighbors; in return, they invited me to brunch. I joined a book club. I asked a co-worker who brought in cinnamon rolls every Monday to teach me how to bake. On Sundays, we worked in her kitchen. Each week was a new recipe. These acts filled me with pleasure. I built my nest, twig by twig.

David suggested I consult with the company lawyers. I explained my situation to them; they felt confident that they could help me get a work visa and later a green card. They also told me about a wonderful concept in California called 'alimony.' The way the lawyers spoke of this phenomenon made me wonder what else I didn't know as a foreigner in America. *Rights, rights,* Oksana had said. *What are our rights?* I would find out.

I didn't want Tristan's money but it was a pleasure to tell Oksana that if she divorced Jerry, she would not be penniless or powerless.

Of course I called Valentina. She'd sold Soviet Unions™ to an American entrepreneur for a million dollars in an off-shore account. She said that when she'd started the business, it had been a buyer's market – the men had the advantage. Now, in just a few years, the tables had turned and Odessan women were on top. 'It's become a seller's market. They get the Americans to take them and their friends shopping and to fancy restaurants. The new owner installed a row of computers and he pays girls to respond to the letters. The clients pay per e-mail sent and received. The women dupe them into sending money for everything from English lessons to plane tickets. He posts indecent photos of models to lure in the men. Ingenious! Why didn't I think of that?' she lamented, with a drop of venom in her voice.

She hadn't changed a bit.

'How are things in Odessa?'

'Changing right and left! Foreign businesses have invaded. Some oligarch is renovating the Mikhailovksi Convent on Uspenskaya Street. Muslims are moving in faster than you can say "Allah." More and more construction going on. More gaudy than anything. I'm ready for a change if you want to know the truth. Maybe I could visit you in America. This old communist has decided capitalism isn't so bad.'

She booked her plane ticket and even helped Boba apply for a passport so she could come help me with the baby. When I spoke with Boba on the phone, she sounded happy, like a teenager in love. I don't think I ever sounded that way about Tristan.

Of course David still called once a week. As we spoke, I realized that in part, my new life was thanks to him. He had hurt me, but he'd also worked hard to make amends. He'd become a true friend. 'Thank you.'

'For what? I didn't do anything.'

'Whatever you say ...'

He said he was leaving Odessa.

'Please don't be offended. There's something I want to ask,' I admitted. 'It's about something Vita and Vera said ... Is it true that you got sent to Odessa as a punishment?'

'In a way.'

'What did you do?'

'You know my grandfather started the shipping company? Well, when he died a little over two years ago, my father decided that he would cut me off if I didn't prove myself. He blocked my trust fund and set me up as the director of the Odessa office. He thought the challenge would straighten me out. He said if I didn't keep the branch afloat, he and his lawyers would make sure the family money would skip a generation and go straight to Melinda. He said a lot of other things, too. They're too nasty to repeat. I arrived here pissed off at the world and ready to drink myself into oblivion.'

'Odessa is certainly the right place for that.'

He laughed. 'I know. During my first week, I gambled away $100,000.'

'No! How could you?'

'Are you going to yell at me again?' he asked.

'I don't believe it! You have everything and you throw it away!'

'You're going to yell at me.'

'If I'd had the opportunities you had, if I had one-tenth of what you have –'

'You have more. You have Boba,' he countered.

I smiled. He was right. I was infinitely richer. Not that I would admit it to him. 'And speaking of Boba, don't get me started. How dare you bribe her with mangoes?'

'Any interest at all in hearing the end of the story?'

I remained silent.

'All right then. Luckily, I lost the money to a gangster, who agreed to hold my stock in the shipping company as collateral.'

'That was sporting.'

'There was a price. If I couldn't pay him back, he got to keep the stock which was worth much more than $100,000.'

'Oh.'

'Vladimir Stanislavski figured it would be easy money.'

Vlad? Of course. 'So that's why he came to our office so often,' I said, feeling disappointed.

'Maybe at first. But I paid my debt and he kept coming.'

'What are you going to do now that your "sentence" is up?' I asked.

'I'm not sure,' he said.

I realized I missed sitting in the boardroom, talking about literature and Odessa. A strange thing to miss.

*　　*　　*

My assistant did not announce him. David just walked through my door. I glanced up from my desk, expecting anyone – Grandfather Frost, even Tinkerbell – but him. He looked good, so good to me. He'd shaved his mustache. He was wearing a navy blazer like all the other men who worked in the financial district. The green of his silk tie brought out the flecks of amber in his eyes. Of course he was tan, he'd just come from Odessa. His dark hair had been cut too short for my taste. No matter. It would grow.

I stood.

He came to me. What would be appropriate? A handshake? Too formal. A hug? Perhaps not. I stroked his arm, touching him to make my eyes believe he was actually there.

'What are you doing here?' I asked, chin thrust out.

He looked me up and down dispassionately. 'Something's different about you.'

He got himself a position on the board of directors and an office right next to mine. The first thing he did was to ask the company lawyers why I was still married. They explained that the paperwork took time. Through the office wall, I heard him yell, 'I don't want to hear any excuses! She needs a divorce and a work visa. And she better have both within a month.' He made sure things happened quickly. Though he denied it, I believe that some goodwill was involved.

Rumors circulated. Would he be the new director of the San Francisco branch? How long would he stay? The women in the company bombarded his elderly secretary for information. Was he single? Was he interested in seeing someone? What were his plans? He told his family and colleagues that he wanted to be involved in ARGONAUT, but needed a break from the ulcers that had come from running a branch. He told me that he wanted to be at my side, even if it meant only at work.

Underneath the snow globe on the corner of my desk sat a copy of my divorce papers. I knew Vlad was waiting for a sign, yet I hesitated to send it. For the first time, I was happy and free. I wanted to enjoy this independence, for the moment, at least. I was free to go out with friends – Jane, Jono, Tans and I went to concerts, galleries, and cafés. Tans and David got on very well. All of us went to dinner often.

Of course, Jane bragged that she would be the godmother.

'If you make me godfather, I'll teach him how to play basketball,' Jono lobbied.

'Make me godfather and I'll pay for his college,' Tans replied.

I looked to David, who was looking at me, and wondered what he would offer. 'What about you?'

'I'm pretty sure you're having a girl,' he said. 'And that she'll be beautiful just like her mother.'

My eyes misted up. In Odessa, we say God loves three, but looking around the table, I thought he must appreciate five even more.

Things weren't perfect. My studio was the size of a room in a *communalka*. Prices in San Francisco were even higher than those in Moscow. Though my job was more straightforward than it had been in Odessa, it was more complicated, too. I had to learn new laws and regulations and worked long hours. Most days, I did not leave the office before 7.30. I missed Odessa. Ask Jane. Anyone who has lived there is unable to forget the opera house (the third most beautiful in the world), the hospitality of the people, the monuments, architecture, the sea. How I longed for my native city. But as David reminded me – once Anna Akhmatova left Odessa, she left for good. There's no use looking back, Boba said. You'll only end up with a crick in your neck.

I was finally living the life I'd dreamed of when I was back in Odessa and looking towards America. When I'd wanted something – though what exactly I didn't know – so badly. A feeling of contentment filled me. I lived in a city on the sea. I had good friends and a challenging job. I spoke English every day. I was bringing a new life into this world. Births happen every day, but it still felt like a miracle to me. I cradled my belly and thought of my little wonder. How much Boba and I would love her.

David walked through my door with a tray of coffee and cookies.

I looked at my watch. 'It took you three minutes and 19 seconds. Better than yesterday. Worse than the day before.'

He poured us each a cup of decaf. I took a sip and looked out the window.

'Not bad,' I said. 'Not bad at all.'

ACKNOWLEDGEMENTS

My love and gratitude to Barbara & Ed Skeslien and Eddy Charles for making all things possible.

My friends Clydette & Charles de Groot have accompanied me on this journey and have helped me in so many ways. Anca Metiu and I meet once a week to write in a café, and her company and friendship have meant a lot to me. Sylvia Whitman of Shakespeare & Company has been a great source of encouragement and inspiration. This book could not have been written without the support that I received from the Soros Foundation and Dr. Robert Hausmann.

I am blessed to have the support and friendship of these writers, my first readers: Emma Jane Kirby, Jack Kessler, Kathryn Clutz, Amanda Bouchet, Anna di Mattia, Carolyn Skelton, Laura Mason, Edward Carey, and Elena Devos. Thanks to Sapna Gupta, Susan Moreau, Katya Jezzard, Jim Branin, Lauren Sinclair, and Josh Melvin. My thanks to Penelope Le Masson of the Red Wheelbarrow, who has been so kind to me over the years. She has the best stories. Thanks to Bridget Larson and Cindy Rogers of the Prairie Peddler in Shelby for their hospitality as I worked on my novel. Thank you to my teachers, especially Mr. Goodan and Miss Hanson. Love and gratitude to Kathy Skeslien, Madame Nathan, Sarah Andrews, and Kris James, who have always supported my work.

Now the road to publication. Many thanks to Laurel Zuckerman for encouraging me to attend the Geneva Writers' Conference, which is organized by the amazing Susan Tiberghien. My agent Laura Longrigg has been a generous and gracious source of editorial acumen and wisdom. She and Stella Kane have exceeded my expectations in every way, and I thank everyone at MBA Literary Agents for their support and enthusiasm. I feel very lucky to have Bloomsbury as my publisher. On both sides of the Atlantic, they have been very supportive. Helen Garnons-Williams is an editor nonpareil, and I thank her for her insight and ideas. It has been a pleasure to work with Justine Taylor and Erica Jarnes, and I thank them for their close attention to Daria and her words. Of course, it is a dream to work with Alexandra Pringle. I thank Colin Dickerman for his initial enthusiasm and Kathy Belden for taking my book and me under her wing. Amy King, Natalie Slocum, and Sarah Morris created gorgeous cover art. In Germany, I would like to thank Joachim Jessen for bringing my novel to the attention of Christian Rohr of C Bertelsmann. He and Astrid Arz have been lovely to work with. I thank you all for your faith in this novel.

Finally, I would like to express my thanks to the subagents and publishers who have shown faith in the novel: Tassy Barham, Trine Licht, Milena Lukic, Vicki Satlow, Caroline van Gelderen, Martijn David of Uitgeverij Mouria in the Netherlands, Luciana Villas-Boas of Record in Brazil, Ornella Robbianti and Patricia Chendi of Sperling & Kupfer in Italy, Vesna Virant of Mladinska Bucuresti SRL in Romania, Jelka Jovanovic of Mladinska Knijiga Beograd in Serbia, Sif Jóhannsdóttir of Forlagid in Iceland, and Marika Hemmel of Damm Förlag in Sweden.

Reading Group Guide

These discussion questions are designed to enhance your group's conversation about *Moonlight in Odessa*, a wry, tender, and darkly funny look at marriage, the desires we don't acknowledge, and the aftermath of communism.

For discussion

1. *Moonlight in Odessa* takes place in Odessa, Ukraine, in the mid-1990s. What is the significance of this time and place: the unstable period after perestroika when mobsters like Vlad and communists-turned-capitalists like Valentina took advantage; when government employees went to work but didn't get paid; and when the Internet was not yet the sophisticated tool it is today? How might the story be different if it happened today? Would the story be the same if it were set in Moscow?

2. Daria's grandmother influenced many of Daria's decisions, from what she studied at college to who she married. Was Daria right to listen to her grandmother? At the risk of hurting Boba, should Daria have tried earlier to become more independent? Was Boba right to push Daria to leave Odessa? Did Daria regret her choice?

3. Mr. Harmon commits a terrible act. What does he do to earn Daria's forgiveness? Do you think he deserves to be forgiven? Which was more convincing—his actual apology or his subsequent acts of atonement, such as continuing to send food to Boba?

4. Anti-Semitism is an insidious problem in the former Soviet Union. Did you see through Olga? Did she hide her true feelings from Daria, or did Daria just not want to see the truth about her neighbor?

5. Daria corresponds with several men over the Internet. How is meeting someone over the Internet different from traditional dating? How is it the same? Are dating sites such as eHarmony or Match.com the same as international matchmaking sites?

6. There are clues that Tristan may not be a teacher. He writes "Should I of waited?" instead of "Should I have waited?" (114), and "Its the most beautiful place" rather than "It's the most beautiful place" (105). Should Daria, who is a stickler for proper English, have noticed these mistakes, or did she simply see what she wanted to in Tristan?

7. Did Tristan lie when he said he lived near San Francisco? How did Tristan and Daria lie to each other? Was their relationship doomed from the start?

8. Daria is bilingual and can communicate with English-speakers. How was her friend Oksana at a disadvantage because she couldn't speak English? Do you think Oksana would have married her husband if she had been able to understand him?

9. What do you think about Daria's response to America? Is she too critical? Do you think that homesickness or depression is a factor in the way she feels? Would she have had the same observations if she had lived in a city and worked in an engineering firm?

10. Daria loves the English language. How is this love expressed? She also loves literature. Does Daria understand something about Harmon when he tells her about his father using a quote from Babel: "You want to live, but he makes you die twenty times a day" (71)? Is literature a form of solace? How do words sustain us?

11. When Daria is anxious, she thinks of irregular verbs; when she is unhappy or nervous she thinks of lines of poetry from Vladimir Mayakovsky ("my forehead melting the glass") (112), or Anna Akhmatova ("And he did not take his eyes,/Staring blankly, from my ring.") (295); when she is happy, she plays with words (*fair/fare*, *board/bored*). How does Daria use poetry and irregular verbs to express what other language cannot?

12. *Moonlight in Odessa* takes place before Skype, low-cost calling plans, and inexpensive pre-paid phone cards were available. Daria's phone bill was several hundred dollars per month, and Tristan explained that they had a budget and couldn't spend so much money. Do you understand his point of view? Was he unreasonable or was Daria? Was he genuinely trying to save money or was he trying to limit Daria's contact with the outside world? How did he try to make Daria feel at home and help her to adapt?

13. Online matchmaking sites enjoy booming business.

Why do you think some American men go abroad to look for a wife? Why would a smart, talented woman like Daria marry a man like Tristan? Can these marriages work?

14. What advice would you give to a foreign woman going to America to marry a stranger?

15. Several foreign women have been brutally murdered by their American husbands—an escalation of domestic violence in their relationships. Do you think that Tristan's abuse would have escalated if Daria had stayed?

16. Who was your favorite character in the book? Why? Who was your least favorite character?

17. Which character was the most interesting to you? What aspect of the book surprised you the most? Could you relate to the dynamics between characters—for example, Daria's relationship with her grandmother or the treacherous office politics at the shipping company?

Janet Skeslien Charles, originally from Montana, divides her time between France and the United States. *Moonlight in Odessa*, her debut novel, was inspired by her two years in Odessa as a Soros Fellow. Visit her Web site at www.jskesliencharles.com.